MW01195710

PRAISE FOR
Welcome to Bellechester

"Captivating from the start! This sweet story unfolds against the backdrop of the bucolic English town of Bellechester with its engaging and relatable residents. The author paints detailed and vibrant pictures of the settings, characters, and events that stimulate the readers' imagination and their connection to the characters. We meet the confident, smart, and compassionate Doctor Mary Elizabeth Senty (Emme), and the kind but intrepid Chief Inspector William Donnelly (Will). Their friendship unfolds along with a mysterious heist and a conclusion that leaves us eager to see where Emme and Will take us next."

—*Dan O'Leary, Esquire*

"Will Donnelly is pleasantly surprised to learn that he has been promoted to chief inspector, but this will require him to relocate to the town of Bellechester on short notice. Bellechester has been struggling with a crime spree, and the hope is that his youth and dedication will help the community to tackle the challenges. Meanwhile, Doctor Mary Elizabeth Senty is preparing her own move to Bellechester so that she can begin serving the community along with Doctor Harold Merton. We get to know the community of Bellechester while the two new members get to know each other. The mystery keeps the reader guessing until the end."

—*Gayle Yanchar Bari, science educator*

"If you liked [*The Doctor of Bellechester*], you will like the second book even more. The characters in the first book are [here] again . . . plus many new characters that you will not forget. I found the book easy to read, and it kept me engaged in the story. . . . Follow Mary Elizabeth's story [and discover] the new twist. I did not see that coming! I sure hope there will be a book three."

—*Paula Brust, former educator and avid reader*

"This is an enjoyable read. The characters are interesting and recognizable. The author does a great job in describing the details as relates to the era. There is a budding romance, a mystery to solve, and questions to ponder. Enjoy a cup of tea and a scone as you visit Bellechester."

—*Barb Kraft, avid reader*

"If you happen to enjoy a cosy (British spelling) mystery filled with interesting, 'fun to get to know' characters, you'll probably enjoy *Welcome to Bellechester* from the pen of Margaret A. Blenkush. Like the first book, *The Doctor of Bellechester*, this is a warm, relaxing sort of novel, the sort of story you can enjoy on a cold, winter's night."

—*The Wishing Shelf Book Awards*

PREVIOUSLY PUBLISHED BY

MARGARET A. BLENKUSH

The Doctor of Bellechester,
Book 1
in the Dr. M.E. Senty Series

Enjoy your visit
to Bellechester.
Blessings!
Margaret A.
Blenkush
2024

PRAISE FOR
The Doctor of Bellechester

Margaret A. Blenkush takes the time to build characters, premises, logical courses of action and illogical challenges to set ideas that will resonate with modern readers. From the (1959) England setting and its culture to the focus on acts of kindness, discovery, and changing hearts and minds, *The Doctor of Bellechester* creates a story that draws connections between different generations and shows how, with little effort, their lives and interests can intersect and complement one another.

—*Diane Donovan, Midwest Book Review*

"A delightfully cosy [British spelling] story, perfect for readers who enjoy medical novels and strong, easy to root for, characters. Highly recommended."

—*The Wishing Shelf Book Awards*

" . . . there was sufficient suspense and intrigue about what would happen to dear Emme that I could not put the book down. . . . I was not disappointed! In this divisive society, it was wonderful to read a book that demonstrates the best that a person can be. It was both heartwarming and uplifting. I heartily recommend it to all."

—*Daniel O'Leary, Esquire*

". . . *The Doctor of Bellechester* is a well-written, cosy (British spelling) novel. Its smooth writing, easy dialogue, and likable characters create an enjoyable reading experience. I look forward to the next book from this author!"

—IPBA Benjamin Franklin Award judge

Honorable Mention for 2023 Best Catholic Fiction, Catholic Media Association Book Awards

Honorable Mention for 2023 Best Front Cover Art, Catholic Media Association Book Awards

Finalist in the 2023 Wishing Shelf Book Awards, London, England

Welcome to Bellechester

Book 2

By Margaret A. Blenkush

Edited by Kerry Stapley
Cover illustration by Lisa Kosmo
Book design and typesetting by Dan Pitts

ISBN 13: 978-1-64343-610-4
Library of Congress Catalog Number: 2023917672
First Edition: 2024
28 27 26 25 24   5 4 3 2 1

Pond Reads Press
939 Seventh Street West
Saint Paul, MN 55102
(952) 829-8818
www.BeaversPondPress.com

Contact Margaret A. Blenkush at www.margaretablenkush.com for school visits, speaking engagements, book club discussions, and interviews.

BOOK DEDICATION

This book is dedicated to my family.

To my parents, Valentine and Dolores, who have proved that love is stronger than death.

To my twin sister, Mary, still my best friend. With her husband Dwight, they kept the family tree growing and prospering.

To Anne Marie, Kathryn Rose, Elizabeth Helen, and Phillip Anders, who regard me as their "second mother."

To my boys Avinash, Oscar, Elias, and Quentin, who gave me my most cherished title, "Aunty Margie Great." They are keeping me young.

Contents

Foreword

Have you ever moved to a new town to begin a job or start school and not known a soul? If you have, then you might relate to the experiences of Dr. Mary Elizabeth Senty and Inspector William F. Donnelly as they settle into their new community. I hope you enjoy meeting the village folk alongside our two main characters in this sequel to *The Doctor of Bellechester*. The first story ended on Thursday, August 27, 1959, and this book begins the very next day in London. While the village of Bellechester, England, is totally fictional, many of the towns mentioned in this book do in fact exist, like Shrewsbury, Ludlow, Birmingham, Worcester, and Leominster. They all help situate Bellechester in the southwestern part of Shropshire County.

All my knowledge of medical conditions and treatments came from internet research. The same is true of British police procedures. Any errors or ignorance of such matters belong to the author alone. Younger generations may find it hard to believe that in the "olden days" of the late 1950s, telephones were not portable and ambulances did not contain EMTs, only attendants whose job was to transport patients to the hospital.

While it is true that Britain and the United States share English as a common language, it is equally true that some British words and terms are unfamiliar to American ears. Therefore, a glossary is included at the back of the book. My American reviewers found that reading the glossary before beginning the story enhanced their reading experience.

My goal was to write another entertaining, gentle story with enough intrigue to keep the pages turning. You will have to let me know if

I have succeeded—I always welcome comments on my website, www.MargaretABlenkush.com. If you are left with a few questions at the end of the book, fear not! Book three is in the planning stages. Until then, settle in, get comfy, enjoy a cup of tea, and allow me to be the first to say welcome to Bellechester!

Friday, August 28, 1959

CHAPTER 1

WILL'S PROMOTION

Detective Inspector William Francis Donnelly walked out of the interrogation room with a pile of manila folders under his arm. "Another confession!" The young detective sent to observe Will's interrogation techniques was close at his heels. "How did you know to use a soft touch on this lad?"

"You get a feel for the demeanor of the accused. This teen was no hardened criminal. Just looking into his eyes, you could see how terrified he was of his surroundings and his situation. A sympathetic ear was all that was needed."

"Sir, if you don't mind, I want to get to my desk so I can copy my notes. I want to remember every word."

"You go right ahead."

The young detective walked ahead down the hallway to the Met's Crime Against Property Division. Will smiled to himself. *Was I ever that eager?* Unlike his mentee, Will was not ready to go back into the office quite yet. He exchanged greetings with the officers he passed. He stopped at the large bulletin board outside the station commander's office. There was a large bare space where the promotions list should have been. Will shook his head, turned, and slowly walked back to the division, enjoying a few more minutes of the cooler hallway air before weaving his way through the maze of desks back to his own. He plopped his large stack of folders down. "Whew! Feels like an oven in here. When is this heat wave supposed to break?"

Inspector Trevor Jones, whose desk faced Will's, looked up from his work. "Thunderstorms possible tonight. Say, how did the interrogation go?"

"It was a doddle. The kid was out with his mates trying to impress a girl. He took a convertible parked outside a shop with the keys left in the ignition. Simple crime of opportunity. I still think we should've arrested the owner of the car too."

"On what charge?"

"Stupidity."

Trevor raised an eyebrow. "If stupidity were a crime, we wouldn't have enough nicks."

Will removed his jacket and carefully hung it over the back of his chair. Before he sat down, he loosened his tie, unbuttoned his cuffs, and rolled his sleeves past his elbow.

The day's heat intensified over the afternoon. The minutes dragged by. Large fans in the corners of the room provided no relief. They only seemed to blow the hot air around, making the blue swirls of cigarette smoke dance above the officers' heads. The usual smell of the room was overpowered by the body odor of twelve overheating officers. Will tried his best to continue his work despite the distractions.

"Will! Will! I think this is it."

Will looked over to Trevor. "What?"

"I think the promotion list arrived. Although the officer who went into the super's office didn't look like one of ours. That's strange."

"If the officer didn't look like one of ours, then he is most likely seeing the super about another matter."

"Aren't you anxious to know if you made the list?"

"I am sure the super will announce it when it comes through. He won't keep us in suspense any longer than necessary."

"How can you be so cool?"

"No one can be cool on a day like this," Will said as he pulled his shirt away from his body. "No, I am a realist. I know that I don't stand a chance this time. The chair of the interview committee told me that they never had anyone as young as me apply for the position. That was as good as saying that I would not be considered, and to try again next time. I wish they would post the results so it would be official."

"I bet they say discouraging things to all the applicants so as not to tip their hand. Besides, I don't think thirty-two is so young. You are practically middle aged," Trevor quipped.

"Trevor, I really need to get this report done today. Tomorrow is the big rugby match, and I don't want this report hanging over my head all weekend." Will reached for his coffee mug, which was filled instead with cold water.

"The kids are excited to see their Uncle Will play tomorrow. Doreen is looking forward to your match too. It will give her the afternoon off so she can have lunch with her girlfriends."

"Then let me finish my work."

"Why don't you let your junior do the reports? We all do it. Good practice for the lads. Besides, delegating tasks shows leadership."

"Is that what you tell yourselves? Everyone knows you lot hate writing reports. I prefer to do my own, thank you." Will waved his pencil. "Now, don't you have some work of your own to do?"

"All right, all right! I'll let you get on." Trevor laughed in good-natured defeat and returned to his papers.

"I would appreciate that." Will reached for his cup but found it empty. He wound his way to the break room. The large clock on the wall read 3:24 p.m. Only six minutes had passed since he had last checked the time. A drink of cold water revived his spirits and cleared his head.

Trevor reached across his desk to answer Will's phone. "Superintendent Billingsby wants to see you. Maybe it's news about the promotion. Good luck," he said when Will returned.

"Thanks, Trevor. Sorry I've been irritable today."

"Ah, forget it."

Will unfurled his sleeves and buttoned the cuffs. He slipped his suit coat over his once-crisp white shirt, now limp with perspiration, and navigated quickly through the maze of desks. He paused outside Superintendent Billingsby's office. Will tugged at his sleeves one last time and adjusted the knot of his tie. A deep baritone voice responded to his knock: "Come in! Ah yes, Donnelly," he said as Will entered. "Come in, come in."

Superintendent Billingsby was a large, barrel-chested man in his early sixties. An able administrator, he ran his department with a tight rein and velvet glove. His suit jacket and tie hung on the coat tree in the corner of his office. A small oscillating fan on the bookcase in the opposite corner fluttered the papers on his desk. Superintendent Billingsby, shirt sleeves rolled up and collar open, turned to the officer standing beside him. "Chief Superintendent Williamson, I would like to introduce Detective Inspector William Donnelly."

Even on this sweltering day, Chief Superintendent Williamson showed no discomfort wearing his full uniform. Will admired his cool, reserved manner. He shook Will's hand with a firm grip. "Very pleased to meet you, Inspector. Superintendent Billingsby has been telling me wonderful things about you. Highest conviction rate in the department!"

"Very pleased to meet you too. Thank you for the compliment, but I don't work alone. We have a crack team of detectives in this division."

"Here, let's all sit down." Superintendent Billingsby motioned toward the table and chairs in the corner of the room.

Chief Superintendent Williamson opened his black briefcase and set several papers in front of him. Will eased his six-foot two-inch frame into the chair opposite Williamson. Superintendent Billingsby reached for a pitcher of ice water that sat in the middle of the table. Streams of condensation had run down the sides of the pitcher, creating a pool of water at its base. After providing everyone refreshment, Billingsby turned to Will. "Earlier today, I received a call from the chair of the promotions board. As you know, there were only three chief inspector positions open here at the Met. I regret to inform you that the positions were offered to officers who had more seniority than you. I am sorry."

As disappointing as the news was for Will, he was glad to finally receive an answer. He was about to utter a sigh of relief when he felt the steady gaze of Chief Superintendent Williamson upon him. At that moment, Will's years of military training kicked in. Whatever he was feeling on the inside, he made sure the expression on his face never changed. "That is quite all right, sir. I knew it was a long shot. But I am glad to have had the experience of the exam and the interview. Thank you for telling me. I will leave you to your meeting. Very nice to have met you, Chief Superintendent Williamson." Will rose and again shook the chief superintendent's hand.

Chief Superintendent Williamson was surprised by Will's move but uttered no response.

"Donnelly, where are you going?"

"I should get back to work, sir. I still have a report to finish before I leave today."

"But Inspector," Superintendent Billingsby continued, "You are not dismissed. I have not yet finished. Please," he said and motioned to the empty chair, "sit down."

"Yes, sir. So sorry, sir," This time it was not the heat that gave Will's cheeks a warm glow of color. Reaching for his glass, he took a large swig of water.

Superintendent Billingsby chuckled. "That's better. You young people today are always in such a hurry. The chief superintendent and I have a few questions for you."

"Inspector, where do you see yourself in five years?"

Will answered the chief without hesitation. "In my years of serving with the Royal Military

Police, I discovered I enjoyed police work. I still find it a privilege to assist people who find themselves in tough situations. I intend to make police work my career. I am happy to serve in whatever capacity best reflects my abilities and training."

Chief Superintendent Williamson pointed at the paper in front of him. "I see on your resume you were a member of the Royal Military Police for twelve years. Why did you leave?"

"I joined the military right from school in '43. Because of my interest in police work, they assigned me to the Royal Military Police. During the war, I guarded our ports here at home. After the war, I was transferred to the special investigation branch, which took me to India, Germany, and Korea. As I reached my late twenties, I had seen enough of the world. I wanted to come home and put down some roots."

Superintendent Billingsby asked, "Now, where is your hometown again? I know you are not a native Londoner."

"You are correct, sir. I was born and raised in the town of Preston, Lancashire," Will said.

Chief Superintendent Williamson asked, "How long have you lived in London? Do you like living here? Is this where you envisioned settling down?"

"I have lived in London since I joined the Met in 1955. London can be an expensive place to live, but it also has a lot to offer. Overall, London is a great city. I don't mind living here. But when I start a family, I would prefer to live in a smaller community, more like Preston—less traffic and cleaner air."

Chief Superintendent Williamson asked, "Do you have any ties that would keep you in London? What about your wife? Does she like living in London?"

Will shifted uneasily in his chair and took another sip of water. "I am not married and have no serious girlfriend at the present time. Currently, my only tie to London is my rugby club."

"Ah, rugby," Chief Superintendent Williamson said with a smile. "Great sport. The only true English sport. How did your club fare this past season?"

Will began to relax and let his professional guard down. "I play with the Met Pips. We had a good season last year and finished third in the city's amateur adult league. Saturday, we play in the Rover Cup's semifinal match."

"Isn't it a bit early to be playing rugby?" Chief Superintendent Williamson asked as he reached for his glass of water.

Superintendent Billingsby explained, "The Rover Cup kicks off the amateur club rugby season here in London. The top eight teams from last year's city standings compete for the cup. It is quite the tournament, second only to the city championship which occurs in the spring. We are very proud of our team around here, Chief Superintendent. I do believe we could go all the way this year."

"I wish your team the best of luck," Chief Superintendent Williamson said.

"Thank you, sir," Will said.

"Do you have any more questions for Inspector Donnelly?" Superintendent Billingsby asked.

"No, I am satisfied," Chief Superintendent Williamson replied.

"Good." He turned to Will. "Inspector, we shan't keep you in the dark any longer. Our promotions board feels you are ready to become a chief inspector. However, because of your low seniority, you would have to wait a long time for promotion here at the Met. They believe you would have a better chance in another jurisdiction."

"Sirs, am I being transferred?"

Superintendent Billingsby chuckled. "Only if you want to be."

"Let me clear up your confusion, Inspector," Chief Superintendent Williamson interjected. "My county of Shropshire does not have the resources to conduct a thorough search for candidates to fill senior positions on our police force. We have a unique arrangement with the Met. Any of our officers who wish to be considered for promotion go through the Met's process. Then the board shares with us the exam results and the interview notes on our candidates as well as those who were not chosen for promotion here at the Met. Our deputy chief constables and local police board review the information and make their selections. My superior, Deputy Chief

Constable Lawson, sent me to conduct the final interview. How would you feel about living in a village out in the country, Inspector?" Chief Superintendent Williamson asked.

Superintendent Billingsby quipped, "That would satisfy your conditions of settling in a smaller town with less traffic and cleaner air."

Will smiled. "Yes, yes it would. Chief Superintendent Williamson, I have no objections to living out in the country. It would be a nice change of pace from London."

"Very glad to hear that. Inspector Donnelly, there is nothing left for me to do but offer you a chief inspector position in the County of Shropshire. You would be responsible for the village of Bellechester and several smaller constabularies. Your jurisdiction would cover roughly one hundred square miles in the southwestern part of the county. You would report directly to me. Take time to think about it. I am not expecting an answer today. Take a drive and check out Bellechester if you like. I just need your answer by 9:00 a.m. Monday."

The only sound in the office was the whirring of the fan. Will took another sip of water before he replied. "Thank you, Chief Superintendent, but I do not need the weekend to think about it. I would be honored to accept the position and work under your command. I only hope I can justify the faith you and the deputy chief constables have placed in me."

"Excellent. Glad to hear it. You have two orders. The first is to implement the new national police standards in your area. I have all that information right here," Chief Superintendent Williamson said. He opened his briefcase and handed Will a stack of file folders.

"Thank you, sir. I will look them over this weekend," Will said.

Then Chief Superintendent Williamson handed Will a thicker stack of folders. "And there is another, more serious matter that needs your immediate attention. Recently, several jewel robberies targeting the wealthier citizens in the county have occurred. The victims have been applying pressure on me and my superiors to get these crimes solved. The deputy chief constables believe that with the success you have had here at the Met, you are our best hope to solve these cases. Your appointment as chief inspector gives us the perfect opportunity to catch them."

"How do you mean, sir?"

"Do you know Lady Beatrice Brantwell?"

"No, I can't say that I have had that pleasure."

Chief Superintendent Williamson continued, "I served under her husband, Lord Geoffrey Brantwell, in the Second World War. Fine chap. They have an estate outside Bellechester. As the most influential couple in the area, they have graciously offered to host a gala to introduce the new chief inspector to the local citizenry. Lady Brantwell's parties are legendary and not to be missed. It will be the social event of the season in our part of the county. It will also be the perfect cover to trap the jewel thieves." He paused for a moment and then asked, "You do own a full mess dress, I presume?"

Will thought, *Are you kidding? On a detective's salary?* But he said, "No, sir. But I will be sure to purchase one."

"Excellent. As the highest-ranking officer in southwestern Shropshire, you will often be called upon to represent the police force at local ceremonial functions. The villagers expect to see you in your finery at these events. It shows respect and it gains respect. Maintaining good public relations is part of your job description. A very important part."

"Yes, sir, I understand. I will do my best."

"I know you will. You seem to be a bright chap. Your official installation as chief inspector will take place at the gala. Be sure to send your guest list to Lady Brantwell. Since you don't have a local residence yet, she will be sending your invitation to the precinct. Watch for it."

"Yes, sir."

"Because your appointment requires you to relocate, you will be granted two weeks' leave. That should be enough time to get yourself settled in Bellechester."

"Thank you, sir. That is very generous."

"Come see me at my office in Ludlow at 9:00 a.m. on Tuesday, September 15, and we will get you squared away. I am afraid your morning will be spent filling out paperwork and getting your warrant card. In the afternoon, we will travel to Shrewsbury, where we will meet with Chief Constable Scott and Deputy Chief Constable Lawson."

"Very good, sir. I look forward to meeting them."

"Before I go, do you have any questions for me?"

"Right now, I cannot think of any."

"Here is my card. If you should think of any questions later, please do not hesitate to call. Now if you'll excuse me, I shall take my leave." The men stood. Chief Superintendent Williamson shook Superintendent Billingsby's hand.

"Very nice to have met you, Superintendent Billingsby. Sorry to be taking your best detective."

"Good to meet you too. Inspector Donnelly will be missed, make no mistake. But I am glad to have given the lad his start in civilian police work. I know he will work as hard for you as he has for me."

Chief Superintendent Williamson shook Will's hand. "Glad to have you on my team, Donnelly."

"I look forward to working with you, sir."

Chief Superintendent Williamson gathered up his briefcase and left the office.

Superintendent Billingsby turned to Will. "Aren't you glad you decided to stay for the rest of the meeting?"

"Yes, I am. Thank you, sir, for your kind words. I only hope I can be as good a supervisor as you. I have learned a lot from you and have enjoyed my time working in this division."

"I meant what I said. I am going to miss you, Donnelly. You are a fine detective. And I know you will make a splendid chief inspector. Chief Superintendent Williamson is fortunate to have you."

"Thank you, sir. Do you want me to turn in my warrant card before I leave today?"

"No, no, you hang onto it until after the rugby tournament is over. In case the Pips make the finals, I don't want you disqualified because you can't prove you are one of us. No, no, Chief Superintendent Williamson isn't going to take you from us until after the Rover Cup. I made sure of that," Superintendent Billingsby said with a wink. "You are too valuable to our team."

"Thank you, sir. I appreciate you letting me finish the tournament with my teammates."

As they walked out of the office together, Superintendent Billingsby slapped Will on the back. "Now the only thing left to do is announce your new appointment to the men."

"That and for me to finish my report," Will said.

CHAPTER 2

Will Shares His News

Will's wet raincoat left a trail of water behind him as he climbed the three flights of stairs to his flat. Darkness and silence greeted him. Will felt a pang of envy for Trevor. He wished there were a friendly voice to welcome him home and ask about his day and a gaggle of kids to come running to the door, screaming to be picked up or tussled with. *Someday*, he thought.

His apartment was exactly as he'd left it that morning. His clean breakfast dishes lay in the dish drainer, ready to be put back in the cupboards. He hung his suit coat in his bedroom wardrobe and changed out of his work clothes. He took a shower before putting on a clean T-shirt and pajama bottoms.

He had intended to come home right after work, but Will's detective buddies insisted on celebrating his promotion at their favorite pub. Will was not a big drinker and had only two pints of ale. The pub served extraordinary fish and chips, so the men had a real feast. Afterward, he stopped at a petrol station to fill his car and buy a roadmap of the county of Shropshire.

Will spread the roadmap on his kitchen table. He'd never heard of Bellechester, but he quickly discovered exactly where the village, and his new territorial responsibilities, were located. Will glanced at the clock and found there was still enough time to share his news with the one person he had wanted to tell all day. He settled on the couch.

"Hello?" came a robust voice on the other end of the line.

"Hello, Dad."

"Are you calling with the results of the rugby game? I thought the semifinals were being played tomorrow."

"You're right. The game is tomorrow. I have other news." Will became so excited he jumped up from the couch and began pacing as he talked. One hand carried the phone, and the other held the receiver.

"I am being promoted! You are now speaking to Chief Inspector William F. Donnelly."

"Congratulations, son. Well done. I'm so proud of you. Your dear sainted mother would be proud too. Our Will, a chief inspector."

Will felt the lump in his throat as he recalled his mother's memory. "Thanks, Dad. That means a lot."

"How did this all come about? You never said you were applying for a promotion."

"I never told you because I didn't think it would happen. I knew a lot of other detectives with more seniority were also applying. I did it mainly for the experience."

"First time the charm, eh? 'Tis the luck of the Irish! That's what it is. Will you still be in the properties division?"

"No, Dad, I won't be with the Met anymore. I will be working for the County of Shropshire. I will be headquartered in the village of Bellechester. I command the Bellechester police force as well as three smaller constabularies. My jurisdiction covers one hundred square miles."

"Bellechester, you say? Never heard of it. Where is it again?"

"Southwest Shropshire County."

"I will have to get the atlas out. But my goodness, Will, your first command. And such a large territory! You must tell me everything. Don't leave out a single detail."

"But Dad, this is long distance. It will cost me a fortune!"

"Oh, I think my newly appointed chief inspector son can afford it," his father teased.

Will settled back into couch and relayed the entire conversation with Chief Superintendent Williamson and Superintendent Billingsby. "My commissioning ceremony is going to be part of a big gala. I was asked for a guest list, so look for an invitation in the mail."

"I'll be there. I wouldn't miss it for the world."

"Jack and Robert will be invited too."

"Great! The entire Donnelly clan will be there to celebrate one of their own."

"I'd like you to be the one to pin the extra star on my epaulets."

"It would be my honor."

"Thanks. It will be great to see everyone again."

"Hey, good luck at the match tomorrow. Don't forget to call and let me know how your team fared. I'll be thinking of you."

"You got it. According to the map, Bellechester is less than a three-hour drive to Preston. I hope I can make it home more often to visit."

"I would like that."

"Well, I better get to bed. Big game tomorrow. Good night, Dad."

"Good night, Will."

Saturday, August 29

CHAPTER 3

THE RUGBY GAME

Saturday was clear, sunny, and cooler. The Rover Cup semifinals were being played in the affluent west London neighborhood of Holland Park. The Met Pips were playing at three o'clock in the second match of the afternoon.

As Will walked from the parking lot to the field, seven-year-old Davy ran to greet him. "Uncle Will! Uncle Will!" Davy threw his arms around Will's waist and gave him a big hug.

Will tousled the boy's hair. "Hey, Davy."

"Unk Will!" It took four-year-old Jane a bit longer to reach Will. She threw her arms around his leg. After that hug, she raised her hands to him: "Up! Unk Will, up!" Will scooped her up and held her so they were face to face. "Kiss!" she demanded. She planted a wet, sloppy one on his cheek, and he kissed her cheek back. She laughed and threw her arms around his neck while he carried her.

Trevor had found the perfect spot to watch the match. It was far enough away from the sidelines that the kids wouldn't get hurt by stray balls or players and near enough that he could still get a good view of the field. He had the baby in the pram and a blanket spread out nearby for the kids.

Will brought the kids over to Trevor. "See you kids after the game." He set Jane down, then bent over the pram and asked, "How is Billy-boy today?" The baby smiled and cooed.

"Say, I have been checking out your opposition. They look awfully young and fast. They should give you a run for your money this afternoon."

"Well, I hope you didn't wager against us," Will told Trevor.

Trevor sighed. "My betting days are over, old man. Doreen saw to that."

"I knew she could straighten you out and turn you into a pillar of society." Will ran out onto the pitch. "Davy, after the game, you let me know how I played," he called.

"Sure thing, Uncle Will!"

It was a hard-fought battle. The Met Pips were a team of men in their thirties. Trevor's assessment of the opposition was spot on. The Mayfair Magpies were a younger, quicker team and kept the Pips on their heels.

Throughout the game, the teams exchanged the lead many times. With time ticking away in the second half, the Magpies had a free kick. The ball went off the side of the kicker's foot at a strange angle. Instead of heading downfield, the ball sailed toward the sidelines. To everyone's horror, a young woman happened to be walking in its trajectory. Realizing the ball was headed straight for her, Will and many other Pips broke ranks. They sprinted toward her, expecting the worst. The woman saw the ball, dropped her purse, and caught the ball as she fell to the ground. There was a collective gasp, then silence, followed by an eruption of cheers amongst the players and spectators.

Will reached her first. "Are you hurt, miss?" He helped her to her feet.

The rest of the Pip players reached them and complimented her catch while asking if she was all right.

The surprised woman kept saying, "Yes, I'm fine. Thank you. Here, what should I do with the ball? You want it? Should I throw it back?" She cocked her arm to throw the ball back onto the field.

At that moment, one of the touch judges appeared. "Here, miss, I'll take it." The players followed him back to the field, except Will. He picked her purse up off the ground and handed it to her. "Here's your purse, miss."

A strand of her long chestnut-brown hair fell across her face. As she brushed it back, her blue eyes met Will's. She smiled at him and reached for her purse. "Thank you kindly," she said in an accent Will found hard to place.

"Are you sure you're all right?"

"Just a little dazed. I didn't expect to see a rugby ball come flying at me. Boy, that kicker really shanked it, didn't he?"

"There is a doctor on the sidelines if you want him to look at you. Here, I can take you to him." Will offered her his dirt-and-blood-caked arm.

"No, that won't be necessary. Really, I'm fine," she said as she brushed off her skirt.

To his surprise, Will realized he would rather stand and talk with her than return to the pitch. He was just about to ask her name when one of his teammates yelled, "Will! Will! Hey, buddy! The doc is coming! He'll take care of her. Come on! We've got a game to win!"

Will said the first thing that popped into his head. "Nice catch." He ran back onto the field. Will saw the doctor reach the woman. The game resumed, and Will lost track of her. When the referee blew the final whistle, the Pips had eked out a win by the score of 14–12.

The Pips' captain called out, "Let's go to Tanner's Pub so we can have a proper celebration!" His announcement was met with hearty cheers from the field. "Donnelly, you coming?" he asked as Will walked toward the sidelines.

"I'm going to have to pass today. I've a lot to get ready before I move," Will said.

"Oh, by the way, congrats on your promotion. Will you be able to make it to the game next week?"

"Yes, the super arranged it so I could finish out the tournament. I will give you a call towards the end of the week to get the details of next Saturday's game."

"Okay. See you next week." The captain hurried off the field to catch up to his teammates.

Will scanned the sidelines, hoping to glimpse the woman who caught the ball, but he never saw her. Instead, he spied two very excited children running toward him. "Yeah! Uncle Will! Uncle Will! You won!"

"Hey, kids!" Swinging Jane up on his shoulders, Will carried her back to where Trevor was folding the blanket. Davy walked by his side. "Well, Davy, what is your report?"

"Lots of ankle tackles today, Uncle Will," Davy said in a serious tone. But then he brightened as he thought of some positive news. "Good runs, though."

"Davy, sharp eyes as always. Looks like I will have to concentrate on my tackling techniques for next week," Will said as he tousled Davy's hair.

Will brought Jane down from his shoulders and helped Trevor pick up the toys. "Thanks for coming to the game. And thanks for bringing my good-luck charms."

"Anytime, buddy."

Trevor handed Davy the blanket. "Think you can carry this for me?"

"Sure thing," Davy said. "Dad, can we come to Uncle Will's game next week?"

"We will have to ask your mum. She's the boss of this outfit. But if you kids are good, I think maybe we can convince her."

Davy and Jane jumped up and down. "Yeah! Yeah!"

Trevor pushed the pram. Will carried Jane on his shoulders as the little group walked to the parking lot. "Say, Will, who was the woman who made that catch? She looked like a pro!"

"I don't know. I didn't ask her name."

"What? The greatest detective inspector that the Met's property division ever had, and he didn't even get her name! Geez, Will, you were talking to her long enough to have gotten her name, address, telephone number, and whereabouts for the past forty-eight hours."

"I wanted to make sure she was all right."

"From where I was sitting, old man, I'd say you were the goner. After that encounter, I am surprised you can even remember your own name. What color were her eyes? Brown?"

"No, they were sparkly blue. She had an accent. Canadian, maybe? Did you see what happened to her? I lost track of her once the game started up again."

"Sad to say, but that doctor who was helping on the sidelines took her under his wing. They were together for the rest of the game and then left together. Sorry, old chap, but the doctor, not the police inspector, caught her fancy."

"Typical. I finally meet a woman I could be interested in, and I am transferred out of town. Where has she been for the last four years?"

"Tough luck, Will."

Will helped Trevor pack his car. "I'll talk to you during the week. Bye, kids. Be good."

"Bye, Uncle Will," Davy said.

"Kiss bye, Unk Will?" Jane asked.

Will obliged. As the car drove off, he waved. Then he found his own car and headed back to his apartment to see how many other tasks he could cross off his to-do list.

Monday, August 31

CHAPTER 4

WILL FINDS A HOME

Monday's drive to Bellechester was long and uneventful. Will had arranged to meet the local real estate agent for lunch at the Ram's Head Pub. He arrived in the village a little before noon, grimacing as he exited the car. Will's body reminded him of every tackle made and hit received in Saturday's rugby match. Trevor liked to call him "old man," and at that moment, he felt like one.

The midday church bells were tolling when Will walked into the pub. There were several men finishing their lunch at the bar.

"Would you have a room available for tonight?" Will asked the bartender.

The barman laughed. "On a Monday night? Yeah, we can accommodate you."

"Great, thank you," Will said. "I am supposed to meet Mr. Lester here. Could you point him out to me?"

"Mel?" The barkeeper nodded toward the back of the pub. "He's sitting in a booth waiting on you. Start walking back there, and he and his jacket will announce themselves." He chuckled and then left to attend to a customer who was waving an empty glass.

As Will walked toward the back of the pub, an older gentleman wearing a red, yellow, and green seersucker-plaid jacket waved, slid out of his booth, and approached.

"Mr. Lester?" Will asked.

"And you must be Inspector Donnelly." Mr. Lester shook Will's hand. "Let's go put our lunch order in."

After lunch, Mr. Lester drove Will out to a new housing development on the outskirts of the village. "A small canning factory is being built to the west of the village. With the promise of good paying jobs, the village is anticipating a growth spurt. Hampstead Place is a development of fifty single-family dwellings."

Mr. Lester stopped the car in front of a home that had balloons lining the walkway up to the front door. "Here is a model home. It will give you an idea of what the homes are like. This is a two-bedroom model. The larger homes have four bedrooms, but the layout is basically the same. The kitchen comes equipped with all the modern conveniences: a hob built into the counter, an oven built into the wall, a washer in the mudroom, and a retractable clothesline built in."

"These are nice and modern, I give you that," Will said after the tour. "But I prefer an older home. All these houses look the same. They're built so close together that you can shake hands with your neighbor by leaning out the bedroom window. And the lawns are the size of a postage stamp."

"You surprise me, Inspector," Mr. Lester said. "I thought that is what you young people want—little upkeep, everything modern and up to date with all the latest gizmos and gadgets."

Will laughed. "I am not that young. No, I prefer an older, well-built house that has some charm and character to it. And I would like to live closer to the police station."

"If that is what you are looking for, then let's go back to the village. There is one house for sale that you might like. Although I must warn you, it will take a little work to get it in shape. But if you have a little imagination, I think you'll see the potential."

As they rode back to town, Mr. Lester explained, "This house belonged to Mr. and Mrs. Hobart. He died in the Second World War, and she taught English at the upper school for many years. Mrs. Hobart spent the last few months of her life in the hospital. She died last fall, so the property has stood vacant for a while. But I always liked that house."

Mr. Lester stopped the car in front of a brick house only two streets from the police station. Knee-high grass filled the front garden. Climbing roses had outgrown an arched trellis. Mr. Lester opened the front gate and used his forearm to hold back the roses. "Watch yourself. These are thorny."

"See what you mean," Will said as felt the prick of the thorns through his suit coat.

"Notice the steps." The steps were made from bricks arranged in a semicircle. Mr. Lester continued, "You will find the same degree of workmanship throughout the entire house."

The instant Will walked into the empty house, he knew he was home. The foyer had a bench for taking off galoshes, coat hooks set into the wall, and an umbrella stand. Another doorway brought them into the sitting room. A set of stairs with an ornately carved wooden banister was to their right. Wood also framed the doorways. The wood trim and the fieldstone fireplace gave the house a nice, warm, homey feel. As Will stood in the middle of the empty sitting room, he could already picture his furniture in place. His sofa and overstuffed chair would fit easily. But most importantly, there would be a place for his state-of-the-art radio and phonograph. His large collection of vinyl records were his pride and joy.

The kitchen could accommodate a table and chairs. A large coal-burning stove sat to one side of the room, an icebox to the other. The kitchen had glass-doored cupboards that ran to the ceiling. One door led from the kitchen to the back porch, and another opened onto a bedroom. The bedroom was large enough for a double bed and dresser, and could also be accessed from a hallway. Will was relieved to see that the house was already equipped with indoor plumbing. The bathroom nearest the bedroom had white-tiled walls and a black-and-white geometric pattern on the floor. The bathtub was footed, and a mirrored medicine chest hung above the pedestal sink. Farther down the hallway was a second bedroom, then a door to the sitting room. At the top of the stairs there was a large open room.

"Plenty of room for storage up here. Later, you could add more bedrooms if you need them," Mr. Lester said. "The house was built in 1928. You might need to update the electrical, heating, and plumbing systems. There is room for a garage out back. The rooms could use a new coat of paint. With all the windows, the rooms are nice and bright. See, the doors all close, the floor is level, and there are no cracks in the ceiling. It's sat vacant for almost a year, and there are no signs of leaks or water damage. With a little modernizing, it would make a lovely home."

"Yes, Mr. Lester, I can see this is a good sturdy house. Do you think I could make it livable in two weeks? I need to report to work on the fourteenth of September."

"You're in luck. I can put you in touch with Ned Manderfield. He is the local contractor who can hire the workers you need."

"Aren't all the local tradesmen working on the Hampstead homes?"

Mr. Lester snorted in disgust. "The developer is some big shot from Shrewsbury. Brought in all his own workers. Shut out our local men. That rubbed folks the wrong way, I can tell you. No, Ned can get you some of our own who will do a right good job for you. And I will tell you why. These men want to look you in the eye when they see you on the street. No fly-by-night workers that do shoddy work, then leave town and never see you again. No, no, our men take pride in their work."

"Sounds good, Mr. Lester. But we haven't talked price yet. I don't know if I can afford this place plus all the upgrades."

"Let's go back to my office. I think you will be pleasantly surprised at the price of the house. The beneficiaries of Mrs. Hobart's estate live out of town. They are eager to have the place sold and the estate finally settled. We can also give Ned Manderfield a ring. He can inspect the house and give you an estimate of the work you want completed."

"I hope I can afford this house."

"If you need more money, I am sure Mr. Drummond over at the bank would be happy to give you a home loan. You will find that our village is ready to welcome you, Inspector. We need nice young people like yourself to settle down here instead of running off to London or Birmingham. For now, how about I mark the house as pending until you get your financing arranged?"

"Sounds good. Thank you for all your help."

CHAPTER 5

Good-bye, London

Mary Elizabeth, a young American doctor, had spent the weekend as a guest at the parental home of one of her colleagues. She checked the bedroom's drawers and wardrobe one last time, latched her suitcase, and set it beside her other suitcase outside the bedroom door. With her purse and medical bag in hand, she surveyed the room to burn a picture of it into her mind. It was the first bedroom she had slept in where all the furniture matched—the four-poster double bed with a pink-and-white flowered canopy, the dressing table and mirror, nightstands, and the chest of drawers were all one set. It was so different from the mismatched pieces of furniture that had decorated the boarding rooms and dormitories she had lived in for the past decade.

Opening the French doors, she walked onto a small balcony. The gardeners were already hard at work weeding the landscaped flowerbeds. A stone water nymph continuously poured water from her jug into a pool that stretched the length of the back garden. Mary Elizabeth watched colorful koi swim among the lily pads. She inhaled the fresh morning air, wondering what adventures the day would hold for her.

Mary Elizabeth descended the long, winding stairway. She dropped her bag and purse on the table in the front hallway and entered the dining room. The Harrington family was already seated at the dining table. Seeing her, both the Drs. Harrington stood up.

The elder, Dr. Stuart Harrington, greeted her. "Good morning, Mary Elizabeth."

"Good morning, Dr. Harrington, Mrs. Harrington, Stuey," Mary Elizabeth answered.

She went to the buffet and filled her plate with Cumberland sausages, eggs, and toast. Dr. Stuart Harrington III pulled out a chair for her. "Ready to spread your wings into the world, Doctor?" he teased.

"Just like you, Doctor," Mary Elizabeth answered.

As soon as she was seated, the servant came and filled her water glass. "Juice this morning, Dr. Senty?"

"Yes, orange juice, please, and tea."

"Very good, Doctor," the servant replied. When he returned with her beverages, he smiled as he placed a silver-plated jam caddy on the table in front of her.

"Oh, you remembered. Thank you." Before she ate, Mary Elizabeth bowed her head and made the sign of the cross, silently praying her meal prayer. Seeing her cross herself for the second time, the elder Dr. Harrington felt free to speak. "Mary Elizabeth, after Stuart drops me off at the office, he will drive you to the dealership to pick up your car. I hope that will not delay your journey by too much."

"No, not at all. I am very grateful Stuey will give me a lift. On our way home from the car dealership on Saturday, I was able to send Dr. Merton a telegram. I told him I would arrive in Bellechester by late afternoon. I never realized how difficult it would be to find a decent car in my price range. I am so glad you suggested the Rover dealership," she said between bites. "I hadn't thought of them because they sell such fancy, high-class cars. Who knew they would have a used car that I could afford?"

Mrs. Harrington leaned over her plate and asked, "The Rover dealer? Doesn't your golf buddy Henry Nelson own that dealership, dear?"

"Well, yes, he does. I suggested they visit him because Henry is always ready to help a young person such as Mary Elizabeth get started in life with a good car. Going into practice in such a rural area as Shropshire, she needs a dependable car to get to her patients."

Mary Elizabeth looked at Dr. Harrington and said, "Oh, I see. Did you have something to do with Mr. Nelson finding that trade-in at the back of his lot for me?"

Dr. Harrington cleared his throat and looked down, unable to meet her gaze. Rearranging the napkin on his lap, he said, "At lunch on Saturday, you sounded so discouraged. I merely gave Henry a courtesy call and told him to expect you. He asked what kind of car you were looking for and what your price range was so he could have some cars ready to show you when you got there. That would save you time. I knew he would find the perfect car for you. Henry is very good at his job."

"That he is. Usually when buying a used car, you take it as is. But Mr. Nelson said he wanted his mechanics to give it a thorough check before I picked it up. That was very nice of him. I guess what my grandfather told me is true," Mary Elizabeth said.

"What did your grandfather tell you?" Mrs. Harrington asked.

"Oftentimes in this life, it is not what you know, but who you know," Mary Elizabeth said.

Dr. Harrington concurred. "So true. So true."

"Well, I am glad she found a car. I was about to suggest she buy herself a motorcycle," Stuey said.

"Stuart!" Mrs. Harrington shot him a disapproving glance.

"Actually, Mrs. Harrington, I was starting to think the same thing. How many car dealerships did we visit on Saturday, Stuey?"

"Three," he said. "I do believe she inspected all the cars in every used-car lot we visited." Seeing his mother shoot him another hard stare, he quickly added, "But at least at the Rover dealership, there was a rugby game going on across the street, so I did not mind."

"Was it a good match?" Dr. Harrington asked as he sipped his morning coffee.

"I'll say. It was a semifinal game of the city's adult league, the Mayfair Magpies versus the Met Pips. The game play was extremely hard fought. It was almost like watching a professional match. I imagine there are some very sore, bruised players walking around today. We might even see some of them in our office."

"How is that, son?"

"Standing on the sidelines, I was able to offer medical assistance. I fixed a dislocated finger and wrapped a sprained ankle. I handed out quite a few of my cards after the game."

"Good thinking. Did you see any of the game, Mary Elizabeth? What did you think of our sport?"

"I only caught the last few minutes," Mary Elizabeth said.

"Come on, Mary Elizabeth. Don't be so modest," Stuey said and began to laugh.

"Stuart! Remember your manners," Mrs. Harrington said.

"My apologies, Mother."

Dr. Harrington asked, "Is there a story here?"

"After I finished at the dealership, I walked along the sidelines of the field looking for Stuey. I saw a rugby ball flying through the air towards me." Mary Elizabeth shrugged her shoulders. "It was no big deal. It was instinct, really."

Mrs. Harrington said with alarm, "Oh my! Did the ball hit you? Were you hurt?"

Stuey was unable to control himself any longer. He stood up and, with his usual dramatic flair, acted out the scene. "Hit her? It was a sight to behold. The spectators and the players were all yelling at her to duck or get out of the way. She looked up, leapt to the side, held out her hands, and caught the bloody ball! For a moment there was stunned silence on the field. Then everyone, including the players, started clapping and cheering."

Mary Elizabeth continued, "It was all so embarrassing. I didn't know what to do. I was going to throw the ball back onto the field, but then everyone was yelling at me to stand still. Luckily, by then, a referee came over, so I handed it off to him."

"I say, Mary Elizabeth," Dr. Harrington said. "Well done. Who won the match?"

"It was a close game, but the Pips won fourteen to twelve," Stuey said, sitting back down at the table.

"I know that the Mayfair Magpies are a neighborhood team, but who are the Met Pips?" Mrs. Harrington asked.

"The Pips belong to the London Metropolitan Police force. They all hold the rank of inspector or higher. Mary Elizabeth made quite the impression on the Pips, on one player in particular. They had quite the romantic interlude on the sideline."

Mrs. Harrington perked up. With her teacup raised, she inquired, "Oh, do tell."

Mary Elizabeth blushed. "We didn't have a romantic interlude. I only met him for a minute when he handed me back my purse."

Stuey grinned mischievously. "Let's see, number nine, wasn't it, Mary Elizabeth? Short chap, blond hair, brown eyes?"

Mary Elizabeth set down her fork in exasperation. "Really, Stuey! He was number twelve, very tall, over six feet for sure, broad muscular shoulders, black hair, blue eyes, and a very nice smile."

"I told Mary Elizabeth she should have invited him to our party Saturday night."

Mrs. Harrington said, "He would have been very welcome, Mary Elizabeth."

"He is probably married. After the game, I saw several children climbing all over him," Mary Elizabeth said. "Besides, he wasn't that interested."

"Wasn't interested?" Stuey was incredulous. "Mary Elizabeth, how can you say that? One of his teammates had to run to the sidelines and practically drag him back onto the field."

"Oh Stuey, how you exaggerate! He was merely checking to make sure I was okay. If he was truly interested, he would have come to the pub after the match. He didn't."

"Oh, so you were looking for him in the pub?" Stuey asked.

Dr. Harrington said, "Stuart! You took Mary Elizabeth to a pub?"

"I hadn't planned on it, but after the match the Pips invited us to the pub to join their celebration. The team captain even paid for our drinks. They made Mary Elizabeth an honorary member of the team. And they asked me to be their team doctor for the rest of the tournament."

"Oh, how nice for you, dear," Mrs. Harrington said. "Now, Mary Elizabeth, how long will it take you to drive to Bellechester?"

Relieved that Mrs. Harrington had changed the subject, Mary Elizabeth replied, "Looking at the map, Stuey and I figured it would take about five hours to make the drive. I should be there by midafternoon."

"Where will you be staying in the village?" Mrs. Harrington asked.

"Dr. Merton has invited me to stay with him in his residence. From the way he describes it, his living quarters are quite spacious."

"That is very generous of him. Have you met his wife? How big a family does he have?" Mrs. Harrington asked.

Mary Elizabeth said, "Dr. Merton is not married."

"Oh, my! Do you think it is a good idea to stay with a single man?"

"Dr. Merton is older than my father by quite a few years. He and Dr. Applegate were classmates in medical school. Dr. Applegate vouched for his character, and I know him to be a very shy, sweet man. He has always treated me with the utmost respect. I told Dr. Merton that I would not make any firm decisions about my housing until I look the situation over. In a small town, people are always going to talk. Nothing we can do about that."

Dr. Harrington said, "Very wise, Mary Elizabeth. Doctors are expected to set the moral tone for the entire village. I am afraid every move you make and every word you say will be scrutinized. It is part of the mantle we wear."

"Dr. Merton did mention that he has a housekeeper. We shall see how it all works out. It is my understanding that the surgery is attached to the residence. I would think it would be advantageous to have both of us living in the same house. That way when people call for the doctor, they need only dial one number," Mary Elizabeth said.

"To be sure, that would make for quicker service in an emergency. But it will all depend on how your living situation is presented to the villagers. I am sure that your Dr. Merton knows his people very well. He will not do anything that would place your reputation, or his, in danger," Dr. Harrington said.

"Before I forget, I want to thank you, Mrs. and Dr. Harrington, for your hospitality this weekend. It is hard to believe that Stuey's and my junior doctor training is now over. You have been so kind to me and Ruhan throughout the last four years, inviting us to spend all the holidays with your family," Mary Elizabeth said.

"You are very welcome, dear. We are always glad to have you stay with us," Mrs. Harrington said. "It was as if we had our own United Nations under our roof, with Ruhan coming from India and you from America."

Dr. Harrington said, "I am going to tell you the same thing I told Ruhan yesterday before Stuart took him to the airport. You are a part of our family now. Don't ever forget that. If you ever need anything, please don't hesitate to ask."

"Thank you. As you know, I do treat Stuey as a brother. I have six of them already, so one more won't matter," Mary Elizabeth said.

"Well, I hope you view me as an older brother," Stuart said, sitting up straighter in his chair.

Everyone laughed. Mrs. Harrington rose from the table, followed by everyone else.

"Are your bags packed and ready to go?" Dr. Harrington asked Mary Elizabeth.

"Yes, I put them outside my room. My trunk is already downstairs here somewhere."

"I will have Mr. Roberts bring down your suitcases and make sure your trunk is also packed in the car. I will meet you out front in ten minutes." Dr. Harrington said as he headed toward his study.

"Thank you. I will be ready."

"First Ruhan left us, and now you," Mrs. Harrington said as her eyes began to fill with tears. "I hate goodbyes, so I am going to say farewell to you here, Mary Elizabeth. You take care of yourself. Please write when you are settled. I would love to know what your new life will be like in Bellechester."

Mary Elizabeth took Mrs. Harrington's hand. "I promise to write. I hope one day, you and Dr. Harrington will visit me. I hear that the County of Shropshire is very beautiful. Goodbye."

"Goodbye, dear," Mrs. Harrington said as she dabbed her eyes with her lace handkerchief. She quickly exited the room, her floral dressing gown flowing behind her as she walked up the stairs to her room.

"And I hope that you will come and visit too. Bring Connor and Reggie, and we will have a grand reunion," Mary Elizabeth told Stuey. "I suppose it is too much to hope that Ruhan would be able to come from Bangalore. But Saturday's party was wonderful. It was a fitting way to end our four years together. I am going to miss you, Stuey. Who will I have to tease now?"

"Now, don't go getting sentimental on me, or you'll start me blubbering too. Are you ready to go?" he asked.

"You betcha. Now remember, I expect to receive an engagement announcement soon from you and Barbara. She is a wonderful girl, although what she sees in you . . ."

"Oh, come here." Stuey opened his arms. "I must say I do approve of this American goodbye tradition of yours."

"It's called hugging. And it's about time someone thaws out your cool British reserve." She gave him a peck on the cheek.

"Well, we better get outside. We don't want to keep Father waiting," Stuey said as he walked toward the front entrance.

"You go on ahead. I want to pop my head in the kitchen and thank your staff for always making me so comfortable."

In a few minutes, Mary Elizabeth joined the Harrington men in the front driveway. The elder

Dr. Harrington's pristine black 1958 Bentley S1 Flying Spur stood in the driveway. "You young people sit in the front. I never get the chance to try out the backseat."

It was a fifteen-minute ride to Harley Street in Marylebone, central London. In the car, they debated the superiority of rugby or American football, cricket or baseball. Soon enough, Stuey pulled up in front of a two-story red-brick building. The large, shiny brass nameplate on the outside of the building declared that the offices of Doctor S. Harrington and Sons, Physicians and Surgeons, resided within those walls.

"It looks like you will have to put up a different sign now that the third-generation Dr. Stuart Harrington has joined the practice. Stuey's grandfather must be so proud."

"He is. But that's a good point, Mary Elizabeth. What do you say, Stuart? Shall I put it on the agenda of the next office meeting?"

"That would be swell!"

As the elder Dr. Harrington got out of the car, he again said to Mary Elizabeth, "Now, please remember, Mary Elizabeth, you have friends here in London. If you ever need us, we are here for you."

"Thank you, Dr. Harrington. I will remember. Goodbye."

As they drove along, Mary Elizabeth looked over at Stuey and saw his furrowed brow.

"Okay, Stuey," she said. "What's the matter? Spill."

"You think I have it easy going into practice with my grandfather, father, and uncles? I tell you, it takes a lot to live up to the Harrington name. It's a bloody nuisance always being known as 'young Stuart' or 'the nephew.' I envy you, starting your practice fresh where no one knows you. You can be yourself."

"Don't worry, you will find your way to make your own mark. Look how easily you fit in with that rugby team on Saturday. Keep hanging around those rugby fields and I am sure you can drum up enough business to keep you busy. One day you can be the team doctor to some national sports team. Who knows? Maybe even an Olympic team!"

"Hey, that's not a bad idea. I wonder if my father and uncles would go for that."

"See, there you go. Give it a chance. Remember, you are a highly trained and skilled GP. And if it gets too bad, you can always move to another practice. I am sure there are any number of doctors who would love to have you join them."

"I'm not sure my family would let me leave."

"Well, if it gets too bad, you and Barbara can always move to Australia," Mary Elizabeth teased. "I hear it's quite nice down under, eh mate?"

Stuey chuckled. "Mary Elizabeth, you can always find the bright side. What about you? Are you nervous about going out and practicing in the sticks?"

"You forget, I grew up in the sticks. Living in a rural area does not bother me. I prefer it to city life. But sometimes it can be hard for an outsider to fit in. I just hope the villagers will accept me. You have never lived in a small town. Folks there have their own way of putting you in your place, or rather, the place they think you should be in."

"If I know you, by next year, you will have the entire village singing 'Yankee Doodle' and celebrating the Fourth of July." Stuey pulled into the Rover dealership. "Here we are. I never did get to see the car you picked out on Saturday."

"Well, there she is." Mary Elizabeth pointed to the car parked in front of the dealership.

"Sweet! She's a beaut."

"Thanks, it is quite the car. I didn't think I could afford a car as grand as this, but the salesman said it had been sitting in the lot for a long time. Most of his customers want the latest model, so he was eager to sell it. You don't think the people in the village will think I am putting on airs, do you?"

"What is this model? A '52 Rover 90?" Stuey asked.

"Yes, I believe that is what the salesman said. Goodness knows I can't keep all those car models straight."

"No, your Rover is a very sensible car. These cars are very dependable. That should give folks confidence that you will be able to get to them when they need you."

"Thanks, Stuey."

Stuey and Mary Elizabeth walked into the dealership. After signing the paperwork and handing over the money, Mary Elizabeth received the keys to her car. The salesman gave her a brief tutorial to show her where the light knobs were and how to operate the windshield wipers. Stuey then transferred her suitcases into the back seat. He hoisted her trunk into the boot.

"Now, do you have your map?" Stuart asked. "We marked your route last night. But if you like, I can lead you out of London to ensure you get on the right road."

"Yes, please! Last night I had a nightmare I was driving my car around London looking for the exit to Bellechester, but I could never find it. It was awful."

"Now we don't want that to happen. Follow me. When it is time for you to turn off, I will honk my horn," Stuart laughed.

"Got it. Well, this is goodbye." Mary Elizabeth jumped out of the driver's seat and gave Stuey another quick hug before she climbed behind the wheel. "Now don't forget me!"

"You? Never!" Stuey shouted over his shoulder as he walked to his car. He led her onto the London streets. Once he was sure she was on the correct road, he honked his horn, and turned right while motioning that she should go straight.

CHAPTER 6

On the Road and into the Fire

The traffic became thinner as Mary Elizabeth continued her journey northwest out of London. Her hands began to ache because she was gripping the steering wheel so tightly. Mary Elizabeth needed a break after driving for three hours. She stopped in Worcester at a petrol station. While the attendant filled the gas tank, washed the windshield, and checked the oil and the air pressure in the tires, Mary Elizabeth walked down the street to stretch her legs. She could tell by the freshness of the air that she was now in the countryside. After paying the attendant, Mary

Elizabeth pulled her headscarf from her purse. She rolled down her front windows so the breeze could blow through the car. As she continued on her way, she looked into her rearview mirror and caught herself smiling. There was no denying it. Mary Elizabeth felt at home in the country.

Her route took her through Leominster. She was getting excited, realizing she was only thirty minutes from Bellechester. She had been traveling uphill and down dales, and the scenery took her breath away. She passed flocks of sheep and herds of cows grazing in green pastures. Walls built of stones separated the fields. She remembered Dr. Merton saying he'd come to Shropshire more than thirty years ago and never felt the need to leave. Now she understood why.

As her car ascended the last big hill, she spied three steeples in the distance. From Dr. Merton's description, she knew the village ahead could be none other than Bellechester. She passed St. Bede's Benedictine Abbey, driving slowly to admire the sites. A half mile further along was the village school. The large two-story brick building housed the lower school. A playground filled with all sorts of jungle gyms, slides, and swings stood in front of the school. Next door was a smaller building which housed the upper school. A group of older students were playing on a field behind the school. A tall metal fence ran for half a mile before a large iron gate marked the entrance to St. Walburga's Convent. A large two-story stone building stood on the corner. The sign in front of the building read "Dr. H. Merton, GP." She drove her car around the back of the building and offered a short prayer of thanks for arriving safely at her destination.

Getting out of her car, her legs were a bit wobbly. She tried to convince herself it was because she had sat in the car for so long, but she knew better. She was nervous. With her medical bag and purse in hand, she walked around to the front of the building. The small painted sign that hung above the doorbell read "Ring Bell and Walk In." She pressed the button, and a dog barked inside the residence. She opened the door cautiously and saw a long hallway. A smiling young woman behind the reception desk greeted her. "Please, come in. May I help you?"

Mary Elizabeth's nose twitched from the strong odor of disinfectant in the air. Her confidence grew as she strode towards the receptionist.

"Hello, I'm Dr. Mary Elizabeth Senty. Very pleased to meet you." She smiled, extending her hand.

"Oh my!" exclaimed the young woman. "You're Dr. Senty?"

"Yes, I am. Dr. Merton is expecting me."

"I'm Miss Sarah Chamberlain. Dr. Merton is out on a call right now, but he told me to take you into his residence as soon as you arrived. Just a moment, please. I will ring Mrs. Duggan to let her know you are here." She picked up the phone and dialed a number. Mary Elizabeth could hear the receptionist say, "Mrs. Duggan, Dr. Senty has arrived . . . yes, right away."

Miss Chamberlain got up and walked around the massive oak desk. Sarah Chamberlain had a slim figure. She wore a pink headband in her shoulder-length light-brown hair. The slightest hint of makeup covered her attractive heart-shaped face. She wore a pink floral-print skirt with a white blouse. A pink sweater hung around her shoulders. "Please follow me," she said as she walked over to the massive wooden doors. "I hope you like dogs. Dr. Merton has a large Gordon setter called Magnus. He is a good dog and very friendly once he gets to know you."

"That's all right. I grew up with dogs on the farm, but our dogs were all outdoor dogs. I've never met an indoor dog before. But I am sure Magnus and I will get along just fine."

Miss Chamberlain knocked on the floor-to-ceiling sliding doors and opened them. Before they could step inside, Magnus came out to greet them. Mary Elizabeth ignored him and let him sniff her. A tall thin woman came out of the kitchen wiping her hands on a tea towel. A cover-all apron with small red roses protected her blue gingham day dress. Her pinned-up black hair was streaked with grey. Mary Elizabeth guessed that she was in her fifties. Her dark eyes, pointed nose, and small mouth reminded Mary Elizabeth of a hawk. She was sure not much escaped Mrs. Duggan's notice. Miss Chamberlain made the introductions.

Mary Elizabeth set down her medical bag, smiled, and held out her hand. "Very pleased to meet you, Mrs. Duggan. Harold—I mean, Dr. Merton—has told me wonderful things about you." Magnus sniffed at her medical bag.

Mrs. Duggan stiffened and frowned when Mary Elizabeth called Dr. Merton by his first name. "Well apparently, Dr. Merton forgot to tell us a thing or two about you."

Mary Elizabeth could not think of an answer and so said nothing. The awkward silence seemed to last an eternity. Finally, Miss Chamberlain said, "Well, I best be getting back to the front desk," and walked toward the sliding doors.

Mary Elizabeth followed her. "I think it would be better if I went with you and waited for Dr. Merton in the surgery." She looked back at Mrs. Duggan.

"Yes, that would be a very good idea. Let Dr. Merton figure out what to do with you." Mrs. Duggan turned on her heels and walked back into the kitchen. The kitchen door swung behind her.

Mary Elizabeth picked up her medical bag and followed Sarah back into the surgery. When they reached the reception area, Sarah said, "You will have to forgive Mrs. Duggan. She is very protective of Dr. Merton."

Mary Elizabeth nodded. "Miss Chamberlain, could you please direct me to the lavatory? It has been a long trip."

"Of course. It is down this hall, second door on the right."

"Thank you kindly." Locking the door behind her, Mary Elizabeth whispered to her own shaken image in the mirror, "Welcome to Bellechester." She splashed cold water on her face to revive her flagging spirits and gave herself a silent pep talk. *It will be better once Harold returns. Keep a positive attitude.* Once set to rights again, she emerged from the lavatory ready to face the world.

"Does Dr. Merton have any patients scheduled for this afternoon?"

"He did. But when he got called out on an emergency house call, I canceled his appointments. I rescheduled as many as I could for tomorrow. That is how it usually works. I write down the information on any new phone calls that come in, and put them in this basket. When he returns, he picks up his messages here. When I leave, I notify the local operator, and she keeps the phone messages for Dr. Merton. He phones her when he returns."

"Sounds like you have a very good system in place."

"Yes, but lately the appointments have gotten backed up quite a bit. Dr. Merton has been working long hours trying to keep up." Miss Chamberlain smiled at Mary Elizabeth. "I am glad he found some help. While we are waiting for Dr. Merton, would you like me to show you around?"

"That would be wonderful, but I don't want to take you away from your work."

"That's all right. I am all caught up now." Miss Chamberlain stepped out from behind her desk and walked down the right wing of the building. "Here is our waiting room."

The waiting room had six chairs along one side of the room and across the back wall. The other side of the room held a single chair and a small children's-sized table with three small chairs. An assortment of puzzles and toys were scattered on the tabletop. Two floor lamps provided extra light. Next to the children's area, a wooden rack held a variety of magazines. "What a pleasant waiting area," Mary Elizabeth said.

"You just visited the lavatory, and across the hall is the first exam room." Sarah turned on the light switch.

There was the usual exam table in the middle and a row of built-in cabinets along one wall. At the far end of the room was a desk with two chairs in front and one behind. The other side of the room sported a large, empty, white wall. "Doesn't Dr. Merton use this room?"

"No, he prefers to use the other exam, which is closer to the pharmacy area. This room would be for you to use," Sarah said.

"This will do nicely. I am amazed at the large size."

"I am glad you approve," Sarah said.

"Oh yes, I am very impressed."

Sarah then led Mary Elizabeth to the next room. "Here is the laboratory and the X-ray room." There was a long table upon which sat a microscope and all the materials to conduct simple blood and urine tests. In the back of the room was an X-ray machine on wheels. An exam table was in front. A light box for viewing the X-rays was mounted on the side wall.

Across the hall was the second exam room; its layout mirrored the first. The only difference was Dr. Merton's diplomas and certificates, which decorated the empty wall. He also had several pictures of Gordon setters. A picture of Queen Elizabeth II hung prominently at the center of the wall. Mary Elizabeth took her time looking at all the pictures.

Suddenly, there was a commotion coming from the reception area. A frantic male voice called, "Is there anyone here? Please help!"

Miss Chamberlain and Mary Elizabeth ran up the hall to the reception desk. A monk in full habit and a well-built teenage boy were holding up a younger boy whose pale face was etched with pain. He was crying, "My knee! Oh, it hurts!" The two teens were clearly teammates.

Mary Elizabeth was right behind Miss Chamberlain. "Here, bring him into this exam room and get him up on the table." She grabbed her medical bag off the front desk and followed the trio into the room. With effort, they got the injured athlete up onto the table.

Mary Elizabeth spoke in calm and soothing tones. "Now, who do we have here? What is your name?" she asked the boy.

"B-B-Bobby Da-Dalton."

"Bobby, I am Dr. Senty, and I'm going to help you. Miss Chamberlain, could you please bring me Bobby's medical record?"

"Right away, Doctor." She hurried out of the room.

"Father, can you tell me what happened?" Mary Elizabeth asked as she went over to the sink and washed her hands.

"I am Brother Hubert. We were having a derby. Bobby was defending, and the opposing player kicked the ball past him. As Bobby turned to follow the play, his cleats caught in the sod. He fell to the ground. John and I got him here as quickly as we could."

Mary Elizabeth examined Bobby's leg. She could tell his kneecap was at an awkward angle. "Ah," she said. "So you zigged and your kneecap zagged. Is that right?" She looked up at him.

"Yeah," he said through gritted teeth.

"Well," Mary Elizabeth said, patting his shoulder, "we will see if we can't get your knee back in shape for you. But first I am going to give you some medicine for the pain. Lie back and rest, and I will return very soon."

Miss Chamberlain arrived with Bobby's records. "Thank you. Let's see what we have here." Taking a few minutes to read it, she laid it out on the desk. Bobby had no drug allergies, so Mary Elizabeth opened her bag and filled a syringe. Assembling all her other materials on a small tray, she stood beside Bobby. "Could everyone wait outside the room while I give Bobby his medicine?"

Bobby cried, "No, I don't want them to leave."

Mary Elizabeth said, "I am American, so I say it differently. But if I were Dr. Merton, I would say, 'Bobby, I am sorry, but I am going to give you a jab in your bum.' They can come back in afterward."

Brother Hubert said, "We will be right outside."

Bobby put his arms over his eyes. Mary Elizabeth put her hand on his shoulder. "Bobby, it will all be over in a few minutes, I promise. The medicine will make you feel better soon." Getting Bobby positioned while minding his knee took some doing, but as promised, the jab was soon over. "Next we are going to take a picture of your knee, so we know what we are dealing with here." She went out to the hallway. "Brother Hubert, we need to take Bobby next door to take some X-rays. I am afraid I am going to need your assistance again."

"Of course. Anything to help." He and Bobby's teammate followed Mary Elizabeth into the room.

Mary Elizabeth said, "So sorry, Bobby, but we must move you. The medicine should begin to kick in about now so that should help with the pain."

Brother Hubert signaled for the other boy to help, and they carried Bobby onto the X-ray table.

"Please wait in the other room while I get these X-rays taken. I will call you when we are finished."

Realizing that any movement would be extremely painful for Bobby, Mary Elizabeth took her pictures as quickly as possible. Brother Hubert and the other boy got Bobby back to the exam room, and Mary Elizabeth stayed and viewed the X-rays. To her relief, she saw that Bobby's kneecap was not broken; it had just slid out of place.

As Mary Elizabeth stepped out into the hallway, she called, "Miss Chamberlain, could you come into the exam room, please?"

When Miss Chamberlain entered the room, Mary Elizabeth asked, "Can you tell me where I could find a splint and bandages?"

"The splints and bandages would be in the back pharmacy area."

"Great. Could you bring a basin filled with warm water, soap, a washcloth, and a towel?"

"Of course. Right away."

"Thank you." Mary Elizabeth walked down to the pharmacy area, found the supplies, and brought them back to the exam room.

"Let me tell you what we are going to do. I say *we* because this is going to be a team effort. Everyone is going to have a job to do."

Miss Chamberlain came into the room with the basin full of warm water and the towels. She put them on the counter.

"Thank you, Miss Chamberlain."

"Bobby, do you know approximately how tall you are?" Mary Elizabeth asked.

"About five feet, six inches," Bobby said.

"Miss Chamberlain, could you call the apothecary shop and see if they could fix up a pair of crutches for Bobby?"

"Right away," she said and left the room.

"Bobby, what does your father do?"

"He works at the bank," Bobby said.

"Brother Hubert, could you please call Mr. Dalton and let him know what happened? Ask him to stop at the apothecary shop and pick up Bobby's crutches. You can use the phone at the front desk after Miss Chamberlain finishes with her phone call."

Brother Hubert said, "Yes, of course."

Turning to Bobby's teammate, who was standing by his friend's side, she asked, "What is your name?"

"John Murray," he said.

Bobby spoke up, "But we all call him *Beef.*"

Mary Elizabeth noticed that the large boy's face fell as he heard his nickname spoken. "John, how are you doing? You aren't feeling queasy or anything, are you?"

"No, I feel fine," he said.

"Do you think you could be my assistant?" Mary Elizabeth asked.

His face brightened. "Oh, yes. That would be swell. What would you like me to do?"

"First, let's go over to the sink and wash our hands. Here, I'll show you how we doctors do it." After washing her hands, she said, "Okay, now it's your turn. When you're finished, please bring the basin to the exam table. I'll bring the soap and towels."

John did as instructed.

"Bobby, I am going to wash your knee. I am going to be as gentle as I can, but we must get all the dirt off. The medicine I gave you should be working, so this shouldn't be too painful. Why don't you tell me about your team?"

The boys were soon telling Mary Elizabeth all about their hopes for the upcoming season. Mary Elizabeth worked quickly. "Thank you, John. You can dump out the basin in the sink and set it on the counter for now," she said when finished.

"Yes, Doctor," John said.

After carefully examining Bobby's knee, she said, "All right. Let's put you back together again."

"How are you going to do that? Is it going to hurt?" Bobby asked.

"The procedure is called a reduction. I am going to position you, and your body is going to do all the work. Once your kneecap is back in place, most of your pain will be gone. Ready?"

Bobby nodded.

Mary Elizabeth bent over the table and cradled his leg. She flexed his hip to relax his quad muscles. Then she gently lowered the leg, and

Bobby's kneecap slid back into place. She put his leg down and examined it.

"Bobby, how does your kneecap feel? Does it feel like it is in the right place now?"

"Yes, it does. It feels much better," Bobby said.

"For now, I am going to put this splint on your leg to keep the knee stabilized. John, could you come and hold the splints in place while I wrap the bandage around his knee?"

"Sure thing," he said, taking a position on the other side of the table.

"Can you lift your leg for me?" Mary Elizabeth placed the splint on Bobby's leg and wrapped it up. "You strained some of the ligaments that keep the kneecap in place. When you get home, I want you to put ice on your knee for fifteen minutes. And then again after supper and before you go to bed tonight. Your knee will be sore for the next few days. Take two aspirin every six hours as needed for the pain. Use your crutches to get around. It is very important that you do not put any weight on your injured leg. Whenever you are sitting, make sure you keep your leg elevated. That will keep the swelling and the pain down.

And come see me again on Thursday. At that time, I will x-ray your knee again to be sure that there is no further damage. If you have any questions or your knee pain gets worse, call the surgery right away. I will write these directions down for you and your family to help you remember."

Bobby asked, "How soon until I can play again?"

"We have to make sure your ligaments heal and become strong so they can keep your kneecap in place. In about six weeks, I will give you some exercises for your knee."

"That long?" Bobby said.

"We have to take it slowly so you don't reinjure that knee. By that time, your knee will be even stronger than it is now."

"Don't worry, Bobby," John said. "You will be back in time for the tournaments, and those are the games that really count."

"Yeah," Bobby said, "I guess you are right."

"Even though you can't play, you can be an extra set of eyes on the sidelines. We can ask Brother Hubert if you can be like his assistant or something."

Bobby's face eased at the thought. "Yeah, that would be cool!"

Mary Elizabeth said, "John, could you go to the reception desk and ask Miss Chamberlain and Brother Hubert to come back here?"

"Right away."

Mary Elizabeth said to Bobby, "You are very lucky to have a good friend like John."

Bobby laughed. "Beef isn't my friend. I don't think he has any friends. He and his mother moved to the village earlier this summer."

"But you are on the same team. He helped carry you from the field."

"Brother Hubert made him do it because he is the biggest guy on the team."

"Okay, Bobby. Here's the deal. You are coming back here on Thursday to see me, right?"

"Yeah, I guess so."

"Before you come back, I want you to introduce John to some of your friends. Be ready to tell me five interesting things you have learned about him. And most important of all, I want you to stop calling him Beef. His name is John. Understood?"

Realizing from the tone of her voice that Mary Elizabeth meant business, he quietly said, "Yes, Doctor."

As Mary Elizabeth walked past Bobby, she put her hand on his shoulder and smiled. "Very good." She went to her desk and wrote in his chart.

Miss Chamberlain and John walked into the room. "Sorry for the delay. Dr. Merton has returned, and I had to fill him in. Right now, he is speaking to Brother Hubert. Is there anything else?"

"Please ask Dr. Merton to join us when he is available. Thank you."

Miss Chamberlain left. Mary Elizabeth continued writing. There was a knock on the door. Both Brother Hubert and Harold came into the room. Harold walked over to Bobby. "Young man, I hear you had a tough go on the field today."

"Hello, Dr. Merton. Yeah, I banged up my knee."

"Well, I am sure that Dr. Senty has taken good care of you." Harold said. "So glad to see you, Dr.

Senty. I see you got a baptism by fire. So sorry I could not be here to greet you when you arrived."

"I am very glad to be here, Dr. Merton. Miss Chamberlain was a big help, as were young John and Brother Hubert. With everyone's help, I think we have done right by Bobby. Let me fill you in."

Harold joined Mary Elizabeth at her desk. After listening to her summary, he agreed. "Yes, another X-ray on Thursday will let us know if the kneecap is in the right place and if the ligaments have stabilized."

"Now we are waiting for Mr. Dalton to bring Bobby his crutches. Thank you to John and Brother Hubert for all your help. Does anyone need a ride home?"

"I live right here in the village. I can walk home. Bobby, I hope your knee feels better soon. The team needs you," John said.

"Thanks, John." Bobby looked over to Mary Elizabeth, and she smiled at him.

John added, "Dr. Senty, I really enjoyed helping you today."

"John, you proved to be an excellent assistant for me."

The smile that lit John's face stretched from ear to ear. "I was? Wow, thanks. Goodbye, everyone." He left the room.

Brother Hubert said, "Dr. Senty, I don't know how you did it, but that is the most I have seen John smile all summer. Bobby, you take care. Hope to see you soon at practice. Thank you, Dr. Senty, for everything. God bless."

CHAPTER 7

WILL LEARNS ABOUT HOME REMODELING

A truck with "Manderfield Contracting" painted on the sides was parked in front of the Hobart cottage. A tall ladder leaned against the house. After Will fought his way past the overgrown rose arbor, he stood in the front garden. A voice from the roof yelled out, "Be right down!"

It was not long before a spry middle-aged man came scrambling down the ladder to him. "You the new owner?" he asked.

The man was of medium height and slight build with sandy-brown-and-gray hair which stuck out the sides of his brown cap. He had a lead pencil balanced behind his right ear.

"Yes, I'm Inspector William Donnelly. Mr. Manderfield?" Will held out his hand.

"Mr. Manderfield is my father. You can call me Ned. Everyone does," Ned said as he shook Will's hand with a strong grip.

"What is your verdict on the roof?"

"My grandad and dad put this roof on for the Hobarts when they built this house in '28. Nice couple. He went away to serve in the Second World War. Poor bloke. Never came home." He put his head down and shook his head. "You see any action?"

"I was with the Royal Military Police in the Korean conflict," Will answered.

"A Redcap, eh?"

"Yes, sir."

"Police work wasn't much of a stretch for you, was it?"

"No sir, it wasn't."

"Well, you being a Redcap and all, some of us vets get together on the second and fourth

Wednesdays of the month at the Ram. You'd be most welcome to join us," Ned said.

"Thank you for the invitation." Will took out his pad and pencil and wrote down the information. "How's the roof?"

"It's a slate roof and still in good shape. Those roofs can last up to a hundred years. Most times, with slate roofs, it's the timbers that rot and cause problems. Once we get inside, I will look in the attic."

"Here, let's go inside." Will unlocked the door.

"What kind of work do you want done?" Ned asked, looking around.

"Could you look at the boiler? Also, I would like your opinion on updating the plumbing and electrical systems."

"In other words, you want me to look over the whole place?" Ned said with a laugh.

"Mr. Lester said you are the expert in these matters."

"Let's start in the basement and work our way up."

That afternoon, Ned gave Will a crash course in home remodeling.

"Mr. Lester and I toured a model Hampstead home. I didn't care for the way the house was built, but it did have a few modern touches that I hope we can incorporate into this house."

"Such as?" Ned had his pencil and small notebook ready.

"In the kitchen, I would like to replace the coal-burning stove and the icebox with an electric stove and refrigerator. They also had a double sink, which would be handy for doing dishes."

"Anything else?"

"I would like to add a shower in the bathroom. I am afraid I do not fit very well in most bathtubs."

Ned laughed as he wrote down Will's requests. "I think we can accommodate you."

"And the last thing is a clothes washer in the kitchen with a retractable clothesline in the back mudroom. I do like the convenience of being able to do laundry in the evening and drying my clothes without depending on our English weather."

"I'm sure it will be doable."

As they walked from room to room, Ned threw out estimates for material and labor. Will stopped trying to keep the figures in his head and concentrated on answering Ned's questions. After checking the timbers in the attic, they ended the inspection in the sitting room.

"Since there is no furniture in the house, you might want to consider having new linoleum put in the kitchen. Easy to keep up. The rest of the floors are wood. Now would be the time to have them sanded, stained, and sealed. You pick out the colors, and my crew can have the ceilings, walls, and floors done throughout the house in three days."

"Actually, I was thinking of doing the painting myself," Will said.

"Son"—Ned put his hand on Will's back and used his kindest fatherly voice—"if I might make a suggestion. Your time and energy might be better spent if you concentrated your efforts on cleaning up the yard. There is enough work out there to keep you busy for at least two weeks. My crew is used to working together and knows how to stay out of each other's way, if you catch my drift."

"Point well taken," Will said. "Since we are doing everything, what about building a garage out back? Would that be possible?"

"Anything is possible. Let's go take a look." They walked through the knee-high grass in the back. "Lots of room back here. The clothes poles are rusted. Easy enough to replace them and re-string the lines. Now, do you want a single or a double garage?"

"A single. I only have one car."

"Maybe your wife will want her own car. Mine is already after me for a car of her own. And my boys are looking to buy their own junker car to fix up. You need to start thinking about the future. If you are putting all this money into fixing up this house, you will want to stay in the home for twenty or thirty years. That way, you can enjoy what your money bought."

This could be my forever home, he thought. "You are right, Ned. Make it a double."

"I don't think you will regret it. Besides, that will give you plenty of room to store your lawn mower and other outside tools."

That's right. I will have yard chores to do. And all those tools to buy.

"Inspector?"

"Sorry, I was just thinking."

"Yes, I could see the pound signs dancing in your eyes. I know it is overwhelming right now, but believe me, there is nothing more satisfying than a man owning his own home."

"I hope you are right," Will said. "What are the next steps?"

"I have all my measurements and notes. I am going home now and will put everything in a proposal. I can get it to you by tomorrow morning. Where should I drop it off?"

"Could you bring it to Mr. Lester's office?"

"Right. I will get the proposal to Mr. Lester by noon tomorrow."

"Do you think you can finish the work in two weeks?"

"It will be tight, but the garage can wait. We will concentrate on rewiring the electrical system and updating the plumbing. That will take the most time. Do you authorize overtime for the men if we need it?"

"Do you think the men will need overtime?"

"In a house like this, we never know what problems we might run into. The good news is that all the basics are here. All our work will meet the new housing codes. Like I say, might be tight to meet the two-week deadline."

"Yes, I authorize overtime. When should I schedule the movers?"

"If you schedule your movers for the end of the second week, you should be fine." Ned saw Will's furrowed brow. "Now don't worry, Inspector. I've got good hard-working men on my crew. You'll get your money's worth out of us. We will also get the phone company out here to install a line for you. When we are through, you will have a lovely home that you and your family can enjoy for many years."

"Thank you."

"Anything else?"

Will shook Ned's hand in the front garden. "Could you please write down what you need from me and when? I just want to make sure everything goes smoothly."

"Of course. This house will be a joy for us to work on, as most of us knew the Hobarts. It will be good to have someone living here again." Ned climbed into his truck and stuck his head out the open window. "Yes, I think the Hobarts would be pleased to have you buy and fix up their place. Good afternoon, Inspector."

CHAPTER 8

Around the Village

Mr. Dalton arrived with Bobby's crutches. Mary Elizabeth went over Bobby's instructions with him. Bobby was busy figuring out how to maneuver with crutches. Once he got the hang of using them, the pair left the surgery.

When Harold first met Mary Elizabeth in London, she'd given him the name used by her family. That name, derived from her initials, was Emme. Harold only called her by the nickname when they were alone, favoring her formal name at the practice. "Emme, I hope you don't have any doubts that you are needed here."

"I'm glad to help."

Harold looked at his watch. "I am anxious to introduce you to my friend, Father Matthias Evenson."

"You spoke so highly of him in London—I can't wait to meet him," Mary Elizabeth said as she continued to clean up her exam room.

"Good. I'll give him a call." Harold went out to use the telephone at the reception desk.

"St. Anselm's Rectory. Mrs. Winters speaking."

"Good day, Mrs. Winters. Dr. Merton here. Is Matt available?"

"Oh, Dr. Merton, Father is upstairs having his afternoon nap. May I take a message?"

"The new doctor has arrived. Could we come around in half an hour or so? I would like to make the introductions."

Mrs. Winters's voice conveyed her excitement. "In half an hour? Oh my, yes, I will be sure he is up by then. What an honor it is that you chose us to be the first to meet the new doctor. We will be ready to extend a warm welcome and make sure the new doctor feels right at home."

"Exactly what I wanted to hear, Mrs. Winters."

"Yes, Doctor. Goodbye to you then."

"Goodbye, Mrs. Winters."

After Mrs. Winters hung up the phone, she sprang into action. She laid out her best blue tablecloth on the large oak table. From her flower garden she picked white penstemon and purple asters and placed them in a crystal vase. The blooms complemented her fancy bone-china place settings, which were white with tiny blue flowers. In thirty minutes, the dining room table was set for tea.

Even though Mrs. Winters was a good ten years older than Father Evenson, she still possessed twice his energy. Her plump figure was testimony to her legendary culinary skills. A few years ago, Dr. Merton and Father Evenson had hinted that maybe it was time for her to slow down and think about retirement. She had met that unwelcome counsel by saying she would be dancing on their graves before she retired. They'd never broached the subject again.

Father Evenson sat at the table and could not resist the tray of cakes and sandwiches set before him. He was about to sample a lemon bar when Mrs. Winters swatted his hand and scolded, "Not till they get here!"

Mrs. Winters continued to fuss. "If this new doctor is young and single, you can bet all the eligible women in the village will be lined up outside his office. The rest of us will have no hope of getting an appointment!"

The ornately carved wooden mantel clock that sat on the buffet chimed four bells. Soon after, there was a knock on the door. Father Evenson jumped up. "I'll get it."

Mrs. Winters heard Father Evenson say, "Welcome, my friend. And welcome to you too. Shall we go into the dining room?"

Father Evenson led the way. Close on his heels strode a confident young woman in a pale-blue blouse, a floral skirt, and black flats. She looked to be in her early thirties. She wore her hair pulled back in a ponytail. A smile filled her face. She wore no makeup as her cheeks boasted a natural healthy glow.

Mrs. Winters was still looking behind Mary Elizabeth when Harold announced, "Mrs. Winters and Father Evenson, I would like to introduce to you to Dr. Mary Elizabeth Senty, my new associate."

Mary Elizabeth extended her hand first to Mrs. Winters and then to Father Evenson. "Very pleased to meet you both. Dr. Merton has told me so much about you, I feel I have known you for years."

Father Evenson soon regained his poise and broke the awkward silence. "Please, call me Father Matt. Here, sit down." He went and pulled out a chair for her. Mrs. Winters still stood there with her mouth open.

"Thank you," Mary Elizabeth replied courteously. "Mrs. Winters, you have laid out such an elegant tea. The sandwiches and the sweets look delicious. Dr. Merton told me he hoped you'd make lemon bars. He said they are legendary."

"Yes, thank you."

Noticing that Mrs. Winters was still standing up, Harold went over to her and said, "Where are my manners today? Here, Mrs. Winters, please, let's all sit down. I am so glad that you are one of the first to meet Dr. Senty." Harold held out the chair for her.

"Harold, why don't you tell us how you came to bring Dr. Senty to Bellechester?" Father Evenson inquired.

"I had been thinking of retiring for a while. My body is slowing down, and I'm concerned that soon, I won't be able to deliver the same level of care I am used to giving my patients. I called a former classmate of mine, Dr. Basil Applegate. He is the head of the junior doctor program at Mother of Mercy Hospital. I decided to travel to London and evaluate his new crop of doctors. I chose Dr. Senty because I found her to be knowledgeable and competent. She also has a very compassionate way of relating to her patients. I asked her, and she consented to come to Bellechester."

"But before I said yes, I had to know the answers to several important questions."

"Oh, indeed?" Father Evenson inquired. "And what might those be?"

Mary Elizabeth counted out the questions on her fingers. "Number one, did he think the people of Bellechester would accept a woman doctor? I cannot be of help to Dr. Merton if people will not come to me. I want to relieve his workload, not add to it. Number two, does Bellechester have a Catholic church? My faith is very important to me. And number three, what is the surrounding countryside like? You see, I grew up on a farm. I need open spaces for my spirit to thrive."

Harold laughed. "She doesn't need much, does she?"

"Well, I like a woman who knows what she wants," Mrs. Winters declared.

Harold said, "Dr. Senty and I agreed a trial period was sensible. I think we will all know in three months whether she and Bellechester are a good fit."

"Very smart and well said," Father Evenson agreed.

Mary Elizabeth wiped her mouth after eating an egg salad sandwich. "And there is one more thing . . ."

"Yes?" Father Evenson said as he reached for another lemon bar.

"Dr. Merton and I thought the two of you might have some ideas on the best way to introduce me to the good people of Bellechester."

Father Evenson had a thoughtful look on his face while he finished eating his bar. "I know. On Sunday, at the very end of Mass, I will ask the congregation to be seated, and then I will have you say a few words."

"And I can organize the ladies so after Mass we can have tea and cakes. That will give the villagers the opportunity to meet you personally. How does that sound?"

Harold said, "Wonderful!"

"I hope that doesn't put you through too much trouble," Mary Elizabeth said.

Mrs. Winters patted her hand. "Not at all, dear."

Father Evenson said, "Good. I am glad that it is all settled."

When the doctors left the rectory, they walked back up the street into the village. "How did you think that went?"

"Emme, you did wonderfully." Then he chuckled. "I will always remember the look on Matt's face when he saw you with me."

"Where are we going next?"

"I thought I should introduce you to Mr. McCafferty, our chemist. His shop is just a few streets up."

The village was mostly deserted, as it was nearing the dinner hour. Whenever Harold passed someone, he tipped his hat and greeted them by name, but he did not stop. Harold was never one to idly chit-chat, and no one dared to stop and question why he was in the company of a young lady. Still, their stares and questioning looks were not lost on Mary Elizabeth.

"Harold, in London, when you were telling me about Bellechester, you painted such a vivid picture for me. Now that I am here, it is exactly as you described. The older part of the village feels like I have stepped back in time. The cobblestone streets and the signs hanging above the shops remind me of a Charles Dickens novel. When we passed the bank, I expected to see Scrooge sitting at his desk."

"Now, that you mention it, Quincy Drummond does look a little like Scrooge. I guess it takes a fresh pair of eyes to see those things. Oh, here we are."

They had walked halfway down the block when Harold stopped before a shop that had a mortar and pestle painted on the sign. The front window displayed a shelf of clear carboys filled with different-colored water. Large black letters on the shelf read "A. McCafferty, chemist." A bell jangled as they entered. Their noses twitched at the strong smell of camphor in the air. Behind the counter stood a tall, middle-aged man wearing a short white medical jacket. He had a long, thin face with a handlebar mustache that curled up at the ends. When he saw them, his face broke out into a wide smile.

"Harold, what brings you in today? Do you need to place an order for medicines to fill your cabinets?"

"No, Angus, not today. I called in to introduce you to Bellechester's new general practitioner."

"Well, where is he?" Angus looked right past Mary Elizabeth, who stuck out her hand.

"Good afternoon, Mr. McCafferty. I am Dr. Senty, Dr. Merton's new associate. Very pleased to meet you."

Mr. McCafferty took her hand. "So, you're Dr. Senty. When Miss Chamberlain called earlier this afternoon to request Bobby Dalton's crutches, I naturally assumed the order came from you, Harold. But then both Miss Chamberlain and Mr. Dalton said the order was from a Dr. Senty. I was confused. Now everything makes sense."

"Yes, Dr. Senty will be joining me in my practice. She just arrived this afternoon. I don't think either of us expected her to need your services so soon."

"I am pleased to meet you, Dr. Senty. I hope you will like our village."

"I am sure I will. I look forward to working with Dr. Merton and collaborating with you. I surely appreciated your help earlier. Now, Mr. McCafferty, if I may have a piece of paper and a pencil, I will show you how I sign my prescriptions so that you are familiar with my handwriting."

"Yes, I have what you need right here."

"When signing prescriptions, I use my initials, M. E. Senty." Mary Elizabeth handed her signature over to him.

"Thank you. I shall keep this for reference."

Harold walked down an aisle and came back to the counter with a pack of razor blades. He removed his coin purse from his pocket while Angus rang it up. "On my last blade. When are the influenza vaccines due to arrive?"

"Should be coming in a few weeks. I'll let you know as soon as they're here."

Mary Elizabeth asked, "Are the villagers good about receiving the vaccines?"

Harold said, "It has always been a struggle to convince otherwise healthy people to take their jab. But '57 was such a bad flu season that last year we had twice as many folks line up for the vaccine."

"We almost ran out, so this year I increased our order. With your help, we might be able to reach even more folks this season."

"I'll be glad to help in any way I can."

Harold started toward the door. "Well, we should be going. We have a few more stops to make. Nice to see you again, Angus."

"Goodbye, Mr. McCafferty." Mary Elizabeth followed beside Harold.

As they continued down the street, Mary Elizabeth asked, "Now where in the village would I find a pair of barn boots?

"Barn boots? You mean *Wellies?*" Harold asked.

"Is that what farmers wear on their feet in the mud?"

"Yes, I believe so."

"Back home, we can get our barn boots, jeans, and work gloves at the seed and feed store. Does Bellechester have a store like that?"

"Oliver's Feed Store is down about half a mile on Abbey Road. Are you thinking of taking up farming?"

"You never know," she said as they continued toward the office. "Actually, I like to go on long walks. When it rains, the gravel roads turn to mud so easily. I want to keep my feet dry."

"You should find what you need at Oliver's."

As they reached the end of the street, Harold stopped and faced her. "Now, Emme, don't be too obvious, but I want you to glance across the street at the building on the corner with the large plate-glass window. Tell me if anyone is watching us."

"There are two men standing at the window. One is an older gentleman wearing a leather apron, and he is pointing at us. The younger man looks to be about in his late thirties. He has blonde hair and is holding a cigarette. They both appear to be laughing at us."

Harold sighed. "I was afraid of this. The man in the apron is Ron Trumble, the printer. The other man is Howard Pritchard, the editor of the *Bellechester Bugle*. I imagine he will want to interview you for the paper. But please, Emme, watch what you say. He has an annoying habit of twisting and turning an innocent comment into something that bears no resemblance to what was said."

"Sounds like you have a story to tell me."

"I can tell you over supper. Do you want to go over there and have me introduce you?"

"No, that is fine. Now that I know what he looks like, I think I will let him come to me if he wants an interview. Besides, I want to hear more about your experience with him. If you don't mind, could we go back to the house now? Today has been a busy day, and I have not yet had a chance to see the upstairs. I still do not know if living together will work. This afternoon, I was only in the sitting room for a few minutes."

"Didn't Mrs. Duggan give you a tour of the residence?"

"I don't think I am what she expected. She told me that you would figure out what to do with me, and then she disappeared into the kitchen. After that greeting, I decided to wait for you in the surgery. But Miss Chamberlain was very welcoming and hospitable. Her presence of mind and how she handled herself when Brother Hubert burst in with Bobby Dalton was amazing for one so young."

"Yes, Sarah Chamberlain was one of the best hires I have made, besides yourself, of course." Harold shook his head. "Emme, I am so sorry that you didn't receive a warmer welcome from Mrs. Duggan. I will speak to her tomorrow."

"Please don't. We knew not everyone would welcome me with open arms." Then Mary Elizabeth laughed. "Actually, her greeting reminded me of my home state of Minnesota."

"How so?"

"Her welcome was frostier than a car windshield on a January night."

CHAPTER 9

Home Again

When Harold and Emme got home, they could hear Magnus's muffled barks coming through the doors. Magnus bounded out to greet them as soon as they entered. Harold petted him; then the dog went to Mary Elizabeth. She bent down to pet him too.

"So, big fella, you remember me. I am glad you think that we can become great friends." She continued to talk to him while she petted him. Magnus made blissful sounds and put his paw in her lap.

"Heel." Hearing his master's voice, Magnus went and sat by Harold's side and looked up at him, awaiting further instructions. Harold scratched behind his ears. "Good dog, Magnus. I can tell she is going to spoil you. Then what will I do with you?" As they continued into the sitting room, Magnus went to lie by the fireplace.

"What a restful room! Harold, I didn't know you were such a keen decorator."

Wallpaper in green-and-gold figures gave both rooms a homey feeling. A large stone fireplace sat between the windows on the west wall. Along the south wall stood built-in bookshelves and a desk. On the desk was a telephone. The large sofa and two matching overstuffed chairs were covered in green velvet. Electric table lamps lit the small end tables. Facing the fireplace was a rather worn-looking recliner covered in brown cloth. Next to the recliner was a small table piled high with medical journals, newspapers, and books. On the other side of the recliner was a standing lamp.

"Thank you, Emme, but it was my predecessor's wife who deserves the credit for the decorating. One day in 1926, her husband went out on a house call and never came home. He suffered a heart attack. The doctor's wife was so grief stricken that she left the village to live with one of her married daughters as soon as the funeral was over. She took a few personal mementos but left the house fully furnished. Over the years, I made only minor alterations. I electrified the entire house, updated the phone system, and purchased my recliner."

"Oh, that is a sad story about the doctor and his wife. I hope going to live with her family brought the widow some comfort."

A warm, enticing aroma wafted from the kitchen. "Shall we go into the kitchen and see what Mrs. Duggan made us for supper?" Harold asked.

He opened the oven door. There sat only one individual cottage pie. He closed the oven door with such force that Mary Elizabeth, who was looking out the kitchen window, jumped at the noise.

"Anything the matter?" she asked. Harold scowled. "Supper smells delicious."

Harold recovered to a more pleasant expression. "How about I take you up to see the second floor? I am sure you are anxious to see if the accommodations are suitable."

The back door of the kitchen led to a narrow porch which ran the length of the building. At one end was the door to the back garden. At the other end, a staircase led to the second floor. Between the kitchen and the stairs there was a long perpendicular hallway.

"Where does that hallway lead?" Mary Elizabeth asked.

"It leads up to the reception area. That door up there comes out next to the reception desk in the surgery. From that hallway, you can go out the front door without having to go through the kitchen or sitting area," Harold explained.

"That will be very handy if I am called out in the night. This way my comings and goings will not disturb you."

"Yes, and it does give both of us privacy. Now let's go upstairs. You know, I cannot even remember the last time I was up there."

At the top of the stairs was a wide foyer. A desk, floor lamp, and comfortable chair were arranged at one end. The two of them walked down the hallway, passing four bedrooms. The upstairs bathroom was situated directly above the surgery's bathroom. The most spacious bedroom was located at the end of the hall. Large windows faced south, east, and west. Underneath the south window was a padded window seat. A double bed with two chests of drawers, a chaise lounge chair, a desk, and a large wardrobe filled the space.

"This is huge. I love having so much natural light. You know, Harold, I believe we could make it work. There is enough separation that we could both have our privacy and yet still have some common areas. And I do like being so close to the surgery. Yes, I would like to give it a try."

"Emme, I am so glad to hear you say that. And I think it would be a good idea to have a telephone up here on the second floor, possibly in this room, if it is to be your bedroom. I will call the telephone company tomorrow. Now let's see about bringing your suitcases up from your car."

After settling in, they went back into the kitchen. "I'm sorry, Emme. I thought I told Mrs. Duggan that there would be two for supper tonight, but it seems we got our signals crossed." He opened the oven and brought out the small pie. "Should we eat out at the Ram's Head Tavern? My treat?"

Mary Elizabeth said, "Thank you for the offer, but no. Mrs. Duggan made this pie for your supper, and I think you should eat it. Do you mind if I open the refrigerator?"

Harold said, "Of course not. No, I couldn't possibly eat the pie. What would you have for supper?"

"Harold, I don't want to argue with you." Opening the refrigerator she said, "Here, I found lettuce, tomatoes, and cheese. I am going to make a nice salad. Now, do you have any bread?"

"Yes, here is a loaf."

"Good. If you slice the bread, I will fix the salad. A little oil and vinegar for the dressing, and if we split the pie, I do believe we will have a nice meal after all."

Over supper that evening, Harold told Mary Elizabeth the story of his encounter with the editor of the *Bellechester Bugle*. "It was when Howard Pritchard first came to town about eight years ago. He did a story on me because, at that point, I had been practicing medicine in the village for twenty-five years. He asked me what I enjoyed most, and I said I liked watching the children grow up into fine young men and women. I said how satisfying it is to be delivering the babies of the babies I had delivered years ago. I think of all of them as my own children."

"Nothing wrong with that." Mary Elizabeth said. "That sounds like a very nice thing to say."

"Well, I thought so too. But when the newspaper came out, the headline read, 'Dr. Merton Claims All Bellechester Babies Are His Own.'"

Mary Elizabeth burst out laughing. "Oh, Harold. Really? He printed that in the paper. Oh, how embarrassing for you."

"The day the paper came out, I had a surgery full of angry men demanding to know if I was the real father of their children. The whole village was in an uproar."

"What happened?"

"Lord and Lady Brantwell put pressure on Howard, so he printed a retraction in the next issue. In a few weeks, the whole episode was forgotten."

"Oh my, I will be very careful what I say around him. You know those days in London when we said the Rosary together?"

"Yes?"

"After you left the hospital, somehow saying the Rosary without you just didn't feel the same. So, if you don't mind, could we continue saying the Rosary together after supper—that is, if neither of us is out on a call?"

"Of course, Emme. Let's go sit in the front room and pray."

"Thank you, Harold. It has been such an eventful day that I fear I shall not be awake much longer."

Tuesday, September 1

CHAPTER 10

A BELLECHESTER MORNING

At 7:10 a.m., Mary Elizabeth walked downstairs. She tried to be quiet, but the stairs creaked and groaned under her feet. Harold stuck his head out from the kitchen. "Off to Mass, Emme?"

"Yes, Harold."

"Well, say a prayer for me if you remember."

"I will. See you later." Mary Elizabeth walked down the long hallway and opened the door to the street. The air was cool and sweet. She wrapped her sweater tightly around her. The village of Bellechester was beginning to wake. As she walked past a block of houses, she could smell bacon frying. Mary Elizabeth's stomach growled. She quickened her pace. The milkman was also on his route. The clank and clatter of full bottles being delivered and empty ones being retrieved added to the morning sounds. When he saw Mary Elizabeth, he tipped his hat. Mary Elizabeth waved. "Good morning."

She walked past the darkened shops with their "Closed" signs prominently featured in the windows. The familiar blue light was still lit on the lamp post in front of the door of the police constabulary. She crossed the street and took the diagonal path that ran through the park.

A man was running up the path towards her. His running attire consisted of a white T-shirt, blue shorts, socks, and plimsolls. Mary Elizabeth could see he had been running for quite some time, for even in the cool morning, his T-shirt was stuck to his chest. Beads of sweat glistened in his black hair. As he passed her, he greeted her with a "Morning, miss."

Mary Elizabeth turned around and called out, "Morning." He acknowledged her greeting by raising his hand as he continued his run. She continued to watch him. For a big man, the runner was a picture of athletic style and grace. She sighed and hurried to church, trying to fill her mind with loftier and holier thoughts.

Birds were chirping in the branches of the tall mature trees. Robins scoured the ground for worms while the squirrels chased each other. Mary Elizabeth laughed as she watched their antics. Crossing the street again, she came upon the rectory and the stone church with the tall square bell tower. Mary Elizabeth stopped a moment to admire the Romanesque architecture of the building. Pulling open the heavy wooden door, she stepped into a world of wooden pews, stained-glass windows, statues of the saints, and paintings of angels and heavenly images which covered the walls and ceilings of the sanctuary. Mary Elizabeth was now in her spiritual home. Even in Bellechester, a village where she had just arrived, she felt safe and secure among all the familiar trappings of her faith. Rows of candle flames danced inside colorful vigil lights. She dug into her purse for a few coins, fitted them into the slot, and lit a candle. She made her way up the aisle, genuflecting by the fourth pew on the side of the church, where a statue of Mary, the Blessed Mother, stood. She settled into a pew, knelt, and bowed her head in prayer.

At the sound of tinkling bells, Mary Elizabeth rose. Father Evenson, accompanied by two young altar servers, entered the sanctuary and the familiar ritual of Mass began. After Mass, Mary Elizabeth stayed in the pew a few more minutes praying for her family back in Minnesota and her friends in London. Once again, the runner intruded on her thoughts, so she prayed for him too. Genuflecting once more before the tabernacle, she made her way outside.

Father Evenson stood by the door greeting parishioners. "Good morning, Dr. Senty. Today looks like another beautiful day."

"Good morning, Father Matt. Thank you for your pearls of wisdom. I will try not to bury my talents today."

Father Evenson laughed. "You better not. That would not bode well for the health of this community. Will you be joining us every morning?"

"I hope to as long as I am not out on a call. I find Mass centers me and reminds me of what is most important in life. It keeps me going. And it helps me feel less homesick."

"Oh, how is that?"

"I find it comforting to know that my grandpa will be hearing the same words at Mass in my home church of St. Ursula, and my older sister Rose will be hearing them in her Benedictine convent in Buffalo Prairie. On some spiritual level, Mass connects the three of us. Does that sound strange to you?"

"Not at all. Someday I would like to hear more about your family."

"I am afraid that would take an entire evening, as I come from a large family."

"I shall look forward to it."

"I best be going. The surgery will be opening soon. Have a good day, Father."

"You have a good day too, and tell Harold that I will be by to pick him up shortly."

When Mary Elizabeth returned from Mass, Sarah was already at her post at the reception desk. She put down the receiver and looked up at

Mary Elizabeth. "Good morn . . ." She never got to finish her greeting, because the phone rang again. "Good morning, Bellechester Surgery. Dr. Merton is not in the surgery today, but Dr. Senty has an opening at eleven thirty. Would you like to come in then? All right, I will put you down. See you at eleven thirty. Goodbye." After she hung up the phone she said, "Dr. Senty, I scheduled your first patient for nine o'clock, so you had better go in to the kitchen and grab some breakfast. Your morning schedule is now full. You won't have a break until lunch. Word has gotten out about you, and folks are asking to see you."

"Thanks," Mary Elizabeth said as she opened the door behind the reception area and walked down the hall into the kitchen. Harold sat the table finishing his breakfast. Instead of wearing a suit and tie, he wore an old long-sleeved shirt with frayed cuffs and a fishing vest. "Good morning, Emme. Better eat a good breakfast. You are going to have a busy day."

"Is the surgery always this busy?" Mary Elizabeth asked as she went to the fridge and got out two eggs. She put a piece of bread in the toaster.

Harold sat at the table, sipping his tea. "No, not usually. I doubt you will have any serious cases today. The village folk are curious. They just want to come and meet you."

"I was going to ask if you will be in the surgery with me, but judging by your attire, I take it you have other plans?"

"Yes, Matt and I are going fishing this morning. I thought it best the village meet you without me around. Sarah is scheduling my house calls for the afternoon. Today, the surgery is all yours."

"So you are going to desert me? I don't even have my exam room set up yet. My diplomas are still upstairs in my trunk."

Harold laughed. "A piece of paper inside a frame is not going to impress them. They only want to get to know you. Just be yourself. Besides, you have already won over the most difficult patient in Bellechester. His opinion is the only one that really matters."

Mary Elizabeth stood at the stove scrambling her eggs. She looked back over her shoulder at

Harold and scrunched up her face. "Bobby Dalton?"

"No, you silly, me. If you can convince me that you are a caring and capable doctor like you did in London, well then, the rest of the village will be a doddle."

There was a knock at the back door, and Matt walked in all dressed up in his fishing attire. An old hat sat on his head with several fishing lures dangling from it. "You ready to go there, Harold? The fish aren't going to wait."

At Matt's voice, Magnus came running in from the sitting room. He stood before Matt, his tail wagging.

"Want your pets?" Magnus immediately rolled on his back so Matt could scratch his belly.

Mary Elizabeth brought her eggs and toast to the table. "Have a good time. But Harold, if your ears start burning, it won't be the sun."

Harold feigned surprise. "Why, Emme!" He smiled and patted her hand as he walked towards the back door. "Don't worry. You'll do fine. You can tell me all about it later at lunch. Let's go, Matt. Magnus, come."

Mary Elizabeth watched as Harold disappeared into the garage and came out with his fishing pole, net, and tackle box. Father Evenson's car was soon loaded, and the two friends and Magnus drove away.

Across town, after his morning run, Will showered, dressed, and packed his overnight bag. He descended the narrow staircase, ducking at the bottom to avoid the lintel.

"Leaving us already, Inspector?" Donnie asked as he stood behind the bar, wiping pint glasses and readying the bar for the day's customers.

"Not quite yet. I wanted to clear out of the room so you could prepare for the next guest."

"That is very thoughtful of you, Inspector. But I hope you won't be leaving before you have breakfast. Your fry-up is included with the room. And you won't want to miss my wife's famous black pudding. It is known throughout these parts."

"I could get very used to your wife's cooking. Last night's lamb chops were delicious. Be sure to give her my compliments."

Donnie grinned widely. "I'll tell her. Now you go pack your car, and your breakfast will be ready in about twenty minutes. If you need reading material, the latest issue of our weekly newspaper is at the far end of the bar. Guests receive a complimentary copy."

"Thank you, Donnie."

While waiting for his breakfast, Will picked up last Friday's edition of *The Bellechester Bugle*. The article on the front page caught his attention. "Inspector Brett Leaves Village After Eight Months; Replacement Yet Unnamed." Will read about his predecessor with interest. Inspector Brett was quoted as saying, "I found a position in Manchester that was better suited for my family. We need a fresh start."

The journalist also interviewed Chief Superintendent Williamson. "We wish Inspector Brett all the best in his new position. Until a new inspector is named, we leave the Bellechester constabulary in the capable hands of Sergeant O'Hanlon. We will be taking our time to find the best possible candidate for your village. Because of the rise in crime in recent months, especially thefts in Bellechester, we are looking for someone who has skills and expertise in those crimes. We are also going to be sensitive to his family situation. We want to be sure that the new inspector and his family will be an asset to the Bellechester community."

Turning to page three, Will read about the most recent crime event in Bellechester. Officer Jenkins gave his account. "I was on patrol when I noticed the door's window was smashed and ajar at Oliver's Feed Store. Upon investigation, I discovered three juveniles inside. Two were passed out on a sack of feed, and the other was trashing the place, tipping over barrels of seed, and throwing merchandise off the shelves. It took a while to subdue this juvenile before I got him cuffed and to the station. Once awakened, the other juveniles were more cooperative. Damage to the store was extensive." The article went on to say that the three juveniles had appeared before the Bellechester Magistrates in a closed hearing. No further information was available.

For Will's breakfast, Donnie's wife made him a full English breakfast consisting of two fried eggs, a rasher of bacon, two sausages, fried tomatoes, mushrooms, beans, bubble and squeak, fried bread, and black pudding. Will savored every bite.

CHAPTER 11

Patients and Patience

Mary Elizabeth finished her breakfast and placed her dirty dishes beside Harold's in the sink. Mrs. Duggan began her day at nine o'clock, and Mary Elizabeth had no desire to run into her. She went upstairs to make sure she was ready for whatever the day would bring. For her first official day of work, Mary Elizabeth chose a navy pencil skirt and a white blouse with short-capped sleeves. Mary Elizabeth felt that was her most professional-looking summer outfit. She wore her hair in a bun and made sure she had plenty of bobby pins to catch any strays. She was satisfied with her reflection. *Remember! You are a highly trained GP. There is no situation today that you cannot handle. Harold believes in you, so you believe in yourself too. Be professional, personable, and compassionate, and keep your sense of humor!* She hurried downstairs and along the hallway to the back of the reception area. She put on her white lab coat and waited for Sarah to be off the phone. "How do we do this? Do I come out and bring the patients back to the exam room, or do you?"

"Dr. Merton prefers that I bring patients back to his exam room. Saves him some steps. But whichever way you want to do it is fine with me."

"Well, if you don't mind, I would like to call my own patients. That way, I can make sure I have finished writing out all my notes before calling the next one."

"That makes sense to me. I put your patient's files here." She thumbed through a hanging folder on the left side of her desk. "I keep Dr. Merton's files on the other side."

"Wonderful. You are very organized. I love it." Mary Elizabeth picked up her first file.

Two middle-aged women were deep in conversation in the waiting room. Mary Elizabeth stood in the doorway. "Prudence Farnsworth."

The women stopped talking. The plumper of the two wore a tall red feathered hat. Her stylish red-print wrap dress clung to her rotund figure. She wore a string of pearls around her neck and had a large red purse draped over her arm. Her red gloves stretched halfway up her forearms. As she walked toward Mary Elizabeth, her red high-heeled shoes clacked on the linoleum. "That is Mrs. Thomas Farnsworth," she corrected Mary Elizabeth.

"Excuse me. Mrs. Thomas Farnsworth, please follow me." Once they were inside the examining room, Mary Elizabeth took her place behind her desk. "Mrs. Farnsworth, please have a seat. My name is Dr. Mary Elizabeth Senty. I am very pleased to meet you. Now, what brings you to the surgery this morning?"

Mrs. Farnsworth made no rush of situating herself in the chair. "Why, you do, of course. My husband is mayor of Bellechester, and as first lady, I consider it my duty to pay you a call. Last evening, I heard the most astonishing news. There is a rumor going around town that Dr. Merton brought a young woman from London to live with him. They said she was a doctor, but I knew that couldn't be true, so I came to see for myself."

"I am so glad you came in this morning. Sometimes people don't always get the story straight. But in this case, what you heard is correct. I am a doctor, and I do share the doctor's residence with him. Now, what can I do for you today?"

"Poor Dr. Merton! He hasn't been himself since his illness last winter. I said to my husband just the other day that I feared Dr. Merton would go off and do something barmy. And he did!"

"Barmy?"

Mrs. Farnsworth stared at Mary Elizabeth as if she were questioning Mary Elizabeth's sanity too. "Why, yes. He left the village without telling anyone where he was going."

"Surely Dr. Merton would not leave the village without a doctor."

"He did arrange for doctors from the hospital in Glendale to cover for him. There was a different doctor here at the surgery for each of the four days he was gone."

Mary Elizabeth listened attentively. "I am sure those doctors did their best to care for Dr. Merton's patients." Mrs. Farnsworth took a sharp breath. Mary Elizabeth studied the contents of Mrs. Farnsworth's medical file.

Mrs. Farnsworth saw Mary Elizabeth hang her head. "I should say, you should be ashamed of yourself, taking advantage of a sweet old man like Dr. Merton."

Mary Elizabeth tried not to let Mrs. Farnsworth's words get to her, but she could feel her cheeks getting warm. In a level and professional voice, she said, "I'm sorry, Mrs. Farnsworth, but I must set the record straight. Dr. Merton asked me to come to Bellechester to join him in his medical practice. And I agreed. No one took advantage of anybody. Now, I see from your medical chart that the last time you were here, your blood pressure was elevated, and you complained of heart palpitations and swollen ankles. How are you feeling today?"

"Fine. Never better."

"I am glad to hear it. Dr. Merton's diagnosis was hypertension, which can be quite serious. Often there are no symptoms. Now, let's go over here to the examining table, and I will take a reading of your blood pressure and listen to your heart so I can update your chart."

"I didn't come here for a medical consultation."

"In the last entry, Dr. Merton wrote that he wanted you to come back in one month for another blood pressure check. That note was written over a year ago, and there are no further entries." Mary Elizabeth got up from her desk and walked over to the sink to wash her hands.

Mrs. Farnsworth was flustered. "I have been extremely busy. I am the head of the local chapter of the Women's Institute as well as a delegate to the national women's conservative party and head of St. Anselm's Altar and Rosary Society."

"You are an impressive woman, Mrs. Farnsworth. I can see you are a leader in this community. A woman as busy as yourself needs to take care of herself to be able to use her time most efficiently. Now, to prevent you from having to make another trip to the surgery, why don't we update your chart now, while you are here? It will only take a few minutes, and then you can get on with your busy life."

"Oh, all right, as long as I am already here."

"Good. That's a wise decision, Mrs. Farnsworth. Please, come sit on the exam table. Here, if you come around to this side, there is a step stool. Let me help you up."

Mary Elizabeth conducted her examinations. She recorded the numbers in Mrs. Farnsworth's chart. Mary Elizabeth slipped off one of Mrs. Farnsworth's shoes and carefully examined her ankle. "Mrs. Farnsworth, do you find that in the evening, your ankles are quite swollen?"

"Yes, yes, I do. I attribute that to the shoes I wear. But by the morning, my ankles are back down to a normal size again."

"Here, I will slip off your other shoe, and then I will have you come over to the scale so I can get a quick height and weight from you. So sorry, but I am afraid you will have to remove your hat." Mary Elizabeth took a moment to admire Mrs. Farnsworth's headdress. "Your hat is quite striking, and it goes so well with your outfit."

"Thank you." Mrs. Farnsworth took out her hat pins and removed her hat.

"Let me help you up onto the scale."

Mary Elizabeth charted the results and helped Mrs. Farnsworth off the scale. "Thank you, Mrs. Farnsworth. I have all the numbers I need from you today. I will let you get yourself back together. Then we can go through your exam results."

After Mrs. Farnsworth had quickly collected herself, she sat in front of the desk. Mary Elizabeth told her, "Mrs. Farnsworth, I am afraid that your blood pressure numbers are still quite high. Having elevated blood pressure means that your heart is working harder than it should. Here," Mary Elizabeth said as she handed a prescription to her. "Mr. McCafferty can fill this for you. Take one pill every day in the morning. It is a diuretic, which will help your body release some of the fluid it is retaining. This pill will cause you to use the toilet more frequently, but it should help with the swelling in your ankles. Most importantly, your heart will not have to work so hard. Do you have any questions for me?"

"No, Doctor."

"Well, I realize I have given you a lot of information to absorb. Mr. McCafferty will go over your medication with you again when you pick up your prescription. If you think of a question later on, you can always give me a call. I am happy to talk with you. Here, I'll walk out with you." She gathered up Mrs. Farnsworth's file and escorted her to the front desk. "Miss Chamberlain, I'd like to see Mrs. Farnsworth again in a month."

"Of course, Doctor." Sarah consulted her appointment book and turned the pages to October.

"You take care, Mrs. Farnsworth. Goodbye."

Mary Elizabeth pulled out the next folder from Sarah's desk. Walking to the doorway of the waiting room, she saw that the waiting room was beginning to fill up. Raising her voice so it could be heard over din of conversation in the room, she called out, "Freda Lester."

At first no one moved. Then the middle-aged woman who had been talking with Mrs. Farnsworth rose slowly from her seat. She clutched her white handbag. Her outfit was simple, a pale-blue dress with short white gloves. She wore a single string of pearls, and her hat was adorned with small pale-blue flowers. Her low-heeled white shoes barely made a sound as she walked toward Mary Elizabeth. When Freda Lester reached the doorway, Mary Elizabeth asked, "Now, is it Miss or Mrs. Lester?"

"Mrs. Lester. Oh, I am sorry. I can see that you are very busy. I should go."

Mary Elizabeth reassured her, "No, please. You have been waiting a while to see me."

Mrs. Lester protested weakly, "It was a mistake for me to come. I only came because Prudy wanted me to come and keep her company."

Mary Elizabeth said, "I am glad that she brought you. Now come with me and we will have a nice chat. I would like to meet you." Mary Elizabeth gently put her arm around Mrs. Lester and shepherded her into the exam room. "Please come and sit in the chair next to my desk."

Mrs. Lester obediently walked up to her desk and sat on the edge of the chair. Her posture was straight as an arrow. She set her purse in her lap and fumbled absentmindedly with the strap. Her eyes followed Mary Elizabeth. Mary Elizabeth thought, *No sudden movements. Mrs. Lester looks like she could bolt out of this room at any moment.* Once seated, Mary Elizabeth said, "This is nice. I appreciate you spending some time with me. I was wondering, as a newcomer to Bellechester, do you have any advice for me?"

"Me? Give you advice?" Mrs. Lester asked.

"Yes, I thought you might tell me how I could best fit in—you know, become part of the community." Mary Elizabeth watched the woman before her begin to relax.

Mrs. Lester sat back in the chair. The features of her face softened as she pondered the question. After a few moments she said, "St. Anselm's Altar and Rosary Society meets the second Tuesday of the month. Many of the women in the village are members. Prudy is our president, and I am the membership chairwoman. Yes, you would be most welcome to join us. We pray the Rosary at seven and then have our business meeting. Sometimes we even have a guest speaker. The talks are always so informative. We take turns bringing treats, and there is always time for us to have a good chin wag. We are all home by nine o'clock."

"Your society sounds like a wonderful organization. Thank you for inviting me." Mrs. Lester's brow furrowed. "Is something wrong, Mrs. Lester?"

"I'm sorry. But our group is only for members of St. Anselm's. I never even asked if you are Catholic."

"Not to worry, Mrs. Lester. I am Catholic born and bred. I don't know how I would get by without the Mass and the sacraments. I have already met Father Evenson. He seems like a very caring priest. He said I could get registered in the parish after Mass on Sunday."

For the first time, Mary Elizabeth saw a smile on Mrs. Lester's face. "Yes, we are very lucky to have Father Evenson for our priest. Oh, that is very nice. You being Catholic will go a long way in getting folks to warm up to you."

"I hope you are right, Mrs. Lester. I do want to become part of this community. You have done me a great kindness. Thank you. Now I would like to return the favor. Is there something I could do for you this morning?"

The smile vanished from Mrs. Lester's face. She began fumbling absentmindedly with her purse strap. "Oh Doctor, thank you. I have enjoyed talking with you too." She hesitated for several moments before she shook her head. "No, there is nothing you can do for me today. Thank you all the same."

"All right, Mrs. Lester. Know that my door is always open for you. If you ever feel the need to come and just talk, know that I am here for you. Anything you tell me is strictly between the two of us. As with Father Evenson in the confessional, we doctors also safeguard your privacy. It is part of our professional code of ethics and something that I take very seriously."

"Thank you, Doctor." Mrs. Lester stood up. "I'm sorry I wasted your time this morning."

"You didn't waste my time. I enjoyed meeting you. I especially appreciated you telling me about St. Anselm's Rosary Society. I will mark the date on my calendar. Here, I will walk out with you." Mary Elizabeth escorted Mrs. Lester back to the reception desk. Sarah looked up expectantly at Mary Elizabeth. Mary Elizabeth just shook her head.

"Now remember, Altar and Rosary, next Tuesday."

"I will remember."

"Thank you, Doctor." Mrs. Lester reached for Mary Elizabeth's hand and smiled at her. "Good day."

"Good day, Mrs. Lester." Mary Elizabeth stood at the desk and waited for Mrs. Lester to exit the building. She turned to Sarah. "How are we doing?" Mary Elizabeth peeked into the waiting room. All the chairs were filled. "Oh my. Have I fallen behind already?"

"Don't worry, Dr. Senty. Some of the village folk have stopped in to get a look at you. They are not expecting to be seen. We are doing fine. No need to hurry."

"That's a relief." She pulled the next file, lingering at Sarah's desk for a few minutes. When she appeared in the doorway of the waiting room, the conversation stopped. "Mr. Dobbins."

"Aye." A burly man in his late forties approached her with a bandaged hand. He smiled and teased, "You's a pretty lass. Sure'n ya know yur stuff?"

Mary Elizabeth returned his smile. She made sure she spoke loud enough for the entire waiting room to hear. "Shall we go see, Mr. Dobbins? I'll let you be the judge of that."

"What brings you to the surgery this morning?" she asked in the exam room.

"Aye, that good Dr. Merton himself said I should come in on Tuesday to get the stitches outta my hand, so here's I am."

"That's good news," Mary Elizabeth said. "I would be very happy to take those stitches out for you. Why don't you hop up on the exam table, and I will take a look."

Mr. Dobbin complied, and Mary Elizabeth unwrapped his hand. "Let's see what we have here. Your wound has closed and is healing nicely. Dr. Merton did a fine job with the stitching. See?"

Mr. Dobbins had his head turned from her the entire time she was unwrapping his hand.

He continued to face the wall as he said, "I'll take your word for it, lass. My stomach is doin' flip-flops jus' tinkin' about it."

"Here. You lie back, and I will extend the end of the table so your feet won't dangle. Are you comfortable?"

The big man took a few minutes to get himself situated. He took great care to not see his hand. "Tanks."

"I must put my instruments in the sterilizer and let them cook for a few minutes. Then we will get down to business. Now, Mr. Dobbins, why don't you tell me about yourself?"

As she worked, she kept up a conversation with Mr. Dobbins, asking about his family and his job. "There. All done, Mr. Dobbins—your stitches are all out."

"So soon? I's never felt a ting."

"Glad to hear it. Now I am going to wrap it up again because your hand will be tender for a day or two. Thursday, you can take off the wrap and have your wife replace the bandage. After that, switch the bandage every two days. Come back to the surgery in two weeks, and we will see if your wound is completely healed. Now, if you notice you hand hurting or getting red, be sure to come back to the surgery sooner. Either Dr. Merton or I will look at it. Promise?"

"Promise. Tanks." Mr. Dobbins got himself into the sitting position.

"Sit there for a few minutes while I finish writing in your chart. And then we can walk out together."

As they walked out to the reception area, Mary Elizabeth stopped at the doorway to the waiting room and asked loudly, "Well, Mr. Dobbins, how did I do?" She gave him a wink.

Mr. Dobbins chuckled and winked back. He turned to the folks in the reception area. He held up his newly bandaged hand and made sure his answer was equally loud: "Jus' fine, lass, jus' fine."

Both of them could hear appreciative murmurs. Mary Elizabeth escorted Mr. Dobbins to the reception desk. "Miss Chamberlain, could you make an appointment for Mr. Dobbins two weeks from today? Good day, Mr. Dobbins."

Mary Elizabeth's morning flew by as she met more villagers and tended to their needs. Shortly before noon Sarah said, "That's it for the morning." She rose from the desk and locked the front door.

Mary Elizabeth hung her lab coat behind the desk and waited for Sarah to return. When Sarah slid open the doors to the residence, the odor of fried fish overpowered them.

"Smells like Dr. Merton's fishing trip this morning was a success."

They walked into the dining room and saw that there were three places set for lunch. Loud sounds of banging pots and pans emanated from the kitchen.

Sarah sat down right away. Mary Elizabeth hesitated, standing behind her chair. "Aren't you going to sit down?" Sarah asked.

"Does Mrs. Duggan eat with us?"

"No. She usually eats in the kitchen."

"Oh, okay." Mary Elizabeth sat at the place across from Sarah.

Harold emerged from his bedroom wearing his brown suit. He walked past the table and went into the kitchen. In a few minutes, he returned to sit at the head of the table, wearing a grim expression on his face.

Mary Elizabeth and Sarah exchanged quizzical looks but said nothing.

"Shall we say grace?" Harold asked.

After the prayer, Mrs. Duggan came out of the kitchen with a plate of battered fish. She set the plate down hard in front of Harold and disappeared behind the swinging door. She brought out bowls of mushy peas and fried potato wedges. The food was served without a word. As Mrs. Duggan set down the plate of lemon wedges and the bowl of tartar sauce, Mary Elizabeth said, "Mrs. Duggan, the meal looks delicious."

Mrs. Duggan ignored her. "Yes, Mrs. Duggan, you have made another fine meal," Harold said.

Mrs. Duggan nodded but spoke not a word as she hurried into the kitchen.

"It looks like your fishing trip was a success." Mary Elizabeth asked, "Do you and Father Evenson have a favorite spot?"

Harold attempted to be cheerful. "Yes, we do, but I am afraid it is a secret."

It was Sarah's comment that set everyone's spirits to right again. She said, "You must have all had a good time. I can hear Magnus snoring from here."

CHAPTER 12

THE INTERVIEW

After lunch, the trio returned to the surgery. Sarah unlocked the door and handed Dr. Merton the patient files for his house visits. She whispered something to Dr. Merton that made his eyes grow big. "Yes, right. Let me know when the coast is clear."

"Yes, Doctor."

Harold hurried down the hall toward his office and closed the door.

"What was that all about?" Mary Elizabeth asked.

"Dr. Merton likes to review the patient files before he goes out on his calls. That way he makes sure he has the medicines and other instruments he needs for his visits."

Mary Elizabeth raised her eyebrow before she slipped on her white lab coat. "Since my one o'clock has not yet arrived, could you give me the files I asked you to set aside this morning? I would like to finish writing my notes before we get started this afternoon."

"Of course, Doctor." Sarah handed her the unfinished charts.

Mary Elizabeth finished her notes in her office, then handed the files back to Sarah. She glanced at the name on the file of her first afternoon patient. "Ah, now I understand." She stood in the doorway of the waiting room and called, "Howard Pritchard."

Howard rose from his seat and began to cough. He took out his handkerchief. Mary Elizabeth waited until his coughing jag passed before she led him to the exam room. "Mr. Pritchard, I am Dr. Mary Elizabeth Senty. My, you have a nasty cough. I am so glad you came into the surgery this afternoon. Shall we get right to it? Now, if you will go behind the screen and take off your clothes from the waist up, I'll see what is going on in that chest of yours."

Howard stopped in front of the screen. "Dr. Senty, I am the editor of the village paper, the *Bellechester Bugle*. I am here to interview you, not to have a medical exam. I thought I made that quite clear to Miss Chamberlain."

"Why can't we kill two birds with one stone?" Mary Elizabeth asked. She paused for a moment and then began to laugh. "Sorry. That is not the best analogy for a doctor to use, is it?" She smiled.

Howard tried to laugh but succumbed to another coughing spell.

"Tell you what. Let me examine you and then you can interview me. That way, both of us can end this appointment having done our jobs."

Howard mused, "A first-hand account will give this article an interesting angle. Yes, Dr. Senty, I consent to your examination."

"Very glad to hear it." Mary Elizabeth walked to her desk and studied his chart while Howard changed behind the screen.

Howard sat on the exam table after being weighed and measured. He brought his notepad and pencil with him. "How long have you been a doctor?"

"I received my medical degree in 1954 from the University of Minnesota."

"American! I thought I recognized the accent. How did you end up in Bellechester?"

"I was given the opportunity to do my residency at London's Mother of Mercy Hospital. How could I pass up a chance to live in England for four years? Dr. Merton came to Mercy last week searching for a junior doctor to join him in Bellechester. I had just completed my training and had all the proper certifications and credentials. Dr. Merton observed me in a clinical setting and apparently liked what he saw. He offered me the position, and I accepted."

"Was it as simple as that?" Howard asked.

"Yes, it was that simple."

"There is a rumor going around the village that you and Dr. Merton are living together. Any comment?" Howard was poised to record any reaction his words might evoke from her.

"Just to be clear, Dr. Merton and I are not 'living together,' in the way your innuendo implies. Yes, we both live in the doctor's residence, but our living quarters are on separate floors in different parts of the house.

Howard turned his head as another coughing fit seized him. When he recovered, he pursued his line of questioning.

"You can appreciate how it looks to the village. A single male doctor and a single female doctor living in the same house?"

"Yes, I suppose it does raise eyebrows. But we already have Mrs. Winters living in the same house as Father Evenson. They are both single. If no one questions that arrangement, why should they question Dr. Merton or me about living in the same house?"

"You are not comparing apple to apples. Father Evenson took a vow of celibacy."

Mary Elizabeth shrugged her shoulders.

"Anything else you would like to say on the matter?"

"Only this. Having both of us in one place makes it easier for us to respond in an emergency.

If one of us is out on a house call, the other is available. People don't have to run to another door or call another number to get help. That should reassure folks that this living arrangement lets us respond quickly to serve the medical needs of this community."

She looked over to Howard, who was busily scribbling in his notebook.

"All right, Mr. Pritchard. I think we have exhausted that topic. Now it is my turn to ask questions. When did your coughing begin?"

"I always seem to cough, but a few days ago the coughing got worse. I spit up this heavy phlegm."

"I see you smoke."

"How can you tell?"

"The telltale bulge in your jacket pocket, yellow stains between your fingers, and the smell of smoke on your clothes. How many cigarettes do you smoke each day?"

"Usually just a pack a day. Sometimes more if I am on a deadline trying to get the paper out."

"All that smoke is not good for your lungs."

"This is incredible! I can't believe what I am hearing! When I was in college, a doctor recommended that I take up smoking to calm my nerves and relax. He even admitted to being a smoker himself. He said smoking helped him keep a clear head so he could better treat his patients. And now you are telling me smoking is not good for me!" He shook his head.

"That is exactly what I am telling you. New studies have been recently published that show smoking increases your chances of lung disease and an early death." Putting her stethoscope in her ears, she said, "Now, I am going to listen to your lungs. Deep breaths, please." Howard complied. But every deep breath brought on another fit of coughing. Taking off the stethoscope, she said, "I can hear lots of congestion in your lungs." She looked into his throat and felt his glands. "Is it painful when you swallow?"

"Yes, I do have a scratchy throat."

She took his temperature. "Mr. Pritchard, your temperature is slightly elevated at 100.5 degrees."

She took a vial from the cupboard and handed it to Howard. "Here, see if you can cough up some phlegm, then spit it into this tube. Meanwhile I will set up the X-ray machine. I would like to take some pictures of your lungs. Come to the X-ray room when you are ready." She quickly left the room.

Moving from the table caused Howard to cough again. By the time he joined her in the lab and X-ray room, he'd filled half a vial with phlegm, which he handed to Mary Elizabeth. She set the vial next to the microscope.

Mary Elizabeth got Howard positioned. "Don't move." She was walking toward the protective screen when they heard several sets of footsteps run past the door. Dr. Merton's voice shouted, "Call an ambulance!"

Howard became agitated. "Sounds like Dr. Merton is being called out on an emergency. I should go out there and see what is happening." Before Mary Elizabeth could stop him, he was out the door. She found him at the reception desk. Miss Chamberlain had barely replaced the receiver when Howard began peppering her with questions. "Who needs an ambulance? What happened?"

"Please, Mr. Pritchard, come back to the exam room. I need to take those X-rays."

"I have to find out what is going on," he said.

"Dr. Merton is going to help a patient. Patient confidentiality will prevent Miss Chamberlain from giving any further information. Please, let's finish the examination."

All the movement gave Howard another coughing jag. "How much longer is this going to take?"

"That all depends on your cooperation. I do need to take those X-rays. While the film is developing, I can look at your phlegm under the microscope. That should solidify my diagnosis and treatment plan. Then you can go on your way. But the longer we are out here, the longer it will take. Shall we finish your tests?"

Reluctantly, Howard walked back to the room, and Mary Elizabeth took her pictures. "You can go back to the exam room, and I will return in a few minutes."

The X-rays revealed spots in the lung indicative of an infection. A small sample of phlegm in a petri dish exposed the telltale configuration of a long chain which supported her findings from his physical examination. Confident of her diagnosis and treatment plan, she hurried to the surgery's pharmacy area to prepare his injection.

Returning to the exam room, Mary Elizabeth found Howard rummaging through a stack of pictures on the floor that were waiting to be hung. She asked, "Find anything interesting?"

Howard turned toward the door, picture in hand. "Hope you don't mind."

"Not at all."

"I can't quite tell what is happening here."

"Bring it over to the exam table and I will tell you. But first I need to tell you what your exam today shows. You have a lung infection caused by a bacteria called group A Streptococcus. Smoking weakens the immune system and the lungs, so your body is having a difficult time fighting off this harmful bacteria. It also increases the likelihood of spreading these germs to your family. Now, has anyone else in your family complained of a sore throat or had a fever?"

"No, I don't think so."

"If they do, please have them come to the clinic so we can test them. Strep is contagious and can be quite serious, especially for children."

Howard nodded. They heard a siren grow louder until it abruptly stopped. "Sounds like the ambulance is here in the village. Are we done? Can I go now?"

"I just need to give you your medicine. Now, if you will stand at the end of the exam table, face the back wall, and drop your trousers, please. I am sure you know how the rest of this goes." She held up the hypodermic needle.

Howard sighed. "I am all too familiar. Can we just get on with this?"

"Of course." Howard placed the picture on the exam table in front of him and complied with Mary Elizabeth's directions.

"I bet that picture does look strange if you aren't from Minnesota."

"What is happening here?"

"I grew up on a dairy farm. When I was eighteen, I won a statewide competition to be an ambassador for the dairy industry."

"Why are you bundled up? Doesn't your fair occur at the end of the summer?"

"Yes, it does. I sat in a revolving cooler and had my face carved in a ninety-pound block of butter. The best part was that after the fair, I got to take my bust home."

Howard laughed. "But what did you do with ninety pounds of butter? Where did you keep it?"

"Here we go, Mr. Pritchard. Try to relax. Deep breaths. One, two, three." Mary Elizabeth administered the medicine. "There. All done." She held a cotton ball on the site. "Now, to answer your questions, I donated the butter to the annual parish corn feed. What was left, we used at home. Although I do believe my folks had to buy another refrigerator to keep it. It lasted us about a year."

The ambulance siren blared again, then grew fainter.

Howard lowered his head and said under his breath, "And I missed the story of the week."

Mary Elizabeth grew concerned. "Mr. Pritchard, are you all right? Are you having a reaction to the penicillin?"

"No. Are we done here?" His tone was sharp.

"Yes," she said as she removed the cotton ball. "You can get dressed." Mary Elizabeth continued to clean up her supplies. When he was fully dressed, Mary Elizabeth gave him information on the medicine and tips to help ease the discomfort at the injection site. "Right now, you need to go home, rest, and drink plenty of fluids."

"Thank you, Dr. Senty. Your story will appear in the next issue of the *Bugle,*" Howard Pritchard said.

"Are you sure you got enough information for a story?"

"Yes, I did. I will be sending over a photographer later this afternoon to take a few pictures for the article."

"When do you want me to stop by your office to check your facts?" Mary Elizabeth asked.

"That won't be necessary, Dr. Senty. If I need further clarification, I will contact you. Otherwise, you will have to wait and read the story when it is published like everyone else."

At the front desk, Mary Elizabeth said, "Miss Chamberlain, please make an appointment for Mr. Pritchard for next week. Good day, Mr. Pritchard."

CHAPTER 13

Miss Hutchinson

Will passed a tidy stone cottage with a beautiful flower garden on his walk to the bank. The owner of the house emerged as he stopped to admire the chrysanthemums.

"Young man," she called waving her hand. "Yoo-hoo, young man."

Will turned around. "Yes, ma'am?"

A spry, elderly woman neatly attired in a pale-green suit and matching hat unlatched the gate and hurried to catch up to him. "Are you the new police inspector who is buying the Hobart house?"

"Yes, I am, but how did you know?"

She laughed. "Inspector, there are no secrets in this town. I don't know why we even bother having a newspaper. By the time the *Bugle* comes out, everyone already knows the news." She held out her white-gloved hand. "I'm Miss Vera Hutchinson, retired schoolteacher."

"Very pleased to meet you, Miss Hutchinson. I am Inspector William Donnelly. I was admiring your flower garden."

"It is a lot of work," Miss Hutchinson admitted, "but it is worth it for the joy it brings me. Ada—that is, Mrs. Hobart, God rest her soul—had a beautiful garden too."

"I haven't discovered any evidence of flowers in the yard. Everywhere I look, I only see tall grass and weeds. The only exception is the roses on the arched trellis. They do give off a lovely scent, but I am afraid I need to cut them down."

"It's a bit early to be pruning roses, Inspector."

"I suppose it is. Unfortunately, the roses have outgrown the trellis. They are blocking the walkway to the front door. The movers will never be able to get past all those thorny branches."

"Yes, climbing roses can run amok with no one to train them. But if you must cut them back, leave at least three inches at the base. Be sure to get yourself a pair of thick work gloves, the kind that go halfway to your elbow. Prune branches no longer than three inches at a time so you won't get pricked by the thorns. I offer you this advice from my own painful experience, Inspector."

"Thank you, Miss Hutchinson. I will be sure to follow your recommendations. Do you happen to know anyone in the village who could help me get my gardens in shape?"

Miss Hutchinson was silent for a moment. "You might try Eddie Hughes and Tommy Clarke. They could use the work. Folks say they are both hard workers. Yes, I think they will do a good job for you."

"Do you know where I could find them?"

"Sergeant O'Hanlon at the police station can make the arrangements."

"Sergeant O'Hanlon? Have they been in trouble?"

"It's best if I let Sergeant O'Hanlon explain. If you wish, after your yard gets cleaned up, I can help you identify the perennials Ada planted in the flower beds. That way you know what you have."

"Thank you, Miss Hutchinson, for your kind offer. Be assured that once I am settled, I will be grateful for any assistance you can give me. But now, I am afraid I must dash. I have an appointment with Mr. Drummond." Will took her hand. "It has been a pleasure meeting you."

"May I walk with you, Inspector? I am headed to the bank as well."

Will offered her his arm. "In that case, it would be my pleasure to escort you, Miss Hutchinson."

Miss Hutchinson sighed. "It has been decades since a handsome young man offered me his arm. I accept with pleasure."

Will asked, "How long have you lived in Bellechester?"

"I came in 1920. My fiancé died in the Great War. I went back to school, got my teaching certifications, and decided to make a new life for myself here. Yes, Bellechester is a good place for beginnings. Now, enough about me. Inspector, what are your impressions of our village?"

"I have only been in the village for a day, but everyone I have met has been very friendly. I think I shall like it here. This morning I read in your local paper that the village has been having problems with break-ins and thefts."

"Yes, our village does have its share of troubles. Oliver's Feed Store was the latest in a string of break-ins. But at least in that case, I do not think our young thieves will offend again."

"How can you be sure?"

"Two of the youths, Eddie and Tommy, are locals. Both are basically good kids from good families. They just got mixed up with the wrong sort. I believe they learned their lessons and will not cause any more trouble. The instigator of the crime is another story. He is a bad apple. Luckily for the village, his family recently moved away. I doubt he will be able to influence any more of our young lads down the wrong path. Oh now, let's speak of more pleasant subjects. When can we expect to meet the rest of your family?"

"I am afraid the village will have to settle for only me. I am not married."

Miss Hutchinson laughed. "A young man as nice as yourself who owns a cottage? I assure you, Inspector, you won't be single for long."

They reached the bank, and Will opened the door for Miss Hutchinson.

"Thank you, Inspector. Now, you must come for tea when you are all settled."

"Thank you for the invitation. I shall look forward to it. Good day, Miss Hutchinson."

"Good day, Inspector." Miss Hutchinson stepped into the bank and made her way to the teller.

Will spoke to the young secretary who was typing a letter. "Excuse me, miss. I am Inspector William Donnelly. I have an appointment to see Mr. Drummond."

She got up and opened the small wooden gate. "Come in, Inspector Donnelly. Mr. Drummond is expecting you."

She led Will to the corner office and announced, "Inspector Donnelly to see you, sir."

Behind the massive mahogany desk sat a large gentleman in a three-piece suit. A gold chain ran across the front of his vest. His round face held a pair of gold-rimmed spectacles which he wore halfway down his nose. Mr. Drummond wore his white whiskers in a mutton-chop beard-and-mustache design, remnants of a long-gone era. "Please have a seat."

Will sat in front of the desk. Behind Mr. Drummond was a large window which looked out onto Market Street. "Welcome to Bellechester, Inspector. You look rather young to be promoted to chief inspector. How old are you?"

Will answered, "Thirty-two, sir."

"Well, I hope the powers that be in Shrewsbury know what they are doing. Of course, you can't be any worse than the last one they sent us. Bentwood or Bradford or something. I have already forgotten his name. He wasn't here long enough for any of us to get to know him. Although we did get to know his son. Yes, his son made quite an impression in the village. But I digress. Now, what can I do for you today?"

Will wanted to ask more questions about his predecessor and his son but decided to stick to business. "I am here to see about a home loan."

"Yes, yes, the Hobart house, isn't it? I do believe Mr. Lester sent over the paperwork earlier." Mr. Drummond pressed the button on his desk intercom. "Miss Randall, please bring in the file on the Hobart house."

Soon there was a knock on the door, and Miss Randall brought a thick manila folder. She handed it to Mr. Drummond. "Has Mr. Dalton had a chance to look over the figures?"

"Yes, Mr. Drummond, his notes are right on top."

"Thank you, Miss Randall."

Will handed an envelope to Mr. Drummond. "At lunch today, Mr. Lester and I went over the estimate from Ned Manderfield for all the renovations on the house. Can we roll those numbers into the home loan? This receipt from Mr. Lester shows the down payment I made on the house today."

"Is Ned Manderfield your contractor? Good choice, young man. He and his crew do top-shelf work." Mr. Drummond laughed. "Just like his father, he is. You will get your money's worth with him. You won't be sorry to have him work on your house."

"That's good to hear."

"Recalculating your loan will take a few minutes. I hope you aren't in any hurry this afternoon."

"No. I want to get the financing on the house settled before I drive back to London."

"While we wait for Mr. Dalton to adjust the figures, we can have a good chinwag." Mr. Drummond pressed the intercom, and his secretary came into the room. He handed her the envelope and the file. "Please have Mr. Dalton recalculate the loan including these new renovation figures."

"Yes, Mr. Drummond. And I have those papers ready for your signature. If you could sign them now, they could go out in the afternoon post."

"Yes, bring them in."

"Very good, Mr. Drummond."

Mr. Drummond turned to Will. "You must pardon the interruption, Inspector, but these papers are time sensitive. It will just take a few minutes."

"Please go ahead."

The secretary returned with the papers. While they were conferring, Will got up and walked to the window in the corner of the office that faced Market Street. The Venetian blinds were up, granting an unobstructed view. The street was deserted except for a man wearing a plaid cap and short leather jacket. He was leaning against the lamppost across from the bank. Miss Hutchinson finished her business and strolled down Market Street. Seeing Miss Hutchinson, the man threw his cigarette butt onto the ground and began to follow her. Will observed that the man had his eyes on Miss Hutchinson the whole time. If Miss Hutchinson stopped to look at a shop window, the man would also slow his gait. He seemed careful to always keep the same distance between them.

Will got an uneasy feeling in the pit of his stomach. He shifted his feet, keeping his eyes glued to the man in the plaid cap. Mr. Drummond finished his business with his secretary. He swiveled his chair around to face Will. "And how long have you worked—"

"Mr. Drummond, get on the phone and call the police station. Have them send an officer to Market Street. Now!"

Mr. Drummond immediately picked up the phone. Will bolted from the room and ran out of the bank.

Miss Hutchinson arrived at the butcher shop. She waved to the butcher through the window and pointed to his meat case. She was about to step into the shop when the stranger ran up behind her and snatched her purse with such force that Miss Hutchinson lost her balance and fell backward onto the pavement. She hit her head on the cobblestones and lay motionless on the ground.

By the time Will got to the scene, the butcher was kneeling next to her. Will put his hand on the butcher's shoulder. "Don't move her! Call for the doctor!"

"Right." The butcher scrambled to his feet and disappeared into his shop.

Will pursued the thief up the street. A policeman came running from the other direction down Market Street. Spotting the man with the purse, the policeman began blowing his whistle. The thief stopped, turned, and spied Will running toward him full-bore.

The thief crossed the street, racing through the village square. The policeman and Will continued to give chase. Will had the better angle and reached the thief first. Employing his best rugby tackling technique, Will burrowed his shoulder into the thief below his waist. Wrapping his arms around the man's legs, they both fell to the ground. The force of the tackle sent Miss Hutchinson's purse flying outward. Will recovered first and grabbed the man's arms behind his back. By this time, the police officer arrived on the scene.

Breathing heavily, Will said, "Got your cuffs, officer? I've got him in position. Here, give them to me."

The officer, also out of breath, hesitated.

Will gasped, "Inspector Donnelly, Met Police. Give me your cuffs." The thief was struggling to escape from Will's grasp. Afraid of losing the suspect, he barked, "That's an order!" The officer complied. Will handcuffed the suspect, hoisted him up to a standing position, and handed him over to the officer. "Can you take it from here?" he panted.

"Yes, sir," the officer said.

"Good, I will stop by the station later to give my statement." Will pulled out his warrant card and showed it to the officer. He went over and picked up Miss Hutchinson's purse. "I want to return Miss Hutchinson's purse to her first. Any objections?"

"None, sir." The officer pushed the thief along. "It's down to the station for you. Get going."

Will jogged back to Market Street. All the commotion brought the townsfolk out of the shops into the street. A small crowd gathered around Miss Hutchinson.

Harold was at the scene in minutes. Kneeling on the sidewalk, he tended to an unconscious Miss Hutchinson. "Please, folks," he implored as he opened his doctor's bag, "give us some room."

Will laid the purse by Miss Hutchinson's side. No other policemen were in sight, so Will took charge of crowd control. "You heard the doctor. Give them some space. Yes, we are all concerned about Miss Hutchinson. But let's move back so the doctor can work."

Because of Will's large stature and take-charge attitude, the crowd complied with his directions. It seemed like an eternity before the faint wail of a siren could be heard in the distance. The ambulance was coming from Glendale, six miles northeast of Bellechester.

When the ambulance pulled up, Harold gave instructions to the attendants. "Be very gentle. Roll her from her left side. Careful! Do not touch her right arm or shoulder."

The attendants, doing their best not to jostle Miss Hutchinson, slid the litter underneath her and carried her to the ambulance.

"I will meet you at the hospital," Harold told the attendants. One of the attendants jumped into the back of the ambulance. The other got behind the wheel. The ambulance left the village, its siren blaring.

As Harold gathered up his instruments, a loud voice from back of the crowd yelled, "Harold! You need me?"

Recognizing the voice, Harold yelled back, "Yes! Come with me!"

The crowd parted, and soon Father Evenson was beside him. "You got everything you need?"

Father Evenson held up a small square satchel. "Right here."

"Good. Peter!"

Another voice from the crowd yelled back, "Here!"

"Get Glendale Hospital on the phone for me."

"Right away, Doctor."

Again, the crowd parted as Harold made his way inside Evans' Butcher Shop. Peter Evans already had the hospital on the line. He handed the phone to Harold.

"Dr. Merton from Bellechester here. Your ambulance is bringing in an unconscious female patient in her late sixties. She sustained traumatic injuries to her right arm and shoulder. Alert the surgeon on duty and ready the OR. They should be at the hospital in ten minutes. I am on the way. Goodbye." He thanked Peter for the use of his telephone.

"Anytime, Doctor. Do you think Miss Hutchinson will be all right?"

"God willing," Harold replied. "God willing." He hurried out the door. "Matt, my car is around the corner." They sped toward Glendale.

CHAPTER 14

THE BELLECHESTER CONSTABULARY

Will had grass stains on the knees of his light-blue suit pants. He looked disheveled as he sat across from Mr. Drummond. "Sorry for the interruption, Mr. Drummond."

Mr. Drummond replied, "Quite all right. No need to apologize. Was the thief caught?"

"Yes, he is now in police custody."

"How is Miss Hutchinson?"

"She was unconscious when she was placed in the ambulance. The doctor and the priest followed her to the hospital."

"Good men, Dr. Merton and Father Evenson," Mr. Drummond said.

"In my brief encounter with her, Miss Hutchinson seemed like a sweet lady," Will said. "I hope she'll be alright."

"Sweet! Vera Hutchinson?" Mr. Drummond chuckled. "That woman is as tough as nails. Just ask any of her former students. Miss Hutchinson is a well-respected member of this community. I sit with her on the magistrates' court. In fact, she acts as our presiding judge. She is the first woman ever appointed to the court. Smart as a whip, she is. I tell you, Inspector, many a time the accused tried to pull the wool over our eyes, but she could always see through their lies. Must have been all those years in the classroom that gave her the gift." He shook his head in admiration. "Yes, a real force of nature, that one. There will be many prayers said this evening for her recovery, including my own. Now, where were we?"

"My home loan," Will reminded him.

"Ah, yes." Mr. Drummond opened the manila folder on his desk. "Your numbers look good, and we have secured all the information we need from your London bank. Inspector, I am happy to announce that your loan is approved. Here is your new monthly payment including the renovations. I hope you find it acceptable."

Will looked at the number. *A little economizing and I can swing this.* "Yes, this amount is fine." He began signing the forms. "The last time I signed my name so many times, I entered military service."

Mr. Drummond shook Will's hand. "Congratulations, Inspector—you are now beholden to the Bellechester Savings and Loan for thirty years."

After Mr. Drummond collected the papers from Will, he handed him two envelopes. "One check is made out to the estate of Mrs. Ada Hobart. I believe Mr. Lester is handling the sale for the family. The other check is for Ned Manderfield. It should cover your renovation work."

After dropping off both checks with Mr. Lester, Will walked to the police station.

Sergeant John O'Hanlon was stationed at the front desk. At five feet, ten inches tall, he had a stocky build. He wore his strawberry-blond hair in a crew cut.

"Afternoon, sir," Sergeant O'Hanlon said. "Can I help you?"

Will pulled out his warrant card. "Inspector William Donnelly. I am here to give my statement regarding the purse snatching and attack on Miss Hutchinson."

"Sir," he replied, "it is a pleasure to finally meet you. I appreciated your help in apprehending the suspect. My young officer was very impressed by the way you brought down Miss Hutchinson's attacker. He wondered where you learned your tackling technique."

"I honed my skills from spending many hours on the rugby pitch. I will be happy to give your officers a demonstration in a few weeks. Now, do you want to take my statement, or should I just write it down for you?"

"If you don't mind, I'll let you write your own statement. I trust you know how it goes." Sergeant O'Hanlon reached into a drawer and pulled out a lined pad of paper. He handed that and a pencil to Will. "Here, you can use the desk in the Inspector's office since no one is using it at present. It will be your office in a few weeks anyway."

Sergeant O'Hanlon escorted Will to the empty office at the front corner of the building, steps from the reception desk.

"Thank you, Sergeant. I will bring my statement back to you when I have finished. Then there is another matter I would like to discuss with you." Will looked at his watch. "What time does your shift end?"

"I'm here until half past three. I will close the door to give you some privacy."

"Right." Will sat at the desk in his soon-to-be-office. He glanced around the room. The only decoration was a map on the wall which outlined the neighboring constabularies. A table with four chairs sat in the corner. An empty bookcase and a coat rack completed the room's furnishings. Two large windows bathed the room in natural light. *How very different from the huge room with many desks and rows of fluorescent lights that was my old office at the Met.*

Alone in the office, the weight of his promotion descended upon him. *Am I up to the task? Can I make a positive impact on this community?* Will shook these momentary doubts from his head. He cleared his mind and concentrated on the task at hand. Years of experience had taught him what judges and prosecutors found most helpful in witness testimony. Will had finished his statement and was reading it over one last time when he heard a woman's angry voice coming from the front desk.

"What do you mean you can't help me, Sergeant? Don't I pay your salary?"

He could not make out exactly what Sergeant O'Hanlon was saying. Will chuckled, recalling how Trevor and his detective pals had given him grief about his promotion. They imagined him sitting in his office with his feet up on his clean desk, bored out of his mind because there was nothing to do in a small village like Bellechester. Will couldn't wait to get back to London to set them all straight.

Again, the woman's voice broke into his thoughts. Curiosity got the better of him, and he decided to see if he could be of any assistance.

The woman wore a red print dress and a hat with tall red feathers. When she talked, her head bobbed, moving the feathers back and forth. From the back, she reminded Will of an exotic hen he had once seen at a county fair. Will did his best to stifle a laugh. He neared the front desk in time to hear the woman say, "I demand to speak to your superior, Sergeant."

Sergeant O' Hanlon replied calmly, "As I explained to you before, Mrs. Farnsworth, the new inspector will not officially take up his duties until the fifteenth of September. Until then, I am the acting head of this constabulary."

"What are we to do!" exclaimed Mrs. Farnsworth. "No, that is not satisfactory. St. Anselm's Altar and Rosary meets on the eighth of September. We meet at seven, and it will be pitch dark by the time we end. How will my ladies get home safely? With all the crime in the village lately, no one is safe. Why, this very afternoon poor Miss Hutchinson was attacked in broad daylight right on Market Street. It is a fine thing that hooligans are running free and poor God-fearing folks are afraid to walk in their own village. What are you doing about it? Now, I want—no, I *demand* that your officers escort my ladies home after the meeting."

"But Mrs. Farnsworth, I only have two officers on duty at that time, and you have at least thirty women who attend the meeting." He paged through the logbook. "Now, I propose that you and I meet on Friday morning, at 9:00 a.m., here at the station. By that time, I will have come up with a plan to ensure all the ladies get home safely from the meeting."

"Make sure you do! As president, I take the welfare of my ladies very seriously." Mrs. Farnsworth set her large red purse on the counter and brought out a pocket calendar. She opened it and studied the page for a moment. "Now let's see, Friday at 9:00 a.m. . . . yes, yes, I can meet with you. May I borrow a pencil?"

"I'll write our meeting here on the desk log too. Now don't worry yourself. We have Miss Hutchinson's attacker safely locked up behind bars. He won't be getting out anytime soon. He will not cause anyone harm."

"Well, that's good news. Until Friday morning then, Sergeant, I bid you a good afternoon." She turned and toddled out of the station in her tight-fitting dress, her stiletto heels clacking and her feathers bobbing. As she passed Will, she gave him a regal nod which made her feathers bob even more.

"Afternoon, ma'am," Will said in the somber, expressionless tone he'd mastered in the military.

"Well done!" he congratulated the sergeant. "You defused that situation with more patience than I could have mustered. Who was she?"

"Mrs. Farnsworth? She is the wife of the mayor, or as she refers to herself, the 'first lady' of the village. I am sure she will introduce herself to you when you take up your duties."

"I shall be ready for her. It was a good idea to give her a few days to calm down before you meet with her again."

"Mrs. Farnsworth was just upset about what happened to Miss Hutchinson today. Lately, folks in the village have been on edge. We have had more than our share of crime recently, as you discovered today."

"Yes, Bellechester is not as peaceful as it looks. Here is my witness statement, if you care to read it over." Will handed the paper to Sergeant O'Hanlon.

"It looks good to me. I see you have already signed it. When do you think you will be moving to Bellechester, Inspector?"

"I am hoping to move into my house on the tenth or eleventh. I need to arrange matters with the movers when I get back to London. Even though my official start date is Tuesday, the fifteenth of September, I want to move into my office on Monday, the fourteenth."

"In that case, could you please add your London phone number in case we need to get in touch with you before your arrival? I, for one, can't wait for you to permanently occupy that front office."

"Thank you, Sergeant. I too look forward to getting back to work. It will be nice to be settled in and become a part of Bellechester's community. Earlier today I spoke with Miss Hutchinson. She said I should ask you about getting the two lads, Eddie Hughes and Tommy Clarke, to help me clean up my yard. I need to return to London for a few days to pack up and settle some affairs. I don't think I can get my yard cleaned up before the movers come. I would like to get everything settled before I begin work here on the fourteenth."

"That is very understandable, sir. Yes, I can arrange for the lads to do the work for you. They might enjoy the change of pace, and they will appreciate getting more of their community service hours completed."

"I don't have any yard tools for them to use."

"Not to worry. I am sure they can borrow their father's tools, and I have some tools too."

"Are these the lads who broke into the feed store?"

"Yes, this is part of their punishment handed down from the magistrate's court. They were each sentenced to one hundred hours of community service."

"I thought I read in the paper that there were three lads responsible for the break-in. Did the third lad receive the same sentence?"

"The third lad was Jerry Brett, the chief inspector's son. Not only was he the instigator of the feed store crime, but this was not his first offense. In the short time his family was in Bellechester, Jerry was caught several times destroying property." The sergeant shook his head. "The magistrates would give the boy service hours that he would not complete. He thought it was a joke. Knowing that restitution and community service hours would not work, they were left with no choice. The magistrates sentenced Jerry Brett to one year in a Borstal up north. The chief inspector resigned soon after, and the family left town about two weeks ago. The whole situation was unfortunate. But I can tell you that the entire village breathed a sigh of relief when Jerry Brett left. Now, do you have any special instructions for the lads?"

Will relayed the instructions on the roses from Miss Hutchinson. "Trim the grass down so it looks like a yard again, and weed the flower gardens."

"That should keep the boys busy for a few days," Sergeant O'Hanlon said.

"Well, if I am not needed for anything else, I will leave you, Sergeant. I am driving back to London. I hope to return early next week to check on the progress of the house. And if you wouldn't mind, if you have any news about Miss Hutchinson, please give me a call."

"I will, Inspector. Have a safe trip home."

CHAPTER 15

DR. SENTY'S BUSY AFTERNOON

Mary Elizabeth escorted Mrs. O'Hanlon to the reception desk. "I would like to see Mrs. O'Hanlon in three weeks."

"Yes, Doctor," Sarah said as she consulted the appointment book. "Mrs. O'Hanlon, how does Tuesday, September 22, at 2:00 p.m. sound?"

"That will be fine. A good day to you both." Mrs. O'Hanlon walked carefully down the hallway, both hands on her pregnant belly.

Mary Elizabeth reached for the next chart. "Let's see, who's next?"

Sarah said, "That is the chart for your 3:00 p.m. appointment. Because of the excitement in the village, several of your afternoon patients canceled, but you do have two visitors from St. Walburga's convent. They are in the waiting room."

"Visitors?"

"They wouldn't tell me their business. They said they would only speak to you."

Mary Elizabeth returned the file to the holder. "Looks like this is our afternoon for visitors. Mr. Pritchard will also be sending over a photographer to take some pictures for the paper."

"With all your cancellations, I think we can squeeze him in."

"Thank you, Sarah."

Mary Elizabeth approached two nuns sitting in the waiting room. They both fingered their Rosaries, their eyes downward and their lips moving in silent prayer.

"Excuse me, sisters. I am Dr. Senty. Miss Chamberlain said you wanted to see me?"

The elder of the two spoke up. "Yes, we carry a message from our prioress."

"Please, follow me to my office. We can speak there." Mary Elizabeth led them to the chairs by her desk.

The elder nun said, "Reverend Mother Bonifacius invites you to tea on Thursday of this week at 4:00 p.m."

Mary Elizabeth wrote the information in her desk calendar. "Please thank Reverend Mother for the kind invitation. I will be most happy to attend. I shall look forward to visiting with her." She flashed a smile at the sisters. Her smile was not returned as the elder sister maintained her serious expression. The younger sister never looked at Mary Elizabeth. Her eyes remained downcast.

In unison, the sisters rose from their seats. "We will give Reverend Mother your response. Good day to you. *Benedicamus Domino.*"

Mary Elizabeth rose from her chair. She responded in unison with the younger sister, "*Deo Gratias.*"

For the first time since entering the surgery, the younger nun looked up at Mary Elizabeth, her mouth wide in surprise.

Mary Elizabeth smiled at her.

The elder nun glared at both the younger nun and Mary Elizabeth before turning to the door. The younger nun immediately dropped her eyes and followed her elder out.

"Thank you for coming. Please, let me escort you," Mary Elizabeth said as she hurried to open the exam door for the sisters. The trio walked in silence until they came to the front desk. "Good day to you both."

The sisters nodded their heads and walked out of the surgery.

Mary Elizabeth turned to Sarah. "What is my schedule for Thursday of this week?"

"Your morning is full, with a few appointments in the afternoon."

"Please do not schedule anything for me past 3:00 p.m. Reverend Mother has invited me to tea at four."

Sarah laughed. "Don't you mean Reverend Mother summoned you to tea?"

Mary Elizabeth laughed. "Yes, I know. I will have to be on my best behavior."

"The photographer from the paper has arrived, as well as your three o'clock patient."

Mary Elizabeth checked her watch. "If the patient isn't in a hurry, I will deal with the photographer first." She glanced at the name on the chart and then walked into the waiting room. "Mrs. Trumble?"

The middle-aged woman looked up from her magazine and started to get up. "Mrs. Trumble, would you mind if I took the photographer ahead of you? I am sure we will only be a few minutes."

Mrs. Trumble sat back down. "No, not at all. Go ahead. That will give me time to finish reading this article."

Mary Elizabeth walked over to the young photographer. He had a camera on a strap slung around his neck. A large bag of equipment lay at his feet.

He rose from his chair. "Dr. Senty?"

"Yes, and you are?"

"Simon Cummings." They shook hands.

"Where would you like to take your pictures, Mr. Cummings?"

"Let's try your exam room. I will need to see if there is enough light in there to get decent pictures."

"Yes, come on back."

Simon waved his light meter around the exam room. "Yes, this will work fine. Plenty of light in here." It took him several minutes to get his equipment set up.

"Where do you want me?"

"Mr. Pritchard was pretty adamant that I get a shot of that picture of you getting your face carved in butter."

Mary Elizabeth brought the photograph over to him. Placing it on her desk, he took several pictures of it. "How about one where you're holding your framed medical school diploma?" Mary Elizabeth found it amongst the pile of pictures and held it up. Simon had to adjust the angle of the picture several times to compensate for the glare of the lights. Finally, he was ready and the flash went off.

"Now for an action shot."

"Action shot?"

"Let's have you stand next to the exam table, stethoscope around your neck, and you filling one of those needles you jab us with. Mr. Pritchard insisted one of the pictures should show you with a needle in hand."

"Really? Why?"

"He said it would fit with his story. Besides, that makes you look like a real doctor."

As Mary Elizabeth got her supplies ready, she murmured, "Look like a real doctor? I am a real doctor!"

Mary Elizabeth posed as requested.

"Could you not look so angry?" Simon asked. "That will scare folks off for sure. No, don't smile. That looks like you enjoy it. Just look, I don't know, serious but compassionate."

Mary Elizabeth sighed and put on her professional face.

"Yes, yes," cried Simon. "That's it." He snapped the picture.

Mary Elizabeth checked her wristwatch. "I am sorry, Mr. Cummings, but we need to wrap this up. I have a patient waiting to see me. Don't you have enough pictures by now?"

"I won't know what I have until I develop the film, but there should be a couple of keepers in the lot. Just one more. How about you sitting at your desk writing a prescription?"

"All right. Last one," Mary Elizabeth said from behind her desk.

"Now pretend you are handing it to a patient."

Mary Elizabeth looked up. "And what face should I be wearing?"

Simon winced. "A concerned, caring expression will do. I'm sure you have one of those. There! Hold it." Once more the flashbulb went off. "Thank you, Dr. Senty, for your cooperation. I have all I need. We are finished. Dr. Senty, when you see the pictures and Mr. Pritchard's article together, I am sure you will see that all this was worth your time and trouble." He packed up his gear.

"I hope so. Here, I will escort you out."

Mary Elizabeth found Mrs. Trumble engrossed in a fan magazine. "Mrs. Trumble, thank you for waiting. I apologize. I didn't think it would take this long."

"No worries. My husband works at the newspaper, so I know how things go. They are always on a deadline. Besides, I got to finish reading my article and copy down a few recipes." She sighed as she returned the magazine to the rack. "That Cary Grant still makes me swoon."

"Me too. Did the magazine say when his next film is coming out?" Mary Elizabeth asked as they walked together to the exam room.

"His next film is an Alfred Hitchcock thriller. It is already out in the States. We should get it in the fall. It's called *North by Northwest.*"

"Where do you go to see movies around here?"

"The nearest cinema is in Church Stretton. But if you want to see the newest releases, then you go up to Shrewsbury or Birmingham. The *Bugle* usually carries the film listings for all the local cinemas."

"Thank you for the information. I'm still trying to figure out this part of the country."

"Yes, I can tell from your accent that you are not from around here."

"Yes, I arrived from London yesterday. But I am originally from the States."

"I can't wait to read all about you in the next *Bugle*. Howard always makes his stories so interesting."

Mary Elizabeth thought, *I wonder how close Howard's interesting is to the truth.* "What can I do for you today?"

Mrs. Trumble removed a prescription bottle from her purse and handed it to Mary Elizabeth. "Dr. Merton prescribed these blood thinners for me. He said I should come back in a month for blood tests to see if the pills are working."

Mary Elizabeth looked at the label and then consulted Mrs. Trumble's record. "How have you been feeling since you have been taking the pills?"

"Much better. My energy has come back, and I feel like myself again."

"That is good news. Would you mind if I gave you a quick exam before we did the blood draw?"

"Go right ahead." Mrs. Trumble moved to the exam table.

Mary Elizabeth took her blood pressure and listened to her heart. Then she drew the blood sample. "I will call you later this afternoon with your results. I will let you know if we need to adjust your prescription. But from everything you have told me, it sounds like the pills are working as they should."

"Thank you, Doctor. It has been a pleasure meeting you. You are nothing like they said you'd be."

"Oh?" Mary Elizabeth smiled. "I will take that as a compliment."

Mrs. Trumble looked at her quizzically. "But of course."

"Thank you, Mrs. Trumble. Here, I will walk out with you."

When they got to the front desk, she said, "Miss Chamberlain, I would like to see Mrs. Trumble again in four weeks."

"Yes, Doctor." Mrs. Trumble scheduled her follow-up and left.

"That was your last patient of the day."

"Has Dr. Merton returned from the hospital?"

"No, not yet. If he doesn't return by four o'clock, I will have to reschedule his home visits once again."

"How many visits are on his list for today?"

"Six."

Mary Elizabeth said, "I have Mrs. Trumble's blood work to process. If you could draw up a map of where I need to go, I can make Dr. Merton's house visits for him."

"Oh, could you? That would be wonderful. I'll get right on it."

Mary Elizabeth emerged from the lab. She phoned Mrs. Trumble to tell her that she should continue with the same dose. Then Mary Elizabeth picked up and studied the charts on Harold's side of the desk. She read his notes and filled her bag with the medicines and supplies needed for the visits.

Being the first of September, it was still light in Shropshire until 8:00 p.m. Sarah advised Mary Elizabeth to start with the patients farthest out and work her way back toward the village. Sarah went over the map with Mary Elizabeth and pointed out the landmarks that would lead her to her patients and home.

The farmers were surprised not to see Dr. Merton, but most were relieved that any doctor would visit them. Mary Elizabeth mentioned that she had been raised on a farm. She asked questions about their herds and crops. They were impressed when she could hold her own in conversations about commodity prices and government subsidies. That won over even the most skeptical farmer. On her home visits, she lanced a boil, performed a checkup on a two two-month-old baby, treated an entire family for pink eye, medicated and changed the bandage on a leg wound, administered drugs for severe back spasms, and diagnosed and treated a pneumonia case.

Mary Elizabeth finally pulled into the surgery parking lot around 9:00 p.m. A light was on in the kitchen. She entered through the back door. "Harold, are you home?" Magnus came running from his place in the sitting room. She dropped her purse and medical bag on the kitchen table and gave him his welcome pets. Magnus then stood by the back door and whimpered.

"Okay, big fella, I will let you out." She grabbed his collar and walked him into the fenced enclosure in the back. Returning to the kitchen, she peeked into the oven. Lunch leftovers were warming within.

She passed through the residence and opened the large sliding doors to Sarah's desk. On Harold's side of the desk were the patient files and the basket, which held only one message. The note was from Sarah. It was a reminder for Mary Elizabeth to check with the local operator when she got home. *Dear Sarah Chamberlain.* Mary Elizabeth picked up the phone and dialed "0."

A pleasant female voice said, "Operator."

"Dr. Senty calling for Dr. Merton. Has anyone called requesting a doctor?"

"No, Dr. Senty. There are no messages."

"Thank you. Good evening."

"A good evening to you too."

Mary Elizabeth hung up the telephone and uttered a loud sigh of relief.

Mary Elizabeth brought the files into the kitchen. She opened her medical bag and removed a small notebook. Getting a plate from the cupboard, she took the leftovers from the oven and filled her plate. She returned the rest to the oven so they'd still be warm for Harold when he got home.

She poured herself a glass of milk and ate her supper. She went over the notes she had made for herself from the home visits.

Taking her dirty dishes to the sink, she looked out the window. *Magnus! I almost forgot about him.* He was running around the enclosure. She walked outside, wrapping her sweater tightly around her. "Ready to come in for the night?" Magnus ran past her and sat at the back door, waiting for Mary Elizabeth to let him into the residence.

Mary Elizabeth spread the files across the table and transferred her notes into them. She looked at her watch—9:50 p.m. and still there was no sign of Harold. She took the files back to the surgery. Magnus ran past her all the way down to Harold's office and scratched at the door. Mary Elizabeth laid the files on Miss Chamberlain's desk with a note that they were complete.

"Magnus." The dog came running. *I wish I had your energy.* She latched the sliding doors. Ascending the stairs to her room, Magnus ran past her and laid down on the braided rug next to her bed. Mary Elizabeth flung her bag on the desk. She drew the shades, kicked off her shoes, and peeled off her work clothes. She hung her clothes in the wardrobe but was too exhausted to wash her nylons. Mary Elizabeth sighed as she slipped into the freedom of her looser night-clothes. When she returned from the bathroom, Magnus was no longer in her room. *Now where did he go?* Finding her slippers, she wrapped her robe tightly around her and made her way down to the sitting room. There she found Harold sitting in his recliner before the dying fire with Magnus at his side.

Harold turned when he heard Mary Elizabeth come into the room. "I didn't wake you, did I?"

"No, I was just getting ready for bed. How is Miss Hutchinson?"

"Her shoulder surgery was a success. The neurologists are still very concerned about her head injury. They will keep a close eye on her. As you know, the next few days will be critical."

Mary Elizabeth nodded. "Does Miss Hutchinson have any family close by?"

"Her younger sister, Violet, lives in Exeter. After Miss Hutchinson was wheeled into surgery,

I gave her a call. Even after all these years, I still find those phone calls difficult to make. I vouched for the expertise of the surgeon, which reassured her. I was grateful Matt was there to lend moral support. He also spoke with Violet. He told her he anointed Vera before she went into surgery. Knowing her sister had the sacrament and the prayers of the Church with her gave Violet some comfort. She caught the half-past-three train from Exeter to Birmingham. Matt and I picked Violet up at the station and drove her to supper before bringing her to the hospital. The hospital will put her up until her sister is out of danger." Harold sighed and stood up. "I'd best be starting my house calls."

"No need. Several of my afternoon patients canceled because of all the excitement in the village. I finished your house calls about an hour ago. I phoned the operator, and there are no new calls. We are all caught up. I can fill you in on the patient visits tomorrow."

Harold uttered a deep sigh of relief. "Emme, you have no idea . . . thank you for covering for me."

"I enjoyed getting out into the country and meeting the farm families. Practicing rural medicine is my passion. Sarah was a big help today. She mapped out the locations for me. Whatever you are paying her, I would like to add to her wages. In the two days I have been here, she has proven her weight in gold."

Mary Elizabeth saw Harold smile for the first time since the morning. "That is very kind of you. I don't think we can afford her weight in gold, but yes, I agree. We can figure a little raise for her later. But for now, sit down for a moment. There is something I need to tell you."

She sat in the overstuffed chair, and Harold moved to the sofa. Magnus jumped on the sofa next to him and lay on the towel placed there for that very purpose. Harold absently reached over, petting his soft fur.

"This morning, Mrs. Duggan informed me that she could no longer work in a residence that has turned into a den of sin and immorality. She said it was indecent for us to live together. Then she delivered her ultimatum that either you go, or she goes."

Mary Elizabeth drew in a sharp breath. "Oh no, I was afraid of this. If I could just stay until I make other living arrangements—"

"Emme, you are not going anywhere. I'm afraid I was rather cross with her. I said that you are a woman of impeccable character and you are needed here. If she didn't trust me after knowing me all these years, then I was sorry, but she would be the one who would be leaving."

"Oh, Harold, how did she take it?"

Harold chuckled. "I don't think Mrs. Duggan counted on my quick response, nor was it the answer she expected. I explained that I hoped she would stay. I was quite clear that if she was in my employ, then I expected her to treat you with common courtesy. However, if she intended to leave, she would need to submit her resignation in writing and give two weeks' notice so that a replacement could be found. That is why I was in such a foul mood at lunch today. I know it's late, but I wanted you to hear the story from me. Goodness knows what version is now circulating in the village."

"Thank you. I do appreciate you telling me. Do you think it would do any good if I spoke to her?"

"No, I think we should let her be. If Mrs. Duggan wants to change her mind, I want to give her space to do so. I don't want her to feel that she is backed into a corner."

"Aren't you afraid of the damage she can do in the village?"

"Oh, there might be a few people who would listen to her, but most know me, and as they get to know you, they will come around."

Mary Elizabeth yawned. "Another eventful day in Bellechester. Good night, Harold."

"Good night, Emme."

Thursday, September 3

CHAPTER 16

Of Laundry and Tea

Mary Elizabeth avoided Mrs. Duggan as much as possible in the following days. Mrs. Duggan delivered lunch to the table before the doctors and Sarah came into the dining room. If Mrs. Duggan did need to bring something into the dining room, she did so in silence.

Mrs. Duggan did the laundry for the surgery and for Harold. Mary Elizabeth dared not ask her to do her laundry. She turned to Mrs. Winters to ask who in the village might take in laundry. Mrs. Winters suggested Mrs. Murray. She gave Mary Elizabeth directions to her house. After work on Thursday, Mary Elizabeth walked to the small run-down cottage on the outskirts of town.

John Murray answered her knock on the door. "Dr. Senty!"

"Hello, John. How was school today?"

"Interesting. We got to dissect a frog in biology class. Two girls and one boy fainted. The teacher was kept busy with them, so we didn't quite finish the lab. We are going to work with the frogs for the rest of the week. It should be fun."

"I remember those days. I am glad you are enjoying school. Biology class was always my favorite class too. I came by to see your mother. Is she available?"

"Sure. Today is another wash day, so she is in the scullery. Come on in and I'll take you back."

"Thanks, John." Mary Elizabeth walked through the door. John led her through a small sitting room with two worn stuffed chairs. A kerosene lamp sat on a desk that stood against the wall. The dining room held a large table with a heavy blanket over it. Two flat irons sat on stands off on the table's edge. To the left of the dining room was a doorway with a curtain pulled across. Mary Elizabeth guessed sleeping rooms were behind it. John continued through the kitchen to the back of the house. Mary Elizabeth noticed the coal-burning stove and another kerosene lamp hanging nearby.

"Watch your step," John cautioned as he stepped down to the scullery floor. Wooden slats lay across the floor, allowing water to flow to the drain in the concrete floor below.

Mrs. Murray had her back to the door, as she was busy scrubbing the collar of a shirt.

"Mum, Dr. Senty is here to see you."

Mrs. Murray turned around. Beads of sweat glistened on her flushed face. Her light-brown hair was pinned back into a bun. Over her day dress, she wore a thick muslin apron.

"John, are you sick?"

"No, Mum. She came to see you."

"Me? I'm not sick."

Mary Elizabeth extended her hand. "So nice to meet you, Mrs. Murray. I'm new to Bellechester, and Mrs. Winters told me that you take in laundry."

After wiping her wet hands onto her apron, she took Mary Elizabeth's hand.

"Yes, as you can see, being a laundress is how I support John and myself. Let me consult my book for a moment." Mrs. Murray pulled down a notebook from the shelf above the laundry sinks. "I can send John to pick up your laundry on Monday afternoons and return your laundry on Thursday afternoons. I charge forty shillings for a pound of laundry, one pound minimum."

"That would be fine. Thank you. John, I will see you Monday afternoon. Goodbye, Mrs. Murray."

"Goodbye. John, you walk Dr. Senty out." She turned and continued scrubbing the shirt collar.

"Yes, Mum."

From the Murray home, Mary Elizabeth walked to the iron gates of St. Walburga's convent. She rang the bell, and an elderly nun appeared at the gate. "*Benedicite.*"

"Benedicite," Mary Elizabeth replied.

"What business have you at this convent?"

"I am Dr. Mary Elizabeth Senty. Reverend Mother Bonifacius invited me for tea."

The nun unlocked the gate with a large metal key and quickly ushered Mary Elizabeth inside. "Oh, come in, come in. Reverend Mother likes punctuality. No time to lose."

Mary Elizabeth continued down the road until she came to a four-story brick building. She hurried up the stairs and rang the bell.

A tall, slender nun opened the door. "Benedicite."

"Benedicite. I have been invited to tea with Reverend Mother."

"Please follow me." Her rubber-soled shoes made no sound on the polished floor. As they walked down the hallway, the chapel bells tolled. Mary Elizabeth was shown into the parlor, which had leaded glass on the top portion of the windows. The sun shining through them made rainbows that danced about the dark wood-paneled room. By the bay windows overlooking the gardens sat an immense figure. The tall nun walked to her and bowed. "Reverend Mother, Dr. Senty is here."

"Let her come," Reverend Mother spoke with a thick accent. The table was already set for tea.

Mary Elizabeth walked over, curtsied, and stood before her. She was glad she had worn her brown houndstooth wool suit. Its pleated A-line skirt and seven-button jacket felt appropriate to the setting. She wore the jacket buttoned to her neck. Her brown low-heeled shoes, matching purse, brown gloves, and brown pillbox hat rounded out the outfit. A small round pin on her jacket was the only jewelry she wore. Since she was in the surgery for the day, she wore her hair in her usual bun. "Good afternoon, Reverend Mother. Thank you for inviting me to tea."

"Sit down, Doctor. My, you look so young. How long have you been a doctor?"

"I received my medical degree in 1954."

"I see you wear the Benedictine pin. What monastery are you with?"

"St. Benedict's Monastery in St. Joseph, Minnesota. I made my final oblation in my senior year at the college. My oldest sister made her final vows there two years ago."

"And you didn't follow her? Why not?"

"My sister is a very talented musician. She told me that there is a lot of singing in the convent.

I can only carry a tune in a feed bucket," Mary Elizabeth said with a smile.

Reverend Mother laughed. She shook her finger at Mary Elizabeth. "I like your humor. How do you take your tea?"

"Milk and sugar, please."

Reverend Mother poured her tea. As she handed her the cup, she said, "You are American. What are you doing in Bellechester?"

"I finished my training at Mother of Mercy Hospital in London. That is where I met Dr. Merton, and he asked me to come to Bellechester."

"Don't you want to go back to America?"

"Yes, eventually I do. But I also want to be wherever I can use my medical training to help people. All that transpired in the three days I met Dr. Merton—it was nothing short of a miracle that I am here." She took a sip of tea. "For some reason, Bellechester is where I need to be. Do you think I will ever know why?"

Mother Bonifacius smiled. "Yes, I believe someday you will."

"May I ask where you are from?"

"My home is Salzburg. I was sent to school in England in 1933. I received my PhD in medieval European history from Oxford in 1938. My superior sent word to stay in England because of the Nazis. I found this convent and never left." Reverend Mother smiled. "We are the same, you and I. Both far from home."

They spent the next hour chatting. Mary Elizabeth found Reverend Mother warm and friendly. When it was time for Mary Elizabeth to leave, Reverend Mother said, "Next time I call, bring your doctor bag."

"I will, Reverend Mother. Thank you for the tea. Benedicite."

Reverend Mother answered, "Benedicite."

Friday, September 4

CHAPTER 17

GALA PLANS

Mary Elizabeth became comfortable finding her way around Bellechester. The village was beginning to feel like home. Some of the villagers now replaced their silent stares with warm greetings. Some, but not all. Several patients called the surgery and said that they wanted to be seen only by Dr. Merton. Dr. Merton started seeing patients in the surgery again, but only in the mornings twice a week and every other Saturday. When he was in the surgery, Mary Elizabeth made the house calls in the country.

The *Bellechester Bugle* came out on Fridays, and Mary Elizabeth had no idea what Howard Pritchard had written about her.

A young woman with a skin rash on her hand was Mary Elizabeth's last patient of the day. "From what you have told me, your skin allergy came from a chemical in your new floor cleaner. Throw it out. Go back to your old floor cleaner. But be sure to wear gloves when doing any housework for the next few weeks." Handing a prescription to the young woman, she said, "Mr. McCafferty should be able to fill this for you. Apply the ointment twice a day and come back and see me in a week. The rash should be gone by then. However, if the ointment causes blisters or makes the rash worse, then call the surgery immediately and come see me. But I don't think you will have any trouble. You can make an appointment with Miss Chamberlain on the way out."

"Thank you, Doctor."

"You're welcome. Make sure you get out and enjoy this beautiful afternoon, now."

"I will. By the way, I enjoyed reading about you in the *Bugle*. I hope you stay in Bellechester."

"Thank you."

The patient left the exam room while Mary Elizabeth stayed at her desk to finish writing in her chart.

A few minutes later, Sarah stuck her head in and said, "Dr. Senty, Mrs. Winters called and asked you to stop by the rectory."

"Thanks, Sarah. Do I need to take my bag?"

"No, she would like to go over the plans for the welcome reception."

"All right. I'll finish tidying up in here and then I'll be off. Has our copy of the *Bugle* come yet?"

"Yes, Dr. Merton has it. He was very anxious to read it."

"He's not the only one!"

"I'm sure it will be a very nice article. If you are done with that file, I can take it for you."

"Thanks, Sarah." Mary Elizabeth handed it to her. A few minutes later, Mary Elizabeth emerged from the exam room and hung her lab coat behind the registration desk. She grabbed her sweater and dashed out the door. After being inside all day, Mary Elizabeth took deep breaths of the fresh air. She felt her spirits lifting as she walked through the park. Mary Elizabeth knocked on the rectory's back door and entered through the kitchen. She could hear Mrs. Winters chiding someone, "There you go again, upsetting the applecart."

In the dining room, Mary Elizabeth saw that Mrs. Winters's remark was directed at an attractive, well-dressed woman in her early sixties.

Spying Dr. Senty, Mrs. Winters made the introduction. "Lady Beatrice, this is our new doctor, Mary Elizabeth Senty. Dr. Senty, Lady Beatrice Brantwell."

Lady Beatrice walked over and extended her hand. "Very charmed to meet you. Loved the article about you in the *Bugle*."

"Thank you, Lady Beatrice. I am glad you enjoyed the article. It is an honor to meet you." She turned to Mrs. Winters. "You wanted to see me?"

"Your ladyship here has gone and changed everything for your introduction to the village."

"But I thought all the plans were set for a reception after Mass on Sunday. What happened?"

"Allow me to explain," said Lady Beatrice. "Besides Bellechester welcoming you, the village is also getting a new police inspector. And a chief inspector at that. Geoff has an old army chum in the home office. I have it on good authority that the new CI is young, single, and very easy on the eyes." Looking directly at Mrs. Winters, Lady Beatrice continued. "*In addition* to your parish welcome, I am hosting an evening gala for you and the new chief inspector. His commissioning ceremony is going to be part of the evening."

Father Evenson piped up. "Oh, a gala! How wonderful! I love a good party! Will you be inviting my old friend Viscount LeBrosse?"

"Of course. Viscount LeBrosse, and a few barons and baronesses and lords and ladies sprinkled in, will add majesty to the evening. The crème de la crème of southwestern Shropshire will be in attendance. Oh, and of course, the leading citizens of Bellechester such as yourselves." Lady Beatrice made over-the-top movements with her hands as she spoke. "Oh, it will be a grand affair. The glitz! The glamour! And Bellechester's newest young professionals front and center."

"And are you matchmaking to boot?" asked Mrs. Winters.

Lady Beatrice said with a gleam in her eye, "You never know what can happen at these affairs."

Mary Elizabeth bit her lip and put her head down. She felt her cheeks starting to redden.

Father Evenson chimed in, "Oh yes, yes, Dr. Senty and the chief inspector should make a handsome couple."

Mary Elizabeth finally spoke up. "Excuse me. I'm not so sure I like this idea. I have never met the chief inspector. He might be engaged or already have a girlfriend. I don't want folks to get the wrong idea and think we are a couple. This evening should be all about him and his commissioning ceremony."

Lady Beatrice dismissed her concerns with a wave of her hand. "My sources tell me he does not have a girlfriend. He is one of those all-work, no-play types. No, he needs a partner for the evening who is his equal. Who better than a pretty, young professional woman like yourself?"

Mary Elizabeth persisted, "But shouldn't he choose his own partner?"

"My dear Dr. Senty," Lady Beatrice said, taking Mary Elizabeth's hand, "that's very American and democratic of you, but this is England. Gracious! The man is thirty-two years old, and he doesn't even have a girlfriend. Trust me, men like that need a little help."

Mrs. Winters said, "Don't you mean a little push?"

Lady Beatrice shot Mrs. Winters a withering look. Then her expression softened, and she laughed. "No, I am determined to make this gala the finest ever. And pairing our new chief inspector with our new female GP will be just the ticket."

Mary Elizabeth said, "But I really don't have anything suitable to wear to such a fancy event."

"Not to worry about your clothes, dear. I love doing Cinderella makeovers. We will go shopping in London tomorrow. By the time we are through, you will be the prettiest girl at the ball. And all charged to my husband's account."

Mary Elizabeth tried again. "But I have my clinic duties tomorrow."

Lady Beatrice said, "Dr. Merton has handled the surgery by himself for over thirty years. One more day won't matter."

"But what does the chief inspector think about this idea?"

"The chief inspector?" Lady Beatrice stopped for a moment as she pondered the question. Then another wave of her hand. "Think? The chief inspector doesn't think. He obeys orders. In fact, it was his superiors who requested the gala in the first place."

"Is that so?" asked Mrs. Winters.

Father Evenson said, "How odd."

"Dr. Senty, can you give me your guest list by tomorrow? My driver and I will pick you up at half-past eight."

Mary Elizabeth reconciled herself to her fate. "Yes, your ladyship."

Father Evenson rubbed his hands together. "This gala will be a night to remember."

Saturday, September 5

CHAPTER 18

OFF TO LONDON

At 8:25 a.m., a maroon-and-silver 1949 Rolls Royce limousine pulled up to the residence. Winston, the chauffeur, large black umbrella in hand, rang the bell. Mary Elizabeth yelled goodbye and went out the door.

"Good morning, Dr. Senty. May I escort you to the car?" He held out his arm. Mary Elizabeth was soon seated next to Lady Beatrice on the soft leather cushioned seat.

"Good morning, Lady Beatrice."

Lady Beatrice wore a dark-teal wool suit with a large diamond-encrusted pin in the shape of an oak leaf. Around the neck of her suit was a multi-colored silk scarf in shades of teal, gold, brown, and red. On her wrist she wore a three-tiered bracelet set in stones that matched her scarf.

"Good morning, Dr. Senty. We shan't have our spirits dampened by the rainy weather. We have a lovely day of shopping ahead of us in London. Plus, the car ride will give us ample time to get to know each other better."

"Yes, I would like that too."

"Good. Now, I am dying to know how a young American doctor ended up in Bellechester."

"Mr. Pritchard's interview in the *Bugle* pretty much summed it up."

"Piffle!" Lady Beatrice exclaimed. "Your explanation in the *Bugle* was only a few lines. No, I want the real story that is hidden between those lines."

"Oh, before I forget." Mary Elizabeth opened her purse and handed Lady Beatrice an envelope. "Here is my guest list for your gala. Now, I would much rather hear your story, Lady Beatrice. I know so little about you. I am very curious as to why you have taken me under your wing."

"Lord Brantwell and I never had children, so I busy myself with various charitable projects. And I love to plan parties that bring people a little happiness for a few hours."

"Oh, I see. And am I one of your charity projects?"

"Hardly. Why, look at you. You are a woman trying to make her way in a man's world. I admire you greatly. Surely your path to becoming a doctor must not have been easy. Yet you persevered. That, my dear, is just as worthy an accomplishment as honoring the youngest man to be made a chief inspector in the county of Shropshire, maybe in all of England. No, I want you to be feted alongside our new chief inspector. Now, tell me all about yourself. Where were you born? What about your family?"

After two hours of answering Lady Beatrice's questions, Mary Elizabeth finally said, "Please, Lady Beatrice, enough about me. You know everything about me, and I still don't know anything about you. Did you meet Lord Brantwell at a ball?"

"A ball?" Lady Beatrice laughed so hard that tears ran down her face. "My dear, I come from a very poor family in Southampton. I ran away from home at fourteen and joined a traveling theatre group where I honed my acting skills. Later, I worked in Cambridge at the Playhouse Theatre. We catered our shows to the university crowd. We would put on light plays or do song-and-dance revues every weekend. As the fourth son of Lord Brantwell, Geoffrey was sent to school to earn a living for himself. He studied architecture and would often come to the shows with his friends. He was very shy. Some of the wealthier boys would send me beautiful bouquets of flowers with notes praising my beauty or my performance and asking me out to dinner. I usually accepted one of the offers because I knew that meant a free meal. But"—Lady Beatrice turned and put her hands up for emphasis—"paying for my meal was all I allowed them to do."

Mary Elizabeth nodded. Lady Brantwell continued. "Geoffrey sent no gifts nor flowers. Instead, he would write a critique of my performance and have it delivered to my dressing room by a stagehand. His notes were truthful and sometimes brutally honest! Yet, he always signed them, 'From a caring friend.' This went on for months. All I knew was that he was a student at Cambridge, because the notes would stop when the college was on break and resume when the school was in session. After a while, I began to look forward to those notes more than to the flower bouquets and supper invitations sent by my admirers. Finally, one night near the end of the term, I paid two strong stagehands to deliver the man as well as the note to my dressing room. That night I told him he either had to take me to dinner or stop writing me. That's all it took. He took me to dinner. After he received his degree in architecture, we were married and moved to London and lived a very happy and quiet life. Then in March of 1922, our lives changed forever. His father and brother were killed in a horrific automobile crash. Geoffrey inherited the title and entered the House of Lords. We moved to Brantwell Manor and kept a place in London.

And that has been my life for the past thirty-seven years."

"I'm confused. I thought you said Lord Brantwell was the fourth son. Why didn't his other brothers inherit the title?"

Lady Brantwell sighed. "I never understood why people pine for 'the good old days.' There was nothing good about them. The Brantwells' third son died in the First World War. He was a decorated pilot of the Royal Flying Corps. His eldest brother died in the Spanish flu epidemic in 1918. The second son died with his father in the car crash. And so, it fell to Geoffrey as the fourth son to take up the family mantle."

"Oh, Lady Beatrice, how very sad to lose all those family members in such a short span of time."

"Because of those tragedies, Geoffrey and I decided to live in the present and to do as much good as possible." Lady Beatrice turned and looked out the window. "Oh, I see we are coming into London. We will stop and visit with my designers. They will take your measurements, and then we will go to lunch—after lunch we will return to see their dress designs."

When they arrived at Monsieur Lloyd's dress salon, Winston helped Mary Elizabeth out first. The sun had now come out. As she stood on the sidewalk, she tried to get her bearings. Looking across the street, she recognized a familiar sight in the distance. "Is that Mother of Mercy Hospital over there?"

"Yes, I believe it is," Winston replied. He tipped his cap once again and opened the door of the salon for Lady Beatrice and Mary Elizabeth.

"Return for us in about an hour."

"Yes, my lady."

A slim, attractive middle-aged woman greeted the pair. "Lady Beatrice, how wonderful to see you again. And who do you have with you today?"

"Madame Giselle, I would like to introduce Dr. Mary Elizabeth Senty. She is going to be one of the honorees at my gala next month, and I know you will design the perfect ball gown for her."

"But of course. How nice to meet you, Dr. Senty. Now, come with me and we will take your measurements. And I will tell Monsieur Lloyd you are here, Lady Beatrice."

A short, rotund man wearing a red boutonniere on his stylish navy suit soon approached her. "Hey, Toots, what's shakin'?"

Lady Beatrice became indignant. "Is that how you speak to a lady?"

"What lady? That's how I speak to Toots Parker from the Playhouse."

They both laughed. Lady Beatrice asked, "Shorty, how's business?"

"Thanks to you and all your high-society friends, we will be moving soon to a new location on Baker Street in Marylebone."

"My, my, you have come a long way since designing costumes for the Playhouse."

"Sometimes I do get nostalgic for the old days, but that doesn't last long. No, I much prefer having a full stomach and a house with heat and hot water. Now, what brings you here today?"

"I brought you a pretty young American doctor whom I am going to fete at my next gala. I want you to work your magic to attract the attention of a certain young, single police inspector." She paused as Shorty shot her a withering glance. "Now, Shorty, don't you dare give me that look!"

He shook his head. "You don't give up, do you?"

"Why should I? I have a very successful track record. How long have you and Giselle been married?"

"Thirty-four years."

"I rest my case. The last match I made? The young couple is blissfully awaiting the birth of their second child."

Monsieur Lloyd laughed. "With you around, I wonder that there are any single men left in England! Will you be requiring a new gown too?"

"Of course." Lady Beatrice opened her large purse and brought out three jewelry boxes. "And I need something fabulous to wear with these." Opening the cases, she produced a diamond-and-ruby necklace, matching earrings, and bracelet.

Monsieur Lloyd whistled. "Lord Brantwell has excellent taste. These are exquisite! Come in back and I'll have you wear your jewelry so I can make some preliminary sketches and make sure the measurements I have on file for you are accurate."

Mary Elizabeth and Lady Beatrice finished getting measured. "If you don't mind, Lady Beatrice, I would like to take you to my favorite restaurant for lunch."

"As long as I can pay, why not? Where are we going?"

Mary Elizabeth said, "Little Italy. It's not very far from here, and they serve the best Italian food."

"Sounds wonderful."

Mary Elizabeth and Lady Beatrice walked into Little Italy, where they were greeted warmly by the owner, Alex. "*Signorina* Maria Elisabetta! It's so good to see you again! Did you bring *un'amica* with you?

"*Si.*" Mary Elizabeth made the introductions.

Alex took Lady Beatrice's hand and kissed it. "Welcome to Little Italy, my lady. It is always a pleasure to meet another friend of Maria Elisabetta's."

"*Grazie,* Alex. Dr. Senty has spoken very highly of you and your family."

Mary Elizabeth said, "*Un tavolo per due, per favore.*"

Alex exclaimed, "You remembered! Right this way."

Lady Beatrice told Alex, "My chauffeur will be coming in shortly. I will be paying for his meal, but please do not serve him any alcohol. We have a long drive home ahead of us."

"*Capisco.*"

Alex led them to a table near the front. He seated Lady Beatrice and then Mary Elizabeth. "What does Mama recommend today?" Mary Elizabeth asked, taking a menu.

"Mama made *Melanzane alla Parmigiana* and her famous chicken soup as well as her usual menu offerings. May I bring you a glass of wine and bread while you look through the menu? Would your ladyship care to see the wine list?"

"Yes, please. Dr. Senty, I hope you will join me in a glass to celebrate our London adventure."

Because she was not on call today, Mary Elizabeth agreed to a glass of wine with her meal. When Alex told his mother that Mary Elizabeth was in the restaurant, she burst out from the kitchen with warm hugs. Mama was still not confident in her English, so Alex translated. She inquired about "that nice Dr. Merton." When Mary Elizabeth told her how he continued to remember his meal at Little Italy with fondness, and still raved about his dessert, Mama insisted on sending a bag of freshly made *cannoli sicilani* home for him.

During the meal, Lady Beatrice asked Mary Elizabeth, "How are you and Madame Giselle getting along?"

"Just fine. I was so afraid, Lady Beatrice, that you would dress me in a style that I would not like."

"Such as?"

"You know, lots of frills and froufrous."

Lady Beatrice laughed, "No, Dr. Senty, I could never see you in such fashions."

"Anyway, Giselle assured me that they were not the style this year. She showed me gown silhouettes and allowed me to choose."

"Oh, what did you choose?"

"I liked the A-line shape. She said I would look good in jewel tones and showed me some color swatches. They were all so pretty; I said I would like your help deciding. What will your dress look like?"

Lady Beatrice laughed. "I have no idea. Shorty, I mean Monsieur Lloyd, has been dressing me for close to fifty years. I let him surprise me, and he never disappoints. His creations are always so lovely."

As they finished lunch, Lady Beatrice said, "I do believe this is the best meal I have eaten in a long time. Thank you for bringing me here. I will have to tell all my friends, and I will be sure to bring Geoffrey here too."

"Oh, please do. And I am so glad you enjoyed your meal. For me, it was so nice to come to a comfortable place and be among familiar faces again."

"The ambience is so restful that I could stay here all afternoon, but I am afraid we must get back to Monsieur Lloyd's. I can't wait to see what designs they have come up with."

At the dress shop, Lady Beatrice said, "You two have done it again. These designs are absolutely perfect. We will be the best-dressed women at the ball. What do you think, Dr. Senty?"

"Oh, I love your dress, Lady Beatrice. It will be gorgeous."

Madame Giselle asked, "Don't you like your dress, Dr. Senty?"

"I do like the lines and the bow tie at the bodice. I will have to get used to the off-the-shoulder part. Isn't it a tad too revealing? The upper part of my chest will be showing. Shouldn't I be covered up more like Lady Beatrice's dress?"

A resounding chorus of "No!" came from all three. Giselle said, "Dr. Senty, your upper chest and neck are some of your most attractive features."

"There will be time later for you to be all covered up. But now, you are still young and this design will show off your assets," Monsieur Lloyd said.

Lady Beatrice added, "You can't catch a fly without putting out a little honey. We have to get that new chief inspector to notice you. Now, that peacock-green satin is lovely. What material do you have in mind for my dress?"

"I was thinking a deep cabernet chiffon with three-quarter lace sleeves and sequins on the lace appliqué bodice should show off your ruby and diamond jewelry beautifully. Either I or Giselle will come and do the final fitting. We will give you a call."

"Yes, and please plan to stay for dinner and overnight. Traveling to Bellechester and back is too much driving in one day. Now, before I go, I must tell you about this quaint little Italian restaurant just a few streets from here. Dr. Senty, what was it called again?"

"Little Italy."

"Fabulous food, generous portions, and reasonable prices. I highly recommend it."

Giselle said, "We will have to check it out. It was a pleasure to meet you, Dr. Senty. Now, don't worry. Our designs are always in the best of taste. When it is all made, I am sure you will love it."

"Please come again, Dr. Senty. And if your dress works its magic like Toots says, we would love to design your wedding dress." Monsieur Lloyd smiled and winked at her.

Mary Elizabeth's eyes grew wide, and her mouth dropped in amazement.

"Shorty! You are scaring the poor girl," Lady Beatrice said as they walked out the door.

Mary Elizabeth was glad to be inside the car again. Their next stop was shopping for shoes. Lady Beatrice advised Mary Elizabeth to get heels no taller than an inch because those were the best for dancing. The shoes also had to be dyed to match their dress fabric. The designers had given each of them several small swatches for this very purpose. Next, they shopped for handbags. Again, Mary Elizabeth deferred to Lady Beatrice's expertise. Lady Beatrice had wanted to take Mary Elizabeth jewelry shopping, but Mary Elizabeth was firm. Lady Beatrice had spent enough money on her. No, she would wear the jewelry she brought from home. The ride home was a quiet one, as Lady Beatrice fell asleep before they were halfway back.

Monday, September 14

CHAPTER 19

Will Settles In

Will carried a small box of personal items to the police station. Sergeant John O'Hanlon was at the front desk. "Good morning, Inspector. Do you need any help?"

"No, Sergeant. This is my only box of office belongings."

"Are you all settled into your new home?"

"Finally, yes. After this, I do not want to see another box that needs unpacking or a picture that needs hanging for quite a while."

"Very understandable, sir. I hope you will like living in our village."

"I am sure I will. It will be quite a change from the hustle and bustle of London, but I am looking forward to village living. Any word on Miss Hutchinson's condition?"

"She is still at Glendale hospital. The surgery to fix her shoulder was a success, although I hear she suffered a stroke a few days ago. She will be recuperating in the hospital for several more weeks. We continue to pray for her."

"Sorry to hear about her stroke. Does she have any family?"

"Her younger sister, Violet, came up from Exeter to be with her."

"Thank you for the information. Can you tell me where there is a florist nearby?" Will made a mental note to stop in at the hospital after work.

"There's a flower shop across the road from the hospital in Glendale. Would you like me to bring you some tea?"

"Yes, please. Milk, no sugar."

"Very good, sir."

By this time the sergeant returned with the tea, Will was seated at his desk. "Thank you, Sergeant."

"Do you find your office to your liking, sir?"

"Yes, very much so. Back at the Met, our whole division was in one room. It was always so noisy. It will take me a while to get used to the quiet."

"Do you have everything you need?"

"Yes, I believe so."

"If you think of anything later, I will be happy to get it for you."

Sergeant O'Hanlon turned to leave, but Will stopped him. "There is something you can do for me." He pulled a manila envelope from his desk drawer and handed it to O'Hanlon. "New national guidelines for officer recertification have been approved by parliament. Chief Constable Scott needs our compliance by the thirty-first of December. Officers will receive annual training in the areas of firearms and de-escalation techniques. We must also receive annual physical exams. I drafted a letter to the men outlining the new requirements. Here's all the forms that need to be completed by each officer." Will shook his head and sighed. "More paperwork for us. It's all in there. Could you have my letter typed and returned for my signature by the end of the week?"

"Yes, sir."

"Very good, Sergeant. After I finish my tea, I was wondering if you could give me a tour of the station and introduce me to the staff?"

"It would be my pleasure, sir."

After the tour, they found a woman sitting outside Will's office. She was wearing a purple dress trimmed in black. Her large black purse was open next to her. She was looking down, writing notes in a small notebook. She wore a large black plate hat that, with her head down, covered her entire face.

"Ma'am, can I help you?"

The woman lifted her head. "Yes, Sergeant. I am here to meet with the new inspector."

"As I told you before, Mrs. Farnsworth, the new inspector does not begin his duties until tomorrow."

"Then who is that?" She pointed her gloved finger at Will. "I was walking past the station, and I saw a light on in the inspector's office. That man was sitting at the desk." She straightened herself on the bench. "As the wife of the mayor, I thought it my duty to introduce myself first thing."

Will stepped forward. "Good morning, Mrs. Farnsworth. I am Inspector William Donnelly. Please come into my office. I will be happy to meet with you. Sergeant, please hold my calls."

"Yes, Inspector."

As Mrs. Farnsworth rose from her seat, Will had to duck out of the way of her hat. Will closed the door behind them and waited for Mrs. Farnsworth to be seated before he sat.

"What can I do for you this morning?"

"As the first lady of the village, I thought I should find out more about you. I went to your house this morning, but no one answered the bell."

"You know where I live?"

"Inspector, everyone in the village knows you bought the Hobart house. It was reported in Friday's *Bugle*. The paper also reported that you were the one who captured Miss Hutchinson's attacker. Mr. Pritchard wrote you were unavailable for an interview."

"Last week was very busy for me, as I was moving from London to Bellechester. I must have missed his call."

"If you came from London, then you must know our new doctor who also arrived from London."

"London is a very large city, Mrs. Farnsworth. No, I am afraid I have not met him."

Mrs. Farnsworth put her gloved hand to her mouth to stifle a giggle. "I guess you two haven't met. Weren't you at Mass two Sundays ago when the doctor was introduced?"

"Two weekends ago, I was in London."

"The reason I ask is that I find it odd that our new doctor arrives in the village the same day you did. And both of you come from London. And you say you don't know each other?"

"That is correct. It must be a coincidence."

"I should say. Do you go back to London every weekend? Is that where your girlfriend lives?

"No, there is no girlfriend."

"Oh, I see. Don't you want a family, Inspector?"

"Yes, I do. Someday."

There was a pause as she leaned in closer to him. "Well, I think you will find that our village has many fine young women who are family minded. I don't think you will have any problem finding a wife here."

Will choose his next words very carefully. "I look forward to meeting all the citizens of Bellechester."

"Well, if you ever want me to make any introductions for you, just let me know. I make it my business to know everyone in Bellechester."

Will thought to himself, *I bet you do!* "Thank you, I will. For now, I want to concentrate on solving the crime issues in Bellechester."

Mrs. Farnsworth sat back in her chair. "Yes, now how are you going to go about it?"

"The first thing I need to do is assess the situation. That means I will be listening to what our officers, the shop owners, and the townsfolk have to say."

"Listening! We need action!"

"I hear your frustration, Mrs. Farnsworth, but before we can act, we need to have a well-thought-out plan. We need to approach the problem of crime from many angles. It will take the entire community to work together to solve this issue. I hope I can count on your support."

"Sounds like a waste of time to me."

"I must disagree with you there. Bellechester's problems will not be solved overnight. Why don't you give me six months. If you don't see an improvement in the crime rate, then please, come back and see me." The noon bells from St. Anselm's tolled in the background. "Is there anything else, Mrs. Farnsworth?"

"No. But mark my words—I will not be waiting six months to see you again if things don't improve in the village." She rose. "Now I must take my leave, as I have a luncheon engagement."

Will opened his office door for her. "Thank you for coming to see me. It was a pleasure to meet you."

Will ducked away from the brim of her hat as she left. "Goodbye, Mrs. Farnsworth."

"Good day, Inspector."

"Any calls?" Will asked Sergeant O'Hanlon.

"Howard Pritchard from the *Bellechester Bugle* called. He wants to come and interview you for the paper."

"He should talk to Mrs. Farnsworth. She already knows most everything about me."

The sergeant couldn't help but laugh.

"Could you call him back and tell him I can see him this afternoon at half-past one? Now, I am going home for lunch."

"Very good, sir."

That afternoon, Howard Pritchard came to the station accompanied by his photographer. "If you don't mind, Inspector, I would like Simon to take a few pictures of you for the article."

"Of course. Where do you want me?"

"Sitting behind your desk would be good. Could you hold up a piece of paper like you are reading it?" Simon instructed.

"How's that?"

"Perfect." He clicked the shutter. "Now how about you looking at the map on the wall?" Will obliged. Simon looked around the room. "Hmm. Let's have you stand next to Sergeant O'Hanlon out by the front desk. Great. I think I have all I need," he said after those were taken.

Will shook his head and blinked hard after the flashes of the camera bulbs.

Simon left, and Will turned to Howard. "Shall we go back into my office, Mr. Pritchard?"

Howard asked questions before Will could even sit down. Throughout the interview, Will thought back to what Chief Superintendent Williamson had said about maintaining good public relations. After covering Will's professional career, Howard began to ask personal questions. Will glanced at his watch. He had been answering questions for over an hour. He stood up to end the interview.

"If you will excuse me, Mr. Pritchard, I have some important police business that needs my attention. Busy first day and all."

Howard looked up from his notepad. "Oh, yes, thank you for your time, Inspector."

"If you think of any additional questions, you can always contact me here at the station," Will said from his office door.

"I will. Your story will appear in Friday's *Bugle*. Good day, Inspector."

"Good day, Mr. Pritchard." Will escorted him to the door and walked to the break room to make himself a cup of tea. "Now I know what our suspects feel like after an interrogation!" he joked to O'Hanlon.

Sergeant O'Hanlon laughed, then introduced Will to the officers on the afternoon shift.

"Thank you for the introductions, Sergeant. Tomorrow I will not be in the office. I will be with Chief Superintendent Williamson all day."

"Very good, Inspector."

CHAPTER 20

WILL VISITS MISS HUTCHINSON

Will stopped at the flower shop before making his way to the hospital.

The curtains were pulled on each side of Miss Hutchinson's bed. She looked very small and frail among her many pillows. Her sister sat in the chair beside the bed and held Miss Hutchinson's hand. Despite their difference in age, the two had strikingly similar facial features. When Miss Hutchinson saw Will, she perked up. Her sister glanced at the tall, handsome young man. "Another one of your former students, Vera?"

Will watched as Miss Hutchinson struggled to answer, "N-n-no! Fr-fr-ie-n." She lay back on her pillow, exhausted from the effort, but with a big smile on her face.

Her sister looked quizzically at Will. "I am Detective Inspector William Donnelly from the Bellechester Constabulary, ma'am."

"Do you have news about the hooligan that did this to my sister?"

"Yes. After his arraignment, he was transferred to Shrewsbury for his trial in crown court. He will not be causing any more trouble. But that is not my only reason for visiting."

Violet Cranston said, "Oh?"

"As Miss Hutchinson said, we are friends. She was one of the first people I met when I came to Bellechester. I came to visit with her if it would not be too taxing for her."

Miss Hutchinson shook her head. She then looked at her sister and said, "You g-g-g-go."

Her sister got up from the chair. "Well, Inspector, it looks like I have been given my marching orders." She touched Will's arm as she passed. He followed her to the middle of the room. "Inspector, I am Violet Cranston, Vera's younger sister. As you can see, my sister has suffered a stroke from the head injury she sustained in the attack. It has affected her speech. But she is as bossy as ever. Her mind is still sharp, and she would clearly relish your visit. So, if you don't mind staying with her for a while, I'd like to get some dinner."

"It would be my pleasure to stay and visit until you come back."

Violet Cranston patted his arm. "Thank you, Inspector."

"Any special instructions?"

"The doctor said it is good for her to practice her speech, but it does tire her out."

"I understand. You go have a nice dinner."

Violet Cranston left the floor. Will took off his coat and put it behind the chair. He set his hat and the small square box which held a bud vase on the tray table. He sat down next to Miss Hutchinson and noticed the nightstand next to her bed. It was filled with floral arrangements of every size. His lone chrysanthemum-and-bud vase looked very small.

Miss Hutchinson saw his box on the tray table. "F-f-for m-m-m-ee?"

Will took out the bud vase and put it on the table. "I stopped at the florist's. The clerk said yellow flowers mean friendship. And this was the prettiest yellow flower in the cooler. It reminded me of the chrysanthemums in your front garden."

Miss Hutchinson was trying with much effort to raise herself so she could smell the flower.

Will brought the bud vase closer to her. She inhaled deeply. "B-b-bu-ful."

Will took the vase and tried to find a spot on her nightstand. Miss Hutchinson became agitated. "N-no!"

"You don't want me to put it with the others?"

"N-no!"

"Should I leave it on your tray table?"

Miss Hutchinson nodded her assent. "B-b-bu-ful. W-w-wa-n-n s-s-ee. C-c-ca-r?"

Will removed the card. He read, "'Get Well Wishes to Miss Hutchinson from your new friend, Will.'" He added, "Underneath I wrote 'Inspector Donnelly,' just in case you know a lot of Wills."

Miss Hutchinson smiled. Will could see that she was trying to move her hand. She could raise it only slightly. "F-f-fr-fr-en?"

Will slipped his hand under hers. Then he brought his other hand on top of hers, careful not to interfere with her IV line. He looked her in the eye and said firmly, "Friends." They held hands in companionable silence for a few minutes. "Would you like to hear the news from Bellechester?"

Miss Hutchinson nodded. "The two lads you recommended did a fine job cleaning up my garden. They followed your instructions about pruning the roses to the letter. Knowing that you might be in the hospital for a while, they asked Sergeant O'Hanlon if they could take care of your garden too. They will be supervised, of course. It seems the lads prefer gardening to whitewashing the village hall and painting the benches in the park."

Miss Hutchinson laughed. "All m-moo in?"

Will enjoyed telling her about the renovations Ned Manderfield had made to his home. She nodded when Will said how pleased he was with the work done by Ned and his crew.

"G-g-goo m-men."

A nurse came entered, carrying a syringe in a tray. "Time for your nighttime pain medication, Miss Hutchinson."

Will stood up. "Do you want me to leave?"

"If we could exchange places for a minute. I need to inject her medicine into her IV. This medicine will make her drowsy."

Miss Hutchinson became agitated. "N-noo. W-w-w-ee t- t-tak."

"I'm afraid your talking is done for the evening."

"N-n-o! Fr-fr-en-en!"

"I promised her sister I would stay with her until she came back from dinner."

"You can stay, but no talking. Miss Hutchinson must rest now."

Will remembered a tactic he'd used to calm his beloved grandmother after her stroke. "Is it all right if I sing to her? Would you like that, Miss Hutchinson?"

Miss Hutchinson calmed down immediately. She nodded. The nurse injected the medicine into her IV line.

After the nurse left, Will sat back down. "You lie back and close your eyes. Here, you can put your hand right on top of mine." In his rich baritone, he began to sing "I'll See You in My Dreams." He could tell Miss Hutchinson was relaxed. As he finished the song, he heard her steady breathing. She had fallen asleep. Violet Cranston returned shortly thereafter. He gently removed his hand from underneath Miss Hutchinson's. "Do you need a ride?" he mouthed while gathering his coat and hat.

Violet shook her head.

"Good night."

Driving back to Bellechester, he thought about the events of Miss Hutchinson's attack. *Was there anything I could have done to prevent it? Should I have intervened sooner?* Will stopped at the Ram's Head for supper before going home.

In bed that night, he considered the shock of seeing a once-vibrant woman confined to a hospital bed, struggling to speak. Will fell into a troubled sleep.

Wednesday, September 16

CHAPTER 21

On the Road to Brantwell Manor

Sergeant O'Hanlon knocked on Will's office door.

"Enter."

"Sir, here is the recertification letter ready for your signature."

"Very good." Will read the letter a final time. "I am entrusting the scheduling of the trainings and the medical exams to you." He signed the document and gave it back to O'Hanlon.

"Yes, sir. I will see to it that all the men receive your letter. Inspector, might I make a suggestion?"

"Yes, of course." Will looked up from the pile of papers on his desk.

"Scheduling the physical exams here in Bellechester would be more efficient than sending the men up to Shrewsbury. So, if it is all right with you, I will set them up with the village surgery."

"Do you think our village GP can handle all the officers in the district?"

"Oh yes. Dr. Merton has a new associate working with him."

"Very good, Sergeant. I was with the RMP for twelve years. Our motto was, 'By example shall we lead.' Start scheduling the physicals and the trainings for the commanders first."

"Yes, sir." Sergeant O'Hanlon turned to leave.

Will stopped him with another thought. "Oh, and one more thing. Have you seen an invitation come through the mail from Lord and Lady Brantwell?"

"Not yet, sir."

"It is very important, so when it does arrive, please put it on the top of the pile."

"Yes, sir."

Later that morning, Will received a call from Lord Brantwell. "I am leaving for a business trip and safari to Tanganyika next week. The only time I can meet to discuss security arrangements for the gala would be today at three o'clock."

"I'll be there."

"Capital! Goodbye, Inspector."

At the surgery, Mary Elizabeth said, "According to Sarah, the number of patients coming in today looks light."

Dr. Merton said, "And I only have a few house calls on my list. This afternoon, I am hoping to visit Miss Hutchinson and a few other patients who are currently in hospital."

"Will you be looking in on Mr. Long today? I hope the medicine I prescribed for him is clearing up his leg infection."

"I will add him to the list."

Sarah joined them. "That was Lady Brantwell on the phone. The dresses for the gala will be at the manor this afternoon. She asked if you could come for your fitting today around 3:00 p.m."

Mary Elizabeth looked to Dr. Merton. "Go. Don't worry about us. Sarah and I will manage."

It was a beautiful mid-September afternoon for a drive. Mary Elizabeth rolled the driver's side window down and was enjoying the warm sunlight on her arm and the breeze on her face. As she drove farther into the country, she could smell newly cut hay. That scent reminded her of home. She felt a twinge of homesickness. *What would they all be doing on such a fine fall day? The apples would be ready for picking. It would be a perfect day for drying the field corn.* The car thumped beneath her. The sound of a tire going flat vanquished any further thoughts of home from her mind. Mary Elizabeth sighed and pulled to a stop on the side of the road to inspect the situation. Her driver's side back tire was flat.

Better get to it, she thought. *This tire isn't going to change itself.* She took stock of her surroundings. The road was empty. She hadn't seen another car in over fifteen minutes. Her only companions were a herd of cows grazing contentedly in a nearby field. She looked down at her attire. She had changed into her best skirt and sweater to visit Lady Brantwell; she couldn't possibly get dirt or axle grease on those. She was wearing a full slip underneath, so short of other options, she slipped off her skirt and sweater and folded them neatly in the backseat. She took the jack, tire iron, and spare tire from the boot. In no time, she had the back of the car jacked up. The tire nuts and bolts were tight. It took all her strength and then some before they finally came loose. She was focused on the tasks in front of her and did not notice a car slowing down and coming to a stop behind her.

Will saw her disabled vehicle blocking part of the road as he drove to Brantwell Manor. *I really don't have time for this today,* he thought. "Miss!" he called, exiting his car to offer assistance. She did not respond. He took a few steps closer to her. "Miss! Police!" he called louder, startling Mary Elizabeth.

She whipped around and stood up in one motion, the tire iron still in her hand.

Even from a distance, seeing a woman in a full slip with a tire iron surprised Will too. "Sorry to startle you, ma'am." Will flashed his warrant card. "Inspector William Donnelly of the Bel-lechester Police."

Trying to regain her senses, it took her a moment before she said, "If you have come to help me change my tire, you are too late. Thank you, but as you can see, I do not need any help." Certain he posed no threat, she bent down and continued reattaching the bolts.

Then she rolled the flat to the back of the car; she was about to lift it into the boot when Will reached her. "Here, let me help you with that," he said.

"No, thank you, I can manage. No sense in both of us getting dirty," she said as she hoisted the old tire into the boot with ease.

Will knew he should walk away, but he found it difficult to leave her. *She looks and sounds like the woman I met at the rugby match in London. But what would she be doing out here on this empty road in southwestern Shropshire? No, she can't be the same person.* Will shook his head, trying to rid his mind of those impossible thoughts.

Mary Elizabeth became concerned. "Excuse me, Inspector, are you all right?" She looked at him closely.

Will took a few steps backward. "Yes, I'm fine."

"Maybe you should go back and sit in your car out of the sun. Do you have any water with you?"

"Really. I am fine." Will's hat covered much of his face. His dark sunglasses hid his eyes.

He sounds like that nice policeman from the rugby game. It can't be him. He worked for the Met police department. What would he be doing on this deserted road? She disassembled the jack and placed the components in their proper compartment, then slammed the boot shut.

Will had still not moved.

"Inspector, are you sure you are all right?"

"Yes, I'm fine."

"Once again, thank you for stopping. But as you can see, the tire is replaced. All is well. Please, don't let me keep you. Isn't there some other place you need to be right now?" She brushed away a wisp of hair that had fallen over her face.

If he did not leave now, he would be late for his appointment with Lord Brantwell. But first he had to know for sure. He blurted out, "It's you!"

"Of course, it's me! Who else would I be?" Mary Elizabeth asked with annoyance. She desperately wanted to finish the conversation, get dressed, and get back on the road. She looked at her watch. "I am sorry, Inspector, but I am late for an appointment."

Not wanting her to get away from him again, he said, "You can't leave yet."

"Why not?"

"Because . . ." Will was desperate to find an excuse, any excuse to detain her until he found out more information about her. He whipped out his citation book and began to scribble furiously.

"What are you doing?" Mary Elizabeth inquired.

"I am writing you a penalty notice for disorder," he said in a calm and clear voice.

Mary Elizabeth was incredulous. "You are giving me a ticket for changing my flat tire?"

"Of course not," he answered. "Don't be daft. I am citing you for indecent exposure."

"You have got to be kidding! Look! I am wearing a full slip!"

"Ma'am, I'd rather not look at you right now, which is why I am writing this citation."

Mary Elizabeth angrily opened the back door and quickly redressed. Slamming the door shut, she said, "I took off my outer clothes to change my flat. The tire is changed. I am now fully dressed." She yelled, "Satisfied?"

Will was silent. He continued writing.

Mary Elizabeth pled her case. "Look around you. This road is deserted." Then, pointing to the cows in the pasture across the road, she said, "The cows don't seem to mind."

Will was undeterred. "Name!"

"Mary Elizabeth Senty . . . S-E-N-T-Y."

"Address."

"23 Abbey Road, Bellechester."

"Here." Will handed her the notice.

Mary Elizabeth grabbed the citation, jumped in her car, and drove off, leaving Will in a cloud of dust.

CHAPTER 22

Two Impressions of Brantwell Manor

Mary Elizabeth drove slowly off the main road. Brantwell Manor rose before her. The four-story red-brick mansion commanded awe and respect. The front of the building had six large white pillars. A set of stairs ran across the entire front of the mansion. One end of the building held a terrace which opened onto an enormous side flower garden. As she drove toward the house, she noticed an elaborate turf labyrinth built into the front lawn. At its center stood a large statue of Bacchus, prone and feasting on grapes provided by scantily clad nymphs. The road curved around it. Mary Elizabeth stopped in front of the mansion. A valet appeared at her door.

"Where would you like me to park my car?"

The valet opened her door. "If you please, miss." Helping her out of the car, he continued, "I will take care of parking your car. Mr. Jameson is waiting for you." He escorted Mary Elizabeth to the top of the stairs, bowed, and went to park her car. Mary Elizabeth turned to thank him, but the valet was already down the stairs. She had never experienced a valet before, so she stood and watched him drive her car around the back of the house before entering.

Mr. Jameson cleared his throat. "Ahem, Dr. Senty. Lady Brantwell is waiting for you upstairs. Please follow me." He led her through the large foyer, which had a cherrywood table and a tall vase of freshly cut flowers. A crystal chandelier hung from the ceiling. At the top of the stairs, Mr. Jameson knocked on the first door on the left. He opened the door and announced, "Dr. Senty to see you, ma'am."

Lady Beatrice stood on a block while Madame Giselle pinned the hem of her dress. "Thank you,

Mr. Jameson. Come in, Dr. Senty. So nice to see you. I was beginning to get worried."

"My apologies for being late, Lady Beatrice, I had a flat tire. I am afraid my hands are dirty. Is there somewhere I could wash up?"

"Goodness, dear, did you have to change it yourself? Was there no one to help you? Oh here, Andrews"—she summoned her maid with a wave of her hand—"show Dr. Senty where she can get cleaned up."

Meanwhile, back on the road to Brantwell Manor, Will angrily brushed his clothes. He had mucked up any chance he had of making a good impression on the woman from the rugby game. At least he knew her name, whatever good that was to him now. And he was now behind schedule. He stepped on the gas and drove faster than he should to make up some time. Any further musings of the woman on the road were replaced by thoughts of his meeting with Lord Brantwell. At the manor, he grabbed his briefcase and exited his car before the valet reached him.

"May I park your car, sir?"

"Yes. Here are the keys. Thank you." Will tossed his car keys to the valet and hurried up the stairs two at a time. Mr. Jameson greeted him. "Welcome to Brantwell Manor, Inspector. Lord Brantwell is waiting for you in the study. Please follow me."

Mr. Jameson escorted Will down a red carpeted hallway. On either wall, pictures of hunting scenes hung in ornate golden frames. The butler knocked on the open door. "Lord Brantwell, Inspector Donnelly has arrived."

A strong, clear voice from inside the room answered. "Very good, Mr. Jameson. Send him in."

Lord Brantwell, a small man in his early sixties with a full head of white hair, stood behind his imposing rosewood desk. The legs of the desk had elephants carved into them. To the side sat a settee covered in red velvet. It had an elaborate lattice-carved backboard. In front of the desk were two chairs that matched the lattice work of the settee.

"Welcome, Inspector," Lord Brantwell said. "I hope you didn't have any trouble finding the place."

"I apologize for being late, Lord Brantwell. I ran into a little trouble on the road," replied Will.

"Nothing serious, I hope."

"No, only a woman who had a flat tire."

"Glad you are here. May I offer you some refreshment?"

"A glass of sparkling water would be nice, thank you," Will replied.

"Nothing stronger, Inspector?" asked Lord Brantwell.

"No, thank you, sir. I am still on the clock."

"Mr. Jameson, sparkling water for the inspector and my usual, if you please."

"Yes, my lord." Jameson went to the credenza to fix the drinks. He returned with refreshments on a small tray. He offered Will his sparkling water and then Lord Brantwell his Pimm's.

"Thank you, Mr. Jameson. That will be all."

"Very good, my lord." Mr. Jameson returned the tray to the credenza and withdrew from the room.

"Here, Inspector, I have the floor plans you requested. My wife is still finalizing the guest list. She will send it to you soon." Lord Brantwell led

Will to the matching rosewood table that sat on the far side of the room. Sunshine streaming through large windows illuminated the floor plans on the tabletop. Lord Brantwell gave Will the general overview of the house.

"Does the manor have an alarm system?" Will asked.

"Yes, of course. Mr. Jameson turns it on after he makes his rounds to ensure the doors are all locked. He is the first to rise, and he turns it off during the day. If you have any questions about the alarm system, please ask Mr. Jameson."

"Thank you, sir. Does anyone else have access to the alarm system?"

"No, only Mr. Jameson and myself."

"Where is the safe located?"

"Ah, follow me, Inspector." Behind Lord Brantwell's desk hung a large picture of a fox hunt. Grabbing the corner of the picture frame, Lord Brantwell swung the picture out to the side. Behind the picture was a wall safe.

Will took out his notepad and made notes on the manufacturer and model number displayed on the front. "Who knows about the location of the safe?"

"Only Mr. Jameson, Lady Beatrice, myself, and now you."

"And the combination?"

"Just the three of us."

"How long has Mr. Jameson been with you?"

Lord Brantwell's tone became sharp. "Now look here, Inspector. Mr. Jameson has been with me for over twenty-seven years. And before that, his father attended my father. I assure you that Mr. Jameson is completely trustworthy."

"Forgive me, Lord Brantwell. These are questions I must ask."

"Of course. Of course." Lord Brantwell became impatient. He looked at his wristwatch. "Do you have any more questions for me? I am sorry, but I must dash back to London. Critical vote in parliament tomorrow. If you need more help, contact my wife or Mr. Jameson."

"Thank you for your time, Lord Brantwell. I will be speaking with Mr. Jameson and Lady Brantwell in the coming weeks."

"Let's see if we can catch these wretched jewel thieves."

"Of course, sir."

Lord Brantwell pressed a button beneath his desk. Will knew the meeting had not gone as well as he'd hoped. He wanted to leave Lord Brantwell on better terms. "Your rosewood furniture takes me back to my time in India."

"You were in India?"

"Yes, India was my first overseas assignment. I served with the Royal Military Police in Bombay from 1946–48 during the British withdrawal."

"Where else were you deployed?"

Will answered, "After India, I served in West Germany from 1948–51. Then Korea from 51–54. I left the military in 1955 and joined the London Metropolitan Police. I worked with them until my appointment last month to Belchester."

"For one so young, you have a wealth of police experience," Lord Brantwell said. "Maybe you are just the chap to crack this string of jewel thefts."

"I will do my best, sir."

Mr. Jameson appeared. Lord Brantwell addressed him. "Mr. Jameson, Inspector Donnelly must leave now, but in the coming weeks, he may need your assistance. Please give him whatever help he requests. Inspector Donnelly has my full confidence." Lord Brantwell extended his hand to Will. "Very pleased to meet you, Inspector. Have a pleasant trip back to Bellechester."

Will returned Lord Brantwell's firm handshake. "Thank you for your cooperation, Lord Brantwell. Good luck in London." Will scooped up the floor plans and followed Mr. Jameson out of the room.

Thursday, September 17

CHAPTER 23

Paying Her Debt

After Mass, Mary Elizabeth made her way up the street to the police station. She was nervous as she stepped through the door, but then was greeted by Sergeant O'Hanlon's friendly voice.

"Good morning, Dr. Senty—what can I do for you today?" She'd met him and his family at the parish welcome reception the previous Sunday.

"Sergeant O'Hanlon, how nice to see a familiar face." She strode to the counter, opened her purse, and produced the citation. "I am here to pay my debt to society," she declared as she handed him the offending notice.

"Now what is this all about?" he asked.

Mary Elizabeth proceeded to tell him the whole story. She did a rather good imitation of the citing police officer. They both shared a laugh. "I am so glad, Sergeant, that you can see the humor in the situation. I almost pitied that officer. He was so very serious. And for the record, I was wearing a full slip, so I wasn't all that exposed. Of course, upon further reflection, I probably should not have made the remark about the cows. I fear that was what sent him over the edge. Now, what do I owe?"

"Seems like one of my officers was a bit overzealous. I don't see any reason for a penalty notice," Sergeant O'Hanlon said. He took a minute to read the citation. As his eyes reached the bottom of the paper, his expression changed into a serious frown. He looked up at her. "I'm so sorry, Dr. Senty. I can't dismiss this citation. It's just that—"

"Oh, don't worry about it. I'm sure that officer thought he was doing his duty. Besides, I am quite fortunate I only have one citation to pay."

"How is that?"

"Your officer could have also cited me for indecent language because of what I shouted at him as I drove away. So, you see, I will gladly pay this one fine. Now, what do I owe?"

Relief spread over the sergeant's face. "One pound ought to cover it."

Mary Elizabeth dug in her purse and pulled out her pocketbook. She opened it and pulled out a pound note. "There you go." She handed Sergeant O'Hanlon the money.

"Thank you, Dr. Senty. That will take care of your penalty notice. Dr. Senty, before you go, may I ask your advice?"

"Of course."

"County Command has directed that all police officers have annual physical exams. They have given precincts three months to comply. What would be the best way to schedule them with your surgery?"

"We usually do physicals first thing in the morning because we need fasting blood tests. I can have Miss Chamberlain give you a call, and you can schedule the exams with her. I am sure we can accommodate your officers within the allotted time."

"That would be wonderful." Sergeant O'Hanlon said. "Thank you, Dr. Senty."

Tuesday, September 22

CHAPTER 24

THE DOCTOR AND THE POLICE INSPECTOR

The autumn rain was coming down in torrents. Mary Elizabeth burst into the surgery out of breath and looking like a drowned rat after attending morning Mass.

Sarah gasped, "Dr. Senty!"

It took a few moments for Mary Elizabeth to catch her breath. She hung her wet raincoat on the coat stand in the front porch and then walked to the reception desk. "I know. I know," she said. "I was running late this morning. I remembered my raincoat but forgot my umbrella. Darn English weather. The sun was shining and there were only a few clouds in the sky when I left for church. Boy, it's really coming down out there. 'A real soaker,' as my dad would say. Sarah, what time is it?" She untied her drenched scarf and held it out in front of her.

"Eight fifteen," Sarah replied.

Mary Elizabeth peeked around the corner and saw an empty waiting room. "Do you think I have time for a cup of tea? What time is my first patient?"

"He has already arrived. I put him in there." She pointed to the exam room.

"Already! Is it an emergency?"

"Dr. Merton assigned you to do all the police physicals. This morning you have your first one," Sarah said. "The officer said he wanted to get his exam over with as soon as possible. He didn't look like the type that would be content paging through a magazine in the waiting room, so I took him on through to the exam room."

Mary Elizabeth said, "Well, I am sorry, but he is going to have to wait a few more minutes. I need to go upstairs and towel off."

Mary Elizabeth walked through the door at the back of the reception area and hurried up the stairs. She found a towel in her bathroom and wiped off her face and hands. She looked in the mirror. Her headscarf had proved no match for the rain, and her hair was plastered to her head. *Drat! My hair will never dry tied up like this.* She undid her bun and toweled off her hair as best she could. She decided to wear her hair down until it dried completely. Even as she vigorously brushed her hair straight, it still curled a bit at the ends. She found a white headband to keep her hair from falling in her face. She looked in the mirror. With her hair down, she did not look like her usual formidable, no-nonsense, professional self. Instead, her long hair framed her face and softened her features. She frowned in the mirror. *Will anyone take me seriously when it looks like I can't even stay out of the rain?* Then she sighed. *This is the best it's going to get today.* She exchanged her wet shoes for dry ones and hurried downstairs.

Mary Elizabeth grabbed her white lab coat from a hook in the reception area. Flicking her hair out from under her lab coat collar, she turned to Sarah, who was staring at her. "What?" she asked.

Sarah said. "Dr. Senty, I have never seen you with your hair down before. You look . . ."

" . . . like someone who forgot her umbrella and now has wet hair?"

"No, actually, you look quite pretty," Sarah said as she held out a thin patient file to Mary Elizabeth.

Mary Elizabeth said, "Not exactly the look I was going for, but thank you for the compliment." She took the file from Sarah, opened it, and glanced at the lone sheet of paper inside. "No records here. The only sheet is for the police physical."

"Your patient is the new police inspector. He moved to town a few weeks ago."

"Did you say the new police inspector?"

"Why, yes. Is anything the matter?"

Mary Elizabeth looked again at the name on the file. "Sarah, this is the policeman who gave me that penalty notice!"

"Oh no!" She started to giggle, and then put her hand over her mouth.

"I don't know if I can do this. Where is Dr. Merton? Maybe he can give him his physical."

"Dr. Merton left a half hour ago to begin his house calls."

Mary Elizabeth sighed. "In that case, can you also hand me a new patient form? Thanks." She walked up to the closed exam-room door. She stopped for a moment and offered a silent prayer to help her focus on the task ahead. Looking again at the name on the file, she raised her eyes to heaven, shook her head, plastered a smile on her face, rapped sharply on the door, and entered.

"Good morning, Inspector Donnelly," she said as she walked toward the tall, broad-shouldered. figure. She held out her hand. "I'm Doctor Mary Elizabeth Senty."

Will stood at the wall. He had been looking at the pictures she had hung. Today he wore a grey suit, a navy-and-maroon tie, and spit-polished black shoes. He had already hung up his raincoat and hat on the coat tree in the corner. "Yes, I gathered as much from all the diplomas you have hanging on the wall. Very impressive." He took her outstretched hand. "I do believe we have met before."

"On the road to Brantwell Manor." An awkward silence hung between them. Mary Elizabeth said, "I hear you are anxious to be on your way, so shall we get started? Since you are a new patient, there are a few questions I need to ask you. Here, why don't you sit in this chair?" She pointed to the chair in front of her desk. Mary Elizabeth walked around and sat behind her desk. "Let's start with your family medical history, shall we?"

The tension in the room was palpable. Mary Elizabeth was direct, leaving no doubt in Will's mind that she was in control of this situation. He could also detect from the tone of her voice that she was still angry at him for giving her that penalty notice. His military training had taught him that he must surrender in the face of an overwhelming force. He would defer to her, but he didn't have to like it. After enduring several minutes of questioning, Will could not hold back any longer. He exclaimed with much exasperation, "How much longer is this interrogation going to last?"

His outburst took Mary Elizabeth by surprise. She put down her pen and looked up at him with searing blue eyes. After taking a moment to compose herself, she crossed her arms on her desk. In a calm, firm voice, she replied, "Until you tell me, Inspector, everything I want to know." She paused. She tried to stifle a laugh, but it was useless. Her laughter rang out and filled the room.

Will bristled. "What's so funny?"

"Oh Inspector, I am so sorry." Mary Elizabeth said. She was trying hard but was failing miserably in her attempt to stop laughing. She used her hands to fan her face. "Oh my! Okay, I am better now. So very sorry." With much effort, she finally got herself under control. "It occurred to me that there is a reversal of roles here. The idea of a police inspector having to answer all these questions. Well, the irony of the situation just struck me. I do apologize. I don't mean any offense or disrespect. Truly, I don't."

Will noted that her blue eyes had now changed. Instead of glaring at him with a cold, steely stare, her eyes now sparkled and danced with merriment. *How does she do that?* he wondered.

"Please, will you forgive me?" Mary Elizabeth asked with true contrition.

Will thought for a moment before he spoke. He noticed that the tone of her voice was now light and friendly. It was as if her laughter were the thunderstorm that had cleared the tension from the room. He decided to stop thinking about this situation as an adversarial encounter. He remembered what Chief Superintendent Williamson had said about maintaining good public relations with the villagers. "No need to apologize, no offense taken." Then, despite himself, he admitted, "And you are right. Usually, I am the one who asks the questions."

"Don't you find this situation a tiny bit humorous?" Mary Elizabeth asked as she flashed a smile at him.

Will did the only thing he could do. He smiled back. "Yes, I guess so."

"That's better. You have a nice smile. You should smile more often."

Will's smile disappeared as quickly as it had come. "Is that your professional opinion?"

Undeterred by his tone, Mary Elizabeth replied, "It is. Did you know that it is scientifically proven that laughter is beneficial to your health?"

Will blurted out the first thought that popped into his head. "Then you are the healthiest person I know."

Will's remark surprised Mary Elizabeth. She sat back in her chair and laughed again. She pointed her pen at him and said, "Good one."

Will was beginning to relax. He began to enjoy their verbal sparring and the way she could even laugh at herself.

Mary Elizabeth once again turned her attention to the paper in front of her. "I'm afraid that we need to get back to business. We are almost done here." Her tone became more professional. "Only one more question, Inspector. Do you know who might have your medical records from the last five years?"

Will answered, "Dr. Hillerman, in London, would have at least the last four years. Before that, I was in the military."

Mary Elizabeth took down the information. "Thank you. That has been very helpful. Okay. That completes the first part of the physical." She put her pen down and got up from behind her desk. "Let's start with the eye exam." When that was finished, she walked over to a cupboard and took out a small container. She handed it to Will. "Here. The lavatory is right across the hall. Bring it back when you are done."

He went out of the room. Mary Elizabeth walked out to the reception desk. "Sarah?"

Sarah answered, "Yes, Dr. Senty."

"Can you phone a Dr. Hillerman in London for me? Let me know when you have his office on the line. Thank you." She walked back to the exam room and started laying out her instruments. Soon Will joined her.

Mary Elizabeth said, "You can put your sample on the counter over there. Now, if you will go behind the screen and take off your outer clothes, we will get on with the examination. I will give you a few minutes to change." Mary Elizabeth left the room with his container and file and walked into the lab. She emerged a few minutes later.

"I have Dr. Hillerman's office on the line."

"Thank you." She took the phone receiver from Sarah. "Dr. Hillerman? Dr. Mary Elizabeth Senty. The reason for my call is that I have a patient of yours, William Francis Donnelly, born January 30, 1927, here for his annual police physical. I would like to ask you a few questions, as he says you hold his medical records. Yes, I can hold." She motioned for Sarah to bring a pad of paper and pencil. "He couldn't recall if his immunizations are up to date. Anything else I should know?" Mary Elizabeth was busy scribbling notes. "Thank you so much for your help, Dr. Hillerman. Goodbye."

Mary Elizabeth handed the receiver back to Sarah. With her notes in hand, she returned to the exam room. Will was sitting on the exam table in his underclothes. When he saw her, Will said, "I thought you forgot about me."

"No, I was in the lab. I can tell you that the results of the tests on your urine sample were all within the normal boundaries."

"That's good."

"Yes, that's a great start."

As his physical examination continued, Will became more and more impressed by Mary Elizabeth's professional competence. Finally, she said, "Only a few more exams, Inspector. You are doing splendidly so far."

"What's left?" She brought a rolling table with a tray on it to the exam table.

"I need to do a blood draw. Now, can you hold out your arm and make a fist for me?" She felt for the vein in the crook of his arm. As she got her instruments ready, she asked, "Now, tell me, what do you like to do when you are not working?"

"I like to listen to classical music. It helps me to relax."

"What is your favorite piece?" she asked as she tied the tourniquet, found her spot, and swabbed his arm.

"That's a difficult question, as I have many favorites. But if I had to choose only one, then it would be *The Planets* by Gustav Holst."

"I'm not sure I have ever heard that one. I like classical music too. I like beautiful melodies and music that tells a story."

"Then you would like this composition. Holst wrote a piece for each of the planets. He gave the planets their own distinct personalities. It is quite fun. What are your favorite compositions?"

"Yes, that does sound like something I would like. Okay, here comes the poke." As she waited for the vial to fill, her features softened, and her voice took on a dreamy tone. "I like Dvořák's *New World Symphony* and Grofé's *Mississippi Suite,* but my absolute favorite is 'The Gates of Kiev' from Mussorgsky's *Pictures at an Exhibition*. Music like that fills my entire being. It lifts me up, and sometimes I feel like I could just float away. I know that sounds silly," she said, shrugging her shoulders, "but that's the way music makes me feel."

Mary Elizabeth's sentiments caught Will completely by surprise. Not only could she speak intelligently about one of his favorite subjects, but while she imagined those pieces, he thought she was the most beautiful woman he had ever seen.

Mary Elizabeth's concerned voice brought him out of his thoughts. "Inspector? Inspector! Are you feeling all right? You aren't going to faint on me, are you?"

"No, of course not. What made you say that?"

"Well, I had asked you to hold this cotton ball on your arm while I got a plaster for you, and you didn't answer. You had a very strange look on your face. Are you sure you are all right? Would you like to lie back on the exam table for a few minutes? Do you need a glass of water?"

Embarrassed that he had lost himself in his thoughts again, he said, "No, no. I am fine. Truly, I am. You don't have to make a fuss over me."

"Well, yes, Inspector, I think I do. That is my duty right now, to make a fuss over you."

Will was desperate. "How can I convince you that I am fine?"

"How about you hold this cotton ball on your arm while I get that plaster for you?"

"Is that all? Are we done now?" Will asked.

"We'll see," she said as she tilted her head and observed him.

Her intense scrutiny made Will squirm as he sat on the exam table. "What do you mean, we'll see?"

"I spoke with Dr. Hillerman earlier." Her voice trailed off as she continued to gaze at him.

"When did you speak to Dr. Hillerman?"

"I talked to him while you were getting undressed. I needed to find out if you were up to date on your immunizations. He said that you are due for a tetanus vaccine. But given your response to the blood draw, I am hesitant to jab you with another needle. Can you tolerate another jab now, or would you rather come back another time for it?"

"No, let's get it done now so I don't have to come back here again," Will said.

"As you wish, Inspector. And I will try very hard not to take your last remark personally," Mary Elizabeth said as she walked toward the door.

Will became flustered and said, "No, please don't. I didn't mean it like it sounded. I was only answering your question."

"Relax, Inspector," she said from the door, "I know what you meant. As you get to know me, you will discover that I like to tease. I wanted to see if I could coax another smile out of you. You know, you really are making me work awfully hard for them this morning." She lowered her voice and said under her breath, "But they are so worth it."

Will leaned in her direction and said, "Sorry. I couldn't hear that last part. Could you repeat it?"

"I was going to say that since you have moved to Bellechester, you could have your medical records transferred to this office. You would need to sign a medical records release form. It would make things smoother next time you need medical attention. Miss Chamberlain has all the forms at her desk. It is totally up to you."

"Oh, I hadn't thought about that."

"London is a long way to drive if you have a sore throat or if you cut your finger. You can take some time to think about it if you like. It doesn't have to be done today. Like I said, it is up to you. Now, you sit tight, and I will be right back." Mary Elizabeth prepared Will's injection in the pharmacy area. She put everything on a small tray and walked back to the exam room. She put the tray on the portable table next to Will. "Before you came to Bellechester, where were you stationed?"

"I worked at the Metropolitan Police Department in London, or as some people call it, Scotland Yard."

"Is that so? Someday you will have to tell me why they call it Scotland Yard when it isn't even in Scotland. Which arm?"

"Right. I'm left handed."

Mary Elizabeth swabbed his arm with alcohol. "Here, we will let that dry for a moment. Now, besides listening to classical music, what else do you like to do? You are in great physical shape. Do you play any sports?"

"Rugby. I used to play on our department's team."

"Okie dokie, here comes the poke. What was the name of your team?"

"The Met Pips," Will said through clenched teeth as the needle pierced his arm.

"The Pips, you say? I caught part of their game once when they played some bird team. All done, Inspector." Mary Elizabeth removed the needle and placed a cotton ball over the site. "Here, can you hold this a moment?" she asked Will.

Will said nothing.

Looking up at him and seeing that familiar blank look, she said, "Oh no, not again. Inspector! Inspector!"

Will said, "It *was* you. You caught the ball! I knew it! It was you, wasn't it?"

Taking his left hand from the edge of the exam table, Mary Elizabeth placed it on the cotton ball. "Here, apply a little pressure." After she removed the tabs, she placed another plaster over the injection site. Then she sighed. "Yes, that was me. It was either catch the ball or get hit in the head with it. Number twelve?" she asked.

"You remembered?"

"You were the rugby player who recovered my purse for me. Of course, I remembered. In fact, I've been wondering for some time." She laughed.

"I admit I didn't recognize you at first without your uniform and all the dirt and blood. You didn't come to the pub after the game. It looked like you had your children with you. I remember they were pretty excited."

"I didn't go to the pub because I had recently accepted the position at Bellechester. I had a million things to do, what with moving here and all. And those weren't my kids. They belong to my best friend. They came to watch me play. I call them my good-luck charms." He paused before he put his head down and softly said, "I'm not married."

Mary Elizabeth seemed to ignore his last remark. "I should say those children were good-luck charms, because if I remember correctly, your team won that day."

"Yes, we won our next game too," Will said with a hint of excitement in his voice.

"You won the city championship?"

"We did."

"Well, let me offer a belated congratulations to you. That was quite a feat. Will you still play with the team next season?"

"No, I'm afraid my playing days with the Pips are over. I no longer qualify since I don't work for the department anymore."

"Maybe you will find a local team in the area to play with next season."

"I doubt I will have much free time anymore with all my new responsibilities."

"Yes, that's true. Well, I won't keep you from them any longer. That's it, Inspector. Your physical is complete. Do you have any questions for me?"

"No," Will answered.

Mary Elizabeth watched him slide off the exam table. She saw him grimace as he put weight on his right arm. "Be sure to take two aspirin every four hours as needed if your arm aches too much." She added, "It will be sore for a day or two."

"Got it." Will said. As he was about to go behind the screen, he turned around again. "I guess I do have one question. I have been trying all morning to figure out your accent. The way you speak reminds me of some men I served with in Korea. Are you Canadian?"

Mary Elizabeth replied, "No, but very close. American. I grew up two hundred and fifty miles south of the Canadian border in St. Ursula, Minnesota."

Will said, "I knew it!"

"Inspector, I am very impressed. You are definitely in the right line of work. While you get dressed, I will finish filling out the certification form so you can take it back with you. On your way out, leave your office number with Miss Chamberlain. I will call you this afternoon with the results from your blood work."

Will finished dressing and retrieved his coat and hat. He then waited at her desk. After she signed her name on the bottom of the page, she folded the paper and slipped it into an envelope she pulled from the drawer.

"Here you go," she said as she handed him the envelope. "I have only one prescription for you, Inspector."

"What is it?"

Mary Elizabeth said, "Before you go back to work, get yourself a good breakfast. You must be famished after fasting for your blood tests. And you should have food in your stomach if you are going to be taking aspirin today."

"Yes, Doctor." As he walked to the door, he turned and smiled at Mary Elizabeth. "Thank you. Good day."

Mary Elizabeth smiled back. "You have a good day too, Inspector."

When he got to the reception desk, Will asked Miss Chamberlain for the medical records release form. He signed the paper on the spot.

CHAPTER 25

Butterflies Are Free?

Later that morning, after breakfast, Will walked into the precinct. Sergeant O'Hanlon greeted him, "Good morning, sir."

Will was lost in thought. "What? Oh, good morning." He handed Sergeant O'Hanlon a business-sized envelope.

"Sir?"

Will replied, "That is my medical form. Please put it in my recertification file."

"Yes, sir," Sergeant O'Hanlon answered. "Did you have Dr. Merton or Dr. Senty for your exam?"

"Dr. Senty."

"The new doctor is nice, isn't she?"

Will said, "Yes, she has quite the sense of humor. Can you bring me some tea and two aspirin?"

"Right away, sir."

He had started for the break room when the phone rang. "Bellechester precinct. Sergeant O'Hanlon speaking. Yes, he is. I will get him for you. Chief?" shouted Sergeant O'Hanlon, as Will had already gone into his office. "Chief, Superintendent Williamson is on the phone for you."

"Thank you, Sergeant." Will picked up the phone, "Donnelly here. Settling in nicely, sir. Plans to implement the new officer recertification program are already in the works. . . . The invitation? Not yet, sir, but I will be looking for it. . . . Yes, I am personally coordinating the security detail for the gala. I have certified overtime for the men, and if we must, we will bring in officers from other constabularies. There will be no jewel heist on my watch. Yes. Goodbye."

Sergeant O'Hanlon brought Will his tea and aspirin. "Thank you, Sergeant."

The long-awaited invitation arrived in the afternoon post. Will checked the envelope carefully. *Funny,* he thought. *There's no "and guest." Must have been an oversight. I wonder if she would . . .* He opened the envelope and read the invitation.

Lord and Lady Brantwell of Brantwell Manor
request the honor of your presence at a welcome gala
for Bellechester's newest residents
Mary Elizabeth Senty, MD,
and Chief Inspector William Francis Donnelly

Friday, 23 October, at 8:00 p.m.
RSVP Bellechester 7364

So she'll be there! he thought. It hit him: the envelope was no mistake. He was to be Dr. Senty's escort for the evening. *What is going on?* The night of the gala, he needed to be at his professional best. He wasn't sure how he would be with her there to distract him. Will realized this assignment was not going to be easy. His arm throbbed. *Pull yourself together, Donnelly,* he ordered himself.

The phone rang again. "Inspector Donnelly here. . . . Oh yes, Doctor. That is good news. . . . My arm? Oh, hardly feel it at all. . . . Yes, I remember. Thank you for calling. Goodbye." *Can she read my thoughts? How did she know I was just thinking about her?* He wondered as he replaced the phone on the hook.

Will called Lady Beatrice Brantwell. He graciously accepted the invitation, then left the office in search of a formal uniform to wear to the gala.

Will found his ceremonial dress uniform at the police supply store in Birmingham. As was the case with all his clothes, his jacket had to be altered to accommodate his broad shoulders and his pants had to be lengthened for his height. The tailor said he would call Will in a week to come for his second fitting.

The aspirin he had taken earlier in the afternoon wore off on his drive home. By the time he reached his house, his arm was throbbing. He did not have any aspirin at home, having used the last of it after the championship rugby match. Will walked down Market Street to the apothecary, but it was closed. The variety shop was still open. Entering the store, he saw a clerk at the jewelry counter waiting on a boy of about thirteen. A pile of coins lay on the counter between them.

"What does your mother like?"

"She likes butterflies." The young teen pointed to a large butterfly pin in the next case that was filled with different-colored stones. He got excited: "That one is perfect! I'll take that one."

"You have excellent taste. But I am afraid that pin is beyond your price range. I am sure your mum would love any of these pins."

From the display case, she brought out a tray of smaller pins and put them on the counter. "Look, these are pretty. I am sure you can find a pin in this tray that will do."

"All of these pins are so small. It's her birthday tomorrow. I wanted to get her something special. She works so hard, and she doesn't have anything nice." His voice got quieter. "I just want her to have something nice for a change."

"I know, but a small pin is all you can afford."

Then he pointed to the sign on the wall. "What about layaway? I could give you all the money I have as a down payment. I can give her the pin tomorrow, and give you the rest when I earn some more money."

"That's not how layaway works. You need to pay the full price before I can give you the pin."

"But I'm good for it. Hey, I could work for you and pay off the balance that way. If you need someone to make deliveries or sweep out the store or stock shelves, I can do those jobs. Ask anyone in the village, They'll tell you I'm a good worker. Please, Miss Holly, please! I need the pin for tomorrow."

"I'm sorry, John. I am already paying someone else to do those jobs for me. I don't need any more help. Now, I am sure your mother will be happy with one of these pins."

Will wandered the aisles until he found the shelf of aspirin. He picked up a brand he recognized and walked back up to the clerk.

The young lad was still at the counter examining the pins. "I'll be right back, John. I want to ring up this gentleman."

"Sure, go ahead," the lad said.

Will followed the clerk to the checkout counter. As she was ringing up Will's purchase, the young teen walked past. "I couldn't decide, Miss Holly. I'll be back tomorrow after soccer practice. Good night."

"All right, John. You sleep on it. See you tomorrow."

"He seems like a nice kid," Will said.

"John? He's a good lad. And you are the new police inspector?"

"Inspector William Donnelly, ma'am."

"Oh, I read all about you in the *Bugle*. My goodness, you are even taller in person than your picture showed. Welcome to our village. I'm Miss Holly, the proprietor of this shop." She gave Will his change.

Will took his receipt and his aspirin. "Good night, Miss Holly. It was a pleasure meeting you."

"Good night. It was a pleasure meeting you too, Inspector."

Will had only walked half a street when Miss Holly came out of the store yelling, "Inspector! Inspector, can you help me?"

"Miss Holly, what's wrong?" He returned briskly to the store.

"John took the expensive pin and left his money behind. It is not nearly enough to cover the cost. I'd go after him, but I can't leave the shop."

"Now don't worry, I'll handle this. Can you tell me where he lives?"

"Down past the church at the edge of the village. Only cottage in the lane."

"Thanks, Miss Holly." Will put the aspirin bottle in his jacket pocket and started to run. The action of moving his arm back and forth was painful, but Will hoped to catch up to John before he made it home. Will took the diagonal path through the village square as a short cut. He heard someone crying. The sound came from one of the park benches. In the fading twilight, he saw the crying figure was John. The lad was crying so hard he did not notice Will. Will removed his handkerchief and his warrant card from his pockets before he sat at the other end of the bench. Will sat quietly until John finished crying. He extended his handkerchief to John. "Here, use this instead of your sleeve."

Will's voice startled John. "Who are you?" John jumped up, ready to bolt. Then looking closer at Will he said, "Say, you're the bloke from the shop."

"Inspector William Donnelly, Bellechester police," Will said as he showed John his warrant card. "And yes, I'm the bloke from the shop."

John sank down on the bench. "Are you here to put me in the nick?"

Will said, "No, I am here to listen. It appears you got yourself in a little jam."

John nodded. "Here," he said as he handed the butterfly pin to Will. Even though the light was fading, Will could see the different-colored stones sparkle. "My, it is a very beautiful pin."

"I thought it would look nice on my mum's brown coat. When we go to Mass on Sunday, all the other women have fancy hats and jewelry. Mum wears her brown coat and her red wool scarf. After Mass, people act like we are invisible. I thought if she wore this beautiful pin, maybe the ladies would stop to talk to her so she could make friends. I don't think Mum has any friends."

"Do you have friends?" Will asked.

"A few at school and on the team. But I don't have much time for friends. I study a lot. Mum's dream is for me to go to university, so I must keep up my grades. I also help with her business, picking up and delivering laundry."

"Your mother is a laundress?"

"Yes, Mum says it is good honest work. She works awfully hard."

"What about your father? What does he do?"

"I never knew him. Mum said he died before I was born."

"Oh, I'm sorry."

"It's okay. Mum and I get by. Tomorrow, she turns thirty. I just wanted to give her something nice to make the day special."

"That is a special birthday, to be sure."

"And now I ruined everything. I'll be in the nick, I'll miss school, and Mum will have no one to make the pickups and deliveries. Instead of giving her a present, I made things worse for her. What can I do? I don't know what to do."

"John, listen to me. You made a mistake, but you're a bright lad. I think you know what to do to make things right again." Will handed the pin back to John.

John took the pin and nodded his head. "I have to return the pin to Miss Holly." He was quiet for a few minutes before he said, "Inspector, sir, will you come with me? I think I would have more courage if you were with me."

"Of course, John."

As they walked back to Miss Holly's shop, John asked, "Inspector, were you ever in a pickle like this?"

"Yes, I was in almost the same situation as you when I was young. Only it was a Christmas present for my mum. It was my grandmother who helped me do the right thing. It wasn't easy, but I returned the item and apologized. My grandmother said I became a man that day. She was very proud of me."

"What did you end up giving your mum for Christmas?"

"I made her a card. And do you know that after my Mum died, I found that card in a box she kept with all her special treasures? I still have it. Whenever I mess up, it reminds me that I always have a choice, and I can choose to do the right thing."

As they got closer to the shop, Will noticed that John's pace had slowed. At the entrance to the shop, John froze. He looked up at Will. Will reassured him, "I'm right here. You can do this. Just take a few deep breaths." Will demonstrated, and they took a few deep breaths together. Will then reached past him and opened the shop door. The bells above the door tinkled, and Miss Holly came to the front. She frowned but didn't say a word. John looked up at Will, and Will put his hand on John's shoulder.

"Miss Holly, I came to return this pin." He held out his hand and offered the pin to her. "I'm sorry I took it. I thought it would bring my mum joy, but now I see it would only make her sad if she knew I stole it. I would still like to get my mum a pin, so if you wouldn't mind showing me the pins I can afford, I will pick out another one."

Miss Holly took the pin from him. "John," she said with eyes glistening, "thank you for returning this butterfly. Come here."

When John stepped forward, Miss Holly wrapped her arms around him. She spoke softly so only John could hear: "I always thought you were a good kid. Now I know you are a good kid." Then, much louder, she said, "Now let's go pick out something nice for your Mum's birthday." They went back to the counter, and John picked out a small butterfly pin with yellow and orange stones.

Miss Holly said, "You come back after school tomorrow, and I will have this pin in a box all wrapped up. Come back here and choose the wrapping paper and ribbon."

"Do I have enough money for all that?"

"You have just enough."

"Gee, Miss Holly, you are A1. I really am sorry I stole from you, and I will never do anything like that again. Are we square?"

"I forgive you, John. And yes, we are square." She looked up at Will. "Being square is a good thing, right?"

CHAPTER 26

One more fence to mend

Will and John left Miss Holly's shop and walked together down Market Street. It was now pitch dark out. "Inspector, you were right. I do feel better after returning the pin. Miss Holly was sure swell about it."

"Yes, she is very forgiving. Since it is so dark out, I will walk you home. I would like to meet your mum."

"You're not going to tell her about tonight, are you?"

"No. I am just trying to meet as many of the villagers as possible."

"In that case, there is one more place I need to go tonight to make things right." They were now walking through the village square.

"Where is that?"

"I made things right with Miss Holly, but now I need to make things right with God. I broke one of His commandments."

When they emerged from the village square, John walked up to the rectory and rang the bell. Mrs. Winters opened the door. "Why, John, come in. Who do you have with you?"

"Mrs. Winters, this is Inspector Donnelly."

"Very nice to meet you, Inspector."

"Mrs. Winters, this is a pleasure. I am sorry that we are calling unannounced at this late hour."

John spoke up, "Is Father Evenson in?"

A booming voice said, "I am most certainly in. Now, what can I do for you, Master Murray?" Father Evenson emerged from his study. He had shed his cassock and stood in the doorway in his black pants and suspenders, his black shirt sleeves rolled up past his elbows. His Roman collar dangled from his open top button. Reading glasses affixed to a chain hung halfway down his large nose. "And who have you brought with you?"

"Inspector William Donnelly, Father."

Father Evenson shook Will's hand. "A pleasure to meet you in person, Inspector. I read all about you in the *Bugle*."

"Very pleased to meet you too, Father."

Turning to John, Father Evenson asked, "Is your mother in good health?"

"Yes, she is fine. I need to go to confession, Father. Can you hear it now?"

"Now?"

"It's very important, Father. I don't think I would be able to go to sleep tonight if I didn't make a good confession."

"Well, yes, then, come on through." He put his arm around John and took him into the study. He closed the door.

Mrs. Winters turned to Will. "Come. You can wait in the kitchen and keep me company. I'll put the kettle on and make us a nice cup of tea."

"Thank you, Mrs. Winters. That sounds wonderful."

Will sat at the kitchen table while Mrs. Winters fixed the tea. "How are you settling in Bellechester?"

"Just fine. Ned Manderfield did a wonderful job on remodeling my cottage."

"Yes, Ned and his crew do fine work."

Will's stomach growled. He had intended to fix his supper when he returned from purchasing his aspirin tablets. It was now half-past eight, and he had not yet eaten. His arm continued to throb. "I apologize for my noisy stomach."

"Inspector, haven't you had any supper this evening?"

"I am afraid not, Mrs. Winters."

"Say no more." She sprang from her chair, and in no time, Will was eating leftover shepherd's pie.

"This is delicious, Mrs. Winters. I really appreciate your kindness." When Will finished, he was finally able to take his pills.

"Are you ill?" Mrs. Winters asked.

"No, I had a physical this morning and received a jab. My arm is just a little sore."

"Then you met Dr. Senty?"

"Yes, I did."

"What do you think of her?"

"She is different, I will give you that. I suppose her being an American has something to do with that. I have never met a woman quite like her before." He shook his head and, unable to help himself, he grinned.

"Nor I. Are you getting excited about the gala? We received our invitations today."

"I just came back from Birmingham, where I purchased my dress uniform. That is why I hadn't eaten yet. I will probably get more excited as the time gets closer. Right now, the gala still seems a long way off. But I do enjoy a good dance." He smiled. "I hope you will keep a space open for me on your dance card?"

Mrs. Winters said, "Oh, of course, Inspector."

The study door opened, and Father Evenson and John emerged. "There you go, Inspector. Master John's soul is now as white as a lamb on a snowy day."

"Thanks, Father, I do feel much better now."

"That's good." Father Evenson looked at Will. "Any more takers this evening?"

Will put up his hands. "No thank you, Father. We had best be going now. I am sure that Mrs. Murray is wondering about John's whereabouts. Good night. And thank you again, Mrs. Winters, for the supper."

"Anytime, Inspector."

"Good night, everyone," John said.

Friday, October 23

CHAPTER 27

THE GALA

It rained most of the morning, but by the afternoon the sun had come out. The weather forecasters had promised a clear evening. By the time Will pulled up to the manor at six o'clock, the place was abuzz with activity. Maids and valets were running to and fro. He grabbed his garment bag in one hand and his briefcase in the other. As he walked through the door, he was met by Lady Beatrice.

"Inspector! So glad to see you!" She looked around and spotted one of the valets. "Harrison, take the inspector up to his room."

"Yes, my lady." A young valet took the garment bag from him.

"Is there a private place where Lord Brantwell, you, and I can finalize the security details?" Will asked Lady Brantwell.

"We'll meet you in the study in ten," she replied.

"Very good." Will followed the valet up the large central staircase. At the top was a landing with additional stairs leading to a row of bedrooms on either side. The valet chose the right side and stopped down the middle of the hall. "Here is your room. Would you like me to set out your things, sir?"

"Yes, thank you," Will replied.

Ten minutes later, Will was in the study and had the floor plans to the second floor spread out on the table. "Lady Beatrice, can you tell me in what rooms the overnight guests will be staying?"

She went over to the table and pointed. "Geoff and I have our suite of rooms here. In that wing will be Father Evenson, Mrs. Winters, Dr. Senty, and the Dowager Lady Phillips. In the right wing will be Viscount LeBrosse, Baron and Baroness Whitacre, you, Dr. Applegate and his wife, Lord and Lady Porter, Chief Superintendent Williamson and his wife, and Superintendent Billingsby and his wife."

Will said, "I will have uniformed officers stationed at either end of the hallway beginning at midnight. I will also station a constable in your study, Lord Brantwell, since that is where the safe is located. Canine units will only patrol the grounds after sunset so as not to alarm the guests. My officers will be patrolling the perimeter of the house. There are also a few undercover police officers here among your valets and servers. That should cover it. Lord Brantwell, can we run through the schedule for the evening again?"

"At eight o'clock Bea and I will introduce you and Dr. Senty from the landing of the main staircase. We will go into dinner and have brief remarks and your pinning ceremony. Then it is off to the ballroom for dancing."

"It will be a night to remember," Lady Beatrice added.

"Yes, I hope it will all be good memories. I had best get these plans back to my room before the other guests see them," Will said.

"Knowing the manor will be crawling with police won't scare the jewel thieves off?" Lady Beatrice asked.

"You would think so, but I have been reading reports of the other thefts. Our thieves are becoming more and more brazen with each robbery. I believe they will try something just to prove they are smarter than we are."

Lady Beatrice had asked Mary Elizabeth to be at the estate by four o'clock. Mary Elizabeth wasn't sure that would be enough time to affect the Cinderella transformation, but Lady Beatrice reassured her that she employed the finest ladies' maids. She told Mary Elizabeth that all she had to do was show up and they would work their magic. Her ball gown and shoes were already at the manor. Mary Elizabeth would bring her own jewelry: the agate pendant her father had made for her, and her tiara.

A few hours later, Mary Elizabeth sat at the dressing table in her room, pulling on her elbow-length gloves. There was a knock on the door.

"Come in," she called out.

Lady Beatrice glided into the room. She wore a burgundy chiffon gown with a full skirt and three-quarter-length lace sleeves. Around her neck hung a ruby-and-diamond necklace with matching drop earrings and bracelet. "How are you doing, dear?" she asked. "Oh my! You do look like a picture. Come, it's time."

"Can you help me with my pendant?"

Lady Beatrice walked over to the dressing table and fastened the clasp around her neck. "You look beautiful, my dear. I am so glad that you are wearing your tiara. It is the perfect finishing touch. Now you look like a real princess."

"I hope the other ladies will forgive me for wearing it. I never knew that in your country, only married women wear tiaras."

"Oh, fiddlesticks! We Brits have too many rules of etiquette anyway. Besides, you being American gives you the perfect excuse. I insist you tell the ladies how you came into possession of your tiara. That story will be the hit of the evening."

Mary Elizabeth rose from her seat and took one last glance in the full-length mirror. She hardly recognized the reflection that stared back at her. Her dress was the perfect shade of green to set off the reddish-brown highlights in her hair. The full-length gown flattered her figure. Mary Elizabeth was not slim, and neither could she be called plump. She had a wholesome, healthy look about her. The dress had off-the-shoulder sleeves which formed a bow-tie neckline. The dress hugged her waist and then flowed into a full skirt. The silhouette was simple and classic, just like Mary Elizabeth.

The maids had swept her hair into an updo. Her rhinestone tiara was then pinned on top of her head. Her agate necklace set off her dress perfectly. The chain was the right length so that it centered on her décolletage.

"Come on," Lady Beatrice cajoled, "let's get this party started."

Mary Elizabeth followed Lady Beatrice out of the room. When they were halfway down the hall, Lady Beatrice stopped her. "Wait here until I introduce you. A lady must always make a grand entrance."

Mary Elizabeth waited halfway down the hallway and tried to get her nerves under control by recalling the times she had performed intricate medical procedures with senior doctors watching her every move. If she could survive those high-pressure situations, surely she could handle this gala. Besides, tonight the focus was not going to be on her alone. She was going to be sharing the spotlight with Inspector Donnelly. That thought brought her great comfort. She wondered if he was feeling nervous too.

Will entered from the other end of the hallway. He was tugging his sleeves one last time. He checked to make sure his medals and ribbons were pinned securely in place. He wondered if anyone actually felt comfortable in such outfits. *Really,* he thought, *how many formal functions can there be in a village the size of Bellechester?*

Will called upon his military training to stay cool and collected. He knew he'd have to employ every trick in the book to keep his wits about him with Dr. Senty nearby. The gala was not a social event for him; it was work. He had jewels to protect and, hopefully, a jewel thief to apprehend. He vowed to keep close guard of his emotions. He repeated to himself, *I am a highly trained professional. I must not let her get to me tonight. Focus!*

Lady Beatrice hurried to the landing, where Lord Brantwell was waiting. He took her gloved hand and kissed it. He then gave a nod to the butler below. The butler raised his mallet and gave the large gong a good whack. The ensuing reverberations silenced the crowd. With plates of hors d'oeuvres and drinks in hand, the guests gathered in the foyer under the gigantic crystal chandelier. The photographer hired to record the evening's events rushed to take his place halfway up the stairs. All eyes were on Lord and Lady Brantwell.

Lord Brantwell wore a black formal dinner jacket and a thin bow tie. For a small man, he had a booming voice which commanded attention in the loud and chaotic chambers of Parliament. "Welcome, dear friends and honored guests. Tonight, we are proud to introduce to you two extraordinary young people. They are each eminently qualified in their fields. Our community will be the richer for their contributions. It is my pleasure to welcome to Bellechester our new chief inspector, William Donnelly. He comes to us highly recommended from the district office. He served with distinction in the Royal Military Police during the Korean conflict. In his short career with the police force, he has earned many commendations and medals for his prowess in bringing criminals to justice. He is one of the youngest officers ever promoted to the rank of chief inspector. Please welcome William Francis Donnelly."

Will tugged one last time at the navy-blue sleeves of his short formal jacket. With his broad shoulders and his muscular, athletic build, he cut quite the handsome figure. He walked down the staircase and shook Lord Brantwell's hand. He then kissed the hand of Lady Beatrice. As he bowed in front of her, she whispered, "Get ready to be amazed." Will gave her a quizzical look and stood next to Lord Brantwell.

"It is with the utmost pleasure that I introduce to you our second honoree of the evening, Bellechester's new doctor, Mary Elizabeth Senty. She comes to us from America, where she graduated magna cum laude from the University of Minnesota Medical School and did her internship at the world-renowned Bentley Hospital; she recently completed her training at our own Mother of Mercy Hospital in London. I give you Dr. Mary Elizabeth Senty."

Mary Elizabeth took a deep breath, planted a smile on her face, walked to the end of the hallway, picked up her dress, and strode down the three short stairs over to Lady Beatrice, who planted two kisses on her cheeks. Lord Brantwell kissed her hand. She held out her hand to Will. He just stood there, staring at her.

Lady Beatrice whispered, "Kiss her hand. Offer her your arm and follow us." Will did as he was told.

Mary Elizabeth took his arm. She whispered, "Nice to see you again, Inspector."

"Dr. Senty, you look lovely this evening."

Mary Elizabeth leaned into him and said, "I am so glad you approve. I cannot afford you giving me another citation."

Her remark took him by surprise. He threw his head back and laughed. Mary Elizabeth smiled at him. She could feel the muscles in his arm relax. At that moment, the same thought was running through each of their heads. *Maybe tonight won't be so bad after all.*

The photographer's flashbulb popped in their faces. Mary Elizabeth was blinded for a moment and almost tripped down the stairs. Will brought his other hand over to steady her. "Easy. I got you," he said.

Mrs. Winters was standing next to Father Evenson on the floor below. Watching the young couple descend the staircase, she whispered to Father Evenson, "Don't they make a handsome couple?"

"They do indeed," he replied. "They do indeed."

The two couples received the guests as they filed into the dining room. When everyone was greeted, they took their places at the head table.

Father Evenson, who was also seated at the head table, stood and offered a meal prayer. First course was a fruit compote; then came the tomato basil soup, poached salmon with hollandaise sauce, Champagne chicken with sautéed green beans, and for dessert, a trifle. At the end of the meal, Lord Brantwell rose and tapped his glass for attention. "Before we proceed to the ballroom, we have two special presentations. First, I present Dr. Basil Applegate, chief of junior doctors at Mother of Mercy Hospital, London."

Dr. Applegate stood and moved to the microphone. "Thank you, Lord Brantwell. Two months ago, my dear friend and classmate Dr. Harold Merton came to see me. He was looking to mentor one of my junior doctors to become his successor as Bellechester's physician. Besides testing their skill, Dr. Merton wanted to experience first-hand their compassion and their care. He decided the best way to do all that was to be admitted as a patient and let my junior doctors have at him. Dr. Merton is a brave, brave man."

He paused until the laughter subsided. "He asked Dr. Senty to practice medicine with him in Bellechester. I do believe Dr. Merton made a good choice. But that is not why I am here tonight. Every year, Mother of Mercy Hospital presents the Mercy Cross to the top junior doctor as voted on by patients and staff. It is my distinct honor to award this year's Mercy Cross to Dr. Mary Elizabeth Senty. Dr. Senty, please come forward to receive your medal." Dr. Applegate presented her with a case that contained the medal.

Mary Elizabeth spoke into the microphone. "Thank you, Dr. Applegate, for this great honor. I am humbled to receive this award. It was Dr. Merton, though, who bestowed upon me the greatest honor of all when he asked me to practice medicine at his side among the people of Bellechester. I did not become a doctor to win awards. I became a doctor to heal people, to help them become whole again. Dear people of Bellechester, please know that I hold sacred the trust you place in me as your physician. Under the guidance of Dr. Merton, I hope to serve this community for many years. Thank you." She walked back to her place. Dr. Applegate pulled out her chair, and she sat.

Lord Brantwell announced, "Our next distinguished speaker is Chief Superintendent Williamson of the County of Shropshire."

Chief Superintendent Williamson rose and walked to the microphone. "The responsibility for the safety and security of a community like Bellechester is a heavy mantle to wear. The office of chief inspector requires a man of courage and compassion. He must have a deep love for justice. But most of all, he must respect the dignity of each person. Every person must be treated fairly under the law. His concern for the welfare of this community and the men under his command must be at the forefront of every decision he makes. My superiors at county command have found such a man in William Donnelly. Detective Inspector Donnelly, please come forward to receive your promotion to detective chief inspector. Detective Inspector Donnelly chose his father, retired Sergeant Patrick Donnelly of the Preston police force, to pin his new rank."

Chief Superintendent Williamson handed Will's father the extra pip to pin on the epaulettes of Will's dress uniform. Mary Elizabeth had a front-row seat as she watched Will's father pin the extra star on each shoulder. She heard Will's father say how proud he was of him. She caught the slight hitch in the elder Donnelly's voice and saw Will swallow hard. Their interaction touched Mary Elizabeth. She instinctively fingered the agate necklace that hung around her neck, reliving the memory of her father saying similar words to her upon her medical school graduation.

Will's father remained at his son's side while Chief Superintendent Williamson proclaimed, "Detective Chief Inspector William Francis Donnelly, by the power vested in me by the Queen's Central Command, I present you with the order of command for the southwestern constabularies in the County of Shropshire. Congratulations." Chief Superintendent Williamson and Will's father shook Will's hand on their way back to their seats.

Will stepped up to the microphone. It took a moment for him to adjust the microphone stand to his height. "As police officers, we not only protect and serve the community, but are also part of the community. Southwestern Shropshire is our home. We all want to live in communities of safety and security where everyone is treated equally under the law. I cannot do the job alone. My officers cannot do it alone. It takes all of us working together to ensure that we build communities of peace and justice. I pledge to you tonight to do my utmost to help you build those types of communities. I give you my word, my industry, and my life. Thank you." Will sat down.

Lady Beatrice rose. "Thank you to the presenters and the honorees. Powerful words were spoken here tonight. But the time for talking is done. Please follow us into the ballroom. Let's dance! We have much to celebrate tonight."

CHAPTER 28

At the Dance

Lord and Lady Brantwell, followed by Mary Elizabeth and Will, led the others into the ballroom.

"Dr. Senty and Chief Inspector, please join Geoff and me for the first dance. What should it be? A waltz?"

The couples walked to the middle of the floor, and the music began. Will bowed. Mary Elizabeth curtsied. She put her hand out, and Will put his hand on her shoulder blade. He took a moment to catch the beat of the music before expertly guiding her around the floor. They danced in silence for a few minutes.

"Congratulations on your medal."

"Thank you. The youngest chief inspector. Impressive. I assure you that there wasn't a dry eye in the place as we watched your father pin those stars on you."

"Including my own. I am so grateful to my brothers for bringing Dad down for the evening. It meant a great deal to me to have him here tonight. Dr. Senty?"

"Oh, please call me Emme."

"Emme?"

"Yes. Dr. Senty is too formal, and Mary Elizabeth can be such a mouthful. All my family and friends back home call me Emme."

Will was silent for a minute. "Mary Elizabeth is such a beautiful name. I don't mind saying it. May I call you Mary Elizabeth?"

"If you like." With a twinkle in her blue eyes, she asked, "And what shall I call you?"

Will laughed. "Chief Inspector Donnelly has a nice ring to it. Don't you think?"

Mary Elizabeth gazed at him for a long time. Finally, she said, "No, I think I shall just call you *Chief*." The smile on her face melted the icy wall

Will had set around his heart. Almost as an afterthought, she asked, "You don't mind if I call you Chief, do you?"

"No, not at all."

As they continued to dance, Mary Elizabeth heard Will softly singing the words to the music. It made her smile.

The music ended all too soon. Lord Brantwell was approaching, but Will showed no sign of letting her go. He continued to hold her as the music started up again. It was another waltz. Will whisked Mary Elizabeth away, leaving Lord Brantwell standing alone in the middle of the floor. He wore a surprised look on his face. Lady Beatrice came up to him and said, "Come, dance with me again or we shall both look foolish."

The floor now filled with dancers.

Mrs. Winters and Father Evenson watched the dancers from the sidelines. Mrs. Winters remarked, "Did you see the way those two were looking at each other?"

"I did, indeed. I believe we are witnessing the start of a budding relationship."

"Such a beautiful couple."

Hearing the music, Father Evenson said, "Ah, a waltz. Shall we?"

"Yes, thank you."

Will released Mary Elizabeth as the second song ended. "I could dance with you all night."

"I wish you would. You are an excellent dancer."

"Unfortunately, I cannot be selfish. Duty calls. I must dance with all the other ladies. Good public relations for the force, and all that."

Mary Elizabeth nodded. "If there is one thing I understand, it's duty. Don't worry about it. And don't worry about me. I know how to have a good time."

"I believe you do," Will said. "Just be sure to save another dance for me."

"You got it, Chief." She watched him ask Lady Beatrice to dance.

Lord Brantwell asked Mary Elizabeth, "May I have this dance?"

"Yes, Lord Brantwell. I want to thank you for hosting this event. It is an evening I will always remember."

"Don't thank me. This is all my wife's doing. She lives for planning parties such as this."

"Well, at least may I thank you for this beautiful dress?"

"I'd say it was money well spent."

"When I'm wearing it, I feel like a princess."

"That's because tonight, my dear, you are a princess. And if I have played any small part in your happiness, then I am well pleased. Now, perhaps you could do something for me?"

"Yes?"

"May I consult you about a medical matter later this evening?"

"Wouldn't you rather come to the surgery?"

"I need your help with some medicine that is time sensitive. It must be administered tonight."

"Of course."

The music ended. "Thank you for the dance. I will send my valet to find you towards the end of the evening."

Dr. Applegate was next to dance with her. He looked at her very seriously. "Just so you know, Dr. Senty, I usually do not dance with my junior doctors."

Mary Elizabeth feigned surprise. "Is that so?"

They both laughed. "Congratulations again on winning the Mercy Cross. I don't know anyone who deserves it more than you."

"Thank you for those kind words." She looked at him quizzically. "Mercy Cross? Why haven't I heard of that award before?"

"Because you were awarded the inaugural prize."

"Oh, I see. Did Lady Brantwell have something to do with inaugurating that award?"

"Now, Dr. Senty, don't be upset. She thought that since Chief Inspector Donnelly was receiving his stars, you should get something too. She thought that receiving a recognition like this might ease your entry into the community."

Mary Elizabeth laughed. "Yes, that sounds like her."

"You know that I would do anything to help my young doctors get off to a good start in their practices. And it makes for—"

"—good public relations for the hospital?"

"Why, yes, that too. She did make a rather large donation to so that we could offer scholarships to more women and doctors of diverse backgrounds into our program."

"In that case, I am honored."

He smiled at her. "Do you think you will be happy here in Bellechester?"

"The villagers have been accepting for the most part. The most controversy came from my living in the doctor's residence. But Father Evenson gave a sermon supporting us, and Dr. Merton and I hosted an open house that put most doubts to rest. And I love the countryside. The Shropshire Hills are so beautiful. Do you know the real reason I am happy?"

"No, why is that?"

"Dr. Merton asked me to come. In the month I have spent with him, I know that he is a good doctor with a big heart. He cares deeply about this area and its people. I am learning a lot from him. Besides," she added, smiling, "I can beat him at cribbage."

"Yes, I think you will do very well in Bellechester."

Her next partner was Superintendent Billingsby. "My dear, you are a vision. I can see now that

Chief Inspector Donnelly will not mind his assignment in Bellechester at all. Great party."

"How well do you know Chief Inspector Donnelly?"

"He worked for me for about four years. I can tell you he is hard working, conscientious, and well liked by his fellow officers. He's also a darn good rugby player."

"Anything else?"

"I am afraid you will have to ask him yourself. But I can tell you that, as far as I know, he has no wife or girlfriend. Now, that is what you really wanted to know, isn't it?"

Mary Elizabeth blushed.

Her next partner was Will's father. Even though he was retired, for this occasion Sergeant Donnelly wore his dress uniform. Like his son, he was tall and broad shouldered. As they waltzed around the floor, it was clear to Mary Elizabeth where Will had learned his dancing skills. Mary Elizabeth smiled to herself as Sergeant Donnelly softly sang the words to the music.

"Thank you for the dance, Dr. Senty. Please come over to the table and meet the rest of my family."

He held out his arm and escorted her to the table. It was empty. Sergeant Donnelly laughed. "I see the younger ones are still out on the floor."

Mary Elizabeth said, "If they are as good of dancers as you and the chief inspector are, I am not surprised."

Soon the family came back to the table and Sergeant Donnelly made the introductions. Even without him telling her, Mary Elizabeth was sure she would be able to pick out the Donnelly brothers in the crowd. All the Donnelly men had dark hair and blue eyes. Jack, the middle son, was married to Bridget; and Robert, the youngest, was engaged to Eileen.

Robert spoke up: "How long have you and my brother been going together?"

Mary Elizabeth could not hide her surprise. "Oh, we aren't going together. Honestly, I have met your brother only a few times." She could feel her cheeks color.

The brothers shared quizzical looks of raised eyebrows with each other. The music started up again, and Sergeant Donnelly said to his daughter-in-law, "Shall we?"

"It would be my pleasure, Da." Bridget went off with him.

Jack held out his hand. "Dr. Senty?"

Mary Elizabeth smiled and let him lead her to the dance floor. "Of course."

"I hope Robert didn't give offense."

"No offense taken," Mary Elizabeth assured him.

"Our eldest brother tends to be very serious and withdrawn. It has been quite a while since we have seen him this happy."

"I am sure he is happy tonight because of his promotion and having all of you here."

"I don't think that is the only reason. All I know is that when I saw you dancing with him, he looked like the Will that we used to know. The family thinks it's because of you."

Mary Elizabeth gave him a skeptical look. "Me? I find that hard to believe."

"Will told Dad about meeting you at the rugby semis in London and then discovering you again here in Bellechester."

"Surely, I am not the first woman he has ever mentioned."

"You are correct, Doctor. You are not the first. But you are the first in a long, long time."

"Really? A handsome, well-mannered man like your brother? And such a good dancer!"

"He has been alone ever since his fiancé broke off their engagement."

"I don't mean to pry, but did the breakup happen recently?"

"No, it was many years ago. He received a 'Dear John' letter when he was stationed in India. That was '47. Shortly after that, our mum died. Will took both losses hard. He volunteered for more overseas duty and kept reenlisting. It was like he didn't want to come home anymore. After he left the military, he moved to London and threw himself into his work at the Met. We really haven't seen much of him these past twelve years."

"Thank you for telling me."

"I fear I have said too much. Will would have my guts for garters if he ever found out I was telling you these things."

"Don't worry. Doctors are good at keeping confidences. You have my word; I won't say anything to him."

Jack breathed a sigh of relief. "Thank you."

"Now tell me, how long have you and Bridget been married?"

When the band took their break, Mary Elizabeth went in search of Father Evenson and Mrs. Winters. She found them sitting at a table near the open terrace. "May I join you? It will be good to sit down for a while."

Father Evenson offered, "May I bring you some punch?"

"Thank you, Father Matt. That would be wonderful."

After Father Evenson left, Mrs. Winters moved closer to Mary Elizabeth. "Were those sparks I saw when you were dancing with the chief inspector? I saw the way he was looking at you. He couldn't take his eyes off you."

"Mrs. Winters, we were just talking. He is a very good dancer."

"That he is. And a very charming man to boot. He will make a nice addition to our village."

Father Evenson returned with the punch. "I see your dance card has been quite full. Do you think you have an opening for me in the next set?"

"Of course, Father. You can have the first dance when the band returns from their break."

Lady Beatrice breezed in. "Everyone having a good time?"

"You certainly have outdone yourself this time," Mrs. Winters said.

Father Evenson added, "Wonderful party."

"You must excuse me if I steal Dr. Senty away from you. There are some people who would like to meet her." Lady Beatrice took Mary Elizabeth to a table where the Dowager Phillips, Lord and Lady Porter, and Baron and Baroness Whitacre were sitting.

After the introductions were made, Mrs. Phillips said, "My dear, you are wearing a most interesting pendant. That stone is very unusual. I have never seen anything like it. What is it?"

"This stone is called Lake Superior agate. It is a very common gemstone at home."

Baroness Whitacre asked, "And where might home be?"

"I grew up on my family's farm in the state of Minnesota."

Lord Porter asked Mary Elizabeth, "From what jewelry store was it purchased? Lady Porter does have a birthday next month."

Mary Elizabeth fingered her pendant. "I believe my father bought the setting and the chain from a store in St. Cloud."

Lord Porter asked, "Is that where he also bought the stone?"

Mary Elizabeth laughed. "He didn't buy the stone. Our fields are full of them. Of course, they don't look like this in the ground. It takes a good eye to find them. Dad can sometimes spot them from the seat of his tractor. After plowing the fields, he would get my mom and us kids to walk the fields looking for agates. Oh my! The fun we had!"

Baron Whitacre said, "Are you telling us that your father made that necklace for you?"

"Yes. Making agate jewelry is his winter hobby. He slices the agate with a diamond saw. He made his own tumbler which smooths and polishes the stones. Then he cuts the agate to fit the setting. It is quite the process, but he makes beautiful pieces."

Lady Porter asked, "How much does he sell them for?"

Mary Elizabeth said, "Sell them? He doesn't sell them. He gives them as gifts to family and friends to mark special occasions."

Lady Brantwell asked, "And on what occasion did you receive your pendant?"

Mary Elizabeth fingered her pendant and replied, "Dad presented this to me when I graduated from medical school."

Baroness Whitacre sighed. "What a lovely story."

The band reassembled from their break and began to play again. Lord Porter asked Mary Elizabeth to dance.

"I am sorry, Lord Porter, but I promised Father Evenson this dance. I will dance the next one with you. Goodbye, everyone. Nice to have met you." She left the group in search of Father Evenson.

Lord Porter said, "I do believe that is the first time I have been rejected for a priest!" He shook his head.

Lady Porter said, "Here, dear. I will dance with you. Maybe I can soothe that damaged ego of yours."

Everyone laughed except Mrs. Phillips. She turned to Lady Brantwell and said, "Beatrice, dear, didn't you teach that girl any of our ways? Imagine, turning down a lord for a priest. And she wears a fieldstone to your gala! How vulgar, but I guess quite appropriate for a farmer's daughter. I suppose that is what you get for feting a commoner!"

Lady Brantwell turned and walked away.

CHAPTER 29

Reconnecting with London Friends

After Lord Porter danced with her, the elder Dr. Stuart Harrington approached. "Mary Elizabeth?"

"Dr. Harrington!"

"May I have the pleasure of this next dance?"

"Of course. I am so glad you could come. I know it was a long drive for you."

"Young Stuart did the driving. We would not have missed your party for the world. It was all Mrs. Harrington could talk about for weeks. Thank you for inviting us."

"Well, you are my London family."

"Just keep remembering that, young lady," he said with a smile.

"Are you staying the weekend?"

"Yes, my wife found a quaint inn in Craven Arms. Young Stuart and Barbara are staying there with us. The womenfolk have already planned a shopping excursion for tomorrow."

"Oh my! I hope you and Stuey can find something to do."

"If the weather is nice, we may take a long country walk, or perhaps we'll find a local football or rugby match to watch. A visit or two to the pubs will help us pass the time."

"Where is your table?" Mary Elizabeth asked when the music stopped. "I would love to see everyone again."

Dr. Harrington led her to where his party was sitting. The elder Harringtons were with Doctor and Mrs. Applegate, and Stuey and Barbara. As usual, Stuey was talking and had his back toward the dance floor. Mary Elizabeth tapped him on the back.

"May I have this dance, Dr. Harrington?"

Hearing her voice, Stuey swung around and almost fell off his chair. "It's about bloody time you asked me! I was feeling like a wallflower."

Everyone at the table burst into laughter. Mary Elizabeth looked over to Barbara and said, "Do you mind if I steal him away for a dance?"

Barbara laughed and with her hand in a shooing motion said, "Take him. Take him."

Mary Elizabeth took him by the hand and led him onto the dance floor.

"You know I am hopeless at this kind of dancing," Stuey said.

"I thought your mother made you take dance lessons."

"She did. But after the first couple of lessons, the instructor paid my mother not to bring me to class."

Mary Elizabeth burst out laughing. "Oh, Stuey!"

Stuey added, "I tell you, I'm hopeless."

"Well, here. We will just sway to the music. Now tell me the news. You and Barbara engaged yet?"

"You are the first person I'm telling. I am going to ask her on the sixteenth of November. If she says yes, we will go ring shopping and she will receive her ring at Christmas. That is when we will tell the families."

"Why the sixteenth of November?"

"That is the date I met her."

"Oh, how romantic! I didn't know you had it in you."

"Now remember, doctor's oath. Not a word. Barbara doesn't even know."

Mary Elizabeth crossed her heart. "Doctor's oath." Then she hugged him. "I am so happy for you."

"How about you? You know, that chief inspector is not bad looking. If I were the jealous type, I would be green."

"Lucky for me, you're not."

"Say, he looks familiar."

"Don't you recognize him?"

"Should I?"

"Met Pips number twelve? The rugby player who recovered my purse?"

"I say! He is the new chief inspector for your village?" Stuey laughed. "Mary Elizabeth, don't you see? The Fates have brought you together."

"Stuey! I hardly know him."

"Don't worry. You will if he has anything to say about it."

"Why does everyone keep saying that!"

"Because it's true. You have put yourself on the shelf for far too long. Now that you have achieved your goal of becoming a doctor, don't you think it's time you climbed down and joined us mere mortals?"

"Oh, Stuey!"

"Hmm. Maybe I should have a talk with him. Check him out. See if his intentions toward you are honorable."

"Don't you dare!" Mary Elizabeth cried. "Say, where are Connor and Reggie? I invited them."

"Don't know. I have neither seen nor heard from them since our party. You and Ruhan were the glue that always kept us together."

"Have you heard from Ruhan?"

"Just a short note last month. He's busy setting up his practice. He's also engaged. His parents arranged the marriage for him."

"Oh my! An arranged marriage! How does he feel about that?"

"Actually, he sounded relieved and quite excited. He asked for your address so don't be surprised if we receive his wedding announcement soon."

The music stopped. Baron Whitacre asked her for the next dance. Stuey returned to his table. Mary Elizabeth began to dance with Baron Whitacre. She looked into his bloodshot eyes. The smell of alcohol on his breath almost made her woozy. His smile looked more like a sneer. "Having a good time?"

"Yes."

"I can show you an even better time."

"No, thank you." Mary Elizabeth prayed this dance would end quickly.

"Here. You are so tense. Let me help you loosen up." With that, he slid his hand from her shoulder to rest on her bottom.

"Baron, I am warning you, remove your hand now." Mary Elizabeth said between clenched teeth.

"Oh, you are even more beautiful when you are angry," he said as he grabbed her bottom harder and pulled her into him.

Mary Elizabeth tried to remove his hand, but he wouldn't budge. She stopped dancing. She tried unsuccessfully to push away from him. "If you don't remove your hand this instant, I will be forced to show you some moves which will be very painful for you."

Suddenly, Viscount LeBrosse showed up at the Baron's side. Viscount LeBrosse was an older man in his late fifties. His brown hair and beard were tinged with grey, which only made him look more distinguished. Dressed in his formal evening wear, he looked quite handsome. His air and his manners spoke of one well versed in courtly etiquette. He tapped the baron on the arm. "May I cut in?"

Being outranked, the baron mumbled something incoherent, released Mary Elizabeth, bowed tipsily, and left the dance floor.

Viscount LeBrosse bowed, smiled at her, and held out his hands in the dance position. Mary Elizabeth peered into his eyes. His gray eyes were clear, unlike the bloodshot eyes of her previous partner. Satisfied that her new dance partner was not under the influence, Mary Elizabeth took his hand, and they began to dance. "Excuse me for cutting in, mademoiselle, but I could no longer wait to dance with the most beautiful woman at the ball."

"You flatter me, sir. However, your intervention was most welcome and your timing impeccable. May I know your name?"

"Viscount Jacques Etienne Henri LeBrosse at your service, mademoiselle. I am a friend of Father Evenson."

"Pleased to meet you."

"I assure you, the pleasure is all mine. May I give you some friendly advice?"

"Of course."

Viscount LeBrosse then became very serious. "Please be careful. Not everyone here tonight is as they seem. Your beautiful pendant may prove to be quite the temptation to jewel thieves."

"Oh, I know all about the jewel thefts in the area. I read about them in the *Bugle*. But I don't have any jewels. I have my rhinestone tiara and my agate necklace. There are dozens of women here tonight who are dripping with real gemstones. Why would anyone bother with mine?"

"Your agate pendant is the prize. No one, including me, has ever seen anything like it. Everyone is talking about it. Be on guard, my dear. At these affairs, avarice is dressed in finery."

His words sent a chill down Mary Elizabeth's spine. Her smile faded.

"My dear, please accept my apologies. I did not mean to alarm you." He paused, smiled, and with a twinkle in his eye added, "I do not believe our new young chief inspector will let any harm come to you or your beautiful necklace. He seems to be quite an accomplished policeman for one so young. Did you see all those medals and ribbons on his jacket?"

Mary Elizabeth returned his smile. "Yes, I did. I wonder what they all mean?"

The music ended. Viscount LeBrosse bowed and was gone. The band took its final break.

Mary Elizabeth went to the refreshment table and got a tall glass of white soda. She searched for Father Evenson and Mrs. Winters and joined them at their table.

"Father, how well do you know Viscount LeBrosse?"

Father Evenson looked a little surprised. "Why do you ask?"

Mary Elizabeth said, "I just danced with him. He said he was a friend of yours."

Mrs. Winters repeated, "Friend?"

Father Evenson countered, "Comrade-in-arms, you might say. We worked together during the Great War."

Mary Elizabeth replied, "He told me to be careful."

Father Evenson said with assurance, "Good advice."

"Why would thieves care about my necklace when there are women wearing real jewels?"

Mrs. Winters said, "There is a lot of talk about your necklace tonight."

"Lots of coveting going on in people's hearts," Father Evenson added. "Should make for interesting confessions this week."

Mary Elizabeth looked at Father Evenson with alarm. "Viscount LeBrosse said something similar to me when we were dancing. Are all these rich people jealous of my necklace?"

"Some people are never satisfied with what they have."

Mrs. Winters chimed in. "They're always on the lookout for what they do not yet possess. A very sad way to live."

Mary Elizabeth sipped her drink. Father Evenson got up from the table. "And now, if you will excuse me, I must find Lady Beatrice and say good night. I still have my Breviary to say."

Mrs. Winters also rose. "I will turn in too. You stay and enjoy the rest of your party. Remember, I am right next door if you need me. Good night." She patted Mary Elizabeth's hand.

CHAPTER 30

On the Terrace

After Mrs. Winters left, Mary Elizabeth wandered out onto the terrace. It was a clear, cool night. The stars were brilliant. The light from the moon lit the grounds below. Her body was tired, but her mind was racing. *Am I in danger?* Mary Elizabeth was so engrossed in her own thoughts, she failed to notice the tall figure standing beside her.

"Mary Elizabeth?"

"Oh!"

"Sorry," Will said. "I didn't mean to startle you. I saw you come out here all alone. You had a worried look on your face. I came to see if you are all right."

"Just getting tired. The last few dances have been more like hand-to-hand combat than dancing. I wish I had my trusty tire iron with me."

Will let out a hearty laugh.

"You don't know how close I came to using it on you that day on the road."

Will got serious. "About that, I must apologize. I—"

"Oh, It's all right."

"No, it's not all right. I behaved very unprofessionally. You didn't deserve that penalty notice. I am sorry."

"But then why did you write me up?"

Will looked into her eyes. "You looked familiar to me, but I just couldn't believe we'd met before. I was desperate to find out more about you, especially your name."

"You could've just asked me. I would've told you."

"I know. But I wasn't thinking clearly." Will gave a half smile. "Seeing you in your lingerie didn't help matters one bit. Please, will you forgive me?"

"Yes, I do forgive you. But you owe me a pound note."

Will burst out laughing. He brought out his wallet.

Mary Elizabeth stopped him with her hand. "Not here! Put that away before someone sees you! That's all we need is for people to think you are paying me for favors or worse." She began to laugh.

He quickly slid his wallet back into his pocket. "I see what you mean. When can I pay you back?"

"No rush. In the village sometime." Mary Elizabeth smiled at him. "Or—"

"Or?"

"Or you could take me out sometime. You do go out and have fun occasionally, don't you?"

He tried to be serious, but he could not help but grin. "Well, I suppose I could make an exception in your case."

"I hope you do."

Will leaned his arms against the terrace railing and looked over the moonlit garden. "Beautiful night."

"That's my realm up there, you know."

Will turned to her. "Pardon?"

Mary Elizabeth said rather seriously, pointing to her tiara, "I will have you know this crown isn't just for show."

Will now gave her his full attention. "Is that so?"

Mary Elizabeth said, "When I was eighteen years old, I was crowned Princess Kay of the Milky Way at the Minnesota State Fair."

Will shook his head. "You continue to amaze me. So, tell me, what do you know about your realm?"

Mary Elizabeth pointed toward the night sky. "Here, I can point out the Big Dipper, Little Dipper, Orion's belt, and I think that bright star over there is Venus."

Will teased her. "That's pretty paltry knowledge, if you ask me."

"Hey, I was a dairy princess, not an astronomer. What do you know about the stars, Chief?"

The night air was getting chilly. Mary Elizabeth rubbed her gloved hands over her bare arms.

Will asked, "Getting cold?"

"A little. But go on. Tell me about the stars."

Will began to take off his suit coat, but Mary Elizabeth protested. "No, you keep your coat on. I will not be the cause of you catching your death out here."

Will thought a moment. "How about if we try this?" He gently took her hand and positioned her in front of him, trying to ward off the night's chill. "Is that better?"

"Yes, thank you," she said quietly.

Will proceeded to point out more constellations. He kept his other hand on the terrace railing. At that moment, Mary Elizabeth felt like she was home. She experienced the warmth of his body. Inhaling deeply, she discovered that his smell, which was a mixture of lavender, orange, and his own scent, aroused and excited her. Letting her guard down, she relaxed and leaned back against his firm, muscled body. It was as if she were melting into him. That was a feeling she had never felt before, and it was wonderful. Emotions that had long remained dormant within her now sprang to the surface. These new feelings were exciting and powerful. She realized she could stay near to him like this for a very long time. Finally, she realized that Will had stopped talking.

"Amateur astronomer?"

"It's a hobby of mine."

"Do you own your own telescope?"

Will could not hide his excitement. "I do. Out in the country like this, with the stars so bright, the planets and galaxies I could show you . . ."

The band began playing their final set of the evening. With his voice under control again, Will said, "We should probably head back in." He dropped his arm from the railing and backed away. The spell was broken.

"If it's all the same to you, I'd rather stay out here. Remember, you did promise me another dance."

"So I did. Shall we?"

They began to dance. Will began to sing the words to the song "The Way You Look Tonight." Mary Elizabeth smiled. Off to the side, a photographer's lightbulb flashed. The noise and bright light surprised the pair. Mary Elizabeth jumped back.

"Whoa! What was that?" Mary Elizabeth asked as the flash blinded her for a moment. She stopped dancing.

Will said, "That was just the photographer the Brantwells hired for the evening. He has been taking pictures of all the couples on the dance floor." Will waited while Mary Elizabeth set herself to rights again. She nodded, and they resumed their dance.

Reassured by Will's calm strength, Mary Elizabeth asked, "Do you think that photo will make the *Bellechester Bugle?*"

"Definitely front-page material if you ask me." Will smiled.

His remark made Mary Elizabeth laugh. "Chief, I have a confession to make."

"Isn't that Father Evenson's department?" Will teased.

Mary Elizabeth took a deep breath, looked deep into his blue eyes, and then admitted softly, "I am feeling a little scared."

"Scared? Did something happen?" Will asked with genuine concern in his voice.

"When I was dancing with Viscount LeBrosse, he told me that I should be careful who I trust. He said thieves might target my necklace. It rattled me, that's all."

"Well, you can always trust me," Will stated firmly.

Mary Elizabeth looked into his eyes and with relief said, "Thank you. I'm going to hold you to that, don't you know."

Looking deep into her blue eyes, Will could hear himself say, a bit too enthusiastically, "Oh, yes. Please do." He also wanted to reassure her with a kiss, but as he bowed his head, a voice called out from the darkness, "Dr. Senty?"

Mary Elizabeth reluctantly answered, "Yes."

As the speaker advanced from the shadows, both Mary Elizabeth and Will recognized Mr. Jameson. "Lord Brantwell is wondering if you can see him now."

Mary Elizabeth replied, "Of course." She turned to Will. "Duty calls. Thank you for the dance, and the astronomy lesson. Good night, Chief."

"Good night, Princess."

After Mary Elizabeth left, Will stayed out on the terrace. The evening had turned out like nothing he had imagined. He had steeled himself to act like the perfect escort for Mary Elizabeth: attentive, laughing at her jokes, and dancing the obligatory first dance. He would check off all the boxes and do his duty. All the while he would keep his heart and his emotions tightly guarded. However, something had gone horribly wrong with that plan. He had enjoyed being in her company.

Mary Elizabeth was different from any other woman he had known. She made him different too. As he had discovered in their previous meetings—at the rugby match, on the Brantwell Road, and in her exam room—being in her presence had a way of disconcerting him. Effortlessly, she surprised him at every turn. But whatever side of her personality she was showing, Will knew she was being honest and genuine. There was no guile in her. Everything he discovered about her made him want to know more. And if that would take a lifetime, well, so be it.

It took all of Will's resolve to release her after that second dance. If she only knew how much he wanted to dance with her all night long. But Will's sense of duty had separated them that first time. This time, however, it was Mary Elizabeth's call to duty that caused them to part. Will wondered if he'd be able to handle being with a woman who could be called away like that. He shivered in the chilly night air. With one last glance at the celestial ceiling above, Will left the terrace and went back inside the manor. He needed to check with his officers to see that everyone was in place for the night.

CHAPTER 31

A LITTLE MISCOMMUNICATION

Meanwhile, Mr. Jameson led Mary Elizabeth to Lord Brantwell's room. He was about to knock on the door when Mary Elizabeth said, "Wait! I'm going to my room first to get my medical bag. I will be back in a minute." In her room she dropped off her purse, removed her gloves, and picked up her medical bag. Then she returned to Mr. Jameson. "Okay. Ready."

He knocked on the door. "Enter," came the voice from within.

Lord Brantwell was standing before them in his pajamas and dressing gown. "Thank you for coming, Dr. Senty."

"What can I do for you?"

"I need you to administer my medicine. It is on the desk. Dr. Winston wrote everything out. His instructions and notes are in the folder."

Mary Elizabeth opened the folder and began to read. "Who usually helps you with this?"

"In London, I had a private nurse, but I don't have one out here. I don't want Bea to know about my condition."

"I take patient confidentiality very seriously. You have my discretion." Mary Elizabeth continued to read Dr. Winston's notes. "Have you experienced any side effects?"

"Just a little nausea and dizziness."

Mary Elizabeth began writing on a pad of paper. She turned to Mr. Jameson. "I am going to need these supplies for Lord Brantwell." She handed him the list.

"Of course, Doctor. I shall bring these right up for you."

"Thank you, Mr. Jameson. Lord Brantwell, while Mr. Jameson gets our supplies, I will get some numbers from you. If you will come and sit in this chair by the desk, we can get started."

Lord Brantwell complied. Mr. Jameson returned with the supplies, and the treatment began. After receiving his medicine, Lord Brantwell was required to lie down for an hour, after which Mary Elizabeth took more readings.

"There. You are all set for the night. It might be a good idea to have Mr. Jameson stay with you tonight, as you have not had this medicine given in this form before. Mr. Jameson, if Lord Brantwell shows any side effects from the medicine, please send for me. I will check on you again in the morning. Good night."

From his bed, Lord Brantwell said, "Thank you, Dr. Senty, and good night."

Back in her room, she removed her tiara and started to undo her pendant when someone knocked on her door. It was a valet. "The baron has asked me to find you."

"Is he ill?"

"Please come."

"All right. Let me get my bag." She followed him to Baron Whitacre's room. He opened the door, she stepped inside, and he closed the door behind her.

Baron Whitacre said rather drunkenly, "It's about time you came."

Mary Elizabeth recognized him as the man with the roving hands from the dance floor. "Why did you send for me?"

"I'm lonely," he pouted. "Let's play doctor."

"Where is your wife?"

Baron Whitacre gestured with his hands. "Off somewhere. She'll never know."

Mary Elizabeth said disgustedly, "You're drunk. Go sleep it off." She turned to go, but before she reached the door, he lunged at her. They struggled.

"Baron! Let me go!" Mary Elizabeth cried. They tussled some more. He tried to maneuver her to the bed. "Let me go!"

The door swung open, and Viscount LeBrosse burst into the room. As he was about to enter the fray, Mary Elizabeth kneed the baron hard in the groin. Baron Whitacre released her, and she pushed him hard. He fell into the bed. Viscount LeBrosse retrieved Mary Elizabeth's bag and quickly escorted her out of the room and into the hallway.

"My dear Dr. Senty, I heard you were in the neighborhood." He nodded in the direction of the baron's room. "Are you all right?"

Mary Elizabeth said wryly, as she adjusted her dress, "Yes, it seems there was some miscommunication. It turned out he didn't need a doctor after all."

"I was coming to your aid, but it seems that you did not need my help. You are quite capable of defending yourself. You are a remarkable woman."

"No, I'm not remarkable. I happen to be a woman with a father who wanted to make sure I knew how to handle myself in these types of situations. Before I left for medical school, he had my brother, who was in the Marine Corps, teach me a few self-defense techniques. Those lessons have come in handy on a few occasions. Thankfully, I do not have to employ them very often."

Viscount LeBrosse said, "Dr. Senty, I believe they would be very proud of you. Please, may I walk you to your room?"

"Thank you, Viscount. You know, you have an uncanny knack for showing up when I need you. You are my guardian angel tonight."

Viscount LeBrosse laughed. "Mademoiselle, I have been called many names in my lifetime, but I do believe you are the first to call me an angel. Thank you, my dear." He took her arm and escorted her to her room. He opened the door for her. "Is there anything I can get for you? A sherry, perhaps?"

"No, thank you. I appreciate your concern, Viscount, but I am fine. Here, I can take my bag now. Good night."

Viscount LeBrosse took her hand and kissed it. "Good night, my dear. Sweet dreams."

Mary Elizabeth set her bag down by the desk and started to get undressed for bed.

Saturday, October 24

CHAPTER 32

Chaos

At 2:00 a.m., Lord Brantwell and Mr. Jameson stood in the foyer receiving the jewel cases from the overnight guests. A policeman stood watch nearby. When Lord Brantwell was satisfied that no more guests were coming, they carried the cases to his study. The policeman followed and watched as the jewels were placed in the safe. Carefully replacing the picture, Lord Brantwell bade good night to the policeman posted in the study. He went upstairs to his room. Before turning in, Mr. Jameson shut off the lights in the foyer.

At 4:30 a.m., a series of loud bangs broke the stillness of the house. The first were heard on the north side of the manor, drawing the outdoor police in that direction. A few minutes later, more loud bangs were heard in the woods on the south side of the manor. Dogs barked, police whistles sounded, and constables ran in both directions at once.

The overnight guests emerged from their rooms in their night clothes. Will sprang from his room fully dressed. He ran down the staircase, spying a crumpled heap at the bottom. Mary Elizabeth, medical bag in hand, exited her room in her nightgown and robe and ran toward them. The lights were now on throughout the manor's interior.

Mary Elizabeth knelt beside the fallen body, opened her bag, and pulled out her stethoscope.

Will turned to her. "Now that you are here, I need to check on something."

Mary Elizabeth nodded. "Go."

Will pointed to the policeman nearby. "Come with me." They ran toward the study.

Father Evenson appeared beside Mary Elizabeth. "Can I be of assistance?"

"Yes, Father. Go call for an ambulance. We need to get Viscount LeBrosse to the hospital as quickly as possible."

Dr. Applegate joined her with his medical bag.

Bursting into the study, Will and the officer found the policeman bound hand and foot. He was not moving. He had been stripped of his uniform. "Quick," Will ordered, "bring one of the doctors in here." He untied the policeman and laid him out.

Lord and Lady Brantwell arrived and saw that the safe had been emptied except for one empty jewel case.

"I am going to need an inventory of everything that was put in the safe tonight," Will barked.

"I'll get right to it." Lord Brantwell began penning the contents.

When the policeman came back to the stairs and asked for a doctor, Mary Elizabeth turned to Dr. Applegate. "Do you think you could continue here? I'll go with him."

"Certainly. Go."

Mary Elizabeth grabbed her bag and followed the policeman. In a minute, she was on the floor next to Will. She quickly checked the victim's breathing, pulse, and eyes. "He's alive but unconscious."

She examined the officer visually, looking for any signs of trauma. Finding none, Mary Elizabeth took a vial of blood from his arm. "He needs to go to the hospital. Lady Beatrice, please call the hospital and tell them to expect two patients—a head injury with possible fractures, and a separate unconscious patient."

Will went outside. He found Chief Superintendent Williamson and Superintendent Billingsby speaking with another officer. Will joined them. Chief Superintendent Williamson said, "Chief Inspector Donnelly, this is your investigation. The entire police force of southern Shropshire will give you any help you need."

"Thank you, Chief Superintendent Williamson."

"And I can offer you my department's services too, should you need us."

"That is very generous of you, Superintendent Billingsby. I appreciate your offer."

Chief Superintendent Williamson asked, "Anyone else injured besides Viscount LeBrosse?"

"One of my young officers was found unconscious in the study. Dr. Senty is with him."

"How very fortunate that both Dr. Senty and Dr. Applegate stayed overnight."

Will then turned to the officer who was standing with them. "What can you tell us?"

"Looks like they had a car waiting for them behind the wall. We can't find them. They are gone."

Will ordered, "I want roadblocks set up within a twenty-mile radius. Stop and search all vehicles until further notice."

"Yes, Chief Inspector."

Will walked over to another officer. "Have the canine units search all the outbuildings around the manor. We will search the grounds more thoroughly in the morning when there is light."

The wail of the ambulance could be heard in the distance. Will walked back inside. He found

Lady Beatrice. "Lady Beatrice, can you ask your butler to come see me?"

"Yes, right away."

"Thank you." He gave orders to another officer. "You and Atwell start interviewing the guests in their rooms."

"Yes, Chief Inspector."

Will addressed the crowd that was milling around the staircase. "Please go back to your rooms. My officers will be coming to take your statements. If you had put anything in the safe tonight, please give the officers as full a description as you can."

As the crowd began to disperse, Father Evenson, who had thrown on his cassock and collar over his pajamas and carried his sick-call kit, approached Will. "Chief Inspector?"

"Yes."

"I would like to accompany my friend, Viscount LeBrosse, to the hospital."

"That would be up to Dr. Senty. She is in the study."

"Thank you." Father Evenson went in search of her. He found Mary Elizabeth still kneeling on the floor beside the officer. "Can I be of some assistance?"

"Yes, Father. This man needs your prayers. I have done all I can for him here. I wish that ambulance would hurry up."

Father Evenson asked, "May I accompany Viscount LeBrosse to the hospital?" He knelt on the ground and opened his sick kit. Kissing the stole, he placed it around his neck and then opened the oil of the sick. He began the prayers and anointed the officer on his head and hands.

Mary Elizabeth answered, "Yes, if there is room in the ambulance. Can you stay here for a moment? I want to talk to Dr. Applegate. If there are any changes in the officer's condition, please send for me."

Father Evenson nodded while continuing his prayers.

Mary Elizabeth got up and went out to the foyer to find Dr. Applegate. "How is Viscount LeBrosse?"

"He is stable. He has a nasty cut on the head. I've stopped the bleeding. He could have a possible concussion. He does not appear to have any broken bones in his extremities, but we won't know for sure until we get him to X-ray. How is the other man?" Dr. Applegate asked.

Mary Elizabeth answered, "Still unconscious. I cannot find any reason for his unconscious state, so I took a blood sample. Oh, here is the ambulance. Thank you, Dr. Applegate, for all your help. I can take care of things from here. Good night."

When the ambulance attendants came in, Mary Elizabeth directed them to Viscount LeBrosse and the policeman in the study.

CHAPTER 33

GLENDALE HOSPITAL

It was late Saturday morning. Viscount LeBrosse was moved from the accident and emergency department to a private room after being treated for his injuries. A policeman stood guard at his door. Father Evenson sat on a chair next to him. Viscount LeBrosse began to stir. He moaned. Father Evenson got up and stood at the head of the bed. Alone with Viscount LeBrosse, he called him by his real name. "Blaise, it's Matt. Can you hear me? Blaise?"

Viscount LeBrosse struggled to open his eyes. He groaned and then closed them again.

Father Evenson called again, "Blaise, can you wake up? You are safe. You are in the hospital."

Viscount LeBrosse opened his eyes again and asked groggily, "Hospital? Why?"

"You took a tumble down the stairs at the Brantwell Manor, remember?"

Viscount LeBrosse answered haltingly, "Yes and no. Oh, my head," he cried. "Yes, I remember. And no, I did not fall down the stairs. I was pushed."

"Do you know who pushed you?"

Viscount LeBrosse, still struggling to wake, said, "No, but it was someone who knew me from my former life. He called me DeMotte." The viscount groaned again and held his head with both hands. "He got to the safe, didn't he?"

"I'm afraid so. Did you recognize the voice?"

"No, it was not familiar to me. But I would recognize it again if I heard it. Do the police have any leads?"

"Not yet."

Mary Elizabeth knocked on the door and entered with a tray of supplies.

"Viscount! I'm so glad you are awake. How do you feel?" She read his chart that hung at the bottom of the bed.

Viscount LeBrosse held his head. "Terrific headache. I hurt all over."

"You had quite a fall. You are badly bruised. The X-rays show you have several cracked ribs. You are very lucky that you did not break any other bones. You also sustained a nasty cut to your head. They had to give you a few stitches. And it looks like the anesthetic is now wearing off. Here, I am going to give you a quick exam to update your chart."

She put a thermometer in his mouth and took his pulse. Then, she listened to his heart and lungs with her stethoscope. "All said, the hospitalist is keeping you here until he is assured you have neither a concussion nor internal bleeding."

"No!" Viscount LeBrosse struggled to get up. "I must get back to the manor. I must find—oh." He held his ribs and fell back on the pillows.

Mary Elizabeth gently held his shoulder to the bed. "Hold it right there, cowboy. Don't try to get up. Lie back and rest. How bad is your pain?"

Viscount LeBrosse grimaced. "Compared to what? Everything hurts, but especially my ribs and my head. I feel like I've been trampled by a bull."

Mary Elizabeth answered, "Here, I am going to inject this medicine into your IV. It should relieve some of the pain." After putting the empty syringe on her tray, she took his hand. "Viscount, the medicine should begin to work shortly. It will make you sleepy. Rest."

Father Evenson asked, "Doctor, how is that young policeman doing?"

"I suspect he was drugged to render him unconscious. It almost killed him. The A&E docs were able to give him activated charcoal, which helped counteract the drugs he had ingested. It was touch and go for a time, but he has since stabilized. He will be kept in hospital for a few days."

"May I visit him?" Father Evenson asked.

"I'm sorry, Father. He is still under sedation. Only his mother and medical personnel are allowed in his room. Chief Inspector Donnelly even put his room under guard," Mary Elizabeth said. "His mother might like to visit with you though."

Father Evenson told Viscount LeBrosse, "I will be back to see you later."

"I believe the medicine is starting to work." Viscount LeBrosse was having a hard time keeping his eyes open.

"Sleep well, my friend."

It was early evening when Mary Elizabeth, Father Evenson, and Viscount LeBrosse returned to the manor. The viscount had convinced the hospitalist to release him and transfer his care to Dr. Senty. The hospitalist had agreed after conferring with Mary Elizabeth. Lady Beatrice had sent a car to bring the trio back to the manor. Mary Elizabeth got out, carrying her medical bag and a bag which contained her night clothes. She was still wearing the scrubs she had borrowed from the hospital. Father Evenson helped Viscount LeBrosse from the car. Two strong young servants carried Viscount LeBrosse into the manor and up the stairs to his room. Mary Elizabeth helped get him settled into his bed.

"It is less painful for the viscount to sit up than to lie in bed, so make sure he has plenty of pillows to prop him up. Leave an extra pillow out, as he can use it to press on his ribs if that will help the pain."

One of the valets went in search of more pillows.

"The viscount will be on bed rest for at least the next twenty-four hours. Please check in on him every few hours and see to his needs." She asked the remaining servant to bring up a tray of food for him. Then Mary Elizabeth dropped her things inside her room and went downstairs into the dining room. There was no formal dinner that night. Lady Beatrice served a buffet so the guests could eat when they wanted. Guests had been talking to police officers and insurance adjusters all day. Everyone was instructed to stay indoors until the police executed a thorough search of the grounds. The mood in the manor was subdued. The guests were exhausted and looking to make it an early night.

Father Evenson and Mrs. Winters joined Mary Elizabeth in the dining room.

Mrs. Winters asked, "How is Viscount LeBrosse?"

"His condition has stabilized. The hospitalist decided I could look after him here just as well as he could at the hospital. All Viscount LeBrosse needs is rest."

"Does he remember anything?"

Father Evenson replied, "Yes. He says he was pushed down the stairs."

Mary Elizabeth was alarmed. "This is new information to me. Does the chief inspector know?"

"No, I don't think so."

"We should tell the chief inspector."

"We will."

Mrs. Winters asked, "And how is that young police officer doing?"

"His doctors say he will make a full recovery. He will be discharged in a few days. A week of home rest, and he should be back to work."

Mrs. Winters exclaimed, "Oh, thanks be to God. That is good news."

Father Evenson inquired, "What is the news around here, Mrs. Winters?"

Mrs. Winters reported, "The guests who lost jewelry in the robbery were Lady Beatrice, Mrs. Phillips, the baroness, and Lady Porter. Mrs. Applegate and Mrs. Billingsby had their jewelry with them in their rooms, so theirs was not touched."

"Interesting," Father Evenson said.

After she had eaten, Mary Elizabeth got very sleepy. "I suggest an early night for all of us. I am going up. Can I take a rain check on our chat until tomorrow, Mrs. Winters?"

"Of course, dear."

"Good night, everyone."

"Evening, Mary Elizabeth," Will said as he passed her on the stairs.

"Oh, Chief. Do you have a minute?" She turned around on the stairs.

Will walked back up so they were eye to eye. "Only a minute. I'm glad to see you back from the hospital. How are our patients?"

"Officer Collins is resting comfortably. The hospitalist is caring for him, but he has released

Viscount LeBrosse to me. The viscount is now back in his room. He won't be cleared for questioning until tomorrow. Tonight, he needs a good night's sleep. He did tell Father Evenson that someone pushed him down the stairs."

"I should go speak to Father Evenson."

"I just left him in the dining room."

Will smiled at her. "Thanks for the information." He turned and continued on his way.

Before she could turn in, she had to see Lord Brantwell and then check once more on Viscount LeBrosse. She walked into the bathroom and splashed cold water on her face. With a deep sigh, she grabbed her medical bag. She knocked on Lord Brantwell's door. There was no reply. She then went to check on Viscount LeBrosse. She took his tray from his bed, and then checked and charted his vital signs. "How are you feeling this evening?"

"Still sore."

"How is your head?" She checked his bandage.

"Still attached."

"Are you still experiencing pain?"

"Yes."

"Now, do you need anything tonight for the pain or to help you sleep?"

"I am tired of sleeping. That is all I do," complained Viscount LeBrosse.

"Right now, that is all you are supposed to do. That is how you heal. So can you tolerate the pain, or do you want me to give you something for it that will help you sleep?"

"What kind of a question is that? Of course, I do not want to feel pain."

"Let me ask the question a different way: Will the pain you are experiencing right now prevent you from sleeping?"

"Yes."

"Did the medicine I gave you in the hospital relieve your pain? I know it helped you sleep."

"I want something stronger that will last longer."

Mary Elizabeth yawned again. "Okay. I will give you something stronger that should last you through the night."

She turned her back to him and pulled out a pill bottle. Carefully reading the label, she shook out two pills. She then poured a glass of water from his nightstand.

"Here, take these pills. These should last you through the night." She watched as he took the pills from her and drank a few sips of water.

"Here," he said as he tried to give her back the glass.

She pushed the glass back to him. "No, these pills are strong. You must drink the entire glass of water."

Mary Elizabeth sat in the chair next to his bed. Taking his hand, she said in her calm, soothing voice, "In a few minutes, you will not feel any pain. Just lie back and close your eyes. I will stay with you until you fall asleep."

"Dr. Senty, I know so little about you. Why don't you tell me about yourself?"

"If you like." Mary Elizabeth began telling him about the farm where she grew up. She stayed with him until she saw him close his eyes and heard his steady breathing. She gathered her bag and quietly left the room. A police officer was stationed outside his door.

"Viscount LeBrosse should sleep through the night. I would appreciate it if you could check in on him from time to time. Please, come get me if Viscount LeBrosse gets restless or shows any signs of distress. My room is the second from the end, down the other hallway."

"Yes, Doctor."

After she left Viscount LeBrosse's room, she once again knocked on Lord Brantwell's door. This time he answered, "Come in."

Mary Elizabeth entered his room and found Lord Brantwell in his pajamas and robe, speaking with Mr. Jameson.

"Dr. Senty, I did not know you were back from the hospital. How are your patients?"

Mary Elizabeth gave him a quick rundown on Viscount LeBrosse and the young police officer. "And how did things go here today?"

Lord Brantwell told her about the police questioning and the meetings with the insurance adjusters. "A horrible mess. Everyone tried to make the best of it. You know us Brits, we soldier on. Everyone is looking forward to a peaceful night tonight."

Mary Elizabeth yawned. "We could all use a good night's sleep."

Lord Brantwell said, "By the looks of it, especially you. I don't want to keep you. Everything is on the desk."

"Mr. Jameson, if you could bring up the same supplies as yesterday, we will get started." Mary Elizabeth checked Lord Brantwell's vitals. As she filled out his chart, she said, "I see you have two more doses to go. We can do the next one before I go tomorrow. But what about Monday? Will you be back in London?"

"With this theft business, I don't know how long I will be kept here." Lord Brantwell said from his bed.

"If you don't mind Viscount LeBrosse recovering here for a few days, I will visit him every day. I could plan Monday's visit for the evening so I could give you your final dose then."

"That will be fine."

"Enter," Lord Brantwell answered the knock on the door.

Mr. Jamison brought the needed supplies. "Do you require me to stay?"

"Yes, Mr. Jamison," Lord Brantwell said.

"Very good, sir."

Mary Elizabeth administered the medicine. After she returned to her room, she set her bag on top the dressing table. One of its drawers was partially open. *That's odd. I thought I closed that drawer after I put my jewelry away last night. My jewelry!* Mary Elizabeth yanked open the drawer. Her rhinestone tiara glimmered in the room's light. She opened the case holding the King's Cross medal. It lay undisturbed. She pulled out the jewelry bag for her pendant. Opening the cinch, she discovered the bag was empty. Her necklace was gone. *Oh no!* She was now fully awake. She ran down the hall and banged on Chief Inspector Donnelly's door. "Chief!"

The officer guarding the viscount's room said, "Sorry, ma'am. The chief inspector has not come up to his room yet."

She ran back to knock on the doors of Mrs. Winters and Father Evenson. "Help!" she cried. "Please help."

Mrs. Winters opened her door. She was already in her nightclothes, and her hair was wrapped in curlers. "What's the matter, dear?"

Father Evenson, also in his nightclothes, opened his door. "Dr. Senty?"

Mary Elizabeth cried, "My pendant is gone. It's been stolen!"

Trying to calm Mary Elizabeth, Mrs. Winters suggested, "Now, maybe it was just misplaced. Come, we will help you look for it."

They came and searched Mary Elizabeth's room with her. Her agate necklace was not to be found.

Father Evenson asked, "When was the last time you saw it?"

Mary Elizabeth sat on the bed and tried to think. "I had it at the dance. I had it when I saw Lord Brantwell. The baron and I got into a tussle, but I am sure it was still around my neck when I left his room. I remember taking it off when I got out of my gala clothes. I am positive I put it into my jewelry bag next to the tiara and my medal in this drawer before I turned in."

"So it was in your possession when you went to bed. What time was that?"

Mary Elizabeth replied, "Around 1:30 a.m. It was a short night. We were all awakened at 4:30 a.m. with the business downstairs and the hospital. This is the first time I've spent a moment in my room, and I noticed the dressing table drawer was ajar."

"Mrs. Winters, did you see anyone coming in or out of her room today?"

"No. But there was plenty of opportunity for someone to take it."

Father Evenson added, "Yes, but after the jewels in the safe were taken."

"Mrs. Applegate and Mrs. Billingsby did not put their jewels in the safe, either. Do you think they might be missing some jewelry too?" Mrs. Winters inquired.

Father Evenson replied, "Yes, that is a good place to start. But that will have to wait until morning."

Mary Elizabeth cried, "How can I sleep? My pendant!"

Mrs. Winters went to comfort her. "Tomorrow we will inform the chief inspector. I am sure he will find it for you. You must trust things will work out," she said.

"It has been a trying day. Everyone is tired. Let's go to sleep. Before we go to our rooms, let's offer a special prayer to St. Anthony, patron of lost things, to help us locate your pendant. We must have faith."

Mary Elizabeth was too exhausted to argue. She knelt beside her bed while Father Evenson led them in prayer. Then Father Evenson and Mrs. Winters returned to their rooms.

Sunday, October 25

CHAPTER 34

An Early Morning Walk

Mary Elizabeth crawled into bed exhausted and fell right to sleep. The next morning, she awoke at her regular time of 6:00 a.m. It was just beginning to get light; the moon and morning stars were still visible. It was Mary Elizabeth's favorite time of day. She'd slept in her scrubs and left them on as she slipped into her wool sweater and tennis shoes. *A long walk will clear my mind. Maybe I can remember what happened to my necklace.*

She was very careful not to wake the other guests as she walked out of her room. Before going downstairs, Mary Elizabeth checked with the patrolman who was guarding Viscount LeBrosse's room. Viscount LeBrosse had slept through the night. When she peeked into his room, she could see that he was still sleeping soundly.

She bounded down the stairs and out the front door. Once outside, she did some stretches. The air was crisp with a little bite to it, perfect weather for a long, brisk walk. She started down the winding driveway and out past the gate. Instead of walking toward the village, she turned in the opposite direction. She followed the road through the woods. Lining both sides of the road was a three-foot-high stone wall that kept the sloping hills from eroding unto the road. The road crested to the top of the hill. *What a view!* She could see for miles in all directions. Turning toward the village, she made out the church steeples of both St. Bede's and St. Walburga's monasteries. She could also see the square twin towers of St. Anselm's Church. After spending time soaking in the view, she turned around and started back to the manor. She was about a mile away when she noticed her shoelace had come untied. She bent down to retie it. As she was getting up, she saw movement out of the corner of her eye. Still shaken from the theft of her necklace, Mary Elizabeth crouched down against the wall, feeling the cold stones on her cheek. After a few minutes, her curiosity got the better of her. Raising her head slightly, she peeked through the tall grass. Mary Elizabeth saw a person wearing a tan raincoat and brown floppy hat walking toward the lone oak tree that stood in the middle of the clearing. The person stopped at the tree, looked all around, and deposited a package in its hollow. The person surveyed the scene once again before walking back through the tall grass in the direction of the manor. Mary Elizabeth waited until she was sure the person was out of the area. She climbed over the stone wall. She looked into the hollow of the tree and spied a wrapped package. She wanted to take it out and unwrap it to see what was inside but thought better of it. She did not want to compromise a police investigation. She knew she had to find the chief inspector. To ensure she would not run into the stranger, she ran back to the road and followed it to the manor. By the time she got back, more life was stirring inside. The early risers were finishing their breakfast or sitting in chairs reading the newspaper.

Mary Elizabeth found a police officer. "Have you seen Chief Inspector Donnelly this morning?"

"No. I don't think he is down from his room yet."

Mary Elizabeth bounded up the stairs and knocked on his door.

"Come in."

Mary Elizabeth entered to find Will standing before the mirror, tying his necktie.

"Good morning, Mary Elizabeth. Looks like you have been up early."

Mary Elizabeth was still breathless from running up the stairs. She tried to talk but couldn't yet get her words out.

Will offered her a seat on the foot of his bed. "Here, sit down. Take your time."

Mary Elizabeth finally caught her breath. She told Will exactly what she'd seen on her walk.

"That is odd, very odd. Do you think the person saw you?"

"I don't think so."

"Do you think you can show me the tree?"

"Of course."

"Let me think a minute. Have you had breakfast yet?"

"No."

"Meet me in the dining room in, say, twenty minutes. If there are other people there, we will tell them that we are going for a walk. Since we don't know who put the package in the tree, we do not want to arouse anyone's suspicions. Now, can you tell me once again where the tree is located? I am going to send an officer ahead to make sure nothing is disturbed before we get there."

Mary Elizabeth did her best to recall the location of the tree and any other landmarks that would be helpful in identifying the exact spot. "There's something else, Chief."

"Go on."

"My pendant. It seems to have gone missing too. I didn't realize until I returned last night." She did her best to hide her mounting sadness.

"Okay." He looked like he wanted to say something more, but what could he say? It was an active investigation with no active leads. "Got it. See you in twenty minutes."

"Twenty minutes it is." Mary Elizabeth left his room, gently closing the door. Turning around, she ran smack into Superintendent Billingsby, who was walking down the hallway with his wife. "Oh, I'm sorry. Please excuse me."

Superintendent Billingsby said, "Good Morning, Dr. Senty. I hope you found Chief Inspector Donnelly in good health?"

Mary Elizabeth replied, "Oh, yes. He's fine. This wasn't a professional call."

Superintendent Billingsby raised his eyebrows and said, "I see."

As soon as the words were out of her mouth, Mary Elizabeth wished she could take them back.

Mrs. Billingsby slapped her husband on the chest and said, "Stop teasing the girl. Come on, Arthur. Let's get breakfast."

The superintendent turned back and gave Mary Elizabeth a wink and a smile.

There goes his reputation, she thought, *and mine.* Mary Elizabeth quickly hurried to her room. She showered and changed into slacks, a plaid shirt, and flats. Redoing her hair into a ponytail, she looked into the mirror. *There, that's presentable.*

In the dining room, Will sat with Superintendent Billingsby and his wife, Dr. Applegate and his wife, and Lord and Lady Porter. Mary Elizabeth filled her plate at the buffet and headed to their table. "May I join you?"

All the men stood up. Will pulled back her chair, and she settled into the empty seat beside him.

"What are everyone's plans for the day?" Mrs. Billingsby asked.

"We will be leaving soon. We have a family dinner tonight in London." Mrs. Applegate replied.

"But first," Dr. Applegate added, "we are going to spend some time with my friend, Dr. Merton, who lives in the village."

Lady Porter spoke up: "Friday, on my walk, I found a pretty little spot to do a landscape painting. I hope to go back today and paint."

Mrs. Billingsby said, "Lady Beatrice is going to take me and Mrs. Williamson on a tour of her gardens and green houses. Whoever wants to join us is welcome."

Superintendent Billingsby asked, "And what about you two?"

Will reached for Mary Elizabeth's hand and said, "We are planning to go for a walk this morning, as our duties will prevent us from spending much time together today."

Mary Elizabeth said, "It looks like a lovely day."

Will and Mary Elizabeth left the dining room hand in hand. Even as they walked down the long driveway, Will showed no signs of letting go. When they were out of earshot of the manor, Mary Elizabeth told Will of her encounter with Superintendent and Mrs. Billingsby outside of his room.

Will laughed, but when he saw Mary Elizabeth's distraught expression he said, "I'm sorry. That must have been embarrassing for you."

"You realize, Chief, that our reputations are shot."

"Or enhanced."

Mary Elizabeth looked at him. "That only applies to men."

Will reassured her, "I wouldn't worry about it. The super will keep it to himself. Besides, the Billingsbys are from London. I think your reputation is safe in the village."

Will didn't let go of her hand until they passed through the gate. Walking behind the surrounding wall, they were now clear of any prying eyes from the manor. Their pace quickened as Mary Elizabeth led him to the spot. Will found the patrolman hidden in the brush. "Has anyone been here?"

"No, sir."

Mary Elizabeth showed him the hollow in the tree. The package lay as she had found it, undisturbed.

"Nice detective work, Princess. You might make the force yet."

"No thanks, Chief. I already have a job, remember? Do you think my pendant is in there?"

"We will have to wait and see. I will have you give a formal statement. Did you ever get a good look at the person who hid this?"

"Not really. It was early morning, and there was fog burning off the grass. But I could give you a description of his general build and the clothes he was wearing."

"That will help. Now, we wait to see who comes to retrieve the package. Can you show me the path the person took after hiding it?"

Mary Elizabeth led the way through the brush toward the manor. When they got to the edge of the grounds, Will again took her hand. They walked along in companionable silence until they got to the driveway.

Mary Elizabeth said, "Chief, you deserve an Oscar for your performance in the dining room this morning. You were very convincing. Even I believed that we are a couple."

Will stopped and looked intently into her face. "I was convincing because I wasn't acting. I told the truth. I do hope when this investigation is over, we can get to know each other better."

Mary Elizabeth gazed into his clear blue eyes for a moment. "I would like that too. Now, what are you going to do?"

"Well, I think this." Will bent down and kissed her lips softly at first. He caught Mary Elizabeth by surprise. He kissed her again. This time she was ready to receive him. It was wonderful. Soft, tender, exciting.

Mary Elizabeth laughed. "I meant, about the investigation."

"Oh, I'm sorry. I thought . . . I hope I didn't offend you."

"No, that was nice, Chief. Really nice." She then threw her arms around his neck to bring his face toward hers and kissed him long and passionately. That kiss left them both breathless for a moment.

They continued up the driveway arm in arm.

Lord Brantwell and Lady Beatrice were alone in the study. "Geoff, what a wretched weekend this has turned out to be."

Lord Brantwell looked out the window and said softly, "Bea, come here. Look at this."

They watched Will and Mary Elizabeth walk up the drive together, stop, and kiss.

Lord Brantwell said, "I wouldn't say the weekend is a complete loss. Look at them."

Lady Beatrice sighed. "Young love."

"Does that remind you of anyone? You know, we used to be like that," he said as he gently caressed her arm.

"That was a long time ago," she said curtly as she moved away from him.

Lord Brantwell said softly, "Yes, I suppose it was. Too late for us now."

The tone of his voice made Lady Beatrice turn and take another look at him.

CHAPTER 35

Sunday Afternoon Chats

Lord and Lady Porter met Will and Mary Elizabeth at the manor's entrance. Will held the door.

"Thank you, Chief Inspector. I am off to do my landscape painting. See you in a couple of hours." Lady Porter carried a blanket and her case of paints.

Lord Porter followed her, loaded down with an easel and chair. "And I am going as her beast of burden."

Mary Elizabeth called after them, "Have a good time." Will and Mary Elizabeth headed for the ballroom, which had been transformed into a police command post. Will spotted Detective Inspector Watson. "Watson, please take a statement from Dr. Senty."

He signaled to Sergeant O'Hanlon. "Sergeant O'Hanlon, do you have a copy of the statements the guests made to the insurance adjustors?"

Lord and Lady Brantwell were in the foyer bidding goodbye to their guests. Mrs. Applegate spoke to Lady Beatrice, "Thank you so much for including us in this memorable weekend. Your party on Friday night was very special."

Lord Brantwell said, "Thank you, Doctor, for lending your expertise when we needed it."

"Dr. Senty had the situation well under control. You are fortunate to have her. She is a very competent and capable doctor. She will serve your community well."

"Yes, I am beginning to realize that. Please visit us again, for a quieter, more restful weekend."

Father Evenson and Mrs. Winters were in their respective rooms, packing their suitcases. Across from them, Mrs. Phillips and her maid were also getting ready to leave. They overheard

Mrs. Phillips say, "Silly girl. Hurry up. The sooner we are out of here, the better."

Father Evenson walked across the hall and poked his head in the door. "Can I be of any assistance?"

"It is so hard to find good help these days."

"I am sorry that your jewels were stolen."

Mrs. Phillips dismissed his remark. "They are easily replaced. But this has been a most eventful weekend. One always picks up the most interesting tidbits at these affairs."

"Anything you care to share?" Father Evenson asked hopefully.

"You will have to come and see me to find out," she said mysteriously. Then she added, "Come for tea next week."

"I shall look forward to it. Safe trip home." He then took her hand, brought it to his lips, and kissed it.

The valets arrived to carry her luggage.

"Here, let me help you down the stairs," Father Evenson offered.

"Why thank you, Father," she said.

After giving her statement, Mary Elizabeth went back upstairs to her room. She glanced across the hall and saw Mrs. Winters sitting on her bed, dressed to go. She stuck her head in the door. "Are you and Father Evenson going home already?"

Mrs. Winters replied with irritation in her voice, "We were. The father said he's anxious to get back to St. Anselm's. But now he has disappeared again. Sometimes, that man."

Mary Elizabeth answered, "Could be a blessing in disguise, Mrs. Winters. That gives us time to have our chat."

Mrs. Winters suddenly perked up. "So, it does. Come in, come in. Now, tell me everything," Mrs. Winters said as she patted the bed. "What happened at the dance after I left?"

"The chief inspector and I talked and danced out on the terrace for a while. Then I was called away to tend to a patient and that was the end of the gala for me. Did you have a good time?"

"I had a few good chinwags. That chief inspector is quite the dancer." Mary Elizabeth smiled, saying nothing. Mrs. Winters laughed. "For a woman my age, my dance card was quite full. It will probably take me all week to recover."

Father Evenson found Will in the ballroom. "Chief Inspector, if I might have a word."

"Not now, Father. Please see me at the station on Monday."

Father Evenson sighed and went back upstairs to visit his friend. Viscount LeBrosse responded cheerfully to the knock on the door, "Come in.

"Oh, it's you," he added, looking disappointed.

"Were you expecting someone else?" Father Evenson asked. "I am feeling most unwanted today."

"I had hoped you were Dr. Senty. She has not been in to see me yet." He sighed heavily. "But I am glad for your company too. Come here. Sit down."

"How are you feeling today, my friend?"

"Sore and bored. Dr. Senty was right. I do feel worse today than yesterday."

"I am sorry to hear it," Father Evenson said as he turned the chair to face Viscount LeBrosse.

"I know that look." Viscount LeBrosse pointed at Father Evenson. "Now, what is going on in that brain of yours?"

"I think we are dealing with two different thefts."

"I'm intrigued. Go on."

"We know about the jewels taken from the safe. That was a professional job. I believe the thieves and the jewels are no longer on the premises."

"Yes, I agree. Lots of people involved in a very intricate scheme. It would have taken a mastermind to plan that heist with all the policemen around the premises yesterday. What is the second theft?"

Father Evenson told Viscount LeBrosse of Dr. Senty's missing pendant. "That theft, I fear, was committed by another person after the jewel thieves were long gone."

"Why do you say that?"

"Mrs. Applegate and Mrs. Billingsby both kept their jewels in their rooms with them, and neither had their jewels stolen."

"Yes, that makes sense. But do you think Dr. Senty was a victim of theft by opportunity? She was gone from her room a long time yesterday. Anyone could have gotten into her room and stolen it."

"Yes, I believe our thief is someone who saw Dr. Senty and her pendant at the gala."

"Well that narrows it down," Viscount LeBrosse said sarcastically. "Friday evening at the gala, all the women were talking about it."

"Her necklace was taken by someone who was in the house between 4:30 a.m. Saturday morning and the time Dr. Senty returned to her room Saturday evening. It had to be someone who would not call attention to themselves or be out of place on this floor. And that does narrow it down."

"But what about the servants?" asked Viscount LeBrosse.

"I suppose at this point, we cannot rule them out."

"How do you suggest we go about finding her necklace?"

"I spoke with Mrs. Phillips before she left. I can't be sure . . ." Father Evenson's voice trailed off as he lost himself in thought.

"Sure about what?"

Father Evenson shook his head. "Not ready to say just yet. Anyway, she invited me to tea next week. She knows something. I am sure of it. Her room was next door to Dr. Senty's. It could be that she saw or heard something that can give us a clue. I am hoping that when you are on your feet again, you can help me. With the police so engaged in solving the jewel heist, I believe, old friend, it will be up to you and me to find and return Dr. Senty's pendant."

"I'll be glad to help."

"Good. This will be just like old times, when we worked for the government during the War. Now, do you have any thoughts on how the jewel theft was pulled off?"

"Well—" There was a knock on the door. Viscount LeBrosse called out, "Come in."

Mary Elizabeth walked in with her medical bag. "Good afternoon, Viscount LeBrosse. And there you are, Father. Mrs. Winters is waiting for you in the dining room. Lunch is being served."

"And what about my lunch? I never knew I could work up an appetite by sleeping so much," Viscount LeBrosse said.

Mary Elizabeth laughed. "I won't let you starve. After I examine you, I will have a tray sent up."

Father Evenson rose from this chair, "Time for lunch already? Oh my, how time flies. Viscount, we will continue our conversation later."

Mary Elizabeth said, "Yes, I'm afraid I'm kicking you out, Father."

Father Evenson replied, "I will leave you to it."

Mary Elizabeth put her bag on the nightstand. She placed her stethoscope around her neck. She walked over and stood by the viscount's bed. "How did last night go for you? Were you able to sleep through the night?"

"Yes."

"Very good. You may have been right to ask for a more powerful painkiller."

"But then, this morning, the pain has returned. I do feel worse than yesterday."

"That is understandable. Your body is beginning to heal. Let's start with the exam, and then we can talk about ways to get your pain under control."

"Whatever you say, Dr. Senty."

"My, you are very agreeable today. There must have been something special in that medicine I gave you last night. Shall we get started?"

CHAPTER 36

Caught!

"Good afternoon, Lord and Lady Porter. How was your time outdoors?" Will asked when they met in the foyer.

Lord Porter replied, "Very relaxing. Beautiful day to spend in nature."

Will looked behind them to the police officer who had just walked through the door. The officer nodded. Will asked the Porters, "Will you join me in the ballroom? I have an urgent matter to speak with you about, and I'd like to do so privately."

"Of course. We will be with you after we return to the room and drop off these things. Do you have news about my wife's jewels?"

"I'd rather not say out here in the open. I hope you understand, your lordship, but I need to speak with you right away."

"Why the urgency? We will return in a few minutes."

"I apologize, Lord Porter. But I must insist that we speak now."

Lady Porter said, "If you gentlemen will excuse me, I must go upstairs and powder my nose." She started toward the stairs, still clutching the paint valise in her hand.

"I am sorry, Lady Porter, but I must ask you to join us." Will was growing stern. He removed a piece of paper from his pocket.

"Can't it wait, man? As you can see, we have come from our outing, and my wife needs to use the facilities."

"Yes. Officer Galloway?" Will motioned to one of the female officers who was standing behind the Porters. "Please escort Lady Porter to the lavatory. I believe there is one on this floor."

The officer took Mrs. Porter by the elbow. "This way, Lady Porter."

"Ah, pardon me, Lady Porter," Will said. "Please leave your paint valise behind."

She angrily dropped it on the floor. "Thank you, Lady Porter."

"I say, what is going on here? I demand to know immediately," Lord Porter shouted.

Lord and Lady Brantwell and Superintendent Billingsby heard the shouting and came to see what the fuss was about.

"Lord Brantwell," Will asked, "may I use your study for a few minutes?"

"Yes, of course. What is this all about?"

"I will explain once we are all in the study. Officer, please bring Lady Porter's valise."

The little group followed Will to the study. The officer brought Lady Porter's valise and set it at Will's feet.

"Thank you, officer." Will said. The officer stood guard at the door. Will unfolded the piece of paper that he had earlier removed from his pocket. "Lord Porter, I have a search warrant in my hand that allows me to search your persons and the contents of your room."

Lord Porter said, "You searched our rooms yesterday. Why do you need to search our room again?"

Will calmly explained, "Yesterday, we were searching for jewels. Today, we were looking for other items."

Lady Porter, escorted by Officer Galloway, entered the room, shook the officer's hand from her elbow, and stood by her husband.

Will said to the officer, "Thank you for your help, Officer Galloway. Please wait outside."

"Yes, sir." The officer left the room.

Will spoke to Lady Porter, "I was just telling your husband that I have a search warrant that allows me to search your persons and the contents of your room."

"I demand to speak to my solicitor."

Will calmly stated, "You may. But I remind you that you are not under arrest. This search warrant has been signed by a judge, which gives us the lawful authority to execute it with or without your consent."

"Cedric, can he do that?"

"Yes, my dear, I am afraid he can. But we have nothing to hide. Go ahead, Chief Inspector. Get on with it so we can be done with this charade!"

Will directed his next remark to Lady Porter. "Were you able to complete your painting, Lady Porter?"

Taking a moment to compose herself, she replied, "The important details are done. It needs some finishing touches that I can do at home."

"May I take a look?"

"I don't like to show my work until it's completed."

Will said firmly, "I am sorry, Lady Porter. I am afraid I must insist. Now, will you open your case, or shall I?"

Lady Porter left her husband's side and bent down to pick up the case. She threw the case at Will and tried to run, but the policeman who was in the room grabbed her and held her while she struggled. "Let me go!"

Lord Porter bellowed, "Officer, unhand my wife! Will someone tell me what in the blazes is going on here?"

The officer looked at Will, and he nodded. The policeman released Lady Porter but blocked the doorway.

Will opened the case. Amongst the canvas and paints was a parcel wrapped in brown paper. Will set the case on the desk and opened the package. It held a diamond-and-sapphire necklace, drop earrings, and a bracelet. "Lord Porter, do you recognize these jewels?"

Lord Porter examined them carefully. "Yes, these are my wife's jewels. But they were stolen! I gave them to Lord Brantwell after the gala. I saw him put them in the safe. These jewels were taken along with the others. You said yourself you found the case in the open safe."

Will corrected him, "What you gave Lord Brantwell to put in the safe was the case, but the jewels were never inside."

Incredulously, Lord Porter said, "But I saw my wife take off her jewelry and put them in the case."

"After she gave you the case, did you ever check inside to see if the jewels were indeed in there?"

"No."

"She pretended to put them in the case but didn't. You were given an empty case to put in the safe. That is why the thieves left it behind when they took the other jewels."

"But that still doesn't explain how the jewels got in my wife's paint valise."

"Knowing that we would search the rooms after the heist was discovered, your wife hid them on her person. We locked down the manor and kept everyone inside all day Saturday. Her only opportunity to hide the jewels was early this morning, when she went out and placed them in the hollow of the tree. Her plan was to put them in her case along with her paints while you were packing up the easel and chair. That way, you could go home and have the insurance company pay your claim, and she would still have her jewels."

Lady Porter screamed, "You can't prove it."

"Yes, I'm afraid I can, Lady Porter. We have already searched your room and have discovered the coat and hat worn by the person who placed the parcel in the tree. We have a sworn statement from an eyewitness."

Lady Porter asked, "But how could there be an eyewitness? There was no one around—"

"Constance, don't say another word!" Lord Porter shouted.

Will continued, "We had the tree under surveillance all day. My officer saw Lady Porter take the package out and put it in her case."

Lord Porter said, "The jewels are returned. No harm done. You can't arrest her for stealing her own jewels!"

Will replied, "No, but I can arrest her for making a report to the insurers with the intent to collect insurance money under false pretenses. You see, I also have a copy of the claim you signed and filed with the adjusters. Lady Porter's signature is also on the document. I am arresting her for insurance fraud." He read Lady Porter her rights. "You do not have to say anything, but anything you do say will be taken down and may be given in evidence."

Will continued, "Now, Lord Porter, would be a good time for you to call your solicitor. He can meet you and Lady Porter down at the Bellechester Constabulary."

He signaled to the officers. They escorted Lady Porter out of the room.

"Cedric! Cedric!" she called.

"I am calling our solicitor right now, my dear. Geoff, may I use your phone?"

"Of course, old chap."

Superintendent Billingsby accompanied Will out of the room. "That was some fine police work, my boy. But very dangerous. Lord Porter is a very powerful man."

"I swore an oath to do my job without fear or prejudice. I did it. Let the chips fall where they may."

"You realize she will probably go free because of who she is and the fact that no money was actually exchanged."

"With all due respect, my job is not to be a solicitor or a judge. I find the evidence, connect the dots, and make the case. I could not let them leave the manor with the jewels. At the very least, I would hope that the experience of a police arrest and detention, no matter of what duration, would be a deterrent to her ever trying something like that again. Now, if you will excuse me,

I need to brief our witness on the case. Then I will be off to the station to question Lady Porter." Will left Superintendent Billingsby in search of Mary Elizabeth.

Will knocked on her door. "Come in," Mary Elizabeth answered while folding clothes. Her open suitcase lay on her bed.

"Are you leaving now?"

"In a bit. I still have some doctoring to do before I go home."

"I wanted to come and give you an update on the package you found in the tree this morning. Can we sit for a minute?"

"Yes," she asked expectantly.

"You were right. There were jewels in the package. It turned out to be Lady Porter's sapphires and diamonds. Thanks to you, I arrested Lady Porter for insurance fraud. I couldn't have done it without you."

"And my pendant?"

"It wasn't in the package. I am sorry."

She removed her hands from his. "That necklace meant the world to me. How can I tell my folks back home that I lost it? My dad made it specially for me. Oh, Chief!"

By now the tears were running down her face and her chest was heaving. Will put his arms around her. She cried for a long time, finally releasing emotions she had long held inside her. She raised her head. He loosened his grip. He reached into his pocket and gave her his handkerchief. She gratefully took it and wiped her eyes and blew her nose. "Look what a mess I have made of your shirt. I am sorry."

"Don't mention it. Mary Elizabeth?"

"Yes, Chief?"

"I am not giving up looking for your pendant. And you shouldn't give up hope, either."

Mary Elizabeth said, not very convincingly, "If you say so."

"I do say so," he said firmly. "Do you believe me?"

Mary Elizabeth looked into his eyes. "I want to believe you."

"Trust me, Mary Elizabeth. Now I must go back to the station. As soon as I have any information about your necklace, I will let you know."

Will left Mary Elizabeth in her room to finish packing.

Before he went back downstairs, he stopped in his room and changed his shirt. He met Lord and Lady Brantwell in the foyer. "We will be clearing out the ballroom tonight and moving the investigation back to town."

Lady Beatrice asked, "Do you have any leads?"

"We have a few. Now comes the slow and methodical work of building a case. Thank you for your cooperation."

"Please let us know if there is anything else you need from us," said Lord Brantwell.

Will shook Lord Brantwell's hand. "I will, sir. Now, if you will excuse me." He turned and walked towards the door. After taking a few steps, he turned and called out, "Lady Beatrice?"

"Yes?"

"Could you look in on Dr. Senty? I believe she could use a friend about now."

"Certainly." And with that, Lady Beatrice went upstairs.

CHAPTER 37

DR. SENTY AND HER PATIENTS

Mary Elizabeth went to check in on Viscount LeBrosse again after dinner. "How are you doing this evening? Have we gotten your pain under control?"

"Yes, those pills you gave me did the trick. And now that you are here, I feel even better."

"Viscount, you always know the right thing to say to make a girl feel good. I am going to miss our chats."

Alarmed, Viscount LeBrosse asked, "What do you mean *miss*? Are you leaving?"

"Yes, I am going back to the village tonight. Shall we get started? You seem to be progressing nicely. I have talked to Lady Beatrice, and she has agreed that you can stay on for a few days. By the end of the week, you will be recovered enough to go and do whatever you viscounts do. By the way, what do you do?"

Viscount LeBrosse laughed. "That, my dear, is a big secret."

"After you leave here, where will you go next?"

"Father Evenson has invited me to stay with him for a while. He has asked me to help him with a project."

"Good. Hopefully, that will keep you away from mischief and away from stairs for a while."

"I make no promises."

"If you are in the village, maybe I will see you. I always try to attend Father Evenson's morning Mass."

He reached for her hand, brought it up to his lips, and kissed it. "Aah, you are sweet, my dear. I won't see you there, but perhaps we can find another opportunity to cross paths."

"I would like that. If nothing else, you can come see me in a week, and I will take out your stitches. Now, for tonight, I think we can continue with the pills you have been taking today. They should be strong enough to relieve the pain and help you sleep. At this point, rest is what is going to help your body heal. How does that sound?"

"Whatever you say. I trust your judgment."

"Thank you," Mary Elizabeth said. She handed him a glass of water and the pills. "I will leave you six pills for tomorrow. Take two every four hours if you need them for pain."

Mary Elizabeth began to pack her things. "Here are some breathing exercises I would like you to do throughout the day tomorrow. Take deep breaths as deep as you can, like this." She demonstrated.

Viscount LeBrosse took a deep breath. "Oooh, my ribs!" He shook his head. "No, it hurts too much."

Taking an extra pillow from the end of his bed, she said, "Here. Hold this pillow to your ribs. That should help with the pain. But you must try. Otherwise, you could develop pneumonia. Let's wait twenty minutes, and then I'll have you try those breathing exercises again. By then, the pills should be working on your pain." Mary Elizabeth pulled a chair over to his bedside. She took his hand. She asked him questions about his life in Belgium.

After twenty minutes had passed, the viscount tried the breathing exercises again. This time he could take several deep breaths.

"Very good!" Mary Elizabeth said. She could see that the viscount was having a hard time keeping his eyes open. She patted his hand. "Good night, Viscount. Sweet dreams."

Mary Elizabeth quietly slipped out of the room after Viscount LeBrosse fell asleep. She spoke to the police officer stationed outside his door. "How are you this evening, officer?"

"Very well, thank you, Dr. Senty."

"Viscount LeBrosse should sleep through the night. But please look in on him a few times. I expect his condition to keep improving. If anything changes, please call the surgery."

"Yes, Doctor," the officer replied.

Mary Elizabeth spotted Mr. Jameson coming from Lord Brantwell's room. "Mr. Jameson, Lord Brantwell will be needing his supplies now."

"Yes, Doctor," he replied, "I will bring them to his room."

"Thank you." Mary Elizabeth then went down to Lord Brantwell's room and knocked on the door. She heard Lord Brantwell beckon her in.

Lord Brantwell was still wearing his street clothes.

"Good evening, Lord Brantwell. You are my last patient before I go back to the village. I know I am a little early, but I wonder if I could give you your medicine now."

"Yes, of course. I will go and change." He went into his dressing room.

Mary Elizabeth walked over to the desk with her medical bag. She had her back to the door and was busy laying out the needed supplies. She heard the door open but thought it was Mr. Jameson.

Lord Brantwell came back into the room in his pajamas and dressing gown and exclaimed in a loud voice, "Bea!"

His voice startled Mary Elizabeth, who turned around. Her stethoscope hung around her neck.

Lady Beatrice asked, "Isn't it a bit early to turn in?" Looking over and seeing Mary Elizabeth, her voice dripped with sarcasm. "Is this a party for two, or can anyone join?"

Lord Brantwell stood in stunned silence.

Mary Elizabeth looked at him and then Lady Beatrice. "I'm sorry, Lady Beatrice. I am afraid I must ask you to leave. This is a professional call."

Lady Beatrice remarked incredulously. "What?"

Lord Brantwell said, "It's true, Bea. Please go."

"Geoff, are you ill?"

"Bea, please leave. I will explain later."

Lady Beatrice left the room, slamming the door behind her.

Lord Brantwell sunk into his chair. "I was trying so hard to avoid this."

Mary Elizabeth went over to his chair and crouched down. "What do you mean? I am sure Lady Beatrice will understand."

Lord Brantwell looked at Mary Elizabeth. "Our relationship is"—he paused for a moment—"complicated." He went on, "You see, I contracted this parasite while I was on my hunting safari in Africa. Bea begged me not to go, but I went anyway. She has not forgiven me. I have not told her that I am sick." He sighed. "I guess I did not want her to know that she was right. I am sure she thinks I am having an affair."

"But why would she assume you are having an affair?"

Lord Brantwell shifted uneasily in his chair. "Because I had an affair many years ago. Bea had suffered a miscarriage, and while she was recuperating, I broke our marriage vow. Afterwards, I was tormented by guilt. I confessed it to her and begged for her forgiveness." He turned to Mary Elizabeth. "You see, I do love her. I always have and always will. I don't expect you to understand, but the affair was my way of dealing with the loss of our baby."

"I am so sorry, Lord Brantwell. Please do not think that I judge you."

"Thank you. And since I have returned from Africa, I have been avoiding her. I began to feel ill on the last days of the safari. I saw my doctor immediately upon my return. He explained that I was still contagious, and if Bea and I had marital relations, I could pass the parasite on to her. I didn't want her to contract the disease, so I stayed away from the manor. Besides, it was easier to stay in London to receive the treatments."

Mary Elizabeth said, "I see."

"The night before I arrived home, Bea called me at my London apartment. She wanted to talk about the gala. During our conversation, the private nurse arrived. I told Bea I had to go to attend to an urgent business matter and that I would see her the next day. Bea heard the nurse's voice in the background talking to my valet. She accused me of having an affair. I told her if she didn't believe my denial, then she could think what she liked. I hung up on her. Our relationship has been strained ever since that night."

"I know it is not my place to say, but don't you think it is time to tell Lady Beatrice the truth? Keeping this to yourself is a heavy burden to bear. And from a professional point of view, it is not doing your health any good, either. Believe me, telling the truth can be healing. Shall we get started?"

Monday, October 26

CHAPTER 38

Back to Business

Mary Elizabeth stayed in the pew and said extra prayers after Monday's Mass ended. She lit two votive candles. By this time, the church had emptied. Father Evenson came to her. "My, my. A two-candle day?"

"I'm afraid so," Mary Elizabeth said. "You know, I always light a candle for my patients."

"Yes, and the other?"

"The other is for me and Chief Inspector Donnelly," she said sadly. "I hope that wasn't too selfish."

Father Evenson replied kindly, "Not at all. Can I help? Would you like to talk?"

"Yes, Father Matt, I would. But I can't today." She checked her watch. "I'm due at the surgery now. I have to run. Please say a prayer for me."

Monday morning found the Bellechester Constabulary full of activity. Chief Inspector Donnelly gathered the senior officers from the other constabularies under his command. "Inspectors, even though we gave our best effort to provide security for the Brantwell gala, another jewel heist has occurred. It will take all of us to solve this crime. I know your constabularies are small, but I would like you to each assign one of your officers to help with this case."

Inspector Brown spoke up. "That will put a big strain on our manpower. These thieves have struck our area several times now, and we have been unable to solve the crimes. What makes you think that this time will be any different?"

Will replied, "Because we will be expanding the members of our team. I have spoken to Chief Superintendent Williamson. He has asked

Chief Constable Scott to supply one officer from the Shrewsbury Office to each of your constabularies. With every office contributing an officer, we are all a part of this investigation. Chief Constable Scott has also authorized overtime pay for this case. I also spoke to Superintendent Billingsby from London's Metropolitan Police Crimes against Property Division. He agreed to send one officer from his unit. He also extended to us the use of their forensics laboratory. I can tell you from experience, their lab is the finest in the land."

Inspector Masterson said, "I can see that the additional manpower and facilities will be useful. But what about the other crimes in our area?"

"For the time being, work on serious offenses only. Solving lesser crimes will be put on hold for now. All vacations are canceled. Leave requests will be run through me and approved on a case-by-case basis. Our investigation must be fluid. The landscape will be changing daily. I ask for your cooperation and your patience."

Inspector Holcomb said, "Sounds good, Chief Inspector. Where do we start?"

"Once I have the names of your officers, I will be assigning men to teams. Like working on a giant jigsaw puzzle, each group will concentrate on a different aspect of the case. We will meet weekly to keep everyone abreast of our progress. The important thing is that we are not starting from scratch. We have the files from past robberies. And our heavy police presence at Brantwell Manor has already yielded some evidence. Now, are there any other questions? No questions? Each of you, please have your member of the team report to this office tomorrow by 9:00 a.m. That is all. Dismissed."

After the inspectors left, Will divided the different aspects of the case into work groups. Officers found empty firework casings in the woods. They had been the source of the loud bangs. Will would give that information to one group to trace.

Another group would investigate the guest lists and the extra help hired by the estates that had suffered jewel thefts. Officer Collins had provided a good description of the maid who had delivered the tea to him. Her sketch would be shown to the butlers and housekeepers in the area. One of the canine units discovered a red wig that had been thrown into the trash.

Dr. Senty also played a role in the investigation. The blood sample she had taken from Officer Collins might show what drug was used on him. The forensics lab at the Met would be doing the analysis. Local doctors and pharmacists in the area could then be interviewed.

One of the detective groups would investigate the orchestra, the photographer, the rental company, and any other business that had provided goods and services for the event. The final group would work with the Met and Interpol to see if the events of the weekend matched any of the modus operandi of known English and European jewel thieves.

Each group would have a piece of the puzzle. Will hoped that by putting together the pieces, a picture of the jewel thieves would emerge.

When Mary Elizabeth returned to the Brantwell estate that evening, she found an empty bed where Viscount LeBrosse had been. She called out, "Viscount, where are you?"

Viscount LeBrosse's voice commanded, "Stay there. I am coming to you."

He strode out from the bathroom dressed in his street clothes. He walked with no assistance except for his trademark silver-handled cane. Standing in front of her, he made a short bow while holding his ribs. He kissed her hand.

Mary Elizabeth cried, "What a nice surprise! You have made my day. What remarkable progress you have made."

"I was hoping you would be pleased. May I go with you tonight? I do not want to stay here a minute longer," Viscount LeBrosse said.

"Why? What's wrong?"

"It all started after breakfast this morning. Lady Beatrice and Lord Brantwell began arguing. Lots of doors slamming. More arguing. It would quit for a while, and then it would start up again. It went on until teatime. Please take me with you tonight. My poor nerves are shot. I can't bear to hear any more doors slamming today."

"I don't blame you for wanting to leave this place. Tell you what. I will give you a short exam. If everything checks out, then I will take you back with me to Bellechester. If there are no lights on at Father Evenson's, you can stay with Dr. Merton and me at the surgery. We have plenty of room. Is that agreeable?"

"Yes, thank you."

Mary Elizabeth took off her stethoscope. "Everything checks out. The stitches in your head are healing nicely. How has your pain been today?"

"I only used four pills."

"That's good news. You can take those other two pills with you. I don't think I need to give you anything else tonight. I will ask Jameson to carry your bags to the car. I don't want you carrying anything yet. Please, please hold on to the railing and to Jameson's arm when you are walking down the stairs. Take it slow and easy. Promise?"

"Promise."

"I will meet you downstairs in about an hour."

After leaving Viscount LeBrosse's room, she spoke to the officer stationed in the hallway. "Viscount LeBrosse will be leaving the manor with me tonight. He will be staying in the village."

The officer replied, "Very good, Doctor. I will call Chief Inspector Donnelly and see if he wants me to continue guarding Viscount LeBrosse."

Mary Elizabeth replied, "Thank you." She knocked on Lord Brantwell's door. She heard voices inside the room, so she called out, "Lord Brantwell, it's Dr. Senty. May I come in?"

Lord Brantwell came to the door and opened it a crack. "Is it that time already? Sorry. Bit of a mess in here. How about I meet you in the study in ten minutes."

"Fine," Mary Elizabeth replied. "Please remember to bring your medicine and your folder with you."

Mary Elizabeth met Mr. Jameson downstairs. "Mr. Jameson, Lord Brantwell asked me to give him his final treatment in the study."

"Very good, Dr. Senty. Will you be needing the usual supplies?"

"Yes. I will also need your assistance with Viscount LeBrosse. He will be leaving with me this evening."

"Yes, Dr. Senty." Mr. Jameson escorted her to the study. Mary Elizabeth set out her instruments on the desk. While she was waiting, her mind went back to the last time she'd been in this room. She could still see Officer Collins lying motionless on the carpet. Will was at her side. *Darn! I wasn't going to think of him today.* The sound of Lord and Lady Brantwell entering the study brought her out of her reverie. They were wearing their nightclothes and robes. Lord Brantwell was carrying his medicine, and Lady Beatrice was carrying his chart. They deposited both on the desk.

Lord Brantwell said, "Good evening, again, Dr. Senty. I hope you don't mind if Bea stays and watches the procedure."

Mary Elizabeth was surprised. "No, if you give your consent, then it is all right with me. Did you tell her about your condition and what the treatment entails?"

Lord Brantwell held Lady Beatrice's hand and gave her a loving look. Then he turned to Mary Elizabeth and said, "Yes, I followed your advice. I told her about my condition, but I will leave the description of the treatment up to you."

Mary Elizabeth turned to Lady Beatrice. "What do you know?"

"I understand Geoff contracted a blood parasite when he was on his African safari."

Mary Elizabeth explained, "Yes, Lord Brantwell contracted African Trypanosomiasis, commonly known as sleeping sickness. Luckily, he saw his doctor in London as soon as he started having symptoms. His doctor prescribed the drug pentamidine. This antibiotic will kill the parasites. Lord Brantwell needed to receive a dose of this drug every day for ten days."

Lady Brantwell turned to her husband. "When I would call your London apartment, your butler would tell me that you were unavailable. I thought you were having an affair. My fears were confirmed when I heard the same woman's voice in the background every night no matter what time I called in the evening," Lady Beatrice said.

"My doctor sent the same nurse each time. It was easier, for she knew exactly what to do. And Mr. Higgins was telling you the truth. In London, I received the medicine through an IV.

Those treatments would last over two hours," Lord Brantwell said.

"But you didn't bring a nurse here to the manor. I saw no IV apparatus," Lady Beatrice said.

"How could I bring in a nurse? I was trying to hide my condition. Since Dr. Senty was spending the weekend, I asked her to give me the medicine," Lord Brantwell said.

"Lord Brantwell received six of the ten doses in London. I have given him three doses over the weekend. Tonight, I will be administering his final dose. Since we don't have the equipment here to do an infusion, I have been giving him his medicine as an injection. Are you sure you want to stay and watch?"

Before Lady Brantwell could answer, there was a knock on the study door. "Come in," Lord Brantwell said.

Mr. Jameson came into the room with an ice bag and towel. "Sir, I brought your usual."

"Thank you. Put it on the desk, Mr. Jameson."

"As you wish, sir. Do you need me to stay this evening?" Mr. Jameson asked.

Lord Brantwell looked over at Lady Beatrice. Lady Beatrice bit her lip and shook her head.

"No, thank you, Mr. Jameson. Lady Beatrice will be with me tonight."

"Very good, sir," Mr. Jameson said. He closed the door as he left the study.

Mary Elizabeth asked, "Shall we get started?"

"Where do you want me?" Lord Brantwell asked.

Mary Elizabeth pulled out a chair from the rosewood table and placed it sideways. "Lord Brantwell, please, if you will be seated, I will get the numbers for today."

Lady Beatrice sat on the red velvet sofa.

Lord Brantwell shed his dressing gown and pajama top and sat in the chair. Mary Elizabeth took his temperature, listened to his heart and lungs, and took his blood pressure. "All your numbers look good," she said as she recorded them in his chart. "Yesterday I jabbed the right, so it looks like I will need access to your left side tonight." She then walked over to the desk and prepared the injection.

Lord Brantwell put his pajama top back on. He took the chair he was sitting in and set it at the head of the sofa. "Excuse me, darling. I am afraid we need to switch places now. Here, you sit in this chair, and I need to lie on the couch."

"Of course, dear," Lady Beatrice said as she got up and moved to the chair.

Lord Brantwell got himself situated on the couch. "Bea, could you bring over the ice pack, please?" he asked.

Lady Brantwell walked over to the table. When she returned to the couch, Lord Brantwell lowered his pajama bottoms slightly. When she caught sight of his bruised bottom, she sharply inhaled. "Oh, Geoff!"

"Now, Bea, I'm sure it looks worse than it feels. Place it on my left side. Up a tad. There. Aaah!"

"Geoff, I am so sorry that you have to go through this."

"It is a small price to pay for the pain I caused you. In some ways, I prefer the jabs to sitting with a needle in my hand for two hours. These jabs are over in a few minutes. Dr. Senty knows a lot of tricks for making these injections less painful. Our doctors could take a few lessons from her. Thank you, Bea. You can take the ice bag off now." He dried the site with the towel. "Dr. Senty, I am ready. Pick a good spot."

"Lady Brantwell, I am going to clean the area with alcohol. We wait a minute for it to dry. All right, Lord Brantwell, last jab. One, two, three," Mary Elizabeth said and slowly injected the medicine.

Lady Brantwell said, "I can't bear to watch any longer." She turned her head and focused her gaze on her husband's face. When she saw Lord Brantwell grimace, she began to gently stroke his back.

"Yes, this medicine does need to be injected slowly so his muscles can absorb it. You're doing fine, Lord Brantwell. Remember to breathe. Almost done. There, a little pressure, and we are all finished."

"Bea, the ice pack, please." Lord Brantwell's voice was a bit strained.

"Of course, dear." She gently placed the ice pack over the site and continued to stroke his back.

"Lord Brantwell, have you made your follow-up appointment with Dr. Winston in London?" Mary Elizabeth asked as she cleaned up her materials.

"Yes, I see him on Thursday."

"Dr. Winston is very respected—a leader in his field. Lady Brantwell, your husband needs to remain in a prone position for about an hour. That helps prevent any side effects from occurring. But so far, he has tolerated the medicine very well. How are you feeling Lord Brantwell? Any light-headedness? Nausea?"

"A little nausea."

Mary Elizabeth handed him a cup of peppermint tea. "Any questions for me, Lady Brantwell?"

"Is he cured?"

"Dr. Winston can answer that question better than I can. It is my understanding that Lord Brantwell will go in for checkups periodically. But since the disease was caught early, and he has finished the treatments, the prognosis for a full recovery is very good."

"Well, I am glad to hear that. I want Geoff around for a long time to come," Lady Beatrice said as she took Lord Brantwell's hand.

The trio talked until Mary Elizabeth looked at her watch. "Lord Brantwell, can you sit up for me? Take it slow. May I take your temperature and blood pressure one last time?"

"Of course." Lord Brantwell complied with Dr. Senty's request.

Mary Elizabeth recorded his numbers. "If you don't mind, I am taking Viscount LeBrosse back to town tonight. He has made a remarkable recovery. Thank you for letting him stay a day longer."

Lady Brantwell said, "It was our pleasure. Here, I will walk out with you."

Lord Brantwell also stood up. "Thank you, Dr. Senty. Good night."

Tuesday, November 3 – Wednesday, November 4

CHAPTER 39

A LITTLE SLEUTHING

On Tuesday of that first week of November, Lady Beatrice dropped in at St. Anselm's Rectory. "I've just returned from the photography studio. Mr. Miller called and said the proofs from the gala were ready to be picked up, and here they are."

She spread them out on the dining room table. Mrs. Winters, Father Evenson, and Viscount LeBrosse all gathered round.

Mrs. Winters said, "Oh, these are lovely."

Father Evenson said, "The photographer did an excellent job capturing everyone at the gala.

Here, excuse me. I'm going to get my magnifying glass so I can get a better look."

Viscount LeBrosse asked, "What are you going to do with all of these pictures?"

"I was thinking of making a photo album for Dr. Senty. She can keep it as a memento to remind her of the gala. And the others, I will send out in my Christmas cards."

Mrs. Winters piped up, "And will you be making an album for the chief inspector too?"

Viscount LeBrosse asked, "Do you think he needs a reminder?"

Mrs. Winters stated emphatically, "Certainly. The gala was over a week ago, and I don't think Dr. Senty has heard a word from him."

Lady Beatrice said, "I suppose he is busy with the investigation."

"That's no excuse."

"Well, two albums it is," Lady Beatrice answered.

Father Evenson inquired, "Lady Beatrice, would you mind leaving these pictures here with me for a few days? I would like to take a closer look at them."

"Do you think they hold some clues to solving the jewelry heist?"

"Well, they do say a picture is worth a thousand words," Father Evenson replied.

On the appointed day, Father Evenson was pacing impatiently in the hallway. While he was always ready to go anywhere in his basic black cassock and white clergy collar, Viscount LeBrosse took considerable pains choosing his outfit for this visit. Now fully recovered from his tumble down the stairs at Brantwell Manor, this was his first foray with Bellechester's social elite since the accident. He finally settled on a gray windowpane-plaid houndstooth-pattern wool jacket with matching trousers. He wore a crisp white shirt, and for a dash of color, he chose a crimson diamond-tip bow tie and matching pocket square. His signature silver-handled black cane completed his outfit.

When Mrs. Winters saw him, she teased, "Oh, be still my heart. Viscount LeBrosse, how dapper you look today. If I didn't know better, I would say you are going courting."

Viscount LeBrosse replied, "Well, maybe I am. Mrs. Phillips is single, yes?"

Mrs. Winters, tea towel in hand, shooed them out the door, laughing. "Be gone with the both of you."

Viscount LeBrosse, always one to ride in style, hired a 1957 blue Rolls Royce Silver Dawn and driver to take them the fifteen miles to Mrs. Phillips's home. The ride through the countryside was pleasant. The trees were bare and confirmed that autumn was giving way to winter.

The great house of the Phillips' estate sat atop a hill. It now belonged to Mrs. Phillips's son and his family. Mrs. Phillips herself resided in the carriage house that was located at the rear of the property. It had been recently refurbished into a two-story cottage with all the modern conveniences. In the front were meticulously cared-for flower gardens. Mrs. Phillips had a housekeeper who doubled as a cook, a gardener-chauffeur, and a maid to look after her.

Mrs. Phillips's maid greeted them at the door, took their hats and coats, and showed them into the sitting room, where the great lady sat in a high-backed chair. She wore a deep-blue dress and a matching three-quarter-sleeve jacket. Her gold, apple-shaped diamond-and-ruby brooch sparkled on her jacket. Her white hair was coiffed with soft curls. She had a regal air about her that commanded respect and deference. Sunday manners were the order of the day when paying her a visit.

Viscount LeBrosse took and kissed her hand. "My lady, you are looking younger every time I see you. You must tell me your secret."

"Oh, Viscount LeBrosse, you are full of it, but I could listen to you all day. And dear Father Evenson, I am glad for your company too. Shall I pour?"

They settled into their chairs and drank their tea.

Father Evenson inquired, "And how did you enjoy Lady Beatrice's gala?"

"Lady Beatrice throws such wonderful parties. Her guests are always the crème de la crème of society. But I must say, her standards are slipping."

Viscount LeBrosse was surprised by her remark. "What do you mean?"

"Going to such elaborate lengths to fete a doctor who turns out to be an American daughter of a farmer and a chief inspector from who knows where; why, they are commoners. Why should we be honoring them? Well, I never!"

Viscount LeBrosse responded, "If you spent any time with Dr. Senty, I am sure you would find her delightful. She is so kind."

"I know she nursed you back to health. I can see now that she has also turned your head. You are taken with her." She wagged her finger at the viscount. "But I am not so easily fooled. What is a woman doing in a man's profession? Doesn't she know her place? I have seen it time and time again: people trying to move up in society not befitting their station. Wearing a field-stone necklace and a cheap tiara! It was as if she were mocking those of us who were wearing the real thing. I found her behavior disgusting," Mrs. Phillips said.

Father Evenson replied, "God sees into our souls. And it should be our souls that are decorated with the jewels of virtue and good works."

"Save your sermon for your flock, Father. More tea?"

Both Father Evenson and Viscount LeBrosse held out their cups. "Yes, please."

As she poured the tea, Viscount LeBrosse said, "Well, Mrs. Phillips, you won't have to worry about Dr. Senty wearing her agate necklace again, because someone stole it!"

His statement disconcerted Mrs. Phillips so much that she almost spilled the tea.

"I hadn't heard," she said, not very convincingly.

"No matter. I hear the chief inspector is employing all his forces to find the thief and bring him to justice," Father Evenson reported.

Mrs. Phillips replied, "Why should he do that with all of those real gems still missing?"

"Anyone who saw the chief inspector and Dr. Senty at the gala cannot doubt their feelings for one another. Did you see how they danced together? Word is, he will be going to any lengths to get that necklace back for her," Viscount LeB-rosse reported.

Father Evenson added, "And you know that love, like jealousy or envy, propels people to do uncharacteristic and sometimes foolish things. I am sure it is just a matter of time before the culprit is caught." He sat back in his chair and looked over to Mrs. Phillips.

Mrs. Phillips shifted uneasily in her chair and averted her eyes.

Viscount LeBrosse asked, "Wasn't your room next to Dr. Senty's? Did you see any unusual activity around her room on Saturday?"

"No. And I find all this talk about Dr. Senty's necklace quite upsetting. Can we please talk about something else?" Mrs. Phillips asked.

Father Evenson said, "I am sorry you left the manor so early on Sunday. There were some interesting developments later that day."

"Oh, do tell." And so, Father Evenson told her all about Lord and Lady Porter.

"That is most interesting, I would never have guessed. I would have put my money on Baroness Whitacre," Mrs. Phillips said.

Viscount LeBrosse inquired, "Why is that?"

Mrs. Phillips suddenly perked up. "I saw the baroness give the server a bottle of pills."

Father Evenson asked, "Do you remember what the server looked like?"

"Very plain-looking, but I remember, she did have red hair."

Father Evenson answered, "Very interesting."

Mrs. Phillips continued, "And it is no secret that their estate is no longer capable of financing their extravagant lifestyle."

Viscount LeBrosse sounded surprised. "I thought their property is located in a most prosperous part of the county."

"But very poorly managed. The baron prefers to spend his time pursuing other, shall we say, affairs. The baroness tries hard to pick up the slack, but the poor woman can only do so much," Mrs. Phillips replied.

Father Evenson responded, "Very sorry to hear it."

"Now, let's talk about more pleasant things. Viscount, how long will you be in the area?"

"Father Evenson has asked me to help with a project. I do not know how long I will be here," Viscount LeBrosse answered. "Now that the weather is turning colder, do you have any travel plans? I hear Monaco is the place to be this winter."

The three of them continued their conversation for a few minutes. Then, Father Evenson stood up and announced, "This has been a delightful visit, but I am afraid I must get back to the parish."

"Thank you both for coming. It was a most pleasant way to spend the afternoon," replied Mrs. Phillips.

Viscount LeBrosse stood up, took Mrs. Phillips's hand, kissed it, and said, "Thank you, Mrs. Phillips, for the tea and the conversation. It is always a pleasure to share your company. Before I leave, may I use the facilities?"

"Of course. It is just down the hall."

Viscount LeBrosse left the room, but instead of going down the hall, he snuck upstairs.

While he was gone, Father Evenson said to Mrs. Phillips, "Do you see much of your son and his family?"

"With my son, it is business, always business. He is just like his father. No time for family."

"What about your grandchildren? Do they visit?"

"The older ones are away at school. And the younger ones are busy with friends." She sighed. "No time for their grandmother."

"I am sorry to hear that. If you ever want to unburden your soul, you just have to call. I do make house calls. Confession can be so freeing."

Mrs. Phillips said, with surprise, "Father, I have no idea what you mean. What would I have to confess?"

"That is between you and God," he replied.

Viscount LeBrosse returned to the sitting room. Mrs. Phillips rang for her maid, who retrieved their coats and hats.

"Au revoir, my dear lady, until we meet again." Viscount LeBrosse bowed slightly.

Father Evenson took her hand and kissed it. "Remember, Mrs. Phillips, I am only a phone call away if you need me."

"Thank you, Father. Please come again, both of you. Goodbye." The maid then showed the men out.

Father Evenson and Viscount LeBrosse got into the car and were soon on their way back to the village. Father Evenson said, "That was a most productive visit. I gathered some interesting and useful tidbits."

Viscount LeBrosse, patting his front pocket, said, "As did I."

Sunday, November 8 through Monday, November 9

CHAPTER 40

Keeping Busy

Mary Elizabeth sat in the rectory kitchen sipping tea with Mrs. Winters. She pulled a list from her purse.

"Usually, I do not mind being so far away from home. It is just during the holidays that I get homesick. One of my favorite holidays is Thanksgiving. This year, I would like to celebrate it with my new Bellechester friends. To pull this dinner off, I am afraid I will need your help, Mrs. Winters. Could you help me prepare some of the food?"

"Certainly, Doctor."

"Oh, please, please call me Mary Elizabeth."

"All right, Mary Elizabeth. What food will you be serving?"

"I would like to make a traditional Thanksgiving dinner, just like we would have at home. That means turkey with apple-and-raisin stuffing, mashed potatoes, giblet gravy, cranberries, relishes, salad, and both pumpkin and pecan pies for dessert. Thanksgiving is celebrated on the fourth Thursday in November, but I would like to move the dinner to the following Sunday, the twenty-ninth of November. That would give me more time to pull everything together."

"How can I help?"

"No one bakes better pies than you do. If I give you the recipe, would you mind making the pumpkin and pecan pies?"

"I would love to. Do you need help with anything else?"

"Could you also make the giblet gravy? I was thinking of asking Father Matt and Viscount LeBrosse to peel the potatoes, Lady Beatrice . . ."

"Lady Beatrice?"

". . . to bring the wine and relishes, Sarah to bring a salad, and I will take care of the rest."

"How many people will you be inviting?"

"If everyone comes, there will be ten of us."

"I will be happy to help."

"Thank you. I knew I could count on you. I will send out the invitations this week."

Superintendent Billingsby had sent Inspector Trevor Jones to be the Metropolitan Police Department's contribution to the investigation. Trevor stayed at Will's house. Trevor's team was following up on the companies that had been hired for the gala. They'd found nothing out of the ordinary. And yet, when it came to the photographer, they made an uncomfortable discovery.

Trevor took Will aside. "Will, I think you will want to investigate Miller Photography yourself."

"Why, what have you found?"

"When we got to the shop, we decided this investigation would best be handled by you. Turns out, this could be rather sensitive for you, and we did not want to pry into your personal affairs."

"Trevor, what do you mean?"

Inspector Jones slapped Will's back. "Trust me, old chap. You want to take care of this one yourself. We still have the rental company for the tables and chairs to check out."

Will decided to visit Miller's Photography Studio later that afternoon. He took Sergeant O'Hanlon with him. Will had one hand on the doorknob when Sergeant O'Hanlon said, "Chief Inspector, before we go in, I think you may want to see this."

"Sergeant?"

Sergeant O'Hanlon pointed at the window display. "You and Dr. Senty."

Will stepped away from the door and walked over to Sergeant O'Hanlon. He glanced in the window and then did a double take. There, in the middle of the window, sitting on an easel, was a very large, framed color picture of him and Mary Elizabeth. They were dancing at the gala. The photographer shot them smiling and looking into each other's eyes. Underneath the picture was a large sign, "Capture the Magic with Miller Photography."

Will was stunned. He understood why Detective Jones wanted him to do this investigation.

"That is a very good likeness of both you and Dr. Senty. Looks like he did."

"Did what?"

"Capture the magic."

"Sergeant! Let's not forget why we are here," Will said in quiet desperation.

"Yes, sir."

There was no clerk in the shop, so they rang the bell on the counter. Shortly, Mr. Miller, an older man in his mid-seventies, came out from behind a curtain. "Good afternoon, gentlemen. What can I do for you?"

"Mr. Miller?"

"Yes?"

Will took his warrant card from his pocket. "I'm Chief Inspector Donnelly, and this is Sergeant O'Hanlon. We are here about the photographs that were taken at the Brantwell Gala a few weeks ago."

Mr. Miller leaned over the counter to get a closer look at Will. "Say, you're the young fellow in the picture in the window, aren't you? You and the missus are very photogenic. I got more business from that one picture than I have ever received off a photo before. Thanks to you, all my photographers are now booked solid through the new year. I suppose you want to buy that photograph in the window for the missus. I will hate to part with it, but it would make a great Christmas gift for her. She will love it!"

Sergeant O'Hanlon was trying hard to keep a straight face.

"Mr. Miller," Will's voice rose. "We are here on official police business. We would like prints of all the photographs that were taken at the gala. We would also like to talk to the photographer who worked that event."

"You don't have to yell. I may be old, but I'm not deaf. Sure, I can get you the prints. It will take me a few days to print them. Gilbert Pimpkins took a lot of pictures that night. All those rich people like to look at themselves. That is how we make our money. Although, I must say,

Lord and Lady Brantwell were most generous in paying for our services. Why, Lady Brantwell was just in the other day to order more copies of some of the prints. If my memory serves me correctly, most of the reprints she ordered were of you and the missus."

"Dr. Senty is not my missus."

"Is she a doctor? That pretty thing? Well, now I've heard everything. A woman doctor. How 'bout that. She isn't married to anyone else, is she?"

"No."

"You aren't married to anyone else, are you?"

"No."

"Well, that's good. Wouldn't want to be accused of promoting any sort of impropriety. We are, after all, a family business. Say, why isn't she your missus? It's as plain as the nose on your face that there is something special between you two. Pictures don't lie. What are you waiting for?" Mr. Miller wagged his finger at Will. "Better be careful, young fellow, before someone else snatches her up."

Will was doing a slow burn.

Sergeant O'Hanlon could see Will was about to erupt. "Mr. Miller, if you could provide us with the contact information for Gilbert Pimpkins, we will be on our way."

"Yes, I have that information in the back. It will just take me a few minutes to find it. In the meantime, go ahead, look around."

Will turned to Sergeant O'Hanlon. "You stepped in at the right time. Thank you. And Sergeant?"

"Yes?"

"I would appreciate it if none of what Mr. Miller said was ever repeated."

"Of course, sir. Mr. Miller consented to reprint the gala photos for us. He is also supplying us with the photographer's information. That is all I remember."

"Thank you, Sergeant for your discretion." Will pulled out his wallet and removed his business card.

Mr. Miller returned with an index card. "Here is the information for Gilbert."

Sergeant O'Hanlon took out his pad and pencil. "Here, I can copy it down."

Will handed Mr. Miller his card. "Please call me at the station when the prints are ready to be picked up."

Mr. Miller looked at the card. "Sure. Like I said, it will take a few days."

"Sergeant? Are you finished?"

"Yes, sir."

"Would you mind waiting for me in the car for a few minutes?"

"Of course not, sir. Nice to meet you, Mr. Miller."

"Good day to you, Sergeant."

Sergeant O'Hanlon walked out of the store and got into the driver's side of the car. A few minutes later, he saw Mr. Miller remove the picture from the window. It was not long to wait before Will came out of the store carrying a large wrapped package.

Sergeant O'Hanlon opened the boot, and Will placed the package inside. As Will got into the car, he said, "Would you mind stopping by my house on the way back to the station?"

Sergeant O'Hanlon replied, "Not at all, sir."

Thursday, November 12

CHAPTER 41

A BREAK IN THE CASE

Inspector Holcomb phoned Will. "Morning, Chief. Our team was able to trace the fireworks to a business in Shrewsbury. The owner said he sold several fireworks to a middle-aged man. He wore a beard, and his clothes smelled like pigs. He loaded the fireworks into the back of an older-model black pickup truck with lots of rust around the wheels. The next week, a young man with blond hair bought a large quantity of fireworks. The owner remembered him because his clothes also smelled like pigs. He drove an identical black pickup truck."

"Great job. Did the owner remember any of the license plate?"

"No. It wasn't much to go on, but a pub owner in Croyton said one of his regulars came into some money recently. He paid his bar tab and was settling accounts all over the village. The pub owner's description of his customer matches the description of the older man given by the fireworks distributor. The pub owner also said the man owns a pig farm west of the village, drives a black pickup, and has a blond-haired son. I'd like to bring them in for questioning."

"See if you can also get a search warrant. I'd like to have the forensics team at the Met go over the truck. We are looking for any residue from the fireworks. We also need a print of the tires to see if the tread matches any of the tracks found in the woods at Brantwell Manor. I believe casts were made of the tracks."

"Right, Chief. I would also like to have our sketch artist from Shrewsbury present at the questioning to see if we can identify who gave them the money to buy the fireworks. Do you also want to be present for the interviews?"

"Yes, I would. But you will take the lead."

"Thanks, Chief. Our team will get right on it."

That afternoon, Will traveled to Inspector Holcomb's constabulary in Clun. The father, Bradley Kingston, and son, Kenneth, were questioned separately. Kenneth said he had answered a classified ad in the local paper in late September. A man with a heavy French accent answered the call. He instructed Kenneth to meet a woman wearing a large floppy brown hat and a tweed cape at a pub in Holdingford at 2:00 p.m. the following day. Kenneth had no problem meeting his contact. He remembered that the woman wore sunglasses inside the pub. She'd given him an envelope full of cash to buy the fireworks. The woman had said Lady Brantwell wanted to surprise her husband for his sixty-fifth birthday. Fireworks were to be set off at 4:30 a.m. on October 24 on the north side of the Brantwell estate grounds and at 4:35 a.m. on the south side of the grounds. Kenneth had received another envelope upon completion of the task. That had been given to him Saturday at 11:30 a.m. by another woman who wore the same hat and cape to the pub.

After interviewing the son for over an hour, Inspector Holcomb asked to speak to Will. "Sorry, Chief, he isn't giving us much to go on."

"No, but he has given us a few leads. Let's see if we can get a copy of the ad that was placed in the paper. Talk to the editor and see if he can give us a description of the person who placed the ad."

"Right. Should we stop the interview and release Kenneth for now?"

"Not quite yet. I think if we go deeper, he might be able to remember something distinctive about either woman. Do you mind if I give it a go and take the lead?"

"Of course not, Chief."

The chief and Inspector Holcomb went back into the room. Will said, "Just a few more questions, Kenneth. Now, I want you to give me as many details as you remember. If you can't remember, that's all right. We just don't want you making something up because you think we want to hear it. Understand?"

"Yes, sir."

"That day you met the woman who gave you the money to buy the fireworks, who arrived first?"

"She did. She was already seated in a booth when I arrived."

"Was the pub crowded that day?"

"No, I was told to meet her at 2:00 p.m. The lunch crowd had already left."

"So, when you arrived at the pub, you could find a parking space?"

"Yeah, easily."

"Thinking back to arriving at the pub. Did any of the cars parked on the street or in front of the pub seem out of place for a small village like Holdingford?"

"How do you mean *out of place?*"

"You know, fancier, newer model, anything that would stick out as unusual?"

"Now that you mention it, when I drove into the village, there was this sweet 1958 MGA Roadster parked in front of a shop. I slowed down and took a long look. But it was a couple of streets down from the pub."

"Can you remember anything special about the car? Color?"

"It was a white convertible with a dark-red leather interior. The tires were white sidewalls. The top was down, given it being a sunny day."

"Do you happen to recall the license plate?"

"No, I'm sorry."

"Anything else about that car? Any scratches, dents, marks?"

"No, sir. It was shiny, clean, like new. It looked as if it had just been washed and polished. No, that car was well taken care of, I tell you."

"Very good. Now let's move on to the woman. You said she was wearing sunglasses inside the pub. Can you describe the sunglasses? Shape? Any special designs on the frames? Did they look expensive or cheap?"

"They looked expensive. They were that funny shape that women wear, like cat eyes, and they had shiny stones around the top and sides."

"Were her eyebrows showing above the sunglasses? Can you describe them?"

"I don't think she had any. It looked like they were drawn with a pencil."

"Great. Now, the woman handed you the money in an envelope?"

"Yes, that's correct."

"Do you still have that envelope?"

"Yes, it is probably still in the cab of my truck."

"When the woman handed you the money, was she bare handed or wearing gloves?"

"Brown leather gloves that went halfway up her arm."

"Any distinct markings or embellishments on the gloves?"

"No, but I could see she wore a large ring on her right ring finger. When she flexed her hands, you could make out the shape."

"What shape was it?"

"Oval."

"Was she right or left handed?"

"Right-handed."

"Could you see any of her face under the hat and sunglasses?"

"Not very much. She was wearing red lipstick."

"Were her lips full or thin?"

"Full."

"What shape was her chin?"

"It looked like she had a cleft chin."

"Can you describe the woman's voice? Was it high pitched? Low? Did she have an accent? Anything distinctive? Would you recognize her voice again if you heard it?"

"Her voice was lower pitched. She spoke Queen's English. Yes, I think I would recognize the voice."

"Now, let's move on to the second woman." Will asked Kenneth the same questions. From Kenneth's answers, the detectives discovered the second woman was shorter than the first. Her sunglasses were large, round lenses with white frames. Very cheap-looking. The hat and cape were the same. Her body shape was smaller and shorter than the first woman, so the cape hung loosely around her. Her gloves were short, black cloth that went to her to the wrist, which exposed some skin. She was right-handed. She wore no lipstick on her thin lips. Her chin was rounded; very nondescript. Her voice was higher, and she didn't have an accent. Kenneth had not recognized any distinctive cars that day, but it was a Saturday, so the shops and pubs had been quite busy. Kenneth no longer had that payoff envelope. He'd given it to his dad when he handed him his cut, and his dad had given the envelope to Kenneth's mom to reuse.

"Kenneth, after we are done here, we are going to hand you over to a police sketch artist. He is very good. I want you to describe to him just what you told me and any other details you might remember about the two women."

Kenneth asked, "Are Ma, Da, and me going to the nick?"

Will said, "The information you have provided has been very useful. It will all be taken into consideration."

When Will and Inspector Holcomb had left the interview room, the inspector said, "Now I know why you had the highest conviction rate in your department at the Met. I thought I was thorough with my questioning. I can't believe the information you got from him. I swear you could get blood out of a turnip."

Will laughed. "That hasn't happened yet. Over the years I observed the interview techniques of my seniors. I tried to emulate them. I have learned that no detail is insignificant. Sometimes, if you get the witness to remember one thing, other details follow. You just never know what might turn up. Like in this case, I have a hunch that if we find the owner of that 1958 MGA Roadster, we might identity the first woman Kenneth met in the pub."

"I'll get my men to trace the car. There can't be too many Roadsters matching that description on the road."

"Be sure to have your men also look for '55–'59 models, just in case Kenneth was mistaken about the year. But a white convertible with a red or maroon interior is a solid clue."

"You got it, Chief."

"Oh, and one more thing. Once we get a sketch of the hat, cape, gloves, and sunglasses, check all the charity shops in the area. Our thieves might be smart enough to ditch their distinctive clothing. When the teams meet on Friday, let's see if we can get some more manpower to help you trace these leads."

"Thank you, sir. Yes, I think we can use some help."

When they got to the front office, the sketch artist was waiting. Inspector Holcomb made the introductions. "Chief, this is Officer North from Shrewsbury."

Will shook his hand, "Very glad you could be with us today. We will be sending our witness to you shortly. He will be describing two female suspects that were heavily disguised. After you have your sketches, I would like to show you photographs of two women. Could you add the hat and sunglasses to both women?"

"Of course, Chief Inspector. I'll draw anything you want."

"Good. Because I will also need enlargements of the items each woman wore. These will come into play when I submit the information for my search warrants."

"Understood, sir. Where do you want me to set up?"

"You can use this empty room next to the interview room," Inspector Holcomb said.

The father's questioning was much shorter, since he had never met the two women. His only part in the caper had been buying and setting off the fireworks on the south side of the manor.

Will charged each of them with trespassing on private property and sent them away with a fine. They were told they could be recalled for further questioning and so could not leave the country until further notice.

Will said, "Have all the sketches copied for our teams. Send only the sketches of the two women to Superintendent Billingsby at the Met and our contact at Interpol. I think we are getting close, but we still do not have the real mastermind. He was too smart to have shown himself to Kenneth. He is still in the shadows."

"Yes, sir. Before you go back to Bellechester, how about a pint at the White Horse Pub?"

Friday, November 13

CHAPTER 42

TEAM REPORTS

At the day's team meeting, Inspector Brown reported that several of the butlers recognized the woman from Officer North's sketch. She had worked other parties where jewels were stolen. Her name was Ivy Petters, and now they had contact information for her. Lord and Lady Porter and Baron and Baroness Whitacre had attended all the functions she had worked. Will did not bring them in for questioning. For now, they were just identified as persons of interest.

Inspector Watson's team received Officer Collins's toxicology report from the lab at the

Met. Barbiturates had been found in his blood sample. Several days later, Will checked with them to see if they had identified the source of the barbiturates. They were having a difficult time. They had already checked with all the local doctors and pharmacies. No prescriptions were written for any of their prime suspects: Ivy Petters, Lord and Lady Porter, or Baron and Baroness Whitacre. The team had hit a dead end. Will suggested they call the Met's club unit to see what they knew about illegal barbiturate drug sales.

Inspector Holcomb was the last to report. Will asked if any of the other teams could lend Holcomb some team members so Holcomb's team could follow up on leads more quickly. Inspector Holcomb received the names of several new members.

"We have been going at this case pretty hard for a few weeks now, and all our work is finally paying us some dividends. We now have solid leads. I am giving all the teams the weekend off. Let's go at it again on Monday when we are all rested and refreshed," Will said.

After everyone had left, Will went back to his office. He was pleased by everyone's reports, but he kept thinking about Inspector Watson's dead end.

He decided to call Brantwell Manor. "Hello? May I speak to Lady Beatrice?" He had to wait several minutes before she came on the line. "Lady Beatrice, Chief Inspector Donnelly. How are you?"

"Chief Inspector, how nice to hear from you. What can I do for you?"

"I am hoping you can help me with something. Say someone in society, like yourself, needed to acquire drugs for nerves or to help her sleep, and she did not want to go through her regular doctor or pharmacy; how might she obtain them? We are speaking hypothetically, of course."

"Is this about our jewel heist and that poor policeman?"

"Yes, Lady Beatrice. Can you give me any information?"

"Not that I would know from experience, mind you."

"Of course not, Lady Beatrice. Remember, we are only speaking hypothetically."

"Well, I have heard that if you ever need anything along those lines, Dr. Cyrus Barnett of Harley Street would be your man. He is reported to be very discreet and able to supply whatever is needed, for a rather handsome price, mind you. But you must be recommended to him: a friend, or a friend of a friend. It is all very hush-hush and under the table, if you catch my drift."

"Lady Beatrice, may we call on you if we need further assistance?"

"Please do."

"Thank you for the information. Now, it is very, very important that you keep this conversation confidential."

"I understand, Chief Inspector. You can count on my discretion."

"I appreciate that. Good day, Lady Beatrice."

After he hung up, Will called Inspector Watson. They discussed the different options available to them and decided they would ask Lady Beatrice to get an appointment with Dr. Barnett.

Monday, November 16

CHAPTER 43

INVITATIONS DELIVERED

Monday morning after Mass, Mary Elizabeth found Father Evenson in the sacristy. "I'm glad I caught you before I head off to the surgery. Here." She opened her purse and handed Father Evenson several envelopes. "I am hoping you can deliver these to Mrs. Winters and Viscount LeB-rosse for me."

Father Evenson took the envelopes and looked at her rather quizzically. "What are they?"

"These are your invitations to my American Thanksgiving dinner. I hope everyone can come.

Mrs. Winters is helping me prepare the food. It should be a wonderful feast."

"Then you can certainly count me in," Father Evenson said.

"Great."

"Say, we haven't had our talk yet."

"I know, Father Matt. Are you available tomorrow evening?"

"Yes, come to the rectory around seven."

"Sounds good. Gotta run. Still more police physicals this morning."

Father Evenson walked into the kitchen at the rectory and found Viscount LeBrosse eating breakfast and Mrs. Winters sitting at the table having her morning tea.

"Tea, Father?" she asked as she started to rise from her seat.

"No, don't get up. I can get my own cup, thank you. Viscount, I ran into the telegraph messenger boy outside the rectory. This is for you. It looks important," Father Evenson said as he handed the telegram to the Viscount.

"Thank you, Matt." He put the telegram in his shirt pocket. "I'll read it later."

Father Evenson got his cup of tea and joined them at the table. "Dr. Senty handed me these envelopes after Mass. She asked me to deliver them to everyone."

"Oh, these must be the invitations to her Thanksgiving dinner," Mrs. Winters said, eagerly opening hers.

Father Evenson noted, "These envelopes are awfully thick for a simple invitation."

"Thanksgiving? Is that one of those quaint American holidays? Is that the one with turkey?" inquired Viscount LeBrosse.

"Yes, now don't make fun," Mrs. Winters scolded Viscount LeBrosse. "This dinner is very important to Dr. Senty. It's not easy for her to be so far from home on these special occasions."

"I was just asking," answered Viscount LeBrosse, amused by her motherly defense of the American doctor.

It became very quiet around the table as they each opened and read Mary Elizabeth's invitation. Mary Elizabeth had personalized each note. Besides including the basic who, what, when, and where information, she also told each person why she was thankful to have them in her life, and why she hoped they would share this meal with her.

Father Evenson rose from the table. "I must begin work on next Sunday's sermon. Best get to it." He took his invitation and his teacup with him to his study.

Mrs. Winters put her note down and busied herself with the teapot. Her voice cracked a bit as she said, "Better fill up the pot."

After Viscount LeBrosse read his invitation, he folded it and put it in his pocket and continued eating his breakfast. After he finished eating, he took his dishes to the sink and excused himself. A little while later he returned to the kitchen. "I am going to run some errands. Do you need anything from the village, Mrs. Winters?"

"Could you stop at the greengrocer's and pick up some carrots for tonight's stew?"

"Be happy to oblige, Mrs. Winters."

Before he left the rectory, he knocked on Father Evenson's door.

"Come in."

Viscount LeBrosse sat before Father Evenson. His desk was piled high with thick books.

"Matt, I will be leaving Bellechester tomorrow. The telegram was from my contact at the VSSE. I must report to them in Brussels by the end of the week."

"Don't they know you retired?"

"I still do the odd job for them once in a while when my particular skills are required." The viscount rose from his chair. At the door, he stopped. "I will be sorry to miss Dr. Senty's dinner. I have become very fond of her. She reminds me so much of . . ." His voice trailed off.

"Yes, she does. I, too, can see the resemblance." Father Evenson got up from behind his desk and put one hand on the viscount's shoulder. They shook hands. "Be safe, my friend. May God go with you. Come back to us soon."

"Thank you, Matt. I will."

At lunch, Mary Elizabeth handed Dr. Merton and Sarah their Thanksgiving invitations. "I hope you both can come. And Sarah, notice your invitation says *and guest*. I hope you will bring that nice young man who walks you home each evening. Dr. Merton and I would like to meet him."

"I will ask him, but Michael is frightfully shy," Sarah said.

"And Harold, don't worry about our patients. I have already arranged for Dr. Simmons from the hospital to cover us that day. He owes me a favor."

"Wonderful. Then we can both relax and enjoy the evening."

Viscount LeBrosse was seated in the surgery's waiting room right on schedule at 1:00 p.m. sharp.

Mary Elizabeth greeted him cheerfully. "Good afternoon, Viscount LeBrosse. How are you today?"

"Fine. Just anxious to get these stitches out."

"Sure, let's get right to it. Why don't you follow me into the exam room." As she worked, Mary Elizabeth tried to engage Viscount LeBrosse in conversation, but all she got back were one-word answers. Finally, she announced, "There, that's it. You are all done. That area of your head may be tender and sore for a few days, but it has healed nicely." She washed her hands at the sink.

"Thank you, Doctor." Viscount LeBrosse got up to leave.

"Viscount LeBrosse?"

"Yes?"

"Could you come over here and sit for a minute?" She brought her chair around her desk and pulled the other chair so they were facing each other. "Please?" She sat and pointed to the chair across from her.

Viscount LeBrosse sighed. "You know I can never refuse you anything." He walked back and sat down across from her.

She took his hands in hers and looked him in the eyes. "Tell me, Viscount. Is something the matter? You don't seem like yourself today."

"I just have a lot on my mind."

"Is there anything I can do for you?"

"No, my dear. Just continue to be the special person you are."

"Did Father Matt give you my invitation? Are you coming to my dinner?"

"Yes, he did. And sadly, I must give my regrets. I am going home. I will be leaving for the Continent tomorrow."

"Are you upset with me about what I wrote to you?"

"No, not at all. Dr. Senty, no one has ever said anything like that to me before. But truly, I don't deserve your kind words. I am not the man you think I am."

"I am a very good judge of character. What I said is true. I meant every word."

"Dr. Senty, you really don't know me."

"I know you well enough. Why are you going now? Can't you delay your departure until after my Thanksgiving dinner?"

"No, I am afraid not. I have several pressing business matters that need my immediate attention." Viscount LeBrosse once again stood up to leave.

Mary Elizabeth also rose from her chair. "When will you return?"

"That, I do not know. Au revoir, Dr. Senty. I shall never forget you." He kissed her hand and turned to leave.

"Viscount LeBrosse?"

"Yes?" He turned back to face her.

She walked over to him, kissed his cheek, and hugged him. She whispered, "I am going to miss you. Please take care of yourself and come back soon."

His voice was filled with emotion. "I will. Goodbye." He turned on his heel and shut the door. Mary Elizabeth walked back toward her desk. She sat down at her desk and attempted to write in the viscount's chart but found her vision to be a bit blurry. She put his chart aside to be completed later.

Mary Elizabeth heard a gentle knock on the door. Sarah stuck her head in the room. "Dr. Senty, should I send in the next patient?"

"No, please. Just give me a few minutes. I will come out and get the next patient as usual."

"Yes, Doctor."

Mary Elizabeth went over to the sink and washed her face with cold water and dried it with a paper towel. After taking another moment to compose herself, she walked to the door, opened it, and went out to the reception desk to call the next patient.

Tuesday, November 17

CHAPTER 44

Special Delivery

The next day, after Mass, Mary Elizabeth hurried to the post office to mail Lord and Lady Brantwell's invitation. Then, she walked to the police station. Mary Elizabeth found no one at the front desk. She rang the bell that sat on the counter. No one came to the desk. She rang the bell again. There was no response. As Mary Elizabeth turned to go, she noticed Will's door was ajar.

Mary Elizabeth knocked on the door. "Chief? William?" she called. There was no answer, so Mary Elizabeth pushed the door a little farther and walked into Will's office. She put the invitation on his desk and turned to go when she saw the double picture frame sitting on the corner of his desk.

It held two 5x7 color photographs of her and Will at the gala. The first picture had been taken when they were standing at the top of the landing, just before they descended the stairs at the beginning of the gala evening. They were looking at each other and smiling. The second picture captured them dancing together on the terrace. The photograph was taken from inside the ballroom. It showed the moon illuminating the terrace, while they appeared in silhouette. Mary Elizabeth picked up the picture frame and let out a heavy sigh. That night seemed so long ago, and yet not even a month had passed. She wondered if she would ever be as happy as she'd been that evening. She put the picture frame back on the desk. As she turned toward the door, she gave a start. "Oh, my goodness gracious!"

There, standing in the doorway, was Will. He had an open manila folder in one hand and a fistful of papers in the other. He wore a bemused expression on his face. "Mary Elizabeth. What a surprise! What are you doing here, besides breaking and entering?"

Mary Elizabeth stood with her hand over her heart, trying to regain composure. "I came to deliver your invitation to my Thanksgiving dinner. See, here it is." She picked the invitation from his desk.

Will walked over and set down his papers and folder. He took the invitation from her hand. "You could have left it at the front desk."

"There was no one there. I did call out, but no one answered. I even rang the bell. I was going to leave, but then I saw your open door . . ."

". . . so you decided to walk in?"

Mary Elizabeth was embarrassed. "I didn't just walk in. I knocked and called your name, but you didn't answer."

". . . and then you walked in."

"Yes, all right. I walked in. But in my defense, your door was partially open. Why would you have your door open if you were not inviting people to walk through it?"

"Ah, you do have me there. I think you just won your case. Ever think of giving up medicine and taking up law?"

"No." Mary Elizabeth repeated, "Your door was open . . ."

"Yes, yes, I do believe we have established that fact. Okay, you have me convinced. I withdraw the breaking and entering charge since, as you say, my door was partially open. But I still find you guilty of burgling my office."

Mary Elizabeth started to giggle. "Burgling? Really? Is that even a word?"

"It is," Will said with a straight face. "I can even quote you the statute."

"Well, when you put it like that, I must concede the point." Mary Elizabeth put her hands out in front of her. "Chief Inspector Donnelly, you have caught me red handed. What is my punishment?" She took a step toward him.

Will wrapped his arms around her and kissed her.

Mary Elizabeth breathlessly asked, "Who says crime does not pay?"

They kissed again. They stayed in that embrace until there was a knock at the open door. Sergeant O'Hanlon cleared his throat. "Sorry to interrupt, sir. Here is the information you requested from Scotland Yard."

"Thank you, Sergeant."

Sergeant O'Hanlon placed the folder on Will's desk and left with averted eyes, closing the door behind him.

Mary Elizabeth laughed. "See what happens when you leave your door open? I should go." She looked at her watch. "The surgery will be opening soon. Be sure to read your invitation. I hope you can come. Have a good day." She gave him a kiss on the cheek.

Will replied, "I will now. Goodbye, Mary Elizabeth."

"Bye, Chief."

Will sat down at his desk. He opened Mary Elizabeth's invitation. He spent a few minutes reading her letter and then, to the photographs, he said, "Mary Elizabeth, you are something else." He wrote the details on his desk calendar and tucked the letter in his shirt pocket. Then he read the information in the folder Sergeant O'Hanlon had brought to him.

That evening, Mary Elizabeth sat across from Father Evenson in his rectory office.

"Finally, we have a chance to talk. Now, what is on your mind?"

"I am afraid, Father, the better question is who is in my mind?"

Father Evenson smiled at her. "Don't we know the answer to that one?"

Mary Elizabeth did not return his smile. "Yes, we do. I am very confused, Father. I am hoping you can give me some clarity."

"Tell me more."

"Ever since I was a little girl, my goal has always been to be a doctor. It seemed an impossible dream, but I was determined. Nothing and no one was going to stop me. It has not been an easy road, but at critical times, there was always someone who believed in me and helped me. Everything seemed to fall into place, and now here I am: a fully certified practicing doctor."

"Not many people can have their life plans turn out so successfully, Mary Elizabeth. You are very fortunate."

"I know. It is quite wonderful."

"What has you confused?"

"It's the next part of my life that is so unsure. Once I became a doctor, I wanted to practice rural medicine."

"Isn't that what you are doing?"

"Yes, but I wanted to practice at home in Minnesota. Now I am here in Bellechester, and I don't know anymore."

"What do you mean?"

"For so long, I focused on becoming a doctor that I never thought much beyond that. And now . . ."

"And now?"

"Now I am beginning to think maybe there is more to life than just being a doctor. Ever since the gala and meeting Chief Inspector Donnelly, I have begun to experience these strong emotions. How can I have such strong feelings for someone I barely know? And yet, everything I find out about him makes me want to know more about him. I want to spend more time with him, Father. I like being around him. I like how he makes me feel. I could easily see myself spending the rest of my life with him."

"Whoa, Dr. Senty."

"Please, Father, call me Mary Elizabeth."

"As you wish. Mary Elizabeth, take it easy. You have only just met the chief inspector. You and Chief Inspector Donnelly are at the beginning. Right now, you are both at the infatuation stage. Take your time. Enjoy getting to know each other. See if you have similar interests. Be friends first. Build your foundation one step at a time. You have just laid the first stone. You both have a way to go before you start to plan your life together. So just relax and see what develops."

"Easier said than done, Father. I have shut down that part of my life for so long, and now all these emotions are rushing out and I don't know what to do with them."

"Ah," Father Evenson said. "What you are experiencing is quite normal. Remember that these feelings are good and natural and were given by a God who wants you to experience them. But they are powerful. Enjoy them, but don't let them get the upper hand. What is it that word you Benedictines like to quote all the time?"

"Moderation?"

"Exactly. Moderation."

"You have given me lots to think about, Father. Thank you."

"Good. Now let's go out to the dining room and see what treats Mrs. Winters left for us. Then you can tell me about that large family of yours."

Wednesday, November 18 – Friday, November 20

CHAPTER 45

FITTING THE PIECES OF THE PUZZLE

Will and Detective Trevor Jones picked up the photos from Miller Photography and combed through them in Will's office.

"Anything special we should be looking for?"

"A lady with a cleft chin and penciled eyebrows, and another lady with a rounded chin and thin lips. Also, anything unusual." Will replied.

"I hope you won't let this one get away." Trevor gestured to the framed photos on Will's desk. "You two look very happy together. When are you going to introduce us?"

"When this bloody investigation is over."

"See that you do. You know, Doreen and the kids will want to meet her too."

"Yes, Trevor, I promise. Now let's get back to work."

The photographer shot candid photos of the gala. Only a few ladies had the facial characteristics they were searching for. Then, Trevor spotted a picture of Baroness Whitacre speaking to a server. "Hey Will! Look at this photo." He handed the picture to Will who studied it closely. Both women matched the descriptions given by Kenneth.

Will said, "About two weeks ago, Father Evenson called. He reported that Mrs. Phillips had witnessed Baroness Whitacre handing a bottle of pills to the red-haired maid."

Trevor said, "If we show her this picture, do you think she could verify that these are the women she saw exchanging the bottle of pills?"

"I hope so. This would be the solid evidence we need."

"It would really bolster our case," agreed Trevor.

"Let me ask Father Evenson if he could set up a meeting with Mrs. Phillips."

"We need the help of a priest to speak to a witness?"

Will sighed. "Out here we do. When dealing with the elderly of the upper class, it is all about minding our p's and q's. Mrs. Phillips is a great proponent of proper etiquette. Being introduced by Father Evenson might pave the way to a more productive visit for us. I'll give him a call. "

Trevor shook his head.

When Will spoke to Father Evenson, he was most amenable to setting up the meeting and accompanying them on the visit.

Other detectives were checking the surrounding places stolen jewels were most likely to be resold. Will had alerted Interpol and Scotland Yard to their prime suspects and had sent them descriptions of the missing jewels in case someone tried to fence them in London or Europe. Ivy Petters and Baroness Whitacre were under surveillance.

None of the teams had yet identified the leader of the Brantwell heist, but Will was not worried. He knew the mastermind would surface soon. There were still many people who needed to be paid for their part. Will suspected the jewels would need to be sold to raise the cash.

On Thursday afternoon, Will received a small package in the mail. There was no return address. The postmark indicated the package had been sent from France. Will put on gloves before he opened it. Inside, he found a box with a note on top.

Dear Chief Inspector William Donnelly,

The princess went to the ball. She danced with the handsome prince. That night, she lost her necklace and her heart. Who stole the necklace and how it came into my possession are not important. It is being sent to you because the one she loves should be the one to return it to her. And then, the prince and the princess can live happily ever after. Please do not delay! The happiness of the princess is of the utmost importance!

Respectfully,

A Friend

Mary Elizabeth's agate necklace was carefully packed in a wad of cotton. Will stared at the necklace for a long time. His first impulse was to grab the necklace and run to Mary Elizabeth but his police brain prevented that. He walked the package to the lab and asked the technicians to call him as soon as they completed their report.

Inspector Watson met Will in his office. His team had put together a plan, and all they needed was Lady Brantwell's help. Will called Lady Brantwell to ask her to play a part in the police investigation. She assented, and they arranged to meet at her earliest convenience.

The following morning, the foyer's grandfather clock was chiming its nine bells as Will and Inspector Watson made their way to the study to meet Lady Beatrice.

"Good morning, gentlemen," Lady Beatrice said, holding out her hand.

"Good morning, Lady Brantwell. How nice to see you again. Thank you for agreeing to meet with us. May I introduce Inspector Watson, one of my most experienced detectives."

"Good morning, my lady." Inspector Watson took her hand.

"Please, sit down," Lady Beatrice instructed.

Mr. Jameson entered with a tea service for three and set the tray on the table before Lady Brantwell. "Now, gentlemen, shall we get to it?" she said while pouring the tea. "What is the plan?"

Will explained, "One step at a time. First, we would like to see if you can make an appointment to see Dr. Barnett. If they need a reference, first try Baroness Whitacre. If that name doesn't work, then we leave it up to you to try anyone else. If they ask why you need to see the doctor, say it's your nerves, and that you are finding it impossible to sleep."

"I assure you, Chief Inspector, my acting skills are quite polished." Lady Beatrice paused, and with a wisp of nostalgia in her voice, she added, "I had quite the promising acting career on the stage, you know, before I married Lord Geoffrey."

"I apologize," said Will quickly. "I will leave it up to you to ad-lib your own script."

"Apology accepted. I do have to say, I am looking forward to this challenge."

They finished their tea before making the call. Lady Beatrice asked, "Do you have Dr. Barnett's number?" Inspector Watson handed her a piece of paper from his pocket. "Thank you." Then with a theatrical flair, she picked up the receiver. "Showtime." She dialed the number.

"Hello? Yes, this is Lady Beatrice Brantwell calling. I would like to make an appointment to see Dr. Barnett. . . . No, I am not currently a patient of his. He was recommended to me by my dear friend, Baroness Whitacre. She says he is the best. The only one who can possibly help me . . . I need to see the doctor about a very private and sensitive issue. . . . I'm sorry, I will only discuss it with him. . . . Yes, I can hold. . . . Next Tuesday at 5:00 p.m.? Yes, that will be fine. Thank you so much. Goodbye." Lady Brantwell hung up the phone with a very self-satisfied look on her face.

"Well done, Lady Brantwell," Will said.

"What's next?" Lady Beatrice eagerly asked.

"We will have one of our younger undercover detectives act as your chauffeur. He will drive you to the appointment. He will also go in with you to the office," Inspector Watson said.

Will explained, "Once you are with the doctor, all you have to do is secure the pills and walk out. Remember, you would like the same pills he gave to the baroness. We are looking specifically for barbiturates. He must accept payment from money we will give you. These will be marked notes."

"What if something goes wrong?" Lady Beatrice asked.

"If you ever start to feel uncomfortable, make any excuse and get out of there. Remember, you have a trained police officer outside in the waiting room. Or just call out, and he will come. Your safety is our top priority."

Monday, November 23

CHAPTER 46

Mrs. Phillips's Confession

Trevor and Will picked up Father Evenson, and they headed out to visit Mrs. Phillips. No one wanted to cause undue upset to the elderly woman, so Father Evenson agreed to speak to her first to calm any misgivings she might have about making a formal statement to the police. The maid showed the trio into the parlor. She then took Father Evenson upstairs to a little hallway sitting area.

Mrs. Phillips was waiting for him. "Father Evenson, how nice to see you again."

"Always a pleasure to see you, Mrs. Phillips," Father Evenson kissed her hand.

"You were very cryptic on the phone the other day. Why did you want to meet me up here?"

"I wanted the chance to speak with you alone before I took you downstairs to meet with your other guests."

"Other guests? Who else did you bring with you today? Is it Viscount LeBrosse?" she asked hopefully.

"No, I am sorry to say that Viscount LeBrosse has gone back home to Belgium. I thought I would give you the chance to clear your conscience before you met with Chief Inspector Donnelly and Inspector Jones."

Mrs. Phillips became distraught. "You brought the police to my home! Are they here to arrest me?"

"No, Mrs. Phillips, they are here to ask for your help with their investigation. Besides trying to find the missing jewels, they are also trying to find out who drugged that young policeman. Why do you think that they came to arrest you?"

"Because I—I took something." Mrs. Phillips began wringing her hands. "And now I can't find the item anywhere."

"Would you like to tell me about it?"

"How can I, Father? I am so ashamed!" she cried.

"I can see you are carrying a heavy load of guilt. Talk to Jesus. Tell Him everything, and He will forgive you."

"But what will you think of me, Father, if you knew my secret?"

"I will think you are very courageous to tell the truth and very wise to seek the forgiveness of our Lord."

"I wish I could believe you, Father."

"You don't have to believe me. Just put your trust in our Lord, the Good Shepherd, who rejoices at finding the lost lamb."

Father Evenson pulled out his stole from his pocket, kissed it, and placed it around his neck. Then, he settled back in his chair and waited patiently.

Mrs. Phillips made the sign of the cross. "Bless me, Father, for I have sinned."

Meanwhile, downstairs in the parlor, Trevor remarked, "Father Evenson has been upstairs with Mrs. Phillips for a long time. You don't think he is coaching her on her testimony, do you?"

"No, he promised he wouldn't do that. Apparently, Mrs. Phillips was afraid to meet with us."

"Are we that scary?"

After waiting a few more minutes, they heard Mrs. Phillips and Father Evenson descending the stairs. Both officers rose from their seats.

Mrs. Phillips looked relaxed. She had a smile on her face. Father Evenson made the introductions. "Mrs. Phillips, I would like to introduce you to Inspector Jones, and I believe you know Chief Inspector Donnelly from the gala."

"Gentlemen, welcome to my home."

"A pleasure." Trevor and Will bowed and kissed her hand.

"How very nice to see you again," Will said.

"Please, be seated. I will ring for tea." The maid brought the service for four and put it down in front of Mrs. Phillips. "Now, gentlemen, what brings you here today?"

"We are working on solving the Brantwell Manor jewel thefts. Father Evenson says you have some information that can help us," reported Will.

"Yes, I would like to help."

"Could you make a formal statement about what you saw with regard to Baroness Whitacre and this server?" He showed her a picture of Ivy Petters.

"Yes, I can. Now, how do we start?"

"Can you tell us when you first saw them together?" Will asked.

"I first saw the baroness and the server at the entrance to the ballroom. They were deep in conversation. As I got closer, I saw the baroness take a pill bottle from her handbag and give it to the server. The server held the bottle up to the light while they continued talking. When the baroness saw me, she pushed down on the server's hand like she was trying to hide the bottle. The maid stuffed the pill bottle into the pocket of her uniform and walked away. The baroness and I exchanged pleasantries. I inquired after the health of the server. The baroness replied that the server had a headache, and she had shared her aspirin bottle with her."

Trevor asked, "Can you describe the bottle you saw?"

"Yes. I remember that it didn't look like a regular, clear-glass aspirin bottle. It was small, round, and dark brown in color. It looked like those bottles a chemist gives you when they fill a prescription. But this bottle did not have any labels on it."

"Did you happen to see what was in the bottle?" Will asked.

"I imagine pills would've been in the bottle."

"But you couldn't say for sure?"

"The bottle was too dark to see what was inside."

"Do you remember anything else from the evening?"

"Only that you are a very good dancer, Chief Inspector. I hope we shall see you at more galas."

Will could feel his cheeks color. "Your testimony has been very helpful, Mrs. Phillips. Thank you for meeting with us. We will be in touch if we need more information." The men got up to leave.

"Thank you for your time," Trevor added.

"I am glad I could be of assistance." Mrs. Phillips rang the bell for her maid to bring the hats and coats. As the men were putting on their outerwear, Mrs. Phillips asked, "Before you go, may I inquire after Dr. Senty's agate pendant? I understand it also went missing that same weekend."

Will answered, "I am pleased to report that her necklace is now in our custody. It will be back in her possession shortly."

Mrs. Phillips looked at Father Evenson. "Truly, I am very happy for her. I know how much it meant to her."

"And with your help, we hope to be able to return the other jewels taken that night to their rightful owners, including your own emeralds," added Trevor.

"I will certainly pray for that happy conclusion," said Father Evenson.

"Tish!" Mrs. Phillips said. "They are mere baubles. The insurance company will pay, and then I can buy new ones. Goodbye to you. Good day."

Tuesday, November 24

CHAPTER 47

Showtime!

On the day of Lady Brantwell's appointment with Dr. Barnett, Officer Ned Turner and Inspector Watson drove early to Brantwell Manor. Officer Turner would play the part of Lady Beatrice's chauffeur. He was outfitted from head to toe in a light grey chauffeur's uniform complete with cap and polished black boots. Inspector Watson would ride along in the car to London so that they could go over the plan. Will was going to meet them in an unmarked car parked on Harley Street near Dr. Barnett's office.

It was 4:50 p.m. when Lady Beatrice's '49 silver-and-maroon Rolls Royce dropped Inspector Watson a block from the office. Inspector Watson walked down the street to Will's car. Officer Turner found a parking spot in front of Dr. Barnett's office. He escorted Lady Beatrice into the medical building. They had no trouble finding the correct office suite.

"Lady Beatrice Brantwell to see Dr. Barnett," she announced to the receptionist.

The receptionist, a young, attractive woman in her mid-thirties, greeted her. "Yes, Lady Brantwell. Please, have a seat, and the nurse will be out to get you in a few minutes."

Lady Beatrice and Officer Turner took seats in the empty waiting room. A few minutes later, a well-dressed woman wearing a full-length fur coat emerged from the exam area. She stopped at the reception desk to make her next appointment before walking out the door. After a short wait, a nurse appeared. "If you will follow me, the doctor will see you now," she said to Lady Beatrice.

She led Lady Beatrice down a hallway into an examination room.

"Please, sit in this chair. Since this is your first visit, the doctor will want to talk to you before he starts his examination. Here, I will take your coat." She hung the fur coat on the coat tree.

"Thank you," replied Lady Beatrice, a little nervously.

Just as the nurse finished hanging her coat, Dr. Barnett walked into the room. He was a small, fine-featured man in his late forties. He wore a very expensive, well-appointed three-piece suit under his white lab coat. He walked over to Lady Beatrice and took her hand.

"Lady Brantwell, how nice to finally make your acquaintance. Baroness Whitacre speaks very highly of you."

"Yes, Gwendolyn and I go back many years. She is a dear friend," answered Lady Beatrice.

Dr. Barnett turned to his nurse. "That will be all for the day, Nurse Chapman. I can handle things from here. You and Diane can go home. I will see you both in the morning."

"Yes, Doctor. A good evening to you both," Nurse Chapman responded as she left the room, closing the door behind her.

"Now, Lady Brantwell, what can I do for you?" inquired Dr. Barnett.

"I don't know if you heard, but a few weeks ago, I hosted a gala. Several couples spent the weekend. During the night, we had a robbery, and their jewels were stolen."

"Yes, I read about it in the paper. Do the police have any leads?"

"No, not yet. But I feel so terrible. I can't eat. I can't sleep. I am a nervous wreck. I am hoping that you could give me something to help steady my nerves."

"Shouldn't you consult your own doctor about this matter?"

"That's the problem. My doctor is in Bellechester, which is a small village. I don't want anyone back home to know how badly the jewel heist has affected me. I must keep up appearances. You understand, Doctor, don't you?"

"Yes, Lady Brantwell, of course I do."

Lady Brantwell worked herself into a frenzy. The words were coming fast and furious. "I am desperate to get some relief. The robbery is all I ever think about. I feel it is all my fault that my friends have lost their jewels. Can you help me, Doctor?"

"Of course, Lady Brantwell. Please, step on over to the exam table, and I will look at you." He took Lady Beatrice by the hand, and she sat on the table. He listened to her heart and lungs. He took her pulse and blood pressure. "It appears, Lady Beatrice, that your anxiety is quite acute. Your heart is racing, and your blood pressure is raised. My treatment plan would be to give you an injection here, in the office, which will immediately relax you. Then I shall give you pills that you can take whenever your anxiety reaches an intolerable level."

"Gwendolyn never said anything about injections," Lady Beatrice said with alarm. "All she talked about was you giving her little blue pills."

"Baroness Whitacre's condition is different than yours. Your anxiety is much more severe than hers. Really, the injection is just a mild sedative. It will do you good. It will calm you so you will feel better sooner."

"Dr. Barnett," replied Lady Beatrice firmly, "I only take pills."

"If you do not follow my recommendations, then I cannot help you. I am sorry your trip today was for nothing. Good evening, Lady Brantwell." Dr. Barnett rose to leave.

"Wait!" cried Lady Beatrice as she grabbed his arm. "I do want to feel better, but I am terrified of needles. Always have been."

"Dear Lady Brantwell," Dr. Barnett said as he removed Lady Beatrice's hand from his arm, "there is nothing to fear. The injection will be quick, I promise. Just a little poke, and it will be over within a minute. You will feel its calming effects almost immediately."

"Then, will you give me the pills? No prescription? I walk out of here tonight with the same pills you gave Gwendolyn?" Lady Beatrice insisted.

"Why are you so adamant about getting the same pills as the baroness?"

"She said they were very effective, like magic, and they helped get her through some very tough times." Lady Beatrice dropped her voice. "You know, her husband's drinking and philandering causes her all sorts of problems. Poor Gwendolyn."

"Yes, I am well aware of her situation."

"So, do we have a deal?"

"I must say, Lady Brantwell, this is the first time I have ever had to negotiate with a patient over a treatment plan. You certainly are persistent. Yes, I will give you the pills to take home with you tonight if you first let me give you that sedative." He added with quiet desperation, "Then, maybe, we can both go home. It has been a very long day."

Dr. Barnett opened the door to leave.

Lady Beatrice stopped him. "Oh, Dr. Barnett?"

"Yes?"

"How much is this going to cost? Gwendolyn says that you only take cash."

"Fifty pounds for the pills. Five pounds for the injection."

"Thank you, Doctor."

Dr. Barnett left the exam room and went into the pharmacy area.

Lady Beatrice also left the room and stood in the hallway motioning to get the attention of Officer Turner. He noticed her from the waiting room and came to meet her.

Just then, Dr. Barnett came out of the pharmacy area with a tray holding the hypodermic needle and a bottle of pills. He stopped Officer Turner. "I'm sorry. Only patients and medical personnel are allowed back here."

"I am here for Lady Brantwell."

"You will have to go back out to the waiting room. We are not quite done. I am just about to administer her medication. She will be out in a few minutes."

Officer Turner looked at the tray and then called out, "Lady Brantwell! Are you all right?"

Lady Beatrice still stood in the hallway. "Oh, Ned!" she cried in alarm. "Dr. Barnett is going to give me a jab. You know how terrified I am of needles! I would feel so much better if you were here in the room with me."

Officer Turner replied, "Excuse me, Doctor. My lady needs me." With that, Ned brushed past the doctor. He knocked into Dr. Barnett so hard that the tray flew out of his hands and onto the floor.

"Oh, I am so sorry, Doctor," Officer Turner said. "Here, let me help you pick everything up." Dr. Barnett picked up the pill bottle. The hypodermic needle lay on the floor. Before Dr. Barnett could reach it, Ned stepped on it with the heel of his boot, shattering the glass syringe.

"Imbecile! Look what you've done!" Dr. Barnett said. "Now I will have to prepare another syringe."

"I do apologize," Officer Turner said. "But I am afraid we are not going to have time for you to do so. I must get Lady Brantwell over to her husband. They are having drinks with the prime minister tonight, and I promised his lordship that I would have Lady Brantwell at his office by six sharp. You know how horrific London traffic can be at this hour."

Turning toward Lady Brantwell, Officer Turner asked, "Are you ready to go, Lady Brantwell?"

"Oh yes, Ned, as soon as I get my pills." She walked over to Dr. Barnett, held out the money, and said, "Here is your fifty pounds. Please, Doctor, just give me the pills. Then we will be out of here and on our way."

"Here!" shouted Dr. Barnett angrily. He grabbed the money that Lady Beatrice held out to him. He shoved the bottle of pills at her. "Take your pills. Now go!"

"Thank you, Doctor," Lady Beatrice said as she took the pills and retrieved her coat from the coatrack. Officer Turner escorted Lady Beatrice out of the exam room.

Once they got outside, Officer Turner walked Lady Beatrice to the car and opened the door for her. Then, he walked over to the unmarked police car and handed the pills in through the window. The unmarked police car quickly drove away.

Safely inside her limousine, Lady Beatrice said, "Thanks, Ned. You were a true lifesaver."

Officer Turner started the car. "Lady Beatrice, you were very brave. Even though it didn't go quite to plan, we got the job done."

"Let's go home."

Officer Turner put the car in gear. "Bellechester it is."

Testing by the Met's lab confirmed that the pills given to Lady Beatrice had the same composition as the drugs found in Officer Collins's bloodstream. Will's applications for search warrants for Dr. Barnett's office and the homes of both Baroness Whitacre and Ivy Petters were approved.

In executing the search warrants, they found several pieces of jewelry that had been stolen in previous southwestern Shropshire robberies. The jewels from Lady Brantwell's gala, however, were not among them.

The bottle of blue pills was found at the home of Ivy Petters. As Mrs. Phillips had said, the pills were in an unmarked prescription bottle.

The arrest of both women kept Will and Inspector Watson at the Met for several days. Will led the interview on both suspects. Because of Will's skillful interrogation, both Baroness Whitacre and Ivy Petters named the Frenchman Yves Fortier as the mastermind behind the jewel thefts in southwestern Shropshire County. Based on their testimony, Will sought a red notice from Interpol asking Interpol to find Yves Fortier. Interpol cannot arrest anyone, but Will's red notice asked the French police to arrest and extradite Yves to England for prosecution.

The search warrant executed on Dr. Barnett's office yielded a bounty of incriminating evidence. Dr. Barnett was a meticulous record keeper. The police found a register dating back several years. It gave names of patients, drugs sold, dates, and cash received. Dr. Barnett was brought to the Met for questioning. He faced a jail sentence and the loss of his medical license for selling drugs for personal profit. In a bid to reach a plea deal, Dr. Barnett told police everything they wanted to know about his operation. He also named his sources for obtaining the drugs. Will was only interested in finding the source of the drugs used in the Brantwell Manor theft. The Met's club and vice unit took over investigating and prosecuting Dr. Barnett's London drug operation.

Thursday, November 26

CHAPTER 48

ALONG THE FRENCH RIVIERA

On a cold November day, Viscount LeBrosse entered a jewelry store in Saint-Tropez. The Belgian State Security Service (VSSE) had uncovered a plot to overthrow the Belgian government. It was going to be financed by selling stolen jewels. VSSE, working with Interpol and the French police, had hatched a plan that required the skill of one of their most experienced and trusted agents, Viscount LeBrosse. His expertise in gemology was well known throughout the international law enforcement community. Even though he was retired and lived out of the country, he was a loyal Belgian. Viscount LeBrosse disguised himself as the Belgian jewel-broker Stefan DeWelt. Clean-shaven with dyed grey hair, he wore thick-rimmed glasses. He wore padding under his raincoat to give himself a portlier shape. He wore a large hat which covered most of his face. To protect Viscount LeBrosse's identity as much as possible, Interpol also sent in one of their young Belgian agents to pose as Georgi DeWelt, Stefan's son.

Yves Fortier, the jewelry-store owner, showed the pair several items. Stefan examined each piece and gave Georgi an extensive description. Georgi wrote down all the details in his small notebook.

"Your father certainly knows his jewelry," Yves said.

"Yes, he has been in the business a long time," Georgi said.

"It is strange our paths have never crossed before. I thought I knew all the brokers on the continent. Do you have a card?" he asked Stefan.

"Of course," Stefan said. "Georgi, give the man our card." The viscount kept his head down as he examined an emerald necklace with his loupe.

Georgi pulled out a business card from his front jacket pocket and handed it to Yves.

"We have been working out of Melbourne for the past twenty years. But my mother said it was time for us to come home. We are just becoming reacquainted with the jewelers on the continent. If you are interested in opals, I can get you the finest in the world. Another year or two, and Father said I will be ready to take over the business."

"Is this all you have?" Stefan gestured to the display case.

"Are you looking for something in particular?"

"I am working with several clients at the moment. One is looking for an emerald necklace. This one might interest him. Price?"

Yves wrote the price on the back of his business card and handed it to Stefan. He then looked closely at Stefan's face. "You look familiar to me. Are you sure we have not met before?"

"Have you ever been to Melbourne?" Stefan asked.

"No, it's just that you bear a strong resemblance to someone I once knew."

"People tell me that all the time. Now, my other client is looking for a diamond-and-ruby necklace with matching earrings. I don't see any in your cases. Are you sure you are not holding your best jewels in the back somewhere?" Turning to Georgi, he added, "Sometimes jewelers keep the best for themselves."

"Really, Father?"

"I am teaching my boy all your tricks," Stefan told Fortier.

"Of course. I do have a few pieces that just arrived. I have not yet had time to put them on display. Let me get them for you."

Fortier disappeared into the back room. A few minutes later, he emerged with a ruby-and-diamond necklace and earring set. "This is a beautiful set. Might this interest your client?"

"We shall see." Stefan examined the pieces carefully under his loupe. He suddenly became indignant. "I thought you were going to bring me your best. These rubies are of inferior quality.

We are done here. Come along, Georgi, we will try another jeweler in town. Good day."

The two men left the store and walked down the street. Viscount LeBrosse turned to the young Interpol agent and said, "Those were Lady Brantwell's jewels, and the emerald necklace belongs to Mrs. Phillips. I am sure of it. I also recognized his voice as the man who pushed me down the stairs at Brantwell Manor." At the corner, the Interpol agent and Viscount LeBrosse went their separate ways. Viscount LeBrosse got into an unmarked VSSE car and was driven up the coast to his apartment in Antibes. When Viscount LeBrosse was safely out of the area, the Interpol agent gave the signal, and the French police moved in on the jewelry shop. They arrested Yves Fortier and confiscated all his jewels.

That evening, Viscount LeBrosse sat on the balcony of his apartment overlooking the Mediterranean Sea. His valet brought him his usual: Grand Marnier neat. "Nice to have you home again, sir. Dinner will be served in thirty minutes."

"Thank you, Louis. Very quiet tonight," the viscount said.

"Just as you like it, sir."

Viscount LeBrosse reread the letter he'd carried with him to France. By now, Mary Elizabeth's letter was looking very dog eared. A floor lamp from the sitting room shone just enough light onto the balcony so he could make out her words. He really did not need much light, as he had long ago committed her letter to memory. It was as if he could hear her soft, steady voice speaking to him as he reread her words. The truth was, he missed her and all his Bellechester friends. In Antibes, there was no one with whom to share his triumphal sting on the mastermind behind the Brantwell Manor jewel heist. Back in Bellechester, he imagined Matt would have been a rapt audience and would have asked all sorts of probing questions.

The blackness of the Mediterranean Sea only deepened his melancholy. Viscount LeBrosse got up, drink in hand, and walked into his sitting room. It was filled with priceless art and antique furniture. Usually, his treasures brought him joy; that night, they left him cold and empty.

He stood in the middle of the room and once again read the crumpled piece of paper. "What strange hold you have over me, I do not know," he said to the letter. "All I know is that I can never deny you anything."

Then he called out, "Louis, pack my bags."

Friday, November 27 – Saturday, November 28

CHAPTER 49

Yves Fortier

Will and Inspector Watson finally made it back to the Bellechester precinct. Will worked his way through the seemingly unending pile of papers in his inbox. The report on the package that held Mary Elizabeth's necklace revealed no fingerprints. Everything had been wiped clean. The note was written on common typewriter paper. While that news was disappointing, it also meant that the necklace did not need to be held any longer as evidence. Will walked down to the police lab and retrieved the box and its contents. He brought the box back to his office. He planned to visit Mary Elizabeth that night to return her agate pendant to her.

The telephone must have read his thoughts. "Donnelly, here . . . yes, I will be there. Thank you for calling. See you tonight." He looked at the photograph on his desk. "Sorry, Mary Elizabeth. Duty calls." He placed the box with her necklace in his top drawer, locked it, and left the office.

Will met an Interpol boat at the London docks. Yves Fortier was onboard, escorted by Interpol agents Willems and Mertens. Will brought a large police van and several of his own officers with him. Willems, Mertens, Fortier, and two of Will's officers climbed in the back. Will got into the front passenger side, and another of his officers drove the van back to Bellechester.

After Fortier was processed, he was brought to the interrogation room. Will and the Interpol detectives grilled him for an hour on the Brantwell theft. Fortier was silent and offered no information.

Will laid out the charges of robbery, taking stolen merchandise across country borders, attempting to sell stolen merchandise, and the attempted murder of Viscount LeBrosse. Will also told him that Baroness Whitacre and Ivy Petters had already been arrested. Both had given sworn testimony implicating him as the mastermind behind the Brantwell robbery and the other jewel thefts in the Bellechester area.

Will transferred Yves to a cell, where he could consider how cooperative he wanted to be. They were done for the night. They would pick up the interview again in the morning. Will posted extra guards inside the cellblock and outside the jail area. Will then invited the two Interpol detectives to the Ram's Head pub for dinner and drinks. He arranged their accommodations and bade them good night.

It had been another long day in a string of long days. Will was anxious to go home. The full dinner and drinks relaxed him, and the exhaustion that he had been stuffing into the background for days came to the fore. His last conscious thought before drifting off to sleep was of Mary Elizabeth.

The next morning, Will was promptly back at his office. At 9:00 a.m., the Interpol agents arrived to talk to Yves Fortier. Will had an officer bring Fortier to the interrogation room. Once more, Will laid out all the charges against him and Detective Mertens laid out their evidence.

Instead of looking defiant, Fortier looked defeated. Will told him if he cooperated and pled guilty, his sentence would most likely be reduced. But if they went to trial and he was convicted of all the charges, the court might not be so lenient. "Do you want more time to think about it, or have you made up your mind?"

"I will confess to robbery and attempting to sell the jewels."

Will asked, "What about attempting to murder Viscount LeBrosse?"

"I don't know any Viscount LeBrosse."

"Viscount Jacques LeBrosse?" Will asked.

"Never heard of him."

"The man you pushed down the stairs at Brantwell Manor."

Fortier snorted. "Is that the name he gave you?" Will looked puzzled, but the Interpol agents remained stoic. "The man I pushed down the stairs was Blaise DeMotte. And if I hadn't stolen the jewels, you can bet he would have. He and my father stole the crown jewels of Belgium during the Second World War, but DeMotte double-crossed my father. My father died in prison, and DeMotte was never caught. That is why I pushed him down the stairs. I see the charge is only attempted murder, so I guess I was not successful. I will have to try harder next time."

Willems replied, "I don't think there will be a next time. You are going away for a long time."

"Don't I get any points for revealing the identity of DeMotte? You guys must have dozens of arrest warrants out for him."

"Quite," Willems said sarcastically. "We'll give you a medal."

Will commanded his officer to take Fortier back to his cell. The officer and the prisoner left the interrogation room.

Will turned to the Interpol detectives. "I will get his confession typed up for him to sign."

Mertens answered, "Once we have a signed confession, we will escort the prisoner to London, where formal extradition charges from Belgium will be processed. You see, Inspector, you are not the only one who wants a piece of Fortier."

Willems remarked, "Thanks to your hard work, it looks as if we have solved the mystery of your Brantwell Manor jewel heist."

"Do you think he was telling the truth about Viscount LeBrosse being Blaise DeMotte?" Will asked.

Detective Mertens replied, "No. I think he was grasping at straws, trying to distract us from keeping our focus on him. I have never heard of this DeMotte character."

Detective Willems, who was much older than his colleague, said, "I used to hear the older Interpol agents speak of DeMotte. Seems like he was a legendary jewel thief, and indeed, had never been caught. But I haven't heard anything about him since the Second World War. Besides, Viscount LeBrosse was very helpful to us in catching Fortier. From what I remember of DeMotte, cooperating with the police would be the last thing he would do."

"Yeah, I guess you are right," Will said.

Later that afternoon, Detectives Willems and Mertens escorted Fortier into the police van. Will was there to see them off. Detective Mertens shook hands with Will before he stepped into the back of the van. "Nice working with you, Chief Inspector. Till next time."

"Thanks for the hospitality. Good job." Detective Willems said.

"Goodbye. Safe trip." Will closed the back of the van and signaled for the driver to go.

Back in his office, Will tackled the stack of paperwork on his desk. A few hours later, he put the last folder into the "out" bin. He looked at Mary Elizabeth's picture. "You have been waiting long enough."

He took Mary Elizabeth's pendant from his drawer. "Officer Kirby, I am going home and will be taking Sunday off. I will be back in the office Monday morning," he said on his way out.

"Very good, sir. I will make a note of it. Enjoy your time away."

Saturday, November 28 – Sunday, November 29

CHAPTER 50

THE AGATE NECKLACE

Before heading home, Will went by the surgery and rang the bell. Harold and Magnus met him in the hallway.

"Well, hello, Chief Inspector. Come on in."

"Thank you, Dr. Merton." Will bent down and petted Magnus. "Good to see you again, big fella."

"What can I do for you?"

"I was hoping to see Dr. Senty. Is she in?"

"No, I'm afraid she is out on a house call."

"Do you know when she might return?"

"That's always hard to say. Would you like to leave a message?"

"Yes, if I may."

"Here, I will get you a pencil and paper. You write it down and put it in her basket here. She will see it when she comes home."

Harold brought him a pad of paper and pencil and left his note in her basket. He returned the pencil and pad to Harold. "Thank you, Dr. Merton. You have a good night."

"You too, Chief Inspector."

The November night air was brisk, so Will walked quickly back past the police station and up another few streets to his home. After hanging up his suit coat, Will began making supper. He fried a steak in one pan, and in another he cut up a leftover jacket potato, added some onions, and made chips. He poured himself a glass of ale. Halfway through his meal, there was a knock on his front door.

Mary Elizabeth was breathing hard, her medical bag in hand.

"Come in. You look cold," Will said as he ushered her inside.

"Are you all right? I came as soon as I saw your note," she said breathlessly.

"Yes, I'm fine. Here, let me take your coat." Will helped her with her coat. "Come on back into the kitchen. It's nice and warm in there."

"Mmm! Something smells good." She saw Will's half-eaten plate on the table. "Oh, you haven't finished your supper yet? Here, you sit down and eat."

"Have you eaten? I can share."

"No, thank you. I had my supper. But a cup of tea would be nice."

Will started to get up.

Mary Elizabeth stopped him. "No, you sit down. Just tell me where you keep your kettle. Believe it or not, even though I am an American, I am perfectly capable of making a cup of tea."

"Kettle's in the bottom-left cupboard, and you'll find the teapot and the cups in the upper right side. Tea is in the upper left."

"Thanks. Got it." Mary Elizabeth put the kettle on the stove and set everything out on the counter. Then she came and sat across from him.

"Now, why did you want to see me tonight? You will see me tomorrow. You're coming to my Thanksgiving dinner, aren't you?"

"Wouldn't miss it. I have the whole day off tomorrow, and there is no one I would rather spend it with than you."

"You mean me and eight of my closest and dearest friends. Remember, you did say you can share."

"Not exactly what I had in mind. I asked you to come here tonight because—" The whistling teakettle interrupted him.

"Hold that thought." Mary Elizabeth went to make her tea. She brought her cup to the table. "Okay, continue."

Before he began, she snitched a chip off his plate. "This is good. You are a good cook. I'm impressed." She looked up at Will.

"Mary Elizabeth, the reason I wanted to see you tonight is because it looks like we have wrapped up the investigation on the Brantwell Manor jewel robbery. All the culprits are behind bars, the jewels are recovered, and the case goes to the prosecution on Monday." Will got up from the table and took his dishes to the sink.

"Oh my, Chief, that's wonderful! I know you have worked so hard to solve it. I am so happy for you." As he walked back to the table, Mary Elizabeth rose to hug him.

"You are the first person I have told."

"Chief, I am honored to celebrate with you."

"Let's go sit on the sofa," Will said.

"You must tell me everything. How did you solve it?" Mary Elizabeth asked eagerly.

"It took a lot of officers following many leads, but it all came together, mostly in the past week. But what I wanted to tell you tonight is that, about ten days ago, a package arrived for me at the station. It was sent anonymously. The only clue was that it was sent from France. Do you know anyone in France?"

"Me? No, I don't know anyone in France."

"Anyway, there was a letter inside that instructed me to give you what was in the box."

"There was something for me?" Mary Elizabeth spoke those words slowly, as if they had to sink in. "What did the letter say?"

"That, I'm afraid, is confidential, for now."

"Why are you being so cryptic tonight? It's late. I'm getting tired," Mary Elizabeth said as she sipped her tea.

"Sorry. Just bear with me a little longer. I promise it will be well worth it." Will got up from the sofa. "I have the box in my room. I'll be right back." He returned and handed the box to Mary Elizabeth. "Here, this is what arrived from France."

Mary Elizabeth carefully opened the box and unwrapped the tissue. For a moment, she sat there speechless. Finally, she said, "It's my pendant. My agate pendant. But how?" She looked at Will. "Chief, will you put this on me? I am never, ever going to take it off again."

Will obliged and fastened the necklace around her neck. "Yes," he agreed. "That is where your necklace belongs."

"But how did this person find my necklace? How did they know it belonged to me? Why did they send it to you? How did they know you knew me?"

"I do not know any of those answers yet."

"Then you must not be a very good detective," Mary Elizabeth teased.

Will laughed. "Now, that's the Mary Elizabeth I know." Much softer, he added, "And love."

"William Francis Donnelly!" Mary Elizabeth exclaimed. "Did you just say you loved me?"

"Did I?" Will feigned innocence.

"Well, that's a problem," Mary Elizabeth said.

"Problem?" Will asked with a bit of concern in his voice. "Why is that a problem?"

"Because," Mary Elizabeth said, "I love you too." She kissed his lips. She then laid her head on his shoulder, fingering her pendant. "So what are we going to do about that?"

Will put his arm around her and kissed the top of her head. "If we both think about it real hard, I am sure we can come up with a solution."

They stayed in that position on the sofa for quite a while. Suddenly, Mary Elizabeth bolted up. "Oh, manure!"

"Mary Elizabeth, what's the matter?"

"Chief, what time is it?"

Will looked at his watch. "12:30 a.m."

"I've got to get home to bed. I have nine people coming for dinner tomorrow. No, *today*, and I have to finish setting the table and get the turkey in the oven, put the stuffing together, go to Mass, and—"

"Take it easy, Mary Elizabeth. I will come over and help you."

"Will you, Chief?"

"Sure. I'm pretty handy in the kitchen."

"That will be great. Thank you."

They both got up from the couch, and Will retrieved her coat from the closet. "Did you walk or drive over?"

"Actually, when I saw your note, I ran over."

"Did you?" Will said with surprise in his voice. "In that case, I will walk you home. Here you go," Will said as he helped her put on her coat.

Mary Elizabeth put on her hat and gloves and picked up her medical bag while Will put on his coat and hat. They went out into the cold November night arm in arm.

"Chief, tell me again how my necklace came to you."

"All right, if you like." Will faithfully repeated the story. "About ten days ago—"

"Wait!" Mary Elizabeth stopped in her tracks.

"What's the matter?"

"You received my necklace ten days ago, and you never told me?" Mary Elizabeth was incredulous.

"I couldn't tell you because I had to turn it over to the lab to see if we could get any prints off of it, or if it matched any prints taken at Brantwell Manor. I followed the usual police protocol."

"You couldn't tell me that it was in police custody?"

"I didn't want to cause you undue anxiety. If the necklace did produce prints, it would have to be kept in evidence for months until the trial. And if no prints were found, then the necklace would be released to you. I wanted to be sure which scenario it was going to be before I told you."

"Oh, Chief, undue anxiety? Have you any idea what I went through these past ten days? How many nights I cried myself to sleep over losing that necklace? Last Sunday, I finally got up enough nerve to call my folks and tell them that the pendant was lost. It was a very difficult phone call."

"I was only trying to protect you." Will's voice was plaintive.

"Protect me?" Mary Elizabeth's voice rose. "What the heck? What do you think I am? Some dainty English rose?"

"No, I—"

"I don't *need* your protection. I don't *want* your protection," Mary Elizabeth yelled.

"What *do* you want? Tell me." Will's voice matched Mary Elizabeth's in volume.

"I want you to be honest and truthful with me. And I want—" Mary Elizabeth's voice faltered. "I want—"

Will was exasperated. "What? What do you want?"

The shrill sound of a police whistle rose above their voices. Another figure stood off to the side. Will and Mary Elizabeth grew silent. They heard the voice of a young policeman. "Excuse me, if I could have your attention. I'm Officer Jenkins, and I am here to help. I could hear your conversation a street away. We will see if we can get things straightened out. Ma'am, if you would stay under this lamppost here."

Taking Will by the arm, he said, "Sir, let's walk over to this lamppost." The officer moved Will about ten feet away. "Now, sir, if you stay here, I will talk to the lady first. In the meantime, I want you to take deep breaths and try to calm down."

"Yes, Officer."

Officer Jenkins approached Mary Elizabeth. "Evening, ma'am. What is your name?"

"Mary Elizabeth Senty. Dr. Mary Elizabeth Senty," she said, pointing to her bag.

"I thought your voice sounded familiar. You gave me my physical last month."

"Oh, that's right. How nice to see you again."

"You were pretty loud. I am here to help. First, take a few deep breaths."

Mary Elizabeth complied.

"Now, if you could say something to your male friend over there, what would it be?"

She took another deep breath. "I would tell him that I want him to be honest and truthful with me. And I need to hear from him occasionally. I can't bear waiting weeks for him to call. I know he's busy, and I'm busy. But I still miss him."

"Anything else?" Officer Jenkins was dutifully copying down her remarks in his notebook.

"Yes. You can tell him that I still love him, and I know he's doing his best."

"Very good," Officer Jenkins said. "Now, you stay here, and I will go talk to your friend."

Officer Jenkins glanced at Will, did a double take, and then shook his head. In an abundance of formality, he asked, "Sir, what is your name?"

"William Donnelly."

The young officer again looked hard at Will. "Do you happen to work for the Bellechester Police Department?" he asked uneasily.

"I do."

"Do you have a title to your name? Would you be—"

"Chief Inspector William Donnelly? Yes, I am."

"Sir!" Officer Jenkins snapped to attention and dropped his pencil and pad.

"At ease, Officer Jenkins. Now, pick up your pad and pencil."

"Yes, sir." Officer Jenkins found his pad right away, but his pencil was more difficult to locate, as it had flown into the darkness out of the streetlight's reach.

Will looked at Mary Elizabeth, who, with her hand covering her mouth, was almost doubled over with laughter. Will bent down and searched the ground. "Here, I will help you look for your pencil."

It took Will and Officer Jenkins several minutes on their hands and knees before Officer Jenkins found the elusive pencil. They both straightened themselves up.

Officer Jenkins said, "So sorry, sir. I did not recognize you at first. Sorry to have detained you. You are free to go."

"Is that how you were trained, officer?" Will asked gruffly. "To release your detainee without finishing your questioning?"

"No, sir!" Officer Jenkins replied. "But you are the chief and all."

"What difference does that make? Now, finish your interview just as you were trained. Where were we?"

"I was just about to tell you what Dr. Senty said."

"Well, go ahead. What did she say?"

He cleared his throat. "Well, Chief Inspector, this is what Dr. Senty would like to say to you." Officer Jenkins read Mary Elizabeth's words back to him, including that she loved him.

"Do you have any response to that?"

"Yes, I do. Please tell Dr. Senty that just as she is bound by patient-doctor privilege, I am also bound by police confidentiality, protocols, and procedures. I can't speak of active police investigations, so I am not at liberty to tell her everything I know or am doing. Please ask her to have patience with me. Tell her I have never met a woman like her, and that I will make mistakes in our relationship. But I do love her, and I am willing to do whatever it takes to make it work. Did you get all of that, Officer Jenkins?"

"Yes, sir. I will go and tell her."

Officer Jenkins dutifully reported to Mary Elizabeth everything Will had said. After he finished, he asked, "Now, Dr. Senty, do you know how you and the chief inspector can bring this conflict to a peaceful and quiet resolution?"

"How about we apologize, kiss, and make up?"

"Let me relay that message to the chief inspector." Officer Jenkins relayed Mary Elizabeth's solution.

"Dr. Senty is very sensible. I agree to her plan."

"Very good. I'll go tell her."

"Officer?" Will reached out and restrained the officer.

"Yes?"

"I think Dr. Senty and I can take it from here. Thank you for your help."

Will walked toward Mary Elizabeth. The officer followed close behind. Will took Mary Elizabeth's hand and said, "I am sorry, Mary Elizabeth, for not telling you sooner about your necklace, and for not calling you more often, and for underestimating you. Will you forgive me?"

"Yes, Chief. And I am sorry for not understanding your work, and for not appreciating how much you care for me, and for raising my voice. Will you forgive me?"

"Of course, Mary Elizabeth. I love you."

"I love you too, William Francis Donnelly. Very much."

They embraced and kissed long and passionately.

After a few minutes, Officer Jenkins cleared his throat. "I believe my work here is done. I will let you off with just a warning this time since you have resolved your conflict in a, um, mutually satisfactory manner. You can be on your way now. But please, keep your voices down. People are trying to sleep."

Will shook his hand. "Yes, Officer Jenkins. We will. Thank you. Good night."

Mary Elizabeth added, "Yes, thank you, officer. Sorry to have troubled you. You take care now."

Officer Jenkins touched the rim of his hat. "Just doing my job, ma'am. Glad to be of service. Good night to you both."

Will and Mary Elizabeth walked hand in hand to the surgery in silence. When they got to the door, Mary Elizabeth said, "Well, it has been quite a night."

"Yes, it has. What time do you want me to come over and help you prepare dinner?"

"You need a good night's sleep. How about you come over at 1:00 p.m.?"

"I will be here. Good night, Mary Elizabeth. I love you."

"Good night, Chief. I love you too."

They kissed. She walked into the surgery, and Will turned around and walked home.

Sunday, November 29

CHAPTER 51

A THANKSGIVING DAY

Sunday morning, the low sun was shining through Mary Elizabeth's window. She was nice and warm under the blankets and could have slept longer. She turned over and looked at the clock. It read 8:10 a.m. The fog in her brain cleared, and she remembered what day it was. She jumped up. She had already missed the early Mass at 8:00 a.m. That was her usual Mass on Sunday. Now she would have to go to the late Mass at 10:30 a.m. She fingered her pendant. It was still around her neck. She had not dreamed it. She showered and dressed. She still had a little time before she had to leave for church, so she finished setting the table.

When Harold moved into the house thirty-five years ago, the previous doctor's wife had left behind her china and crystal service for twelve. Harold insisted Mary Elizabeth use these place settings for her dinner. He said that was his contribution to the feast. The crystal was a beautiful Lismore pattern by Waterford. The dishes were Royal Worcester English bone china. It was white in the center and had a deep-green pattern of small flowers along the edge.

Mary Elizabeth had never seen anything so elegant. It even had all the serving pieces. It looked beautiful with the gold linen tablecloth and napkins. The china hutch also contained a set of silver candelabras, which she had dutifully polished a few days before. They sat in the center of the table with six dark-green candles. Once the table was set, she left for Mass.

When she arrived at the church, she still had time to light her candles. She lit three: one in thanksgiving to St. Anthony for helping to return her necklace; one for her patients; and one for Will and her family. This Mass was the High or choir Mass. While she enjoyed listening to the choir, she was getting antsy. Mass lasted longer than she had anticipated.

After Mass, she waited to speak to Father Evenson.

"I'm looking forward to your dinner tonight. Mrs. Winters has been baking up a storm."

"Father, I have a special request for you."

"Do you want me to say a special blessing over the food?" he asked.

"Of course, Father. That goes without saying. But I have been thinking. I really don't know Sarah's boyfriend very well, and I have been wondering how to make sure he feels at ease. Do you have any name tags I could use for tonight?"

"I think Mrs. Winters has some in a drawer. I will be sure to find some and bring them along."

"Thank you, Father. And, I have another request of you."

"Yes?"

"Would you be offended, if just for tonight, you left your Roman collar and your cassock at home, and just wore normal, non-black clothes to my dinner? The dress code for tonight is casual, American-style comfy-casual."

Father Evenson laughed. "No I am not offended. I think I have in my closet just the clothes to fit the bill."

"Thank you. See you in a few hours. Don't forget to bring your appetite and the name tags. Gotta run. Bye."

When she got home, she broke her Eucharistic fast with eggs, toast, and juice. She changed into comfy wool slacks, a pale-blue sweater with three-quarter-length sleeves, and black flats. She fixed her hair in a ponytail.

Harold had been a huge help in the days leading up to the party. She had included him in the planning, and she could tell he was getting excited about hosting an event at their home. At first, Mary Elizabeth only wanted to serve soft drinks, but he convinced her to offer a modest selection of hard liquor. In addition to greeting the guests, Harold was responsible for the bar.

When Mary Elizabeth decided to host her Thanksgiving dinner, she wanted to have her guests experience what a Senty family Thanksgiving celebration was like. At home, the family always played games together, so Mary Elizabeth came up with a few parlor games to be played before dinner.

When she was satisfied with the state of the dining and sitting rooms, she turned her attention to the kitchen. She put on a cover-all apron and got to work peeling sweet potatoes.

True to his word, Will rang the front bell at 1:00 p.m. Harold answered the door.

"Good afternoon, Chief Inspector. Come in. Here, let me take your coat. You are here early."

"Yes, I am. I promised to help Mary Elizabeth with the dinner."

"She's in the kitchen. Go right on through." He took Will's coat into his bedroom.

"Thank you." Will walked into the kitchen and found Mary Elizabeth busily cutting vegetables for the dressing.

"Chief Inspector Donnelly, reporting for duty, ma'am," Will announced cheerfully.

"Hi Chief. Right on time. That is one of the things I love about you."

"One of the things. You mean there are others?" he asked hopefully.

"I will reveal all in due time. Wouldn't want you to get a swelled head. But I will tell you another one."

"Yes?"

"It's that you take direction really well. Now go to the sink and wash your hands."

"Yes, Doctor."

As she passed him in the kitchen, she gave him a kiss on the cheek. "I am really glad you are here."

"If that is how you treat the help, then I am glad I am here too." Wiping his hands on the hand towel, he said, "Now, what do you want me to do first?"

"Put this apron on." She threw one to him. "Please get the turkey from the refrigerator and put it in the roasting pan. Here, I will turn the oven on. After you have it in the pan, brush this melted butter on it and then season it."

She finished chopping vegetables, cleaned her knife, and brought over two apples. Mary Elizabeth got a large mixing bowl and dumped the toasted bread cubes, sage, poultry seasoning, raisins, and melted butter into the bowl, mixing it all together.

"The turkey is all set. Do you want me to put it in the oven?"

"Yes, please. What time is it?"

"1:20 p.m."

"Good. Four hours would be about 5:30 p.m. We should be eating at 6:00 p.m., just as I planned."

"Sounds good. What is next?"

"Open that cupboard on the right side. There should be some knives hanging on the door. Choose one, and you can help me chop these things for the dressing."

"All right. I found my weapon of choice."

"Here, I will get you another cutting board. Tell me, Chief, how did you get to be so handy in the kitchen?"

"My gran, my mum's mother, used to live with us, and I loved to hang out with her in the kitchen. My dad was away in the war, and my mum worked the evening shifts at the ammunitions factory, so I used to help my gran out."

"Did she share any of her cooking secrets with you?"

"Yes, she did. But I will never tell. However, I will cook for you sometime."

"I would love that."

Will and Mary Elizabeth worked well together. In no time, the dressing was made and in the casserole dish. She wrote down when the dressing was to go in the oven. She'd made the cranberries earlier in the week so they were chilling in the fridge. Her guests were going to provide the rest of the menu.

CHAPTER 52

The Party Begins

By 3:30 p.m., Will and Mary Elizabeth had finished preparing the food. They'd even washed some of the dishes. The kitchen looked presentable. There was enough clean counter space for Mrs. Winters's pies. They were able to take off their aprons and visit with Harold in the sitting room as they waited for their guests to arrive. Father Evenson and Mrs. Winters were the first to ring the doorbell. Father Evenson was carrying a box that held two pies.

"Here, let's bring those pies into the kitchen." Mary Elizabeth led the way. "You can set the box on the counter. Thank you, Father Matt. Did you remember the name tags?"

"Yes. Where do you want them?"

"You can put them on the table by the telephone."

She was busy unpacking the box and had her back to the kitchen entrance. She heard another voice say, "And where would you like the bread rolls?"

Without turning around, she responded, "Oh, you can put them on the counter too." Recognizing the voice, she turned around and exclaimed, "Viscount! What are you doing here?"

Viscount LeBrosse replied, "Well, I thought I was invited to a Thanksgiving dinner."

Mary Elizabeth said, "You were. You are. Oh, you came." She went over to him and gave him a big hug and kissed his cheek. "I am so happy you are here." She hugged him again.

"If this is the welcome reception I get, then I should go away and come back more often," he said with a laugh.

"But what about all of your business affairs?" she asked as she wrapped the bread rolls in foil so they'd be ready to heat.

"It turns out I was able to finish my business more quickly than I thought."

Mary Elizabeth gave him a big smile. "Come on, let's go back into the sitting room. Here, let me take your coat." After depositing his coat with the others, she quickly set another place at the table for him.

Mrs. Winters said, "If your food tastes as good as it smells, we are going to be in for a real treat tonight."

The doorbell rang again, and it was Sarah and her date. Harold welcomed her. "Come in, Sarah. Now, who is this gentleman you brought with you?"

"Dr. Merton, I would like to introduce my friend, Michael Whiley."

A short, stocky young man with blond hair stood beside Sarah. He stuck out his hand. "Good afternoon, Dr. Merton."

Harold greeted him warmly, "Welcome, Michael. Come on in. Here, let me take your coats.

Sarah, why don't you ask Dr. Senty where she wants your salad?"

They moved from the entrance way into the sitting room. Mary Elizabeth saw Sarah and rushed over.

"Dr. Senty, this is my friend, Michael Whiley."

Mary Elizabeth extended her hand. "Welcome, Michael. Very pleased to meet you."

"Nice to meet you too, Dr. Senty. Sarah has told me so much about you and Dr. Merton."

"All good, I hope."

"Of course, Doctor. Sarah admires you both so much." Michael wrinkled his brow. He was unsure whether his compliment could be misinterpreted.

Mary Elizabeth said, "Here, let's get the salad into the kitchen. Thank you for bringing it. It looks delicious." Mary Elizabeth put the salad in the refrigerator. "Tonight, Dr. Merton is serving as our bartender. He will fix you up with whatever you want to drink."

The doorbell rang. Harold, who was getting Sarah and Michael their drinks, looked up.

"I've got it." Mary Elizabeth opened the door to find Lord and Lady Brantwell on the doorstep.

"Come in. Happy American Thanksgiving!"

Will came up behind her. "Here, let me take your coats." He helped Lady Beatrice with her fur coat and took Lord Brantwell's hat and coat into Harold's room.

Lord Brantwell brought in a large box with wine and relish trays. "I have brought a nice pinot noir to serve with the turkey and an Italian dessert wine to complement the pies."

"Wow, two different wines. Thank you. How do we serve them?" Mary Elizabeth asked.

"The front hallway is cool enough to keep the pinot noir until dinnertime, and the dessert wine can stay out there too. We will just bring it in a little bit before we need it."

"Thank you for bringing them."

Lady Beatrice handed Mary Elizabeth one large relish tray and continued to hold another one. "Here are the relishes you requested."

"I think we can put those in the fridge." Mary Elizabeth replied.

When everyone was seated with their drinks, Mary Elizabeth stood by the fireplace. "I want to thank everyone for coming to my American Thanksgiving dinner. If I could, I would've taken all of you back home with me to Minnesota to experience firsthand what an American Thanksgiving is really like. I can't do that. But what I can do is try to give you a taste, pun intended, of what that day might be like.

"Those of us who live far away come home the night before, which would be Wednesday night. Thursday morning starts like any other day. We do the outside chores and go to the barn to start the milking process.

"Inside chores consist of getting the turkey ready for the oven and putting the dressing together. After those working outside come in, everyone gets cleaned up, and the family goes to Mass. After Mass, we all come home and have a big breakfast.

"The breakfast dishes are cleared, and then we get to work on the main meal. Everyone brings an assigned dish, just like you all did today. I have three sisters and six brothers, and three of my siblings are now married and have families of their own. When we get together, it is loud and crowded and lots of fun.

"That is all I will tell you for now. But during the evening, I will share more of what a Senty Thanksgiving is like. All you need to know for now is that we will eat, enjoy each other's company, relax, and have fun. Hence, the casual attire request. I asked Father Matt to bring name tags tonight."

"Name tags? Haven't we been introduced to one another?" Lord Brantwell asked.

"Tonight we are going to be family. And in my family, we have names, not titles. We call each other by our first names or our nicknames. My family certainly doesn't call me Dr. Senty. So just for tonight, you can call me by the same name my family calls me." Mary Elizabeth got up and passed out the name tags and the crayons.

Viscount LeBrosse asked, "And what name is that?"

Mary Elizabeth took her name tag and wrote M. E. Underneath, she wrote it phonetically: Em-ee. She put her name tag on and explained,

"My family calls me Emme, and that is what I want everyone to call me tonight. Now, you write down what name you would like to be known by tonight. Just for tonight. When you leave, you take off your name tag. Tomorrow, we go back to Dr. Merton, Lady Beatrice, and Father Evenson."

When the guests put on their name tags, they discovered that they would be spending the evening with: Emme, Harold, Will, Mike, Sarah, Matt, Martha, Geoff, Bea, and Jacques.

"Now, it is time for a turkey hunt." Mary Elizabeth divided her guests into three teams. "Remember to find the turkeys in order. The sixth clue tells you what to do after you have collected all your turkeys. Okay, here are your clues." Mary Elizabeth distributed colored envelopes containing clues to the groups. "Now have fun."

"Fun?" Will called out. "This game sounds just like my work to me."

Everyone laughed. Mary Elizabeth watched the teams huddle in their groups before she returned to the kitchen.

She put the dressing in the oven. The turkey was browning nicely. Everything was on schedule.

From the sitting room, she heard gobbles, clucks, and even a cock-a-doodle-do. Mary Elizabeth laughed. She ran to see the orange team: Geoff, Sarah, and Jacques, flapping their arms and pretending to be turkeys.

The other guests were stunned into silence for a few moments before they burst out laughing.

"Well done!" Mary Elizabeth cried.

"How long must we keep this up?" Geoff asked.

"Oh, I think that is quite enough," Mary Elizabeth said. "Now, you can just sit back and wait for the other teams to finish. How did you manage to find your turkeys so quickly?"

"Great teamwork. Sarah is very bright at solving riddles, and Jacques just seems to have a knack for finding turkeys," Geoff replied.

Next to finish the hunt was the brown team: Matt, Bea, and Mike. After they crowed and strutted around for a bit, they sat on the couch with very satisfied looks on their faces. Soon to follow was the green team: Martha, Will, and Harold.

Mary Elizabeth could not help herself. She had to tease Will. "Not so clever of a detective when it comes to turkeys, are you Will?"

"Well, thank goodness, most Bellechester criminals are the human variety."

"Okay, everyone find a place to sit down," Mary Elizabeth announced.

She handed everyone paper and a pencil. "For this next game, you have three minutes to make as many words as you can using only the letters in *Thanksgiving*." Mary Elizabeth turned over the egg timer. Pencils scratched on paper. As the last grain filtered down, Mary Elizabeth cried, "Time."

They took turns reading their lists. There were plenty of groans when someone made a word or a plural the others had missed. In the end, when they tallied up their score of one point per letter, Harold was the clear winner.

The smells that were coming from the kitch-en were getting intense. Mary Elizabeth asked to see Matt and Jacques in the kitchen for a few minutes.

"I have a job for you two. Here, you will need to put these on." She handed them aprons. "Now go to the sink and wash your hands."

"Looks like we will have to work for our supper," Matt said.

"Did you know she could be such a tough boss?" Jacques asked.

"Your job is to peel potatoes. You can peel, and I will cut them up."

Mary Elizabeth got out two peelers and found a paring knife for herself. She brought out a large kettle.

"I haven't announced it yet, but last night, Will returned my agate necklace to me. It was sent anonymously to him at the station."

"Congratulations, Emme," Matt said. "You must be so happy to have it back."

"Oh, I am. I don't think I am ever going to take it off again. But there are still so many unanswered questions."

Jacques asked, "For example?"

"If the person knew the necklace belonged to me, why was it sent to Will?"

Matt said, "Maybe the person didn't know the necklace was yours and just sent it to Will knowing he would find the owner."

"Oh," Mary Elizabeth said without much conviction.

"Was there a note with your necklace?" Jacques asked.

"Yes, but I don't know exactly what it said. Will said he would share it with me at another time. All day, I have wracked my brain, and I cannot figure out who sent the package. Will said the postmark was from France. I don't remember meeting anyone from France at the gala. Do either of you know someone who was at the gala and lives in France?"

Jacques replied quickly. "I know I never met any French guests that night."

"I don't believe I did, either," Matt said.

"It's just that I would like to meet this mystery person and thank him or her in person for finding my necklace and returning it to me," Mary Elizabeth replied.

"Maybe someday you will get that opportunity," Jacques said hopefully.

"For now, it is just one of those mysteries of life. I wouldn't spend too much time thinking about it. The important thing is that your necklace has been returned to you. And I am confident that, wherever this person might be, he or she knows how thankful and happy you are to have it back."

"Matt's right. Maybe for now, this person wants to stay in the shadows," Jacques said.

"You are both right. But I am going to continue to pray for that good Samaritan. I will leave it up to God to bless their good deed. Because of the time difference, I have not had the chance to call my folks and tell them the good news. But I will call them before I go to bed tonight."

"They should be very pleased," Matt answered.

"Jacques, where do you live on the continent?" Mary Elizabeth asked.

"My summer home is outside Givry, Belgium, and I have a little place in Antibes, right along the French Riviera, where I spend the winters."

"Oh, please tell me about Antibes," Emme said.

Jacques described his apartment and the view from his balcony.

When he finished, Mary Elizabeth said, "It sounds grand. Matt, have you ever been there?"

"No, I haven't. But it sounds like the perfect cure for an English winter."

Jacque laughed. "Looks like I have some entertaining to do."

By that time, all the potatoes were peeled and Mary Elizabeth had put the pot on the stove.

"Thank you for all your help. Now, once they are done, which of you will mash them?" she asked.

"Age before beauty. Isn't that how it goes?" Jacques said with a smile.

"In that case, I will be happy to do the honors," Matt said.

The men took off their aprons and joined the others in the sitting room. Mary Elizabeth stayed in the kitchen and snuck a peek at the bird. She set the timer, then joined the others.

When Matt saw Mary Elizabeth enter the room, he said loudly, "Emme has some news she would like to share with us."

Everyone quieted down and looked to Mary Elizabeth expectantly. Mary Elizabeth was taken by surprise and said, "I do?"

Jacques made a motion with his hand pointing to an imaginary necklace around his neck. "Oh, yes. Last night, Will brought me this." She produced the agate necklace out from under her apron.

There were all sorts of gasps, and Martha exclaimed, "Oh, your necklace!"

Bea said, "Tell us how you got it back."

"Well, it is really Will's story to tell." Will once again repeated all that had happened.

Matt asked Will, "How are the other investigations going?"

"I am happy to report that we have solved the Brantwell Manor jewel thefts."

Martha said, "Oh, Will, you must tell us all about it."

"I don't think everyone wants to hear about it."

Bea said, "Oh yes, we do."

Will began, "From our investigation, this is how we believe the theft happened. During the gala, Baroness Whitacre passed a bottle of barbiturates to a servant, Ivy Petters. After all the jewels were in the safe, Geoff retired for the evening.

"Around 3:00 a.m., Ivy Petters brought tea to Officer Collins, who was guarding the safe inside the study. She drugged his tea, rendering our officer unconscious.

"Then, Yves Fortier, who had been posing as a server, put on Officer Collins's uniform and broke into the safe. He gave Ivy the jewels, which she hid on herself. She walked out of the manor and went home after her shift ended. She and the jewels left the manor well before the firecrackers were set off. Yves then went upstairs and replaced one of the officers in the hallway.

"At 4:30 a.m., when the firecrackers were set off, Jacques left his room. As he was going to investigate the noise, Fortier came up behind him, hit him over the head with his nightstick, and pushed him down the stairs. Then Fortier left unnoticed during the mayhem. When the second round of firecrackers went off, he sped off in a car that had been waiting for him behind the wall.

"They traveled down back roads to evade our roadblocks. Their plan was to lie low for a while and then take the jewels to the Continent to fence them."

Just then, the oven timer went off. Will said, "Ah, saved by the bell. The case goes to the prosecutors on Monday."

Geoff said, "Well done, Will."

Mary Elizabeth jumped up. There was a flurry of activity in the kitchen and dining room as Mary Elizabeth gave her guests assignments. Soon, all the food was on the dining room table, and everyone was seated at their place cards. The turkey was set before Harold at the head of the table. Mary Elizabeth asked everyone to hold hands, and for Matt to say the blessing. He prayed, "God, Creator of All, we come together tonight as a family, forged by friendship to pause from our daily lives to thank and praise you. From the bounty which you have provided, may this meal nourish our bodies and bring us closer together in friendship. Bless this food, bless us, and bless our time together. We also pray for generous hearts. May there always be room at our table for the stranger at our door. We pray in your name and through Your Son, Jesus Christ, who, with the Holy Ghost, lives with you forever and ever. Amen."

Everyone responded, "Amen."

Geoff said, "Please raise your glasses in a toast to our host and hostess, Harold and Emme."

"To Harold and Emme," everyone chimed.

"Harold, please show off your surgical skill and carve the turkey."

There were plenty of jovial conversations as everyone tucked in to their meals.

When the meal ended, Mary Elizabeth rose from her place. "I promised to tell you more about how my family celebrates Thanksgiving. At the end of the meal, the women clear the remaining food off the table. The men relax for a few minutes. When the women are finished, the men clear everyone's dishes. They are responsible for washing and drying. There is no desert until all the dishes are cleaned and put away."

That last remark elicited several groans from the men at the table.

"Look at it this way," Mary Elizabeth said. "By the time dishes are done, you will have more room for pie, and it will give me time to whip up some fresh whipped cream to go on the top."

"Well, when you put it like that, I guess doing dishes won't seem so bad," Jacques replied.

Mary Elizabeth asked her guests if anyone wanted take-home containers. Martha volunteered to take the turkey carcass home to make soup. While Mary Elizabeth filled the containers, the men washed and put away the dishes and set the table for dessert.

While the men worked, the women sat in the sitting room and talked. Bea said she had something for Mary Elizabeth. She went out to the front hall and brought back two picture albums. The women divided into two groups and paged through the albums.

Sarah exclaimed, "Emme, you look beautiful. What a gorgeous dress."

"Thank you. Bea and Geoff purchased it for me."

"You and Will look so happy. It all seems like a fairy tale," Sarah said.

"In many ways, it was," Mary Elizabeth replied.

"Before I met Will, I wasn't sure if he was going to be a prince or a toad. But he turned out to be a prince of a guy," Martha concurred.

"The first time I met him, I thought he was a nice guy."

"At the gala?" Bea asked.

"The gala wasn't the first time I met him," Mary Elizabeth replied.

"Was it when he came in for his physical?" Sarah asked.

"No. That was our third meeting, actually," Mary Elizabeth answered.

Bea asked, "And your second meeting was?"

"You know, I think I would like to keep that between Will and me. And, oh yes, Sergeant O'Hanlon."

"Sergeant O'Hanlon knows and not us?" Martha sounded hurt.

Mary Elizabeth laughed. "Let's just say that meeting was quite memorable, but neither of us left a favorable impression on the other."

"But what was your first meeting?" Martha persisted.

"Actually, our first meeting happened in London at a rugby game." Mary Elizabeth told the group about catching the rugby ball and Will handing her back her purse. "Even though he was covered in dirt and sweat, I thought he was quite handsome. But what really got my attention was that he was so kind and attentive. He didn't ask for my name, so I thought he wasn't interested. It was just one of those chance meetings that didn't seem to go anywhere."

"But at my gala . . ."

"Yes, Bea, at your gala, that is where we finally got the opportunity to know each other. Sarah, you are right. There was something magical about that gala, especially when we were dancing. Really, throughout the whole weekend, he gradually turned into that prince for me. Do all your parties have that effect on your guests, Bea?"

"Well, they either fall in love or go to jail."

"Jail!" Sarah sounded alarmed.

Lady Brantwell was eager to share what she knew from her grapevine. "Apparently, both Baroness Whitacre and Lady Porter were in some kind of jewelry theft gang with Yves Fortier. They were responsible for all the jewelry heists in the area. It seems that the baroness needed the money to keep her estate afloat. Lady Porter was bored and just wanted some excitement. Besides solving the jewel thefts, Will also uncovered an illicit drug operation."

"Will never mentioned anything about drugs," Mary Elizabeth said.

"Well, we know that Officer Collins was drugged the night of the gala."

Mary Elizabeth answered, "Yes."

"It turns out, the doctor who sold the drugs to the Baroness was running an under-the-table drug operation that catered to wealthy patients."

"But how do you know about that?" Martha asked

"Well, I was part of the sting operation," Bea stated proudly. She then told them all about her experience.

"Weren't you scared?" Sarah asked.

"Not really. I knew that Officer Turner would protect me, and he did."

"Will you have to testify?" Martha wondered.

"Honestly, I don't know. I did give a statement to the police, but because Officer Turner was also there, Will thinks that his testimony will be used in court. Plus, after we left, the police raided Dr. Barnett's office, and they uncovered quite a bit of evidence of him running this scheme for a long time. The police are trying to keep me out of it if they can, but you never know how these things will go. And if the newspapers ever get a hold of the story, well, let's just say Geoff and I might not have too many social engagements in London after that. But to me, it was worth it to help that poor officer."

"Yes, that was very good of you," Mary Elizabeth said.

"Yes, if your rich friends ostracize you, you will have to spend more time socializing with us common folk," Martha teased.

"Is that so bad?" Sarah piped up.

"Honestly, I have had more fun tonight than I have at a dozen swanky affairs."

"I'm so glad," Mary Elizabeth said. "I think I will go check on how things are going in the kitchen and start whipping up the cream."

"Well, I haven't heard any dishes break, so I think that is a good sign," Martha quipped.

Mary Elizabeth walked into the kitchen. "Looks like a well-oiled machine out here. You are doing a great job."

"I'm getting a new appreciation for how hard my servants work when Bea and I have a dinner party. Will says he is going to give me a crack at washing when we get to the silverware, pots, and pans. I don't think I can break them," Geoff said.

"It is amazing all the new life skills you have picked up tonight, Geoff." Matt teased.

"You never know when I might need them."

Mary Elizabeth got the bowl that was chilling in the freezer and brought out the whipping cream and the bottle of vanilla. When everything was assembled, she used a hand mixer and started to whip the cream. "I didn't know you also stopped an illegal drug operation. How come you never mentioned it?" she asked Will.

"Oh, I was tracing the origins of the drugs used on Officer Collins. Uncovering Dr. Barnett's drug business was just icing on the cake. The Met is taking charge of that prosecution. There, I have finished the glassware and the china. Silverware is next, then pots and pans. Time to change the guard." With that, he let out the dishwater and wiped his hands.

He peeked into Mary Elizabeth's whipping bowl. "Do you want me to take over here?"

"No, I've got this. You have been working pretty hard. Why don't you go sit in the other room for a few minutes and look at the photo album Bea and Geoff made for you from the gala?"

Will turned to Geoff, "Thanks for doing that. Although I don't think I will ever forget that gala, for many reasons."

"And is one of those reasons standing right in front of you?" Jacques teased.

Will turned to Mary Elizabeth, grinning. "Yes, indeed."

"Now, be off with you. You are making me blush."

Martha spotted Will as soon as he entered the living room. "Sit here, Will." She patted the empty space next to her.

Will obligingly sat. "I hear there is a photo album out here with my name on it. Thank you, Bea, for putting it together."

"My pleasure," Bea replied.

Will looked at the pictures.

Sarah commented, "Will, you looked so handsome in your dress evening wear."

Will laughed. "It cost me a pretty penny! No, make that several pretty pennies. Chief Superintendent Williamson suggested I purchase it. Bea, I hope you have many more galas so I can get my money's worth."

"I'll see what I can do."

Will continued to page through the book.

"Which one is your favorite picture?" Sarah asked.

"Any picture that has Emme in it."

"Well, they all have her in them! Now, if you had to choose one, which would it be?" Martha persisted.

Will paged through the book two more times. "I think this one," he said, as he pointed to the picture of Mary Elizabeth and him dancing on the terrace in the moonlight.

"Why that one?" Sarah asked.

Will became serious. "I don't know if this makes any sense, but the previous times we met, I witnessed her competence and her sense of humor. Everyone sees that in her. But when we were dancing out there on the terrace, she shared something with me that allowed me to see a different side of her. A side I don't believe she shows many people. In that moment, it was as if she handed me a gift, a precious gift. I felt special and honored. That's when I knew she was the one."

Sarah got misty eyed. "That is the most romantic thing I have ever heard."

"And it was my gala that brought them together," Bea sighed.

Geoff emerged from the kitchen. "The dishes are officially done. Emme says it is time for dessert."

He then went to the front entranceway and brought in the dessert wine. He opened it and poured it at the table.

"Here's how we are going to serve dessert. Please pick up a plate and then come into the kitchen. Your choices for tonight are pumpkin, pecan, or the Senty special: a slice of each."

Everyone went into the kitchen and came out with a plateful of pie.

When Mary Elizabeth was done serving, she brought out the silver coffee pot and other refreshments.

"Does everyone have their drink of choice? Now, please raise your glass and toast Martha for making these delicious pies."

Everyone raised their glass. "To Martha!"

At each bite, more compliments poured toward Martha. "Thank you, but that is enough. Now, Emme, what does your family do now?"

"This would be the time when everyone just shares announcements or news that they would like everyone to know."

Harold, who had been very quiet all evening, rose from the table.

"If I may, I would like to make two announcements. When Emme, first came last September, I suggested a three-month trial period. I have seen enough and heard enough from our patients that I would like to formally invite Emme to stay and practice medicine with me for as long as she wants."

"Truthfully, Harold, I forgot all about the trial period." Laughter erupted at the table. "Yes, I would like to stay in Bellechester and practice medicine with you for as long as you want me."

"Good," Harold said. "Then that's all settled."

"And what is the second announcement you wanted to make?" Martha asked.

"The second follows from the first. Having Emme here has relieved much of the caseload from me. With her around, I feel ten years younger. As a result, I have decided not to retire next year. I want to keep going. I believe that Emme and I make a great team. We will know when it is time for me to retire."

"Oh, that is great news, Harold," Mary Elizabeth cried. "And don't forget the third member of our team, Sarah. She makes this office run like clockwork. She makes both of us look good." Mary Elizabeth raised her glass. "To Sarah."

Everyone joined in the toast. "To Sarah."

"Would anyone else like to say anything?" Mary Elizabeth asked.

"Yes, I would," Jacques stood up. "Before this, I had no idea what Thanksgiving was all about. Then, I received your invitation. I did not grow up in a particularly close family. But tonight, I learned that family is not only the one you were born into; family can be created. Tonight, for the first time in a very long time, I felt that I was part of a family. Maybe it was because I had to peel potatoes and do the dishes. So, thank you, Emme, for bringing us all together. I am forever grateful."

He raised his glass. "To Emme." Everyone joined.

Mike was next to speak. "The only person I knew before tonight was Sarah. I only came because she said I had to." When the laughter subsided, he continued, "But now, I am glad I did. It was very much like being home with my family.

What I learned tonight is that you can be a part of more than one family."

Will said, "Tonight, I have learned how important it is to take time to just relax and enjoy life."

"The Americans have the right idea: to devote a special holiday to giving thanks for life's many blessings. Taking time to gather with family and friends is important. I would like to propose that this family make Thanksgiving dinner an annual event. I would like to host it again next year if that would be agreeable to everyone," Harold said.

"I am deeply touched by your words. You have all become very dear to me in these last few months. You are my Bellechester family, and I am very grateful. Thank you for the food you brought, the help you gave, and for sharing yourselves so we could get to know each other a little better. Matt, will you send us out with some final words?" Mary Elizabeth asked.

Matt rose. "Meister Eckhart, the great thirteenth-century Dominican philosopher, once said, 'If the only prayer you ever say in your entire life is *thank you,* it will be enough.' Tonight, there have been many words of gratitude. May we keep that sense of gratitude in our hearts all year through. Amen."

"Amen," the group echoed.

Everyone instinctively got up and cleared the table. Jacques washed the dessert dishes. Geoff picked up the dish towel to dry. Martha took out the turkey carcass and pulled the leftover containers out of the refrigerator and placed them on the table. Bea put everyone's dishes on the table to be taken home. Harold brought out the coats from his bedroom and draped them over the couch.

Finally, the dessert dishes were once again washed and put away. The kitchen was clean, and it was time to say good night. Will and Harold helped the women with their coats. There were hugs and handshakes as everyone left with their empty serving dishes and leftovers. Finally, it was only Will, Mary Elizabeth, and Harold who remained.

"Emme, your American Thanksgiving was a big success. It was a wonderful evening. Thank you. Now, Monday morning will be here before we know it. Good night, Will and Emme." Harold excused himself.

"Good night, Harold." Will said.

Mary Elizabeth kissed Harold's cheek. "Good night, Harold. Thank you for everything. But especially, thank you for choosing me to come to Bellechester."

"Remember, Emme, it was you who first found me. Asking you to join me in Bellechester was the easiest decision I ever made. Good night." Harold went into his room and shut his door.

"I should be going home. Tomorrow is a workday for both of us."

"Don't forget your photo album and your container of leftovers for your supper tomorrow." She added, "You know, Chief, we make a pretty good team."

Will kissed her. "Don't ever forget that, Mary Elizabeth."

"If I ever do, I hope you will remind me."

"You got it. Good night." With that, he walked out into the crisp November night.

"Good night." She closed the door. Mary Elizabeth climbed the stairs to her room. She called her parents to tell them the good news that her agate pendant had been found. She also told them of her Thanksgiving celebration and asked how the Senty Thanksgiving had gone in Minnesota.

As Mary Elizabeth lay in bed that night, a peace settled into her heart. For the first time, Bellechester felt like home.

GLOSSARY

Accident & Emergency (A&E) – The emergency room of a hospital.

Benedicamus Domino - Latin for *Let us bless the Lord*. Sometimes used as a greeting among Benedictines.

Barmy - Odd, crazy, bonkers, or foolish.

Black pudding - A type of blood sausage from Ireland and the United Kingdom made from pork blood, pork fat, oats or barley stuffed into a casing. It is traditionally eaten for breakfast.

Boot - The trunk of a car.

Borstal - A reformatory for youthful offenders with an emphasis on physical, mental, and moral development. Offenders were also taught a skill. These institutions existed from 1902 to 1982 in England and other parts of the Commonwealth.

Bubble and squeak - A traditional British dish made from leftover potatoes, cabbage, and other green vegetables formed into a patty and fried. Can be served for breakfast, lunch, or dinner.

Chin-wag – A chat.

Deo *Gratias* - Latin for *Thanks be to God.*

Derby - A sports contest between two teams.

Doddle - Easy. The American expression would be a *piece of cake.*

Flat - A set of rooms on one floor; an apartment in a lower to middle class neighborhood.

Football - Soccer.

Hob - Stove burner built into the counter.

Muck up – To mess up, bungle, or do something very badly.

Nick - British slang for jail.

Pimm's - A gin-based liqueur favored by the upper classes served with ice and fruit in the summertime.

Plaster - A bandage.

Plimsolls – Training shoes; sneakers or running shoes.

Redcap - British slang for a member of the Royal Military Police because of the distinctive red cap that's part of their uniform.

Surgery – A doctor's office or clinic.

VSSE – The Belgian intelligence and security agency. Established in 1830, it protects the country from any internal or external threats against the country.

"Wellies" - Short for Wellington boots; worn to keep your feet dry in the rain or mud. They are named for Arthur Wellesley, First Duke of Wellington, who in the early 1800s asked his shoemaker to make him a tall boot. The style caught on.

Acknowledgments

"Now. remember to say thank you." How many times did we hear that from our elders when we were growing up? How many times have you uttered those same words to your children or grandchildren, hoping that one day gratitude would become an automatic response in their lives?

The person who brought the importance of cultivating gratitude and thankfulness into my life was Archbishop Harry Flynn of the Archdiocese of Saint Paul and Minneapolis. When he arrived in the Twin Cities, I was already working for the archdiocese. He used to gather the employees together periodically as our different departments were scattered among several buildings. These meetings gave him the opportunity to share his thoughts with us. It was also a chance for us to meet our colleagues face-to-face instead of only speaking on the phone. At the end of each talk, he would start thanking people. His list would go on and on as he never wanted to forget anyone. Any liturgy or gathering with Archbishop Flynn in attendance would also end with a litany of thanks. Honest gratitude and sincere thankfulness were the virtues he embodied. Serving under him for ten years made a difference in my life. I couldn't help it. His sense of gratitude became contagious! Archbishop Flynn will always be a happy memory.

Against that background, it is now my privilege to express my gratitude to the people who helped created this beautiful book. First, I would like to thank my project manager, Evan Allgood. He kept me on task and provided wise counsel and encouragement throughout the year. He also gathered together a host of talented professionals to work on the book. Kerry Stapley was the perfect choice for editor as she was in tune with me and the story. Her experience of living in England for a time was invaluable in helping me with British idioms. Working on this book together was a joyful experience. And I hope I was able to add to her body of knowledge as to what life was like in 1959! Abbie Phelps was the proofreader who corrected the typos and made the text a smooth and easy read. Dan Pitts skillfully designed and typeset the book and covers. He met the challenge of duplicating the easy-to-read large print of the first book with double the chapters. For the cover art, I turned again to Lisa Kosmo. How could I not? Her beautiful cover on *The Doctor of Bellechester* earned a 2023 Honorable Mention for Best Front Cover Artwork from the Catholic Media Association Book Division. Congratulations, Lisa!

When the story was finally complete, I held my breath. I was satisfied with the book but what would my readers think? Gayle Yanchar Bari, Barbara Kraft, Paula Brust, and Dan O'Leary read and reviewed the story. I would also like to thank Edward Trayer and the Wishing Shelf

Gang for reviewing the story from their European mindset. Since the story is set in England, I was very curious to receive feedback from the natives!

I hope you enjoyed your visit to the English village of Bellechester. Please come back again soon. More adventures await you in the next book.